THE KISS COUNTDOWN

THE KISS COUNTDOWN

ETTA EASTON

BERKLEY ROMANCE

NEW YORK

BERKLEY ROMANCE
Published by Berkley
An imprint of Penguin Random House LLC
penguinrandomhouse.com

Library of Congress Cataloging-in-Publication Data

Names: Easton, Etta, author.
Title: The kiss countdown / Etta Easton.
Description: First edition. | New York: Berkley Romance, 2024.
Identifiers: LCCN 2023031477 (print) | LCCN 2023031478 (ebook) |
ISBN 9780593640227 (trade paperback) | ISBN 9780593640234 (ebook)
Subjects: LCGFT: Romance fiction. | Novels.
Classification: LCC PS3605.A863 K57 2024 (print) |
LCC PS3605.A863 (ebook) | DDC 813/.6—dc23/eng/20231016
LC record available at https://lccn.loc.gov/2023031477
LC ebook record available at https://lccn.loc.gov/2023031478

First Edition: April 2024

Printed in the United States of America
1st Printing

Book design by Shannon Nicole Plunkett

THE KISS COUNTDOWN

CHAPTER ONE

Homeboy has ten seconds to divert his eyes from my ass before I lose it.

Ten . . . nine . . .

I face the pastry case filled with freshly baked donuts and scones, frowning at the reflection of the man behind me. I say homeboy, but in reality, he looks old enough to be my granddad, with his full gray mustache and a pair of reading glasses perched atop his shiny head. Like most patrons flooding Moon Bean this early, he wears a business suit with wide tan slacks and a black blazer that lends no credibility to his character. Not when he's eyeing my backside like it's one of the butter croissants on display.

One.

"This is my first time here. What do you suggest I get, sugar?" he says, close enough for his Brut aftershave to wrap me in a choke hold.

Nope. We are not playing this game. Not today, when I'm already on edge, anticipating the meeting that will help launch my new beginning—or see it fail at groundbreaking speed.

I whip my head around and glare, reaching deep into that ancestral pool of fortitude handed down from generations of resilient women who perfected the *mess with me and die* look. In two seconds he slides back to a respectable distance and raises his phone to his nose.

That's more like it. Satisfied, I pivot to face the front of the line once more, but it isn't long before another glance toward the glass case tells me he's back to ogling.

As the person in front of me moves up, I'm distracted when my phone buzzes. It's my best friend, Gina, texting that she's leaving her apartment. I let her know I'm already in line so she can grab us a table when she gets here.

Gina rarely makes the three-minute walk it takes to get from our respective apartments to the coffee shop more than twice a week, and when she does, I can always count on her to be at least ten minutes late. The conversion from central standard time to Gina time works in my favor today. No doubt, if she'd witnessed the exchange between Pops and me just now, she'd be harping on me for not entertaining his nonsense and applauding his willingness to risk it all for someone half his age, all the while laughing her ass off.

"I can help the next person in line," a barista with a hot-pink face mask says, and I move forward, dismissing the man behind me from my mind.

After ordering our drinks, I don't dare approach the pickup counter yet. Against the *burr* of multiple grinders and blenders going at once, a blockade of thirsty patrons watch the baristas furiously topping off drinks with pumps of syrup or oat milk, silently praying their hit of caffeine comes next. The only other time you see a crowd this anxious to get their hands around something hot is when it involves turkey legs at the rodeo. You can never know what someone is liable to do when deprived of coffee or poultry, so I keep looking around the shop until I spot Gina.

She waves at me from a table by a large window decorated with hand-drawn candy canes and Christmas ornaments, and I head that way.

The heavy green chair scrapes against the floor as I pull it out and sit across from her. "Hey."

"Good morning," she sings, and it's hard to believe she likely hopped out of bed five minutes before texting me.

Gina is one of those unnatural people who wake up with a good stretch and wide smile, ready to face the day. Not a drop of coffee in her system and she's brighter than a ray of sunshine in her long-sleeve white shirt and knitted yellow scarf.

Technically, I'm a morning person too. After years spent waking up before the sun to prepare for large-scale events, my internal alarm rarely allows me to sleep past six in the morning. But it takes me a nice long walk, usually around the golf course behind my apartment complex, and a cup of coffee before I'm ready for human interaction. Add in a couple of slices of bacon, and it's on.

"So, what's on the agenda for today?" I ask, keeping an ear out for my name to be called.

"I'm going to Sugar Land for a bridal party," Gina says. "The bride is seriously the sweetest. She's getting an updo, and I'm doing blowouts for the bridesmaids."

As Gina effortlessly uses the green silk scrunchie around her wrist to pull her curls into a low ponytail, I inwardly pout. My hair never goes up that easily. Certainly not without me feeling like I've just finished a full upper-body workout at the gym. I guess it's one of the perks of her being a hairstylist.

I try not to visibly shudder at the thought of brides and weddings. If I never have to attend another wedding in my life, I'll be just fine.

Gina's eyes widen. "Oh, I almost forgot. Don't you have that quinceañera consultation this morning? Look at my girl. Ready to take on her first client. How exciting! I take it after we're done here, you'll rush home to get camera-ready." She gives my hairline a pointed glance.

Since all I did was throw on a headband to liven up my worn bun, I'm not offended by Gina's blatant dig at my hair or at the concern evident in her brown eyes. I can't blame her when it's been only two months since I managed to claw my way out of a downward spiral that began when I almost lost my mom and worsened when my employer of eight years tossed me out like hot garbage. But being broken up with by my boyfriend was the exact push I needed to snap out of my despair and right my upended life. So I called Gina and told her I was going to start my own business.

Ever the queen to my bee, she didn't question if I was having a midlife crisis at the age of twenty-eight. She was at my door within minutes to congratulate me, then said I couldn't even think of starting a business until I'd swapped my sweat-stained sheets for new ones.

This morning I awoke to the sweet scent of lavender fields, knowing today was the day when, once and for all, I took control of my life. So, despite my current appearance, I'm ready.

"Don't look at me like that," I tell Gina. "When we're done here, I'm marching to my apartment—and yes, fixing my hair—then sealing the deal with my first client."

"You've got this, Mimi. And here's some extra good luck coming your way." Gina mimes throwing balls of glitter at me, and I indulge her by closing my eyes and basking in it.

"Medium roast and caramel latte for Amerie!" is shouted from the pickup counter, and I get up.

I maneuver around tables and furniture easily enough, but have to fight my way through two particular people who have zeroed in on the workers like their unmovable focus will make the baristas move any faster than they already are. It's a miracle more elbows aren't thrown in every coffee shop across America in the time between when customers place their orders and have to fight the masses to actually get them.

Relief comes when I finally reach our drinks, grab two cup sleeves, and turn to head back, feeling sorry for (and a tiny bit better than) everyone still waiting.

"I went with the cappuccino," Pops says from beside me, and I almost drop the drinks.

I knew he wouldn't be discouraged for long. These old-school dudes are a different breed of tenacious, but I've got no patience to deal with his foolishness today. I grit my teeth as I turn away from him without making eye contact.

I'm halfway to Gina when I realize I forgot to add cinnamon to my coffee. That won't do. I abruptly turn around, only to have my right elbow connect with something warm and solid, accompanied by a man's surprised grunt.

After catching my footing, I'm grateful the lids have held and neither of the cups in my hands spilled. As good as the coffee is, some of the baristas are notoriously awful at putting the lids on, so I always make sure to snap mine tightly before grabbing them. Foresight and planning for the win.

I'm ready to lay into Pops for his stalkerish tendencies when I look up and realize not only did I *not* collide with Pops, but the man I did bump into didn't fare as well as I did.

Coffee blots what I'm sure was once a pristinely pressed white shirt like paintball splatters, while dark spots coating the zipper of fitted navy slacks make it look like he had a suspicious accident in the restroom. The coffee stops mid-torso, so I let my eyes travel up to a wide chest and broad shoulders, then momentarily lose my breath once I reach my victim's face.

He's tall, standing a good head above me, with skin that's a rich, warm brown. He's clean-shaven, with the barest hint of a five-o'clock shadow, and gorgeous full lips that stand out in perfect proportion to a cut jaw. His eyes are a beautiful golden brown, like topaz. You'd think he'd once been foolish enough to stare into the sun long enough to capture its beams. I don't know how else someone would get eyes that brilliant. As our gazes hold, the ground begins to feel unsteady, like the earth might collapse right out from under me, and for a second, I wish I'd worn something more stylish than leggings and an old U of H hoodie. I tear my focus away from his face and focus on his shirt.

I blink, back on solid ground, then grimace at the mess covering his lower half. "Sorry about that."

In the silence that follows, I wait for him to say something like, *It's okay* or *Oh no, it was actually my fault for walking right on your heels.* But he says nothing, and I look up to find his eyes still rooted to my face. Though his stare appears a little dazed, my neck begins to prickle. What *is* it with people today? All I want to do is enjoy my morning cup of coffee. Not get hit on by old men who should know better, and definitely not bump into handsome strangers.

Under his piercing gaze, my annoyance hedges toward guilt, and I try to swallow my irritation. I am the one who turned around without being aware of my surroundings and should probably offer more than an apology.

"I can pay for your shirt to get cleaned," I say grudgingly. I hate the thought of adding a stranger's dry-cleaning bill to my already tight budget, but it *is* my fault he'll likely go around smelling like stale coffee grounds all day. "There's a dry cleaner's just a few stores down."

"Dry cleaning?" he finally says, and wow. That voice. It's as rich and smooth as my favorite brew. And judging by his slow response, he probably needed every drip of the coffee that just spilled.

"Yes. For your shirt."

He looks down, and I think he's finally snapped out of whatever trance he was in. Thick eyebrows shoot up as his eyes land on the white cup with a black lid that now sits askew and then his shirt cuff that's soaking wet.

His eyebrows draw together as he looks back at me, seemingly stunned. "You bumped into me."

I might've clapped if my hands weren't full. I settle for a nod instead. "I know. That's what I'm apologizing for." I sigh and look around, noticing how Gina has switched to the opposite side of the table and now has a straight line of sight to this spectacle. Great, she'll be talking about this for weeks.

That's it, dry cleaning is officially off the table.

"How about you let me buy you another coffee?" I offer instead.

He frowns. "But I don't have time to get a cup with you."

Something isn't clicking here, and I am holding on to my last shreds of patience with everything in me. "What is your name?" I ask slowly.

"Vincent. And you are?"

"Don't worry about that. Look, *Vincent*, I was offering to replace the coffee I spilled, *not* whatever it is you're thinking."

My answer amuses him for some reason, as he tilts his head to the side with half a smile. "'Don't worry about that' is an interesting name."

So he's got jokes. Not funny, and definitely not appreciated. But jokes.

"Do you want coffee or not?" I demand.

His eyes light up even more as he chuckles, and I roll my shoulders to deflect the pleasant sensation the sound tries to elicit. I am not about to be seduced by a nice laugh.

Tearing his gaze from me, he quickly sobers when he checks his watch, which, luckily for him, is still dry. "I better hurry home and change before I'm late for the Monday meeting," he mutters, then sighs and looks at me. "Maybe you can make up for the coffee another time."

My eyes bug out at his words. I am too stunned to speak. And before I can think of a good comeback, he's out the door.

"You can buy *me* another coffee if you want." Pops steps close and eyes me as he raises his cup to his mouth. "I know how you independent women these days like to pay for everything, so you can take me to breakfast too."

Heaven help me.

I look at the ground, where two drops of coffee lie on the light wooden floor. "Watch your step. Don't want to have you fall and break a hip."

Walking away, I shake my head. My mom would tear me a new one for not respecting my elders, even if he did deserve it.

Back at the table, I set our cups down and regard Gina sternly. "Do. Not. Even."

"What?" Her eyes are all rounded innocence. She takes a small sip of her latte, but I can see she's ready to burst.

I may as well have her get it out of her system now instead of badgering me later. With a sigh, I fold my arms across my chest and wait for her to crack.

It doesn't take long. She leans forward on the table and

covers one side of her mouth like she's telling me a big secret. "Okay, but did you see how fine he was?"

"He's still here if you want me to get his number for you."

"What?" Her eyebrows knit before she scowls. "Don't play. You know I'm not talking about Grandpa. I'm referring to Hottie with the Body."

"Oh, you mean the aggravating man with the . . ." Damn, I can't think of anything catchy like Gina.

She shakes her head. "Tell me you gave him your number, or at least got his?"

I grab my drink but set it down again, leaning back in my chair and shaking my head at Gina's ridiculous question. "Of course I didn't get his number."

"I don't see why not. You could do with a little love in your life now that you're done wasting time with Derrick."

"Now that Derrick and I have broken up, my focus is on me, myself, and my business. No distractions, especially from men."

"But—"

"Especially from *that* man."

Him and his *You can make up for the coffee another time.* That is not how this works.

Gina pouts and I sigh. I know she wants me to find the happiness she has with her boyfriend, Mack. It's the same kind of happiness my parents have. I used to want that too. Derrick hadn't been the love of my life. I knew it even when we were together, making plans to someday move in with each other and get married. But what if he *had* meant more? What if, when everything had ended, I'd spiraled even further and lost all of myself? For one, I wouldn't be here drinking coffee with Gina.

Which is exactly why I won't pursue any relationships. I can't afford to fall apart ever again.

"I'm just not in the market to get involved with anyone," I say.

"Fine. Get your business up and flourishing. *Then* we'll find the love of your life. You won't be able to run from the man you're destined to be with forever."

I shake my head at her and take a sip of my coffee. It's only then that I realize: After my run-in with the stranger—Vincent—I still forgot to get my cinnamon.

AFTER COFFEE, GINA AND I BID FAREWELL AS SHE SETS OFF TO MEET her client, and I head to my apartment, leaving behind thoughts of men and untimely collisions. I live in a nice little fusion of residential and commercial real estate. For a stretch of three blocks, the street is lined with boutiques, restaurants, and essential businesses. Gina and I live in the same apartment complex, but she lives with Mack and Mack Jr. (aka Human Mack and Dog Mack), while I live in a one-bedroom by myself.

On my way to my apartment, I pass through the courtyard. It's a large rectangle of Astroturf framed by metal tables and chairs, with a black marble fountain stretching across the front. The farmers market and other small vendors attract shoppers twice a week, on Sunday and Wednesday. I've set up a booth for the past two weeks. It's how my potential client found me.

My stomach tightens at the thought of what awaits me. Closing my eyes, I inhale deeply. I've got this. Planning quinceañeras is my jam. Planning anything is my jam. It's what made me such a valuable asset at Jacob and Johnson for eight years. My vision and legendary parties helped launch them into being one of Houston's top event planning firms. Just because I no longer work there doesn't mean I've lost my touch.

So today I will charm this client with my great personality. Wow her with my ideas. And dazzle her with my follow-through. Then, once I've made her daughter's big moment the event of a lifetime, she will recommend me to her friends, and everyone will know Amerie Price is back. And everything will make sense again.

When I climb the stairs and land on the second floor, I see bright pink papers attached to all the doors. Someone's been busy this morning. It's probably a notice about upcoming maintenance visits or reminders to the pet owners to clean up around the building.

God, I hope they're not reassigning the parking spaces again.

I unlock my door and step into my one-bedroom apartment. Once I place my keys down and turn on the lights, I read the paper, and the words threaten to derail me from the measured footing I just gained. It's a notice for the structure of new rent prices. Starting in the new year, my unit is going up by 30 percent.

I resist balling up the paper and throwing it in the trash.

With the money I've been saving up for years and the severance package I received from my old job, I have enough to ride out this price increase for another lease term, but not enough to pay for rent *and* help my parents.

How did this catch me off guard? I should have expected it when new management took over. The apartments were renamed the Hidden Palms three months ago; I'd just been too focused on my misery to care. It's always the same story. First, rebranding: new name, new paint, balloons out front. Next, they start promoting social events to "get to know your fellow tenants," along with perks like free massages on Wednesdays. A few months later—when they know they've got you—the price hikes kick in. Shit like this should be illegal.

This, however, is a worry for another day. In fact, an increase in rent won't be a worry at all if I get my business up and running with a bang.

On that thought, I place the pink paper beside my keys and head to my bedroom. My hoodie is exchanged for a cream silk blouse. Powder and lip gloss give my complexion a little life. With Gina's voice in my head, I put my hair in a low curly ponytail and smooth my edges, and I'm camera-ready.

I get out my brand-new computer. It was one of the pricey but necessary purchases I had to make when I decided to venture out on my own, since the one I'd been using for years belonged to Jacob and Johnson. I forked out even more money to load it with planning software.

Pulling up Zoom, I click on the link and wait with bated breath for my potential client to show up.

After ten minutes I send her a text message.

> **Me: Hey, I just want to make sure you've got the link. Here it is again. I can't wait to chat about your daughter's quinceañera!**

Right away, I see the message has been read, but she doesn't respond. Maybe she's running behind or just now waking up. Nine is still early for some, especially parents trying to shuttle kids to school and fight Houston traffic, so as I watch the clock in the bottom corner of my screen change from 9:14 to 9:15, I try to cling to the hope that she'll join me any second. Unable to help myself, I glance toward the front door, where the too-bright pink paper shouts at me from beside my keys, and force down the rising fear that wants to swallow me whole at the thought of what I'll do if this venture doesn't pan out. Then, after twenty more torturous minutes, I leave the virtual meeting. No one is joining me.

My reputation has preceded me, and not the one I painstakingly created over years of being one of the best event planners Houston has to offer.

I turn off my ring light, wash my face, and curl up in bed.

CHAPTER TWO

As my phone rings on my second loop around the golf course, I pull it from my front pocket to see a picture of my mom cradling a bundle of purple yarn.

I do my best to muster a smile I don't feel, knowing she'll be able to hear it through the distance, and answer. "Hi, Mom."

"Hey, Mimi. How's it going?" Her voice is warm and loving, doing the trick to turn my brittle smile real, if only for a second.

"I'm okay," I say. "You're up early. Have you and Daddy made it to Las Vegas?"

"Not yet. We decided to visit the Grand Canyon first. And my Lord, what a sight it is." Her carefree laugh squeezes my heart. "Imagine the widest, deepest, most beautiful wonder you've ever seen on TV, and multiply it by ten. Words don't do it justice. And the stars! So many light up the sky at night, you don't even need a flashlight once your eyes adjust. A group from the local university set up telescopes for guests to look through, and we even saw the International Space Station pass by. Oh! Your dad did one of those tours on a donkey and got some unbelievable pictures. It's amazing out here, Mimi." She sighs into the speaker. "I wish we could've come here as a family when you were younger."

I love hearing about my parents' adventures. We were nomads when I was a kid, though not in the sense that we traveled from city to city, exploring all that the world had to offer. More like we hopped from apartment to apartment throughout the years. They were always cheap, mostly sketchy and cramped, but more than accommodating to renters who couldn't commit to long leases. With my dad working one stable job that barely covered rent and Mom's constant medical bills, it was all we could afford. It wasn't until I graduated high school and my dad was promoted to a manager that they broke the cycle of endless moving. Now my parents have a cute three bed, two bath. They aren't rich by any means, but their reversal of fortune is nothing short of amazing. And as happy as I am for them, I'd be lying if I didn't also wish it had happened before I was an adult.

Sure, I have my own designated room in their house that I stayed in during college breaks, but I've always felt more like a guest there. My apartment is the only place that's ever truly been mine, and the possibility of losing it and turning into a rolling stone again fills me with unshakable dread.

"You know I don't like heights, Momma," I say, trying not to let my somber thoughts leak through my tone. "But you and Daddy eat your hearts out. Make sure you're having tons of fun, and send me pictures when you can. You've been taking your medicine, right? How have you been feeling?"

"Don't worry about me, Mimi. I feel good. This RV trip is just what the doctor ordered. Who knows, I may even be able to convince your dad to sell the house, and we'll just travel full-time."

"Tell your mom to quit dabblin' in whatever she's been smokin'." My dad's booming baritone voice comes through clearly, and I realize I must be on speakerphone.

"Hi, Daddy. I hope you're not letting Momma run you too ragged," I tease as I begin walking toward Moon Bean.

"Have you met your momma? Supposed to be out here workin', but she's got me stoppin' at every monument, museum, and Waffle House like she's the one paying me." After a second, Dad laughs, and I can imagine him stroking Mom's hand while she glares at him.

"Hardy-har-har," Mom says drily. "Now tell me, how are *you*, Mimi? We missed you so much on Christmas. I'm sorry we couldn't call, but how was it? What did Derrick get you? For your dad's sake, I hope it wasn't another Titans jersey."

Mom and Dad are doing the double duty of checking in on each warehouse that answers to Dad while also taking the opportunity to sightsee. Since they often travel through back roads, I couldn't get through to wish them a Merry Christmas. Gina also went out of town to visit Mack's family, so for the first time in my life, I spent the holiday alone.

"Christmas was fine. But, um, Derrick and I decided not to exchange gifts. So no jerseys, Daddy." Technically, it's the truth.

While I've always known my mom is living on borrowed time more than the average fifty-year-old, when she was hospitalized from complications with her sickle-cell anemia ten months ago and needed an emergency splenectomy, I was the one who took it the hardest. I was tortured with thoughts of what living in a world without her to turn to would encompass, leaving me unable to eat, sleep, or hold conversations. Once she was released from the hospital, she and Dad worried more about my emotional stability than her follow-up appointments and rest. If they knew the call I took when I stepped out of the room was not my boss checking on her but actually firing me, they never would have left for their trip. So I've kept from them the truth of my job and my breakup with Derrick to ensure they'll focus on the time they have together, not me.

"We can talk more about the holidays later," I say. "I want to hear more about the Grand Canyon."

By the time I make it to the coffee shop, the connection is bad enough that everything they say is a garbled mess. We hang up, with my parents shout-promising to send pictures, and I pull the phone away from my ear, once again alone in every sense. My smile falters, and I let my shoulders fall under the combined weight of feeling like a failure for not being able to get my business off the ground and feeling guilty for keeping secrets from my parents. Especially about the hospital bill.

While they've been traveling, I've been the one checking their mail to make sure their post office box doesn't get too full. Two weeks into their trip, a letter from the hospital arrived. I've been around long enough to know what an outstanding bill looks like, and wrong or right (yes, I know it was wrong—wrong *and* illegal), I opened it. My heart sank when I saw the large amount for the portion Dad's insurance didn't cover.

It was tough enough convincing Mom to join Dad on the trip. The only reason she agreed is because she met a family at her church looking for a short-term rental while their house is under construction. They're using that extra money to fund their trip. In the almost thirty years that they've been married, the only kind of vacations they've taken are day trips to the beach.

If I told them about the bill, or about me losing my job, I already know what would happen. They'd turn around and come home, and Dad would get a second job, just like he did when we moved to San Antonio when I was a kid.

In San Antonio, we stayed with my paternal grand-mother, a woman who'd worked so hard her entire life she couldn't comprehend that my mom's condition made it impossible for her to do the same. I was miserable. I'd met Gina the year prior and had to move away from the only person who ever called me their best friend. Wanting to make his girls happy, Dad took on two extra jobs to save up enough that we could come back to Houston.

But he's older now, and while he'd probably say his body can handle the stress of working so much, he doesn't need to. I have the money to pay off their bills. Though after the notice of the rent increase, I don't have enough to do that and remain in my apartment. It's one or the other, and I choose my parents' happiness.

I'm still holding out hope that by some miracle I'll hit the clientele jackpot and be able to stay in my apartment, as slim as the odds are.

After the first client ghosted me, I haven't gained any new leads. It's no surprise, really. When someone looks me up on the Internet, a picture of a crying bride pops up. It's a stain I can't wash out and a reminder of the worst weeks of my life.

But I still woke up in clean sheets, and as I look up to the predawn sky, there's a break in the clouds with two stars shining through. When I was a little girl who still believed in the magic of the universe, I used to wish on stars all the time. It almost seems like fate that I've looked up at the exact right moment, and it would be a waste of cosmic energy if I didn't make a wish now.

I focus all my energy on the brightest one. "Please, just give me one client."

Just one. That's all I need to get the momentum going. Then I'll work so hard to make it a success.

"Wait," a voice says behind me, and I immediately stiffen as I recognize the deep drawl. "You didn't just make a wish, did you?"

The slight chuckle accompanying the interruption makes the hair on the back of my neck stand up, even as unwanted shivers race down my spine. I asked for a damn near miracle for my business, not another infuriatingly awkward run-in. Clearly the universe has jokes.

I grind my teeth and turn around, steeling my nerves—only to be met with the man I collided with last week. Vincent. In the dark light of the early morning, he's no less devastatingly handsome than the first time I met him, which turns my annoyance up a notch as I cross my arms. "Don't you know it's rude to eavesdrop on people?"

The same topaz eyes I stupidly thought shone as bright as the sun brush over me from head to toe, lingering a little too long on my hips, before their owner shrugs one shoulder. "It's not eavesdropping if you speak loud enough in a public space to be overheard. Anyway, I thought you might appreciate knowing that you weren't looking at a star."

Lord, give me strength.

I look up to make sure I haven't been imagining the bright dots in the sky. For all I know, I've been staring at a UFO and the whole reason I felt the lights were speaking to me is because aliens have been studying my sad life, trying to decide if I'm worth abducting or not. It's a relief to see them still in place, even as wisps of clouds threaten to dull their brightness. I face Vincent again, raising both eyebrows.

He gives me the kind of smile one might bestow on a kid so proud of themselves for "reading" as they sit with a book upside down. He's standing close enough that the smooth material of his jacket grazes my nose when he points up and behind me. "That is a planet. Venus, to be exact. Its dense clouds reflect light from the sun, making it one of the brightest objects from our perspective here on Earth. Morning or night, as you can see." He regards me expectantly, then continues when I remain silent. "Remember this when studying the sky: The light that stars generate travels so far that it's bent by our atmosphere. The bending looks like twinkling to our eyes. Planets, on the other hand, are much closer to us. The light they reflect from our sun comes in a steady beam. The other planet you see there is Jupiter."

While he drones on, I massage the bridge of my nose as pressure builds. This man needs to read the room, because I am ten seconds away from losing it. *Of course* it's a planet. I can't launch a successful business. Can't afford to be honest with my parents. And now, apparently, I can't tell a planet from a star.

I take a deep, cleansing breath, along with a much needed step back so his cologne isn't clogging my senses. "You know what? Thanks for the science lesson, but I really don't have time for this."

I turn back toward the doors, but as I reach for the handle, Vincent grabs it first. He flashes straight white teeth, looking for all the world like a perfect gentleman extending me a common courtesy and not like someone who's managed to once again throw off my entire equilibrium before I've had an ounce of coffee. Thankfully, he doesn't follow me inside, as the phone in one of his pockets begins to ring. The door shuts behind me and I let out a sigh of relief.

The relief is short-lived as I take my place in the line, replaced by a gnawing from that responsible part of my brain that says I need to be smarter about how I spend my money. Before I lost my job, I was saving up to buy something I'd never had—a house. I was going to be living in gorgeous Black Girl Luxury in a space that would be all mine. I'd planned to go all out, settling in a two-story with cathedral-style ceilings, bay windows, and a front yard that would be the epitome of curb appeal, with fragrant mountain laurel trees, rose bushes, and grass so lush it would look like it belonged on a golf course.

Now, without a steady source of income and the money I'll be putting toward my mom's hospital bills, my dreams of home ownership are nothing but a hazy mirage. Maybe someday, if I'm smart about every penny I spend and find people willing to give a disgraced party planner another chance, I'll be able to afford to dream about separate garden tubs and walk-in showers again.

That doesn't stop me from ordering a coffee for myself and two of Gina's favorite scones when I get to the counter. I justify the purchase, knowing how much Gina will appreciate some comfort food after being stuck with Mack's mom for a week. I plan to save them for when she comes back to town tomorrow.

The normal large morning crowd is cut in half like it always is when winter break rolls around, so it doesn't take long before my order is ready. I grab my coffee cup and small bag and move to the sugar-and-cream station.

Coffee and I go way back. I loved the smell when my dad would make his cups in the morning and would always ask him for a sip. He'd relent only when Mom wasn't in sight, and it always caused my face to scrunch up when the bitterness hit my jaw. But the next time, I'd ask again, and Dad would give in. By the time I was old enough to actually drink coffee, I'd gotten used to having it black, though later I discovered cinnamon adds a nice woody flavor.

After sprinkling a dash of the spice in my cup, I snap the lid on and turn around, stopping short when I almost crash into some unsuspecting soul. Again.

"Sorry," I say to a man's back, only to immediately recognize his silver beanie with the Tennessee Titans logo—a grave insult in Texans territory. "Derrick?"

My ex turns around.

Under his atrocious beanie, he keeps his head shaved. He has a deep tan complexion, a small goatee, and groomed eyebrows. He's the tallest man I've ever dated, and wherever we used to go out—it never failed—someone would ask if he played basketball. His response was always "I don't care for the basketball court, but I do run game in the courtroom."

Yeah, he's a lawyer. A corny one at that.

His eyebrows shoot up when he spots me. "Amerie. What are you doing here?"

I barely resist rolling my eyes. I'm hunting rabbits. What does he think I'm doing?

"Well, you know me: morning walk, then coffee." I raise the cup in emphasis. "I'm surprised to see *you*."

While Derrick lives only about fifteen minutes away, coffee shops litter every street corner between our apartments. He literally could have gone anywhere else, but decided to stop at Moon Bean. *My* Moon Bean.

"I was just in the neighborhood," he explains with a shrug, looking me over. "You doing okay?"

"Oh, I'm fine," I say quickly. He knows full well how tough this past year has been, with my mom's health and then losing my job. Gina was right: He is so full of himself.

Derrick holds out a hand in surrender. "Just keeping tabs on you."

"You should be keeping tabs on yourself," I say, then force myself to take a mental step back.

The last thing I need to do is waste energy playing the bitter ex just because he's caught me at a bad time. Maybe if we run into each other next year, I won't feel like ripping that dumb cap off and stuffing it in the trash.

It's not like I hate Derrick. But seeing him now, I can't help but think about his parting words. He had a notable list of my shortcomings: I'm fake in front of crowds and don't know how to take a joke, to name a couple. But the one that really makes my blood boil is my apparent inability to understand true intimacy.

Actually, the idea makes me want to laugh. I witnessed intimacy in my parents' marriage every single day of my life. I know that what my parents have can't necessarily be forged from a truly, madly, deeply in-love-at-first-sight connection. It takes a foundation of friendship and getting to know each other's ins and outs. The good and the crazy.

Derrick and I didn't have that solid foundation. However, while breaking up was the right decision, it doesn't mean I have to pretend to be happy to see him.

A woman with dark hair in a sleek bun walks up to Derrick, sliding her hand in his. "I just looked up the reviews, and everyone raves about the scones here. I want to make sure to try some." She turns her head to me and jumps in surprise. "Sorry, I didn't realize I was interrupting."

Again, I'm not mad or bitter over the breakup with Derrick, but damn that sting in my chest at seeing the new woman he's obviously moved on with.

At least he has the decency to look uncomfortable as he glances between us and clears his throat. "Baby, I ran into my old friend. You remember how I told you about Amerie, right?"

Derrick's girlfriend smiles. "Of course! It's nice to meet you." She sticks out her free hand. "I'm Nora. I've heard nothing but great things about you from Derrick. You can always tell the good ones by how they speak about their past, right?"

"That you can," I mumble, fumbling to place the bag of scones down on a nearby table to shake Nora's hand. "It's nice seeing Derrick's obviously found someone so lovely. And so soon too." The smile I aim at them is the same one I used to wear whenever I showed up at Derrick's work functions and had to pretend to like all his pretentious colleagues.

Nora places her beautifully manicured hand over her heart. "Sometimes the stars align, and when you know, you just know. Hey, you're not here alone, are you? You can sit with us for a while and chat."

"Thanks for the offer, but I'm actually waiting on someone." The white lie rolls off my tongue with ease. If I say I won't sit with them and chat because I have to go stalk the streets like a town crier, letting people know I'm desperate to plan their parties, I will look exactly like my life has gone up in flames since the breakup. It's petty, but I just can't give Derrick that kind of win.

He nods. "Oh yeah? You must be waiting on Gina, then."

I narrow my eyes, not liking how he makes it a statement instead of a question. "No, not Gina," I sneer. Then, to wipe the knowing smirk off his face, I keep going. "I'm meeting my boyfriend for coffee."

We stare each other down. Derrick regards me through eyes full of suspicion, and I hold still, trying not to scratch at my prickling neck.

I don't usually lie to save face. Once I brought home a progress report with a D in math and said it was because the teacher kept losing my assignments. When my mom surprised me by sitting in my class the next day and talking to the teacher after, I realized how being outed was so much more painful and embarrassing than simply owning up in the first place.

And yet here I am.

"You have a boyfriend?" Derrick says, disbelief obvious in his tone.

"Why would I make up something like that?" A careful evasion rather than outright lie.

He makes a show of looking first behind me, then to the right where a few people stand in line, and then behind himself. "Where is he? I'd love to meet ol' boy and give him my congratulations. Make sure you're in good hands."

See, that's the thing with lies. It doesn't matter what label you try to slap over them—white, black, flashing neon— a lie is a lie. And they tend to take on a life of their own. But now I'm committed. I can't backtrack.

I frantically look around the café for some kind of inspiration on what to do next.

Come on, universe. Help me out here.

From the corner of my eye, I see a familiar figure. When I turn my head, I realize it's Pops. He catches my eye and smiles with a wink, and I recoil. Good Lord, no.

I'm ready to abandon all hope of trying to come up with a believable emergency that will allow for a quick escape when the bell above the door jingles.

I understand now why people put so much stock in wishing on stars. It's for moments like these, when the universe answers pleas with a gift of Providence, even for the misguided who wish on planets.

As elation surges through me, I smirk at Derrick before calling out, "Vincent!"

CHAPTER THREE

When I call his name, Vincent's head jerks toward me. He does a double take when I wave, and it stops him in his tracks.

After I walked away from him minutes ago, he probably thinks I'm trying to lure him into some sort of trap. Which, okay, he would be right, but I have no other recourse. I flash my teeth at him, trying to channel that same coaxing energy one might use to get a scared puppy to crawl out from under the couch. Vincent's eyebrows snap together, and he looks even more suspicious.

Welp, that tracks. It's not like I have experience coaxing puppies since I'm allergic to them.

I drop the smile and wave him over again. After a few seconds of hesitation, he walks in our direction.

"I see your phone call wrapped up," I say as he stops at the periphery of our group. Latching on to his forearm, I tug until he's standing by me. "Let me introduce you to some friends of mine. Meet Derrick and Nora." I turn to the couple. "This is Vincent. My boyfriend."

The weight of Vincent's stare settles over me like a boulder. I can practically hear him shout, *What are you talking about, woman?*

Derrick and Nora regard Vincent silently, as if trying to

see if we're really together or if I lassoed the first man to walk through the door and he's about to take off running.

I step right into Vincent's bubble, almost pushing up against him, in case he tries.

Standing this close, my head hits right below his shoulder, and with each inhale, I get a whiff of his clean aftershave mixed with the cold rain that must have picked up again. It filters through the heavy scent of coffee in the air, and I recognize the subtle undertones of spices and sage. While I need his help, I don't *want* to like anything about this man, even the way he smells. I'm tempted to put a good two feet between us, but Derrick is watching us intently. I put my hand over my mouth to cover a fake cough, and press my elbow into Vincent's side as I bring the arm down.

Vincent lets out a quiet chuckle, and the vibrations travel from his stomach and up my arm. "It's nice to meet you two," he finally says.

I won't lie. I enjoy how Derrick's jaw tightens as he eyes the man beside me. After all, Derrick did say I would grow old alone if I didn't learn to put my partner before my mom. Now he can take his words and eat them.

"How long have you and Mimi been dating?" Derrick asks Vincent.

I almost jump as an arm snakes around my back, and Vincent's large hand lands on my waist. He lets out a contented sigh. "You know, it's been one of those relationships where it somehow feels like the blink of an eye and forever simultaneously. Isn't that right, Mimi?"

The way my nickname rolls from his lips leaves me unsettled. The only people I allow to call me that are my parents and Gina. Even Derrick's use of the name was rare, unless he was showing me off in front of colleagues.

Still, I manage a "Right you are," making it as cheerful as I can.

Vincent squeezes me tightly to him. "Yeah, she came barreling right into my life and caught me off guard."

I pat his chest—his hard, muscled chest—as I look up at him and shoot daggers from behind my smile.

I've thought about that morning when my first client stood me up, running over each detail in my mind. When I get to the accident with Vincent, I've realized that he *must* have been too close to me. I know I pivoted on the balls of my feet, so the only way I could have knocked into him was if he was already there, invading my personal space. Really, we're both to blame.

"So is it pretty serious between you two, then?" Derrick says.

I shrug and borrow Nora's wise words. "When you know, you know. Thank the stars and all that."

Derrick transforms from confident lawyer to sullen teenager, and I know the taste of satisfaction. I may not have a job or a clue about how to turn the tides of my business, but at least I've managed to keep my dignity.

"Listen," I say. "It was good catching up with you, but we'll let you two get on with your day."

Derrick ignores my attempt at a polite farewell and keeps talking to Vincent. "What is it you do?"

I'll ignore him too. I step away from Vincent, my body instantly growing cooler, and pick up the coffee and scones from the table. "Once again, it was nice meeting you, Nora."

"I work with NASA," Vincent announces. "I'm an astronaut."

I freeze, hoping against hope the dismay I feel isn't evident on my face. Of all the career choices. Is this guy for real? If he's salty over the shirt I ruined, he could have just said that. Better yet, he could have kept walking when I called his name. Because if Derrick didn't suspect anything before, I'm sure he does now.

I matched with a few guys before who claimed to be in NASA's training program, yet the simplest of social media digging proved otherwise. And Derrick knows this.

Derrick now cocks his head to the side and regards me with a look that says he's onto me, but he'll indulge me anyway. "An astronaut, my man? What an admirable career choice. You must be living the dream." He all but snickers.

"Yes, sir." Vincent gives one quick, affirmative nod, and I wish I could wipe that confident smile off his face.

I'm praying Derrick won't ask any follow-up questions when Vincent smirks, then slips his right hand into an inner pocket of his suit and pulls out a badge. A badge with a red-white-and-blue NASA logo clearly visible for all to see.

"Vincent Rogers. NASA class of 2020," Vincent says.

Nora snaps her fingers. "I knew you looked familiar. My niece is obsessed with space and astronauts. Every time I visit her and my nephew, she asks me to read your book to her." She smooths her already flawless hair. "The picture on the back cover doesn't do you justice."

"Wow, that's great," Derrick says, his tone contradicting his words. He casts one more glance at me before tugging Nora's hand. "Nice seeing you, Amerie. We better order our coffee, honey."

I smile and wave. Once they're out of earshot I turn to Vincent, ready to profusely thank him for his lovestruck act. But as soon as I open my mouth, he stiffens as another woman approaches us. She's eyeing me in particular, and I get the sinking feeling this encounter won't play out as well. If this is Vincent's *real* girlfriend, this might be the day Moon Bean sees some actual 'bows thrown.

This woman is dressed in black scrubs under a puffy gray coat. She holds two large coffee cups, passing one to Vincent as she regards him with a raised brow and mischievous glint in her dark brown eyes. "Vincent, you didn't tell me you were bringing your girlfriend along." Her attention turns to me, and she looks like she found her favorite new toy. "He's been telling me and Mom that he was dating someone, but since he kept you from us for so long, I was beginning to doubt you were real. It's nice to finally see you in the flesh. I'm Camille, Vincent's sister."

My mind whirls. So, ignoring the fact that apparently eavesdropping runs in the family, Vincent's sister heard enough of the whole exchange to think Vincent and I are a couple.

I look at Vincent, waiting for him to set the record straight.

He sighs and shakes his head. "Actually, she's not—"

His sister puts her hand out. "Hold that thought, please." She grabs the buzzing phone clipped to her hip and reads a message. "Just when I thought I'd get an easy morning, duty calls." After replacing her phone, she looks at Vincent through narrowed eyes like she's contemplating something. Her eyes slide to me. "I was trying to convince Vincent to come to my New Year's Eve party, but he always claims he has to work. You can get him out for one night, right?"

"Camille, this really isn't what it loo—"

This time I'm the one to cut Vincent off as I spot Derrick and Nora moving to the sugar and cream, mere feet away. "A New Year's Eve party sounds great. I'm sure I can get him out of the house."

Camille beams. "Great. It's a black-tie affair at Skylawn." It looks like she's about to leave, but she pauses and smirks at Vincent. "Mom's going to be so jealous I got to meet her first. See y'all soon!"

Once she's gone, I count to ten to make sure no one else is going to pop up, then turn to Vincent. "Do you want to sit?"

He sighs. "Sure."

He grabs a handful of sugar packets and individual creamer cups, then follows me to the vacant table farthest from the door. As soon as I sit down, I take a large gulp of coffee. By now it's cooled and doesn't scald my tongue, so I greedily sip it while trying to get my bearings.

First Derrick, then Vincent's sister Camille. Good Lord.

Vincent sits across from me, looking much more composed than I feel. And I don't know him well, but I swear he appears to actually be enjoying himself. Or maybe he likes seeing me all flustered.

Vincent leans back in his seat. "Let me guess, old boyfriend?"

So he's going right in.

"Yes. We broke up a few months ago." I let out a sigh and roll my neck, trying to get rid of some of the tension. When I open my eyes, Vincent is looking at me, but he quickly averts his gaze. "Vincent, thank you so much for having my back just now. I know I put you on the spot."

He nods once. "Don't sweat it."

I take another sip of coffee, this time savoring the smooth brew. Caffeine doing its job? Check. Ex-boyfriend gone, thinking I'm thriving and have moved on? The bell jingles and I turn to watch Derrick and Nora leaving. Check. I'm golden and can now get on with the rest of the day.

"Well, I better head out. Thank you again," I say.

Vincent frowns as I stand up. "Wait, that's it?"

I guess it is pretty rude to simply walk away after he's

helped me. I hold out the bag of scones to him. Gina will understand.

He takes the offered treats in his hand and sets it on the table, but still doesn't look satisfied. "What about my sister's party?"

Oh. That.

I sit back down, and Vincent relaxes. Vincent, the astronaut. No wonder he gave me his little sermon about being able to differentiate between stars and planets. He'd probably felt it was his moral duty.

"My sister was extending the invitation to both of us," he says.

"Well," I begin slowly, "I just assumed you'd tell her I couldn't make it or something."

Pretending to be his girlfriend for a conversation was one thing, born of desperation and bad planning. Attending a party hosted by his sister? That's a whole new ball game, and a complication I don't need.

Vincent shakes his head. "I can't. Look, this may not make a lot of sense to you, but if I don't show up with a girlfriend now, that being *you*, it's going to cause a lot of issues for me with my mom."

"But won't your real girlfriend be upset if you try going with someone else?"

Vincent scratches the back of his head and clears his throat. He's staring hard at the table instead of at me, and I narrow my eyes as I consider his sister's words. Specifically, her doubting his girlfriend was real. Hmm.

I lean forward and narrow my eyes. "Don't tell me you've been lying to your family about having a girlfriend."

He runs a hand over his face. "I have my reasons, as I'm sure you had reasons for lying to your ex," he says pointedly, and I scoff. "Besides, don't you think you owe me?"

"How do you figure that?"

He tilts his head like it should be obvious. "I just helped you impress your ex."

"Well, I helped you by pretending to be your girlfriend in front of your sister."

"Which you wouldn't have had to do if I hadn't helped you first."

He has a point. Damn Derrick. This is why I like planning events. Everything gets written down and carefully considered, then the best and most creative course of action is picked. When I walk into situations blindly, shit like this happens.

"Not to mention," he continues, "you ruined my favorite shirt *and* wasted all my coffee last week."

"What? I offered to pay you back for both!"

As I see the barely suppressed smile and satisfied glint shining from his eyes, I clamp my lips shut, mad at him and at myself for rising to the bait. His smile only grows as he removes his coffee lid, picks up the sugar packets he grabbed (all six of them) and empties them into his cup. Next, he adds three single-serve creamers and stirs it all with a wooden stick. It figures he'd be the type of person who likes his coffee too sweet. Or, as my dad would say, he adds a little coffee to his cream and sugar.

He holds my gaze as he brings his cup to his mouth and sips. I try not to notice how some of the liquid lingers at the indentation of his full upper lip, and instead focus on his apparent aversion to securing coffee lids. The one he took off has been transformed into a holder for the empty packets. But ultimately, Vincent's trash is nowhere near as interesting as his lips, and my eyes zero back in on his mouth in time to see his tongue swipe out and capture the rogue drops.

He sets his cup down and leans forward. "It was really good coffee. Ruined my whole day when I had to go without." His voice has taken on a lazier drawl, and in the midst of a sudden hot flash, I have to wonder if he's from the country.

I move back in my chair and fold my arms over my chest. He's too close. Too big for this tiny table meant for cozy couples or as a solo workspace, and his presence closes in on me like we're in a crowded elevator.

"Why don't you call your sister up and tell her you were simply helping me out before she tells your mom?" I ask.

"My mom and sister work together. And Camille probably called her as soon as her foot hit the sidewalk." Vincent sighs. "Come on, please? It'll just be one night, and we won't even have to stay for the entire party. You'd be doing me a huge favor."

I really need to put all my focus on my business, but my conscience pricks at me. Vincent could have kept walking after I called his name, or run off as soon as he realized what game I was playing. But he didn't. He helped me out, and everything played out better than I could have dreamed. Would going out for one night really be that bad?

I look into his eyes and let out a long breath. "Fine. I'll go with you to the party, and then my debt is paid."

CHAPTER FOUR

This time last year, I was already out with Gina, ringing in the New Year at a party hosted by my old job, with a lot of the heavy planning done by yours truly.

Like now, it was one of those perfect weeks in Texas when, although we were technically in winter, temperatures made it feel like fall. In between dancing and eating way too many fried mac-and-cheese balls, we took dozens of pictures against the silver backdrop.

I still have the photo where Gina is holding a cardboard mustache against her mouth and I'm holding a small sign that reads **CHEERS!** and we're both draped with tinsel boas. We had a bet as to who would be the tipsiest by the night's end, but going off our glassy-eyed smiles and snippets of memories of us singing while Mack drove us home, I'm pretty sure we both lost. I also remember waking up with a massive hangover, realizing that alcohol just hits different once you're over twenty-five.

This year, however, as I stand in front of the bathroom mirror and try to preserve my curls, I'm contemplating doing a Big Chop right here and now.

"Oh, come on," I whimper.

I spent all afternoon getting ready for my evening with Vincent, performing my usual routine before a big party.

While the Bluetooth speakers blasted my favorite playlist, I gave myself a facial, took a steaming-hot bath, and set my hair in twists. After that, I tried on at least five dresses before deciding to go with the first one and pairing it with my black stilettos that tie at the ankle.

Then I took my hair down, only to discover it was still damp. If I leave it like this, by the end of the night my curls will lose all definition and shrink, and I'll come home resembling Samuel L. Jackson in *Unbreakable.*

I stare at my reflection and shake my head.

Why am I putting myself through so much stress when I don't even want to go to the party? I would rather turn on the TV and watch the Times Square ball drop as a whole bunch of celebrities and TV personalities I'm not even up to date with talk about nothing of importance, then watch the fireworks light up the skyline from my window before calling it a night. Up until two days ago my plan had been exactly that.

The sound of the front door opening and closing stops me from doing anything drastic like calling Vincent to cancel—or switching the bottle of oil in my hands for a pair of scissors. Two seconds later, Gina's voice fills the apartment as she announces her arrival by trying to sing over the Jazmine Sullivan song playing. I use my phone to turn off the music.

Gina appears in the doorway pouting. "What happened to the music?"

"It was over." I meet her eyes in the mirror. "Did you bring it?"

Gina's arm disappears into her oversize purse before she pulls out a small pink-and-black box and waves it in the air with a triumphant smile. "Got it right here."

I knew she wouldn't let me down. Her bag is like a chic

survival kit, always full of things like granola bars, flash-lights, travel-size Tabasco bottles, and makeup. In the event of a zombie attack, alien invasion, or the apocalypse, I'd be able to count on her keeping us fed and beautiful.

I turn around with my palm out, but Gina keeps the box close to her chest.

"Let's not get ahead of ourselves," she says. "I want to know why you need my last box of booby tape first. It's New Year's Eve, and as far as I knew, we didn't have any plans. What gives? Also, I had to rush through my last client and then sit in an hour of traffic to get here in time. And you already know how much of a hassle it is to even get this brand."

"Look, Gina," I cut in when she takes a breath. "We can stand here all night while you go on and on, or you can let me get a word in and give you all the answers you seek."

She clamps her lips shut. As I reach for the box again, she stuffs it back in her purse and raises her eyebrows expectantly.

"Fine," I grumble and turn back to the mirror. "Do me a favor. Google Vincent Rogers."

Gina narrows her eyes but gets out her phone.

While she types, I grab my makeup bag from the bottom cabinet. I spritz my face with primer and use my hand as a fan to dry it.

"Okay, Mr. Astronaut. Come through in that blue one-sie," Gina says, ignoring the look I give her when she says onesie. Then, squinting at the screen, she gasps. "Isn't this the guy from Moon Bean?"

"Yup."

"Noice," she says, giving the word an *oy* sound. "How did you find out what he does? Did you Internet-stalk him?" She smirks at me.

I huff. "You know I did not Internet-stalk him."

Gina makes herself comfortable on the granite countertop, sitting with her legs swinging while I give her a half-hearted stank eye. I don't truly mind if Gina sits on the counter. One thing I've loved about this apartment is the spacious bathroom with his-and-hers sinks. The tub is a good size too. What I love even more is how the complex was newly built when I moved in, so I've been the first one to experience the great amenities. It's so very different from what I was accustomed to growing up, where the showerheads were typically coated in rust before we even moved in. Is that what I have to look forward to again if I can't keep this apartment?

"Well, don't tell me you joined him for a nice civil chat over coffee and he told you all about his life," Gina presses. "As much as you complained about him, there's no way I'll believe that."

"No, he didn't tell me about his life over coffee. It was a little more complicated than that."

"Oh? Do go on."

I pick up my blending sponge and try not to grimace. When Gina returned home yesterday and texted me, I deliberately put off telling her about my run-in with Derrick or the favor I owed Vincent. I knew she'd make it a bigger deal than it is. But with Gina here in person, there's no more hiding. I start blending my concealer and foundation while relaying the whole story. With each new sentence, Gina's jaw drops half an inch, and I'm surprised it doesn't pop out of its socket by the time I'm done.

"Mimi, I cannot believe you did that," she says when I end the tale. "And for the record, there is no way to convince me Derrick just happened to drop in with his new girlfriend. He was trying to make you jealous, and it backfired gloriously. He must have been crying and throwing up all night when he found out you upgraded to an *astronaut*."

"The look on his face was pretty satisfying," I admit. "It made the whole ordeal worth it."

"Look at you. All petty and stuff. I love it."

My lips twitch, then I continue applying makeup while Gina goes back to her phone.

"Vincent Rogers. Age thirty-four. Six feet, one inch. Unmarried with zero children," Gina reads. "It says here that he graduated from UCLA with an engineering degree as well as a degree in geology. He did Search and Rescue for three years, got his pilot's license, and was teaching at UCLA before being selected for NASA's training program."

I make a small humming sound, like these are facts I'm hearing for the first time. In actuality, I spent more time than I care to admit reading up on Vincent through NASA's web page and Wikipedia. I even watched some of his interviews on YouTube.

In the media he comes across as the stereotypical astronaut—capable, knowledgeable, and brave. A hero working toward the advancement of humankind. He's one of four astronauts who will go on a historic six-month mission to the moon. They'll study its surface to help NASA understand how humans will survive in deep space long term.

Vincent always seemed passionate yet humble in the interviews. In not one did he interrupt or give unsolicited advice. Or antagonize his interviewers. *Not* like he did around me.

Derrick claimed I had a bubbly persona in public that was perfect for engaging people on a superficial level, but then in private I was too closed off. Clearly, Vincent also has an alter ego for the public, while in person he's irritating. Hot, but irritating.

"He's had more careers than most people I know," Gina says. "Who does he think he is, Barbie?"

"Don't you mean Ken?"

She shakes her head. "Nope. Do you know what Ken is mostly known as? A beach bum. Barbie's been the one bringing home the bacon since the 1950s."

"Why are we even talking about Barbie?"

"I have no idea, because what I really want to know is why a man like Astronaut Hottie even needs someone to pose as his girlfriend?"

I pause from considering which eyeshadow to pick and shake my head. "Your guess is as good as mine. He said he had his reasons."

"Don't we all?"

When I can't decide which color to go with, I finally give up and throw my head back.

"What's wrong?" Gina asks.

"I don't know about this. Do you think I should even be going out with him tonight? This is crazy, right? It's crazy."

"Hell yes, I think you should go out there! It's been forever since you loosened up and had fun. What else are you going to do if you don't go? Hole up and watch Times Square?"

It's eerie how well Gina knows me.

"You already made the commitment, so you need to see this date through."

"It's not a date," I correct her. I need Gina to get that fact straight. "It's a favor. A onetime deal to pay him back for helping me with Derrick, and that's it. And you're right." I sigh. "I did make a commitment."

Gina waves a hand in the air. "Favor. Date. Whatever you want to call it. Just go." She slides from the counter and grabs the eyeshadow palette, pointing to the shimmering gold square. "Put this one on."

"You don't even know if this will match what I'm wearing."

"Let me guess, the green dress with one shoulder?"

I snatch the makeup back and grudgingly admit, "Yes. I swear, either you know me too well or you've been spying on me through some crystal ball."

Gina narrows her eyes. "Have you been talking to Mack's mom? Because you know she thinks I'm a vixen who's warped her son's mind with my magical vagina. I mean, yeah, in the immortal words of Mya: 'My love is like . . . wo.' But I'm only human."

"I take it that the recent visit didn't go too well?"

"Can you believe Mack's mom is still complaining that I haven't gotten rid of my dog? She thinks it's disrespectful to have an animal around with the same name as her precious son." Gina makes a gagging motion. "Never mind the fact that I adopted Mack Jr. before I even met her son and that my pooch is as sweet as can be. At this point, I don't even think her dislike of me is about the names."

I shake my head but notice how Gina runs her thumb over the large area on her arm where brown turns cream. I know it hurts Gina that Mack's mom hasn't fully accepted her. I don't know if she thinks Gina's vitiligo is some kind of defect that reflects badly on her son or if she's simply upset over the fact that her son has a new number one in his life. I'm glad to have met the woman only once. Seeing my best friend sad raises all my hackles, and I don't know if I'd be able to maintain civility around her. She reminds me of the grandmother I haven't reached out to since we left San Antonio all those years ago, with her antiquated mindset that women, Black women especially, should be infallible. Strong, hardworking even at the expense of their health, and looking perfect while doing it.

"Hey," I say softly. "You do know it's her loss if she doesn't want to get to know the future mother of her grandchildren. I mean, I can't speak to the state of your vagina and if it's some cauldron of magic, but I've known you more than half my life and can confidently say the real magic is in your heart."

"Aww, thanks, Mimi. You know you're the queen to my bee," Gina says, using the silly saying we made up in middle school when we started a girl band called the Queen Bees. We had convinced ourselves we'd someday tour with Beyoncé. These days we use it whenever one of us is feeling particularly sappy, or as a placeholder for *I love you.*

And I love Gina too.

She's always there for me. My ray of sunshine in the midst of all the storms. When my mom got sick, Gina dropped off a self-care basket filled with tea, cozy socks, and a ridiculous candle that looked like a bowl of cereal. It didn't fit in with my aesthetic at all, but it smelled amazing.

When this night is over and I've got my business flowing with a good pipeline of clients, I'll have to treat Gina to a special girls' trip.

"That is not enough color," Gina complains as I set the makeup brush down.

She grabs the makeup and turns to me. Instantly, I close my eyes, lest I end up losing one due to Gina's impatience. Smooth bristles sweep my lids as she picks up where I left off.

"We need to have you glowing like the diamond you are."

I open my eyes just to roll them. Yeah, I'm a real diamond in the rough. *Rough* being the operative word. I can't even get my hair right, yet I'm supposed to show up on Vincent's arm, all smiles like we're in a happy relationship. This night is going to be a disaster, and all because I had to save face in front of Derrick. Not only will the night be a disaster, I'll never get my business off the ground. I'm a walking mess, throwing away money on a pointless investment.

Gina runs her thumb over my forehead to smooth out the frown. "Nuh-uh, none of that. How can you say all those sweet things about me but then deny what's plain to see about yourself? You *are* a diamond; you've just forgotten how bright you can shine. Don't worry, we'll get you there." She pauses. "Where are your falsies?"

"I don't have any false eyelashes."

Gina's sigh is full of all kinds of attitude.

"What?" I ask. "Where would I have worn them in the last year? Should I start dressing up for my morning walks around the golf course?"

"If that's what it takes to get you out of this funk, then yes." Gina uncaps the top of my dried mascara, not even bothering to look at me before chucking it into the metal trash can with a *clang* and pulling an emergency tube from her purse. "Look up."

I relax and let her continue to pamper me as she applies a few coats of mascara on my lashes and then color on my lips. She makes a disapproving sound in the back of her throat when she feels my damp hair, then tackles it without a word.

"I know you've been through a lot lately with the breakup and losing your job, and I know that scare with your mom still affects you more than you're willing to acknowledge. But I want you to take this one night to let the old Amerie out and let loose. When midnight strikes, kiss that astronaut until all he sees is stars." Gina's words pierce through me. Who is the old Amerie? It's like I've been in survival mode for so long, I don't remember what anything else feels like. Sure, I'm good at putting on a convincing genial face, but most days are still a struggle. I certainly don't feel like the same person who not only loved going to parties but also enjoyed planning them so much I got a degree in hospitality. All I've felt for so long is tired, worn, and useless.

"Promise me you'll at least try," Gina presses.

I look past her to admire my image in the mirror. Gina is a miracle worker. My hair is braided into a halo around my head, and my face is done in a soft glamorous look. The gold eyeshadow and dramatic mascara look good against my almond skin, and I can't help but think I'm staring at someone I haven't seen in a long time.

I pick up the fan brush and dust highlighter along my cheekbones, nose, and chin. Meeting Gina's approving gaze in the mirror, I softly smile. "I'll try."

CHAPTER FIVE

An hour later, Gina has left to meet up with Mack, and I'm pacing back and forth in my living room. The pacing serves two purposes. For one, I have too much nervous energy. I'm set on seeing this night through, but that doesn't erase my apprehension about pretending I'm in a relationship with a total stranger. And two, my feet need to get reacquainted with stilettos. Gina would disagree, but these Aminah Abdul Jillils aren't exactly the type of shoe one wears to walk around a golf course. Not unless you're trying to find a sugar daddy.

At exactly nine o'clock, three knocks sound at my door. Despite myself, dozens of tiny butterflies take flight in my stomach as I move to answer it. I smooth the skirt of my dress before undoing the dead bolt, opening the door, and . . . *wow.*

Vincent stands tall in the quiet apartment hallway, wearing the hell out of a fitted black tux.

I drink him in from his gleaming ebony oxfords to his slate-gray tie and fresh edge-up. I've seen him in nothing but business suits at Moon Bean, so it's hard to believe he cleans up even more.

"Hey," I say.

"You—" His voice comes out on a rasp, then he clears his throat and tries again. "You look amazing."

The frog in his throat and undisguised appreciation as he takes in my outfit help to quell some of my apprehension as my confidence kicks up a notch, and I tamp down the grin threatening to break through. "Thank you, Vincent. You look great too."

We lock eyes for a second before he clears his throat. "Are you ready?"

"Let's do it." I grab my clutch before following him to a silver Mercedes-Benz. I clock that it's an electric vehicle, not surprised in the least that an astronaut would be conscious about his carbon footprint.

We ride in silence for the first few miles, and I can hardly keep my eyes off him. The fifth time I glance from the street to Vincent, he finally looks back at me. "What?"

"I'm trying to figure you out." I squint my eyes, hoping it will allow me to see through his head. "You're obviously successful. What could you possibly have to prove that you need to show up to this party with a woman by your side?"

I had wanted to keep things simple. Flash a smile here, charm a little there, then go home having paid my debt. But Gina posed the question, and now I can't stop the curiosity that's eating at me to know his motivations.

Vincent rolls his shoulders. "It's complicated."

"You mentioned as much the other day."

He drums on the steering wheel and lets out a long breath. "Okay. For years, my mom has harped on about me settling down and starting a family. Typical mom stuff, right? It was easy to dodge and ignore when I didn't live so close."

"California is quite the distance."

He flashes me a toothy grin and I instantly wish I'd kept my mouth shut.

"Have you been checking up on me?" he says.

"Don't get too full of yourself. I had to make sure you are who you say you are and that I wasn't about to step out with a psycho. Although, I guess that's still debatable."

Vincent chuckles. "Yes, I was in California. I came back to Texas to work with NASA, and while it brought me back home, starting a career as an astronaut really sent my mom over the edge. Don't even get me started on how she reacted when I went to the International Space Station."

"She doesn't like what you do? Other than, say, firefighters, I can't think of any other occupation that's more revered or regarded as heroic."

"Heroic," Vincent echoes with a proud nod.

I make a mental note that compliments go straight to his head.

"To answer your question, the thought of me taking off into space terrifies my mom," he continues. "I don't blame her. While we try to mitigate risk as much as we can, a safe return home is never fully guaranteed." His jaw ticks like this truly concerns him. "But that can be said about any occupation, right? Anyway, each conversation usually ends with her trying to get me to switch careers, and I end up feeling like the bad guy because she's upset."

"And you having a fake girlfriend helps . . . how?"

"I think her hope is that if I had a family, I wouldn't be so willing to risk my life. Having a . . . fake girlfriend"—he shifts uncomfortably—"it allows me to focus on my mission. Ever since I told her I was dating someone, the complaints have stopped. Don't get me wrong, she's still upset about my going to the moon, but our conversations have shifted. Dodging questions about future wedding plans is a lot easier than dodging questions about when I'm going to find a desk job."

"Were you ever seeing someone?"

Even in the interior of the car with nothing but intermittent streetlights to highlight Vincent's dark profile, I see the slight wince in his eyes and can't help but feel just a little joy at his discomfort.

"My profession doesn't exactly make room for extra personal time. I've been training for this mission for the past two years. When I'm not training, I'm researching or providing ground support for other astronauts on missions."

I'll take that as a no, he was never dating anyone. Not that I blame him. His life sounds exhausting.

"I see," I tell him. "Well, okay, then."

We come to a red light and Vincent gives me a dubious glance. "That's it? Okay?"

"That's it." He's got a busy life, but I also understand wanting to spare your parents unnecessary worry. That's exactly why I've put off telling mine about the state of disaster my life is in. "I can't imagine it's easy dealing with your mom if she's not encouraging of your career on top of pressuring you to settle down."

The thought of a marriage-minded momma pushing Vincent makes me think he'd easily slip into *Bridgerton* as a Simon replacement. They may not look the same, but Vincent is handsome enough for the big screen. I bet he does all sorts of experiments and handles sciencey things with those large hands that grip the steering wheel. His muscular thigh flexes as he moves his foot from the brake to the gas pedal, and I just know he'll get some good hang time when he walks on the moon. Is it possible to blast off the moon's surface from a single leap? Gravity is different there. Nah, probably not. Okay, so he definitely has the body, but will he be able to do justice to the love scenes?

"And you?" Vincent says.

"What about me?" My voice comes out more abruptly than I intended. He caught me off guard, in the midst of picturing him as Simon and me as Daphne in that steamy scene where they put the library ladder to *very* good use. And damn, it's definitely been a while, but I don't need these kinds of thoughts about Vincent running through my mind.

"What made you feel like you had to lie in front of your ex?"

I inwardly grimace. There's that word again. *Lie.*

"There's really not much to say. Like I told you before, we broke up a few months ago. After seeing how quickly he's moved on, I didn't want him thinking I was pining after him."

"And are you pining after him?"

"That's a hard no. He's not a bad guy, but deep down I knew our relationship wouldn't last. Especially once my mom got sick and I couldn't put in the effort needed to keep a relationship strong. Who wants to be with someone who won't pull their weight emotionally?"

I say everything matter-of-factly, but my failed relationship really was a letdown. I've always wanted someone who would stand by my side in the good and the bad like my dad has stood by my mom, but by breaking up with me, Derrick proved I was right to hold myself back and not rush anything. When we began dating, he was intentional about wanting a life partner to settle down with. But if he couldn't handle a few months of disconnect when my focus was on my mom—couldn't be my rock when I needed someone to anchor me—he never would have stuck around in a marriage when the going got tough.

Out of all the guys I've dated, none of them have been able to rise to the standard my dad has set, and now I'm not even interested in looking for a partner. How can I when my life is skittering like a car in need of alignment?

"Is your mom okay?" Vincent cautiously asks.

My nod is automatic. "She is. She and my dad are doing a cross-country RV trip. So far they've made it through Arizona and New Mexico, and she says it's a dream come true." I focus on the skyscrapers growing larger as we approach downtown and all the architectural beauty Houston is known for. "But she does have sickle-cell anemia, so some days are a struggle. And, of course, we don't know how much longer she has."

"I'm sorry to hear that," he says quietly.

Most people don't know much about the blood disorder, other than the fact that Black people are more susceptible to it than any other group. I've often wondered if a cure would have been found by now if all those brilliant scientists, doctors, and big pharma companies had to deal with seeing their loved ones in excruciating pain on the regular instead of it being a plague to a group of people who too many doctors still inconceivably believe feel pain differently.

All at once, flashbacks of seeing Mom in pain at the hospital, with the threat of losing a limb or her life, sear my brain. I take a slow breath, trying to dislodge the pressure in my chest that always comes with the devastating reminder that I could lose her at any moment.

I take my phone from my purse to see if my mom ever responded to the message I sent earlier. Once I was all done up in my dress and shoes, I snapped a selfie in front of the full-length mirror and sent it to my parents.

There's a message from her that reads **Looking good, Mimi! Enjoy your night**, followed by three heart emojis. The load on my chest lightens, and I focus my attention back on Vincent.

"Yes, it was hard at times to watch her while I was growing up, but my mom is the strongest woman I know and the best role model I could've asked for." Not wanting to bare my soul anymore to a virtual stranger, I clear my throat. "So, don't you think there are some basics we need to cover for tonight? For starters, how long have we been dating?"

"Eight months," Vincent says.

"Okay. And what's my profession? What do I say if your sister asks about my family? Do I have any siblings?"

"Slow down, Mimi. You're making this more complicated than it needs to be."

My back stiffens. "First, I am not making this complicated. I'm trying to help you by making this relationship seem more believable. I'm pretty sure your sister's not going to buy that we've been seeing each other over half a year if you've told them my daddy is a doctor but then I say he's a warehouse worker. Second, do not call me Mimi. Only my family calls me that."

"But won't it seem more believable if I use your nickname too? If you ask me, Mimi suits you. Did you know it has different meanings in Hebrew, French, and English? My favorite is the Hebrew definition. 'Rebellious.'" The word rolls off his tongue with an infuriating smile.

I silently count down from ten.

"One would think," I say through gritted teeth, "that you would be more thankful toward the person doing you a favor and not purposefully try to antagonize them."

Vincent chuckles, and despite myself I actually find the low sound sexy.

"I am thankful," he says. "But just in case you need to hear it—thank you, Mimi. I mean Amerie." He gets ahold of his laughter, but his grin is wide as he reaches over and pats my knee. Just as quickly, he places his hand back on the steering wheel. "I'm just trying to get you to loosen up a little. I've never said anything other than the fact that I was seeing someone. We'll only be there for about an hour. Long enough for my sister to see us enjoying the evening together. Whatever questions she has, you are free to answer as you like. And for the record, it won't matter to my family what profession your dad is in. Or you, for that matter. The only thing I need you to do is pretend you like me so she reports back to my mom with positive praise."

I'm tired of people trying to get me to loosen up. First Gina, now Vincent. If there's some commandment that says "Thou shall have fun," I've missed it.

We come to another red light, and Vincent looks at me nervously. I haven't verbally agreed to pretend to like him, and I think I'll let him sweat it out. I turn back to the window, and Vincent lets out a low groan. I fight back a smile.

As we continue the rest of the ride in silence, I fight the urge to touch my knee in the spot where his hand was.

CHAPTER SIX

According to Vincent, Camille finds any reason to host a party to be a good one. I haven't felt much in the festive mood lately, but I have to agree with her.

After inching our way through downtown traffic, we park at the venue and find the elevator. Even though I'm in an enclosed space with a man who sets all my senses on edge, I feel surprisingly good. The bass pulses through the handrail and up my arm, and it's like I've just woken up from a long sleep. When the doors slide open and we step onto the open rooftop, a spontaneous burst of laughter almost escapes. I tamp down the instinct, however, lest Vincent think I've lost my mind.

We're at Skylawn, a five-acre rooftop park and urban farm that sits on what used to be the historic Barbara Jordan Post Office. There is a scenic 360-degree view of skyscrapers and highways, but paved pathways lined with trees and large lawns help you forget how high up you are. I planned a wedding here two years ago. The open fields are a blank canvas ready to be transformed for any occasion, and that day it was decorated with vases of purple hydrangea, roses, and calla lilies. The featured drink had been the Purple Rain, a vodka-based cocktail. At the end of the night, a drone show dazzled the guests with the most amazing designs in the night sky before the bride and groom took off for their honeymoon.

I worried I'd be weighed down by memories of the wedding and my old job, but that's not the case. The festive atmosphere won't allow it. Tonight, black, gold, and clear balloons filled with confetti are tethered to strings marking a path from the elevator to the largest of the lawns. A live jazz band plays an instrumental version of the "Cupid Shuffle." As we get closer, I smile at a woman wearing a black cocktail dress who's part of a group dancing right on top of a huge white floor light. Her shoes are off, and she sends a flirty look over her shoulder to a man kicking it out behind her in a maroon velvet blazer.

"Camille is probably somewhere in the crowd," Vincent mutters beside me.

I beam at him before taking a step toward the lawn. "Okay, let's go find her."

"Let's get some drinks first." He places a hand on my back, guiding me to the refreshments.

I am not prepared when his hand touches my bare skin. Ripples of awareness radiate from the middle of my back, racing to the nape of my neck, and those little baby hairs stand on end. The baby hairs aren't the only thing standing at attention, and I'm grateful for the booby tape. I fight the urge to pull away, instead focusing on the sparkly outfits and the aroma of appetizers.

"You seem eager to get in there," Vincent says. "I take it I've got a regular socialite with me tonight?"

I clear my throat. "Socialite? Hardly. I do enjoy a party that's put together well though. Not too long ago you would have had no choice but to come solo. I would've been out with my best friend, or behind the scenes making all the magic like this happen."

We stop at a tall table lined with flutes of champagne. Vincent grabs two and passes one to me. While I take a small sip, he downs his in a few gulps before reaching for another.

"Whoa." I regard him warily. "How about we not get carried away. The night just started, and if you get tipsy, believe I'm calling an Uber home. Or at the very least, *I'll* be the one driving that pretty car of yours. I know how touchy you Benz owners are."

Vincent grimaces and blinks. "That burned a lot more than I thought it would." He sets the second drink back down, untouched. "Sorry. I needed something to take the edge off, but I'll take it slow from now on."

"You don't like parties?"

"I'm more comfortable in a simulation capsule or surrounded by nature." He looks down and scuffs his shiny shoes against the Astroturf. "Real nature."

"Weren't you telling me how I needed to loosen up in the car? Where'd that energy go?" I tease, trying to get him to relax.

When I do events, it's my duty to make the process go as smoothly as possible. Tonight I've let my starving senses be immersed in the glittering lights, and I didn't realize how stiff Vincent was beside me. I may be here only for the sake of him keeping up appearances in front of his sister, but I also want him to have a good time.

"I'm using it to make sure we have an escape route in the event of an emergency. Or do you think everyone's just going to line up single file to get down the stairs?" He's busy scanning the rooftop, probably preparing that exit plan, so he doesn't see me roll my eyes. Though when his eyes land back on me, something in his look shifts. "But to have the most beautiful woman attached to me tonight, I'll endure."

I cock an eyebrow, waiting for him to throw in some smart remark. But he radiates nothing but honesty and appreciation, and I'm thrown off by his attention. Warmth floods my cheeks and I'm unable to hold his gaze. "Thank you."

I look up as Vincent offers a nod of acknowledgment to a middle-aged man passing by with two white cups filled with ice cream and neon-green spoons. Vincent seems to be relaxing; still, I think we can do better. Neither of us planned on a New Year's Eve outing, but now that we're here, maybe we can make the best of it.

"I have a deal for you," I say.

Vincent's eyebrows jump up. "What kind of deal?"

"You loosen up. Forget about the crowd and the fake grass and just enjoy the night."

"If I do, what then? What will you do?"

"Then I'll enjoy the night as well." I shrug. It may not be much of an incentive for him, but now that I'm here, I realize how much I need this. To be out in the fresh air and just forget about everything.

"How can I resist an offer like that?" Vincent says with a small smile. "You've got a deal. What should we do first?"

I look in the direction the man with the ice cream came from. Among caterers walking around with a never-ending supply of champagne and meatballs, there's one lone college-age vendor set up at an ice cream stand. I smile at Vincent. "Let's get some ice cream."

Vincent follows close behind me and we join the line. "What's your favorite flavor?" he asks as we wait for the couple in front of us to make their selection.

"Chocolate, though I can't even remember the last time I had any. You?"

"Strawberry."

When it's our turn, I step forward. "Hi, can we get two, please?"

The worker looks at both me and Vincent with an apologetic smile. "I'm sorry, I'm waiting for more cups. The ice cream's been going fast, and there's only one left."

"It's okay," I tell her. I'm a little bummed, but I won't cry over a treat I don't need anyway. I turn to Vincent. "We can come back later if you want."

"Or," he says, "we can share. We'll take one chocolate. What? We're livin' it up tonight, right, Mimi?" He gives my back a playful nudge. I glare at him for using my nickname but don't protest.

Vincent thanks the worker after she loads the cup with two hearty scoops of ice cream, but before we walk away, I grab one more spoon. He looks at me, mildly insulted, and I lift one shoulder. I'm willing to share the treat with him. But a spoon too? I don't know him like that.

"So, Vincent," I say as we walk on and the first cold bite melts on my tongue. "If parties aren't your thing, what do you like to do for fun?"

"You know, hiking, rock climbing, skydiving. Stuff like that," he says nonchalantly, while my heart races at even the thought of hanging in the air.

"You don't like parties, but you'll willingly spend time in a confined capsule or throw yourself out of a plane. I guess that would make you an antisocial adrenaline junkie?"

He chuckles while spooning ice cream into his mouth. An action I absolutely do not watch closely. Not even when his tongue darts out, licking the excess off his lower lip like he did with his coffee a few days ago. It's not like I'm wondering if the ice cream would taste better from his lips than the spoon.

I press a hand to my stomach to ward off the butterflies

trying to take flight and shake my head when Vincent holds the cup out toward me. "Mind if we check out the decorations while we're here?" I ask. Nothing like some pretty sparkly things to distract from pretty men.

Vincent shrugs, and I lead him to the group of tables covered in white cloth. I move to an empty one, leaning over a chair to admire the centerpiece. It's an arrangement of gold roses in a tall vase with lit candles and large old-fashioned gold clocks. "You know, if they swapped out the gold mats and instead had everything sitting on top of a mirror, the tables would practically glow."

"I don't think I understand," Vincent says behind me.

I wave my hand. "Don't mind me. I can never shut my brain down when it comes to parties and decorations. If I get started, I'll talk your ear off all night."

"You won't hear me complaining."

I stand straight and turn to Vincent, not missing how his eyes quickly dart up, like while I was checking out the table, he was checking me out. And there go those butterflies again. Instead of looking away, I let my eyes travel over him. If we're both letting loose tonight, there's no harm in a little flirting. But when I see the now empty cup he grips in one hand, I frown at him. "You ate all of it?"

Vincent blinks at the cup, then at me. "I tried to offer you some and you shook your head. I thought that meant you were done."

I'm about to question how he finished the ice cream in the small amount of time my back was turned, but then we hear a deep voice call through the crowd, "Vince!"

We both turn to see a man in a sparkling black blazer and gold party hat. He stands a few inches shorter than Vincent and wears gold wire-frame glasses that complement his dark umber complexion.

He shoots a wide grin at Vincent as he stops before us and sticks his hand out. "As I live and breathe."

Vincent ignores the outstretched hand, instead going for a hug. "Lance. Man, it's good to see you." Both men are beaming like long-lost friends when they step back. "It's been too long."

"Way too long. You know, Camille said you might be here tonight, but I didn't believe her. She also said you wouldn't be alone." Lance looks at me, losing all trace of humor. "I don't know who you are, but I do know a woman wouldn't put up with the likes of him. If you're here under duress and need help, blink slowly two times."

I look up at Vincent with wide eyes. "What is he talking about?" Turning back to Lance, I say, "I'm happy to be here with Vincent, and I'm totally here of my own free will."

On the heels of my two slow blinks, Lance barks out a laugh. "Oh yeah, she's a keeper, Vince."

I meet Vincent's suspicious gaze and smile up at him innocently.

Vincent sighs. "Why do I have the feeling introducing you two was a bad idea?"

There's no sympathy to be found from Lance. "Maybe if you came around more often, I wouldn't have to give you a hard time all at once. Excuse me," he says to me. "I know Vince will act like his momma raised him with no manners, so I'll introduce myself. I'm Lance. And you are?"

I take his outstretched hand. "Amerie. It's a pleasure to meet you."

"The pleasure is all mine. It's not every day, or ever, actually, that Vincent brings a beautiful lady around to meet the family."

"Family?" I raise my eyebrows to Vincent.

"Of course he hasn't talked about me." Lance casts an accusing glance at Vincent. "I'm Vincent's brother-in-law."

"Pain-in-the-butt-in-law," Vincent says under a badly disguised cough.

Lance winks at me. "He only gives the people he likes a hard time. You should see him and Camille in the same room together." He holds up his hand and waves behind me. "Speaking of the lovely devil."

"I can't believe you found him before I did." Camille joins our group, first hugging Vincent, then, surprisingly, me, before she stands beside her husband.

Aside from the gold party hat that matches Lance's, Camille is the epitome of class in a long black gown with a square neckline. One side of her hair is swept up, while the other swoops over her eye in loose waves to her shoulders. Her whole look is very much giving Old Hollywood Glam, like a young Sheryl Lee Ralph in *Dreamgirls*. And now that she's here, it's time to turn the act up a notch.

I wrap my arm around Vincent's bicep and smile.

CHAPTER SEVEN

'm so glad you were able to come," Camille says to me. "I was sure Vincent would send me a last-minute text saying he was ditching after all."

"Oh, not at all. He was excited about coming."

She raises her eyebrows at Vincent. "Well, that's a first. I can only assume he wanted to show you off." Her eyes dance between Vincent and me. "It must be serious, then."

I keep my expression pleasant but wonder if I made a misstep by saying Vincent was excited. Then again, I did try to find out information on the way here. If I've portrayed Vincent as someone he's not, he has only himself to blame.

"How long have you two been dating?" Lance asks us.

"Eight months," Vincent says, and I nod.

"Eight months and you couldn't bother to bring her over for Christmas or Thanksgiving." Camille *tsk*s.

"Yeah, we missed you over the holidays, Vincent." Lance kisses the top of Camille's head. It looks like a silent communication between the couple, as if he's telling her to play nice. "It's not the same without you there. Maybe we can get you to come hang out with everyone before you take off."

Vincent's "Maybe" is noncommittal, and I don't miss how Camille stiffens.

"So what do you do for a living, Amerie?" Lance says.

"I'm an event planner."

Lance nods. "That's awesome. What kind of events do you work on?"

"Anything, really. Baby showers, birthdays, family reunions." Everything but weddings.

"Vincent is dating an event planner?" Camille smirks. "How ironic. Does he avoid your parties as well, or is it only family?"

"Oh. Um . . ." Yikes.

I glance up to Vincent for guidance. His jaw tenses. "Camille . . ."

"Don't mind her. Someone misses their big brother coming around," Lance cuts in. "We won't hound you with a hundred questions. We're just happy Vincent has someone to make sure he's not trapped in his office all the time." He winks at me and turns to Vincent. "So what's NASA got you working on?"

Vincent goes on to detail the hours of training he's been putting in for his mission, and I let out a slow breath, glad the conversation has moved on from our relationship and my career.

Until Camille catches my gaze. "It looks like you need a refill. I'll go with you for a new glass."

On second thought, maybe I'm not out of the hot seat yet. My drink is still more than half full, but it's obvious Camille wants to get her brother's girlfriend alone. "That would be lovely."

"We'll be back, boys," Camille says, and aims a meaningful stare at Lance.

Before we walk off, I send Vincent a reassuring smile. I

haven't picked up any mean-girl vibes or the feeling that Camille wants to warn me off. And since Vincent hasn't elaborated on his supposed relationship, I'm not worried about mixing up any details.

Camille and I head back in the direction of the refreshments, and when we're a good twenty feet away she lets out a sigh. "So I have a confession."

"Oh?" I've known her all of ten minutes and already she wants to spill the family tea? While I am curious about anything she may divulge about Vincent, I'm also cautious. I don't want to know anything Vincent wouldn't willingly tell me himself. Everyone is entitled to their privacy.

"Vincent probably has his suspicions, but the main reason I wanted him here tonight was so I could convince him to come to our mom's birthday celebration. It's this big thing where we spend the week out at our cabin. Vincent hasn't shown up in years, which normally wouldn't be a problem, but our parents' anniversary is the same day Vincent is set to launch."

"So your mom must be even more upset he's going to miss out," I muse.

Camille nods. "Exactly. Celebrating life is kind of our thing. It would mean the world to her, Dad too, if Vincent could at least make it for her birthday."

We reach the refreshment tables, and I place my glass down without picking up another one. I'm relieved Camille didn't reveal any deep secrets, but now I have a gut feeling about what she's about to follow up with, and I wish I hadn't left Vincent's side.

She waves to someone passing by before setting her jaw. "I was hoping you could try to convince him for me."

I try not to grimace. This is a one-night-only deal between Vincent and me, and even though I won't be seeing

Camille again, I don't want to get in the middle of their family's business or give her false hopes.

"Please?" Camille presses. "You got him here tonight, which is more than I've been able to do in years."

She looks at me, and I wonder if Vincent taught Camille how to use wounded-puppy eyes or if it was the other way around.

She sticks out her bottom lip in a pout, and I let out a sigh. "I can't make any promises." *Vincent and I are strangers, and my words have no sway over him.* "But I'll strongly insist that he consider it."

"Thank you so much!"

On the way back, Camille gets pulled aside by one of the guests and motions me ahead. Vincent and Lance are still in the same spot chatting, but now both men face the crowd. Vincent's eyes continually scan the area, and when they land on me, my heart trips at the way he lights up. Like he's been looking for me his whole life. It may sound absurd, but I can't think of the last time someone looked that excited to see me.

"Where's Camille?" Vincent says when I get closer.

I will my heart steady and point my thumb behind me. "Hostess duties called."

"Uh-oh," Lance says when he spots her. "She got held up by Noelle. Sweet lady, but she'll never let Camille go without catching her up on everyone and their momma's business. And now she's giving me her *save me or die* stare. Off I go."

I smile as Lance winks and heads for Camille.

Once we're alone, I raise my eyebrows at Vincent. "How'd we do?"

He beams down at me, looking equal parts happy and relieved. "Perfect. You were perfect. Assuming my sister didn't ambush you with a million questions?"

His smile is contagious, and I can't help but match its energy. "No ambushes."

"Good."

We're both staring at each other, and I notice how two small lines appear at the corners of Vincent's eyes. He also has a small, barely there dimple on his left cheek that hardly stands out against his five-o'clock shadow. He's clearly over the moon about his cover remaining in place, and I'm pretty pleased too. We nailed our fake relationship. I may not have everything in my life figured out, but I still have my people skills.

Someone bumps into me, and I stumble forward, bracing my hands on Vincent's chest.

He steadies me with his hands on my upper arms. "Are you okay?"

His hands are hot against my skin, and there's something so secure in being pressed close to his body as he holds me up. His eyes scan my face, stopping at my lips. Instinctively, I lick them and my heart beats so hard I feel it in my throat. I curl my fingers into his jacket, preparing to feel his mouth against mine. But then he drops his hands and pulls back so suddenly cold air whips at me. It's such a contrast from the heat previously blazing between us, I'm surprised our breaths aren't puffs of fog.

What is happening here? This is a fake date. *Fake.*

Wishing I had a drink or something to occupy my hands, I reach for the small diamond pendant on my necklace and take a small step back. "I'm fine. Thanks for the save."

Vincent regards me, regret lurking behind his eyes. I look past him and into the distance where illuminated blue letters from the aquarium dominate a portion of the skyline, not allowing myself to feel anything but relief that he didn't go in for the kiss I could swear everything in his body said he wanted. It's not like we're a real couple.

Vincent opens his mouth, but before he can get anything out, I gesture behind him. "Do you want to check out the gardens?"

He looks at me a beat longer before dipping his head in a nod. "Sure."

We stray from the dancers and refreshments to follow one of the concrete paths. Here, there are no balloons or people we're forced to squeeze between. It's just Vincent and me hidden behind raised garden beds filled with bushes and flowers, with lit-up buildings in the distance. It all feels very clandestine, *like a real date*, and I realize this was the exact wrong path to take if I want to keep some distance from him. When I look at Vincent, however, he seems content to stroll as we pass a line of palm trees and short shrubs. Maybe I'm the only one who's wound up right now. I need to try to loosen up, like Gina said, and enjoy my night out. Lord knows tomorrow will bring a new set of challenges.

"Look." I point to a concrete staircase as we round a corner. "There's our escape in case of emergency."

Vincent lets out a relieved "Hallelujah" and looks at me, eyes twinkling, when I can't help but laugh.

Biting down on my lip, I turn away and dip my finger in a large fountain full of cool running water.

"So you're an event planner, huh?" he says. "No wonder those clocks and candle decorations had you so hypnotized."

"They're called centerpieces, Vincent."

"Right," he says with a half grin, and I get the feeling he already knew that. "How long have you been in the industry?"

"Going on nine years now. I originally started as an assistant at my old company and planned my way to the top one event at a time until I was their most requested coordinator." I let out a satisfied sigh, thinking of the numerous Employee of the Quarter awards I received with certificates to spas or restaurants.

"Old company? Did you start your own business?"

I wrap my arms around my middle. "Yeah, I did."

He places a light hand to my back as we come across one couple taking selfies. They're putting a lot of trust in the metal fence that encompasses the rooftop as they lean against it, trying to get a shot with the building behind them lit up in red and green lights.

"I would think you'd be more excited about being your own boss," Vincent says.

"I am. It's just that it's a very new business. And even though I have all this experience, I can't find any clients." I shrug. "I guess that's what happens when you're one of the city's most talented-turned-notorious planners. It's a long fall from grace and an even longer climb back up."

Vincent moves from my side, stopping right in front of me.

"What do you mean, 'fall from grace'?" he says.

I'm surprised to find that I'm not fully annoyed by his questions. It's hard to be when he watches me so intently and curiously. As if he really cares what I have to say. It makes me want to spill all my secrets to him.

"My mom was hospitalized earlier this year. It wasn't the first time, but it was the closest I've come to losing her." He watches me with complete understanding. The kind of understanding that says I'm not at fault for not being able to pick up the pieces of my life after it was tossed in a whirlwind. "I was actually set to oversee a wedding the morning

I got the call that my mom was about to be rushed for surgery to have her spleen removed. Once I hung up, all that mattered was getting to her. Not bridal parties or venues or checking in with florists—just my mom. I ended up being a no-call, no-show."

"Your company didn't have backup plans for emergencies?"

"Typically, they did. But this happened on Valentine's Day. Everyone had an event they were working, so I had no one to cover for me. The wedding that should have been my bride's dream come true was a catastrophe. We're talking bridesmaids missing their cues, the DJ playing the wrong songs, kids getting to the cupcakes. You name it."

Vincent frowns. "Was it really your fault if the kids got into the cupcakes?"

"It's not just about averting disaster, but also knowing how to recover quickly. I wasn't there to do that. The whole event became a PR nightmare for my company, with clients canceling left and right for months. My old bosses at least waited for my mom to be in stable condition at the hospital before they fired me. I used to have a whole team I could count on, but now it's just me. Trying to make something out of nothing."

"It really takes someone brave to start a business from the ground up with no guarantee of success."

"Brave, or bad at making good choices."

Vincent shakes his head. "You don't really believe that, do you?"

"Well, let's see. I managed to get myself fired with no backup plan. I'm trying to hang on to an industry that wants nothing to do with me anymore. And, oh yeah, the whole morning of bad choices that landed us here." I spread out my arms to encompass the rooftop.

Vincent tilts his head and regards me with speculative eyes. "You know what you need?"

"What?" I'm breathing like I've been running, but it feels good getting everything off my chest. I thought I needed this night to forget my problems, but maybe what I needed instead was an opportunity to yell about it all.

"You need to dance."

His suggestion is so unexpected, all I do is blink for a few seconds. "Dance? Where?"

We're standing in the middle of the pathway, with nothing around us but trees and another one of those huge floor lights.

Vincent takes three steps back until he's standing over the light. His whole body glows like a star fallen down to Earth. "Yes, dance. Right here, right now."

I stare at his outstretched hand. His inviting, almost daring smile—it's a call to adventure. It's a challenge to grab hold of something new and exciting. And though I've never been one for grand escapades, I step forward and take his hand while notes of a '90s slow jam float to us.

Vincent rests his hands on my waist as I take hold of his broad shoulders, and we begin moving with the beat. "You are brave, Amerie. It sounds like life has thrown a lot of curveballs your way, but you haven't given up. Don't discredit the courage needed to keep standing."

"You know, Vincent, you're actually pretty sweet."

"First heroic, now sweet. I could get used to all these compliments." I snort and he smiles down at me. "Better now?"

Yes, but I don't let him know that. Instead, I lay my head against his chest.

He runs a hand along the small of my back. "I'll take that as yes."

"I'm almost having a good time. Don't ruin the moment with your talking," I say, and his chest vibrates with a chuckle against my ear.

He's silent once again, and I realize I've misjudged Vincent. He isn't all annoying. He's actually pleasant to be around. Right now I can't bring myself to be upset that his sister overheard us at Moon Bean.

Speaking of his sister, that reminds me. I lift my head from his chest. "I almost forgot to mention, your sister told me she had ulterior motives for getting you here tonight. It was all a ploy to convince you to go to your mom's birthday celebration. She thought I might be able to do a better job than she could."

Vincent shakes his head. "I know. Lance was talking to me about it too."

"Oh. I told her I couldn't guarantee anything but promised to at least try."

"Well, you tried," he says flatly.

Yup. I knew I hadn't imagined the tension between Vincent and his sister. It's obviously a sore subject and none of my business.

However, unbidden, Vincent opens up. "Look. I love my family. And I couldn't have asked for a better mom growing up. However, at this point so close to my launch, it's critical that I not have any distractions. If I'm subject to a week of her guilt trips, I might have a nervous breakdown. Unless you're up to the task of being my fake girlfriend for a whole week?"

I snort. "Maybe I would if I wasn't trying to keep from having my own nervous breakdown. Come tomorrow, I'm back to spending all of my energy thinking of a way to keep a roof over my head."

He lets out a low hum in the back of his throat. There's a certain kinship between us after I opened up about my parents and business in a way I haven't even opened up to Gina, and Vincent shared with me the issues he's having with his family. It makes the quiet between us feel comfortable as we sway side to side.

When I feel his chest expand against my cheek at least three times like he's about to say something, I tilt my head up. "What is it?"

He's all sexy pensiveness as he meets my gaze, but then his eyes slide away.

"Well?" I push.

He clears his throat. "I was thinking . . . I live alone and have an extra bedroom. It's nothing special, but it's yours, rent-free, if you'll come with me to my family's cabin and any other events where I might need a girlfriend at my side."

I stop dancing. "You can't be serious." But he certainly seems serious as he watches me steadily. "You don't even know me."

"I know that you stick to your commitments. You kept your word about tonight. And I know an arrangement like this would help both of us out. We'd only need to do this for three months, until I leave for my mission."

Vincent may not be so bad, but he is clearly out of his mind. It's a horrible idea to even think of continuing to play his girlfriend long-term for the chance to save money.

Right?

Yes, definitely.

"Vincent, I appreciate the offer, but I have to say no. I just don't see how it could work. I'm sorry."

He sighs and shrugs. "Don't apologize. I get it. I knew it was a long shot, but figured I'd try anyway."

The song ends and "Wobble" begins playing. There's no way I'm wobblin' or backing *anything* up for an audience of one, so I take that as our cue to head back.

We return the same way we came, passing the fountain and palm trees, and I look up at Vincent. When he glances down with a quick smile, there's a small flutter in my chest.

Yes, turning down his proposition is absolutely the right thing. Going beyond tonight would be asking for a complicated mess.

But Vincent's comment about staying *rent-free* keeps playing in my mind on a loop while visions of stupid pink papers and hospital bills flash behind my eyes. What if there's a way to ensure that accepting Vincent's offer doesn't become complicated or messy?

As we approach a hanging garland of silver and gold triangles, I stop Vincent with a hand on his elbow.

"What's up?" he says.

"Vincent, I think we should do it."

He looks me up and down and swallows. "Do *it*?"

Realizing how that must have sounded, I quickly say "No" even as a pulse of heat strikes me. "I mean, continue this." I gesture between us.

I can see it's still not clicking, because Vincent's gaze is steady on my hips. Instead of shouting so the groups of people nearby can hear us, I step closer to him. "I want to take you up on your offer and move in with you."

His eyebrows jump before his eyes dart around and he angles his head toward me. "You do?"

"Yes." Why does it feel like we're so much closer than when we were dancing? I clear my throat. "But I have conditions."

"Shoot."

"This is strictly a business arrangement. I'll go with you

to your mom's birthday and wherever else you need, given that you provide me with plenty of notice. I don't like surprises, so no last-minute crap. And when we're alone, the act is over. You do your thing, I do mine."

"Strictly business." He confirms. "But we will have to make an effort to get to know more about each other to make our relationship convincing."

"Fine. Also, instead of three months, I get to stay until you get back from your mission. That will give me time to build up my clientele and save for a new living arrangement."

"And that will save me from having to pay someone to stop by to check on the house. Do you do yard work too?"

"Yard . . . work?" I've lived in apartments my whole life.

My face must say it all as he twists his mouth to the side, and it looks like he's trying to suppress a smile. "Never mind. Anything else?"

"My parents can't know anything about this. They'd think I've lost my mind. It shouldn't be a problem since they'll be traveling out of town, but I don't know . . . Try not to yell loud when you're watching sports in case I'm on the phone with them."

"No problem. And I have a condition of my own."

"And that would be?"

"You keep at least five feet away when I have a cup of coffee in my hands." At this he doesn't hide his smile, and I grit my teeth, partly in irritation, partly to hold back my answering grin.

Before I can respond, the saxophonist speaks into the mic. "All right, y'all, it's time for the countdown. Grab someone special and let's get this new year started right."

"My favorite part of the night," Lance says from beside us, and I almost jump out of my skin.

Camille is standing with him, and I wonder if they were hiding out of sight, waiting for the perfect moment to pop out. If that's the case, did they overhear Vincent and me making our bargain?

Looking at them, I realize my fears are unfounded. Neither of the two seems concerned or like they're about to bust out some high-beam flashlights and yell *Gotcha!* Instead, Lance hauls Camille close. "Get ready, woman, because I'm about to lay it on ya." He looks at Vincent and me. "Now this is how you ring in the new year."

Vincent imitates Lance, wrapping his arm around my waist. "You got that right."

Oh Lord. How bad will it look if Vincent and I ditch before the countdown is over? The night wasn't supposed to last this long or go this far, but our whole charade will be over before we can truly get started if we bail. I'll have to kiss him.

The countdown begins. *"Ten . . . nine . . ."*

I raise my eyes to Vincent and find him watching me. "This okay?" he asks quietly.

I nod. It's one kiss. What harm will it do?

"One. Happy New Year!"

With the first notes of "1999" by Prince, as champagne bottles pop, couples embrace all around, and fireworks crackle overhead, Vincent and I lean into each other.

Instead of the quick peck-and-scram I was anticipating, Vincent's lips linger over mine. They're soft and warm, and the taste of our ice cream from earlier is much, much sweeter when coming from them. He presses into me once. Then twice. And on the third, I part my lips, allowing the kiss to deepen. Allowing my arms to wind around his neck as he pulls me against his hard frame. Allowing myself to get lost in something other than surviving and thinking about the future, if only for a moment.

When the kiss ends, I fight to catch my breath. That was no ordinary kiss. It was both sweet and scorching. Toe-curling. Over way too soon.

"Happy New Year!" Camille shouts. Her lipstick is smeared, but she's smiling without a care in the world.

I touch my lips, wondering if they have that same just-kissed-silly fullness. "Happy New Year."

"Happy New Year," Vincent says to everyone, then lower so only I can hear, "You've got a deal."

Shivers race down my spine. That damn silky voice. Those damn full lips. They're stained with a tinge of red from the transfer of my lipstick, and he sweeps his tongue across them like he's savoring the last taste of a delicious dessert.

He meets my gaze with hooded eyes, and I could easily fall into those dark depths. At the very least, be persuaded into spending a full night with him. And I've just committed to living with him for the foreseeable future.

CHAPTER EIGHT

I should've known the only way to get you out here on time was to do something juicy enough you'd be dying to hear about it," I say, shaking my head as I walk up to Gina, who is leaning on a large water fountain. Dog Mack is with her, already straining against his purple-and-white-gingham leash in an attempt to reach me. The only time I get to see the adorable rescue lab is outside where the fresh air helps keep my allergies in check.

After the party (as in 1:15 in the morning, when I was already snuggled in bed), Gina sent a text asking where and what time I was taking my morning walk. I told her the name of the park and decided to come ten minutes late so I wouldn't have to wait around. It seems, however, I underestimated how nosy she is.

"And now for something amazing," Gina says in a dramatic hush, adopting a bad Australian accent, with her phone up to her mouth like a microphone. "After what had to be a grueling hibernation, we now witness the reemergence of the stunning Amerie Price."

"What are you doing?"

"Just what will we learn about her first night back in the wild? Did she go big with a midnight kiss? Did she get lucky with a midnight fu—"

"Would you stop?" I look around to make sure no one is paying attention to Gina's foolishness. "Why do you act like this?"

"Like what?" she says, stretching her legs.

I narrow my eyes. "You know exactly what."

"You know you love me. Now, tell me how your date went."

"It wasn't a date." I start walking and Gina follows. "And it was fine. Fun even, if you can believe it."

"Oh, I believe it. You two have sizzling chemistry. Him fire, you ice." Gina nods. "Yes, ma'am."

"Wait, did you just call me cold-hearted?"

"You know what I mean. Did you kiss him?"

I try to keep a straight face, but Gina sees right through me, and her eyes grow big. "Oh my God. You did!"

"His sister was right there when midnight rolled around, and we had to play the part. What else was I supposed to do?"

"Exactly that. You were supposed to do exactly that. And I bet the kiss was out of this world." Gina pauses and smirks. "You see what I did there? 'Out of this world' because he's an astronaut?"

I smother a smile. "Yes. I get it."

Gina giggles, bumping her shoulder against mine. "Now tell me honestly, what did you think of him?"

"Honestly? He wasn't what I expected. When he's not getting under my skin with impromptu science lessons, he's not so bad."

Truth be told, everything about my night with Vincent surprised me. Sure, before he came to pick me up, I wanted to stay home knowing I'd do nothing but wallow in self-pity. But once I stepped one heel on that rooftop, slipping into party mode and playing his better half felt as easy as slipping into my favorite pair of leggings. And I think, I *hope*, it's a sign that this outrageous plan we've concocted will work.

"Can you see yourself going out with him again?" Gina asks.

Just before a speed walker reaches us, I say, "I'm actually moving in with him," then move to the side before casually continuing my stroll.

The speed walker moves on, and it's only once Mack starts whining that Gina begins walking again. Hurried footsteps and panting quickly close in on me before she's at my side again. "I'm not going to ask if you're serious, because you wouldn't be able to pull off a joke like that."

"Hey! I can pull off jokes."

"Of course you can," she says placatingly, and I give her a side-eye. "I'm just at a loss for words. I'm speechless. Dumbfounded. Flabbergasted. Bamboozled."

"You're shocked, I get it."

"Mimi, what is going on? This is totally unlike you."

I sigh. "I know, but I need a place to stay. As much as I miss our college days rooming together, you don't have the space, and I can't be around Mack for too long. And it can't be with Mom and Dad since they have their renters." I don't tell her about the hospital bill, knowing she'd definitely say I need to tell my parents about it. "Vincent is letting me move in, *rent-free*, while I work everything out."

"Rent-free?" Gina looks me up and down. "And just what is he getting in return?"

"You know better than that. I'm going to continue playing his girlfriend in front of his family. That's it."

"Free housing in exchange for a few rounds of playing pretend? Still, Mimi, that's one hell of a deal—for you."

"You're not wrong, but . . ."

Gina watches me with wide, cautious eyes. "Girl, what more can there be?"

"We'll be spending a week at his family's cabin to celebrate his mom's birthday."

Gina opens and closes her mouth two times, but nothing comes out, and I know I really have shocked her.

"When is the move-in date?" she finally asks.

"Next week. I have until the seventh to vacate my apartment without getting charged extra."

She nods. "So six days."

"Six days." I'm still trying to come to terms with the gravity of the situation.

"And this will all be for show?" she says.

"Yes. The New Year's Eve party was for show, and going to his family's cabin will be for show as well. Absolutely nothing will be going on between us otherwise."

She snorts. "You can't tell me you seriously believe that. What, are you gonna go all Mandy Moore in *A Walk to Remember* and make him promise not to fall in love with you? Because you know he's totally going to fall, right? He's already halfway gone."

"No, he's not. Why would you say that?"

Gina looks at me deadpan. "Aside from the fact that you're gorgeous? Well, let me tell you this. Before you ran into him that day at Moon Bean, he was walking right behind you. I swear, he was literally calculating all the ways he wanted to break your back."

"Break my back? Gina, you are too much."

I can admit (to myself, never Gina) that there is mutual attraction between us. But I've come across many attractive guys and never acted upon it. It's part of life. There was attraction between Derrick and me from the very beginning, but it didn't help our relationship survive.

I blow out a breath. "Really, Gina, I'm not interested in starting anything with him. In case you've forgotten, the man is leaving. To outer space. *And* he's got momma issues." I shake my head adamantly. "My focus remains on my life and my business."

"If you say so," she singsongs, sounding in no way convinced.

I REACH DOWN TO RUB MY THROBBING KNEE AND GROAN. SOMETHING has got to give. I'm in my farmers market booth seated at the six-by-eight-foot table I banged my knee on at least four times as I was trying to drag it down from my apartment. It's days like this that make me miss having (a) a team to help with setup and takedown, (b) a cache of items in storage so I wouldn't have to use my own money to buy decorations, and (c) a stellar reputation so I wouldn't have to be out here hustling instead of already planning events.

My table looks good at least, decorated with a gold cloth that sparkles in the sunlight, and in the middle is a clear flower vase full of electric twinkling lights and one dozen pink roses. Many patrons glance as they pass by, but since I'm obviously not selling homegrown food or handmade soaps, I've gotten no takers interested enough to stop by. All I need is one person, but I'm not sure if I'll find them in this crowd or if the continued bruises to my knees and bank account make this gig worth it.

My phone rings, and I glance at it, happy for the distraction.

"Hi, Mom."

"Hey, Mimi. How's it going?"

"Okay. Where are y'all today?"

"We finally made it to Las Vegas, baby! How's work going?"

"Good." I stand up, grimacing at the jolt in my knee, and move to the side of the curtain that separates me from my neighbor who's selling goat milk. "I have a few events coming up that I'm looking forward to."

"That's good, honey. Real good."

From here, I can see the window to my apartment. Four years I've been here—longer than most of my childhood apartments. In front of my window is a tall palm tree that seemed to shoot up during the summer and survived the unexpected freeze last October.

When I first moved in, dancing to "It's My House" by Diana Ross was part of my Saturday morning ritual. I spent the first six months meticulously decorating it just so, purchasing larger items with each paycheck, like my favorite navy accent chair and a large painting of a chandelier.

If the burgundy curtains were open, I'd be able to see my small round dining table that has a Christmas centerpiece with sprigs of pine and red candles on it right now.

That apartment has been my sanctuary, but as I learned long ago, they come and go. And even though I'm more than used to it—this next phase of packing and moving items into storage—I wish I wasn't. It's like I'm in one of those old commercials where a water bottle keeps blowing in the wind until someone finally picks it up and recycles it, allowing it to become something new. I'm that water bottle, only there's no Good Samaritan out there to pick me up. I have to do it myself.

"Mimi, are you there?" Mom's voice says in my ear.

"I'm here. What did you say?"

"I said, are you sure everything is all right? I'm worried about you."

"Mom, I . . ."

I'm so close to telling her about the crazy deal I struck with Vincent, but her words hit me. She's worried about me. She can't have a good time if she's worried about me. She and Dad can't focus on all the new experiences and wonders in the time they have together if they're thinking about me. So, as much as it kills me to have to continue to deal with this on my own, I'll keep silent.

"Mimi?"

"Sorry, I'm fine. I'm actually at a work event now. That's probably why I sound a little distracted."

"You should have told me you were at work," she admonishes.

"It's okay. I wanted to hear your voice." I grip the phone tighter, wishing she really were here.

"Well, you can call me anytime. You know that. But I'll let you go now. We wouldn't want Jacob or Johnson getting on you."

If she only knew. "Okay. I'll talk to you and Daddy later. Love you."

I put my phone in my back pocket but remain by the side of the partition. I hear a familiar woman's voice asking my neighbor about the age of their goats. I walk forward and poke my head around.

Just as I suspected, I see Ms. Katrina. I planned many events for her when I was with Jacob and Johnson. Her company's business party, her family reunion, and her daughter's wedding to name a few. She always has some big event to celebrate, and she's been the best type of client. She'd give us a list of her must-haves and leave the rest of the vision and execution to us. Countless times, she mentioned how I was the best thing to happen to Jacob and Johnson, and I knew it wasn't lip service, because the woman is honest to a fault.

I wonder if she's heard of my being fired yet and who's been assigned to take over her future events.

Would she be willing to give me a chance?

I rub my necklace and chew on my bottom lip as she picks up a bar of soap and smells it. Sure, she liked what I had to offer when I was with Jacob and Johnson, but now everything is different. I don't have the same resources.

I mentally shake my head and stand up straight. No doubts allowed. I'm still Amerie Price. I can still rock the hell out of a table centerpiece, and I can still get shit done. All I need is one client, and she's less than twenty feet away.

Ms. Katrina pays for a glass bottle of goat milk and soap, placing them in a green mesh tote before she begins walking to another booth. My palms are sweaty, but I take a chance and call her name. "Ms. Katrina!"

She stops and turns around, and her eyes immediately light up. "Amerie." She rushes to my booth. "I am so happy to see you."

I pause. "You are?"

"Yes, dear. Laurie is pregnant, and I'm ready to throw her the biggest and best baby shower. She's already thirty weeks, so how soon can we make this happen?"

I blink fast and let my brain catch up with what's happening. Ms. Katrina has never been one to waste time. "Wait, Ms. Katrina, I'd love to help you, but first I need to let you know I'm no longer with Jacob and Johnson."

"Well, I already know that. It's a crime and a shame." She shakes her head. "After all you've done up there, for them to toss you aside after one bout of bad press is despicable. They tried to get me to go with one of the other coordinators, but you know I don't trust them like I do you. You've started your own business, right? That's what you're doing out here?" She looks past me to my table setup and points. "I want that setup if Laurie is having a girl. She's finally going to let us know this weekend. I'm sure you'll come up with something equally nice if it's a boy."

I've always liked Ms. Katrina. A woman who knows what she wants. And I'm not about to dissuade my first sure client.

I step back and gesture toward the table. "How about we have a seat and chat a little more."

My cheeks hurt from grinning so much as I take a seat, but with this step, a clearer future is beginning to form. Living with Vincent for a few months may be just the extra time I need to get on my feet, because Amerie Price is back.

CHAPTER NINE

I n fifty feet, turn left."

The skinny blue line draws nearer to the destination marker on my phone's navigation app, and my shoulders tense up. In less than ten minutes, I'll be at my new temporary home. I'll have a roommate.

It physically hurt my soul to check my bank account and see that the payment for my mom's hospital bill cleared, but I find peace knowing it will never be a burden to my parents. Old muscle memory carried me through the process of boxing up my pots and pans, wrapping framed photos in old newspapers to prevent chipping, and cleaning every square inch to ensure the return of my deposit. I got it all done and didn't bat an eye as I closed the door to apartment 2323 for the last time and handed the keys to the front office.

But now that I'm on NASA Road 1, I can't breathe.

Who in their right mind would think it's a good idea to move in with a stranger—no, to practically blackmail a stranger—all to avoid relying on their mom and dad? Me, apparently. Because when you boil everything down, that's exactly what I've done. I realized Vincent had a need and made sure everything worked for my benefit. Now, I'm not only keeping things from my parents but also taking advantage of someone.

"This is going to be a disaster."

Instead of turning left at the upcoming intersection, I see a Starbucks on the corner and pull in. I order an iced coffee and park, trying to think of any good reason I shouldn't find the nearest extended-stay motel. Yes, it would be pricier compared to the free-ninety-nine option Vincent is offering, but I wouldn't be putting myself in the middle of a complicated mess.

I don't find a motel, though. Instead, I do what every other person who grew up glued to their cell phone does when stressed: disassociate from life by browsing social media as my mind wanders and blood pressure returns to normal.

For one, I am not blackmailing Vincent. I haven't threatened to expose him to his family if he doesn't comply. Two, he's getting a lot out of this arrangement as well. Three, he's a grown-ass man capable of getting himself into and out of deals. Four . . . well, those are the only points that matter in this instance, because I'm still lying to Mom and Dad. But for good reason.

Steady breath in and ease it out. Yes, this is the way.

I go for a sip of my iced coffee only to be met with the hollow sound of ice. It's just as well. I've wasted enough time, and I know I won't, or can't, back out.

When I set the cup down, my phone pings with a message from Vincent.

> **Vincent: In case it's hard to see the house number, mine is the one with pink camellia bushes.**

> **Vincent: The Benz will be in the garage, and I'm going to move my truck to the street. Feel free to park on either side of the driveway.**

Two texts in less than a minute. Is Vincent also nervous about this arrangement? Yesterday I sent him a text that I would be there by twelve, but thanks to my pit stop it's twenty minutes past. Maybe he thinks I'm having a change of heart and am going to leave him high and dry.

I send him a message to quell any fears.

Me: Thanks. I'm about ten minutes out.

Vincent: Don't text and drive.

I roll my eyes and bring the navigation back up. It's time to get to Vincent's house.

Eight minutes later, I arrive at a traditional-style red-brick house with white trim around the windows and a black door. As soon as I park on the left side of the three-car garage, Vincent comes outside, and my pulse picks up.

Seeing him here, out of his pressed slacks and Oxfords and instead sporting a fitted navy sweater with dark-wash jeans, it's undeniable that I'm here in his territory and this is happening. I'll have to get used to seeing and interacting with this version of Vincent. What else will I have to get used to? Him walking around with no shirt? Or worse, no pants?

Knowing he can't see me that well through my tinted windows, I take a few moments to center myself. This doesn't have to be a big deal. We're temporary roommates, and that's it. I kill the engine and step out.

As soon as I pop the trunk, Vincent is all over my things. "I'll get everything inside for you," he says.

I meet him at the back of the car, frowning as he reaches in for the first box until I notice how his muscles flex as he pulls it out.

"Ready to see your new home?"

I snap my gaze away from his arms. "You mean temporary home." I'm here until his mission is over—sooner if business takes off—then I'm out. "Oh, let me grab that."

He's got my Vera Bradley weekender hooked onto his forearm, but when I reach for it he sidesteps me to walk toward the house. I cross my arms and follow him. One thing I won't do is beg a man to let me help him. Living by myself on the second floor, I had to do all the heavy lifting myself, be it groceries or packages dropped at the front office. That damn farmers market table. And though I grew up to the likes of my mom jamming out to "Independent Women Part I," Vincent can take it from here.

Still, I can't resist digging at him. "Me man, big muscles," I say with a deep voice.

Vincent quickly looks back. "Ah, so you admit it."

"Admit what?"

"You've noticed the guns."

Welp. I walked right into that one.

Gritting my teeth, I keep silent and focus as we pass a bush with beautiful pink flowers. "Do you have a landscaper come out?" The HOA here must be proficient, because the surrounding houses all have trimmed lawns and not a trash can in sight, but Vincent's is the only yard with anything blooming in this cold weather.

"I am the landscaper," he says. "Been doing yard work since I was strong enough to push a lawnmower, which, you can probably imagine, happened when I was pretty young." He chuckles at my snort while balancing the box on his knee to turn the door handle. "Unless I'm out of town for an extended time, I take care of everything." He nudges the door open with his foot and steps inside.

I've always enjoyed meeting clients in their homes to

see what insights I can glean about their lives from walking into their personal space, and visiting the occasional model home to get an idea of what I'd do with my own someday used to be my favorite downtime activity. As Vincent disappears inside, I pick up my pace, curious to see what I'll learn about this successful astronaut who will be my temporary roommate.

The house has an open floor plan, so walking into the living room gives me a view of the kitchen with black appliances, a fixed island, and a round mahogany table. There is an L-shaped black couch that takes up most of the space in front of a large mounted TV. With a perfect view into the backyard through a sliding glass door, I spot one lawn chair and a telescope.

What I don't see is anything on the walls. No family pictures, no art, no floating shelves. Nothing to spruce up the generic eggshell color and give me a glimpse of who Vincent really is.

"How long have you lived here?" I ask.

"Going on four years."

I feel my eyebrows jump. Four years, and it still looks like this? At the very least, I would have painted an accent wall as soon as I had the chance. "I'm guessing with all the traveling, decorating isn't on your list of priorities."

Vincent's head moves from the barren wall in the living room to the kitchen. "I just remodeled the kitchen and installed hardwood. You don't like it?"

"Your house is great," I assure him quickly, instantly feeling bad for insulting his home. I need to remember not every kid was like me—hoarding magazine clippings of furniture and free paint swatches from the hardware store in order to create old-school vision boards. I also need to remember that I'm a guest in Vincent's house and act accordingly by not insulting him. And really, it isn't bad at all. With a few personal touches, the place could easily be transformed from "This is my home and I live here" to "Welcome to casa de Vincent, my fortress, comfort, and place of peace."

"Your room is back this way," Vincent says, snapping my attention back to him, and I can't help but notice his voice is beginning to sound a little strained under the weight of the box. My dad always said there was an art to packing. One I've never mastered, always prone to over-stuffing boxes to save time. And I'm pretty sure Vincent grabbed the box with my books. I bet now he's wishing he hadn't pranced off with my bag instead of letting me take it to lighten his load.

He leads me down a hallway, past a closet with French doors and into a room on the right. I can tell he tries to put the box down lightly, but it makes a loud *thunk* as it hits the floor. I clench my lips together to keep from laughing at the pained look on his face.

"Do you need a breather before you get the rest?" I say.

He lets out a gruff "No," but is slow to straighten. Poor guy.

I shake my head and look around the room, stifling a gasp of horror. Scuffed slab is exposed from the floor having been ripped up, and there are only two pieces of furniture. A twin-size bed with a gray blanket and a dresser with a vicious layer of dust on the top. It might be my imagination, but simply looking at it makes my throat itchy.

When I meet Vincent's eyes, he rubs the back of his neck. "Yeah, I didn't expect to have a guest so soon."

"You've lived here four years," I say incredulously.

I'm trying not to freak out, but this room makes Motel 6 look like a four-star hotel. Did I really worry I was blackmailing him, when all the while he knew I'd be walking into this?

Vincent winces. "I know. I'm sorry. I'd planned on laying carpet down before you got here but got held up with work. I should be able to get to it this weekend so at least you won't have to walk on the cold floor."

Dumbfounded, all I can do is nod before taking in the room again. My gaze lands on the window. No curtains. At least it has those sturdy wooden blinds that will keep anyone from being able to see through at night.

"You hate it," Vincent deadpans.

Smart man.

I sigh, and this time I know I'm not imagining the scratch in my throat. "I'll be honest, this isn't quite what I was expecting, but I'll make it work." I pause to clear my throat as the tickle intensifies. "I'll get some of my stuff out of storage to make it homier. After you lay down the carpet, of course."

Vincent looks unconvinced. "Are you sure?"

I force myself to nod. If anything, this room serves as even more motivation to get my life together and find my own place.

"I'm sure," I get out before a fit of coughing overtakes me.

"What's wrong?" Vincent asks, once my hacking subsides.

I'm caught off guard by how quickly he comes to stand before me, peering down with obvious concern. "It's the dust," I say, fighting the urge to take a step back. Why does his presence always make him seem so much larger than he is? "It's messing with my allergies. I'll be fine, I just need to use your vacuum and duster."

After a moment of studying me, Vincent shakes his head. "No. I knew I shouldn't have brought you in here." He retraces his steps back to the box, squats with his feet braced and shoulders back in perfect form, and hefts it up again. "Come with me."

My throat burns too much to ask any questions, so I tag along, right on his heels, shutting the door with a firm *click*. This time he leads me to the room at the end of the hall.

Now this one is cozy. There's a king-size bed with a cream comforter and navy knitted throw blanket at the foot. One side of the bed has an ebony nightstand to match the headboard, while the other has a full-length mirror. It's framed in white wood rather than the gold I would have chosen for my own room, but still a nice touch. And the large window has cream curtains. It immediately dawns on me that this must be the master bedroom.

"You want me to take your room?" I ask.

Vincent sets my overnight bag on the bed. "Yup. Feel free to move anything to your liking."

I shake my head. "No, I can't impose on you like this." Lord knows I want to, because this is a million times better than the guest room, but I can't.

"Amerie, it's not an issue."

"But it's your room." If any place is sacred in a person's home, it's their bedroom.

Vincent shrugs. "Half the time I fall asleep in my office or on the couch anyway."

"Are you sure?" I play with the necklace at my throat. I don't want to stand here and argue all day about sleeping arrangements, but just thinking about going back to the guest room makes my throat close up.

"Yes, Amerie. You're my guest and I want you to be comfortable," Vincent says. "As long as you don't mind sharing the bathroom, then I'm all good."

"Well, okay."

He nods. "Good. That door leads to the bathroom. You'll find a closet in there with towels and toiletries. I spend a lot of time in my office, which takes up the floor upstairs. Can I get you anything right now?"

"No, I think I'm all set."

"Then I'll be back with more boxes," he says, and I swear he groans as he walks out. Luckily for him, the rest of the boxes are filled with lighter items like my clothes, a small portion of my shoe collection, and knitted scarves from my mom.

It's a little overwhelming as I once again take in the room. I'm literally invading his personal space.

I take stock of my new surroundings. The pillow feels nice as I push against it. Not too hard, not too soft. The sheets are made of high-quality cotton, feeling almost silky against my palm, and I know it'll be luxurious once I lie down. No scratchy threadbare linens here. Moving on to the nightstand, I open the top drawer where I'm met with a black box of condoms. I'm tempted to pick them up and see how many have been used, but I manage to close the drawer. I'm already taking over his room, I don't need to violate his privacy.

I move to the bathroom and open the door, intending to get a quick peek. But what I see has me nearly ripping the hinges off to get inside. It's the bathroom of my dreams.

A clawfoot tub large enough for two people to comfortably sink into sits below black casement windows, and I instantly imagine steaming water, floating rose petals, and a glass of wine waiting for me after a long day. The shower *chamber*—since *stall* doesn't adequately describe the area with more space than the walk-in closet at my old apartment—has two showerheads. A detachable one against the wall, and a large square showerhead mounted on the ceiling. I know, with every fiber of my being, hair wash days will never be the same.

"Doing okay?" Vincent calls from the room.

"Mm-hmm," I squeak. I am, in fact, not doing okay. I don't know if I'm even alive.

The tiles on the floor and walls look like marble, so the room gleams with light from the window. The only thing missing is a chandelier above the tub. Vincent couldn't have had the foresight to know I would one day be staying with him, so its absence is understandable.

"Soon," I promise the bathroom, running my hand over the long counter. "Very soon."

When I step back into the room, I see Vincent has left my suitcase and another box near the door. I didn't even make it to the closet to see if my clothes will fit or if I'll have to store them in the guest room. At this point, however, I think if I go back into the bathroom, I'll never make it out.

I go to the bed and open my overnight bag to begin unpacking. The first thing I grab is my makeup bag, which I place on the dresser. Reaching in again, this time I pull out the box with my pink vibrator. Good ol' Little Rocket. I don't know how much use I'll get out of it here. I think it would feel weird to use it in Vincent's bed. Just in case, I take it from the box to test the sound. Once I turn it on, I immediately switch it back off. It sounds ten times louder than it did in my apartment. There's no telling if Vincent will be able to hear the buzzing from the guest room if the mood strikes. I don't think I'll use it outside of the shower, where running water can mask the sound.

"Do you have bricks in this thing?"

At the sound of Vincent's voice, I fumble with the vibrator, almost dropping it before I manage to get the night-stand open and throw it in. Right with the condoms.

Real smooth.

When I turn around, Vincent's face is carefully blank, letting me know he absolutely saw what was in my hands. My body turns up a thousand degrees, but I try to find consolation in the fact that at least it was a small, simple thing, and not some large, triple-suction contraption I considered after binge-reading alien romances.

Well, I am a woman who enjoys her orgasms, and it is the twenty-first century. When Vincent finally meets my gaze, I lift my chin, daring him to say something funny. "What was that?"

He coughs into his hand. "This is everything. You can make room in the dresser or closet."

"Thank you."

He nods once before booking it out of the room, closing the door behind him. I collapse onto the bed and groan into my hands. Good Lord.

CHAPTER TEN

I am in heaven. I have to be. There is no earthly explanation as to why I'm cocooned inside a literal cloud that's so soft it can't be man-made. And why angels are singing throughout the sky.

Only these angels are off-key. And way too loud.

Do they really sing jacked-up versions of Usher in the heavenly halls? I don't think this is right.

Now half-awake, I toss to the other side of my cloud and try to burrow in deeper. Try to fall back into the best sleep of my life and ignore what I now realize aren't angels, but my neighbors being uncharacteristically loud.

My neighbor to the right is an EMT who usually works this early. My neighbors to the left both work from home and keep it pretty low-key. There is nothing low-key about the loud, deep singing that's hardly muffled through the door.

Welp, I'm awake now. Squinting into the dark room, I see the time on an unfamiliar digital clock. Where I am and why I'm here finally dawn on me, as well as the fact that the absolutely non-angelic voice belongs to none other than Vincent.

I groan and sit up, reaching for my phone on the nightstand. There are only another ten minutes before my alarm is set to go off, so there's no point in trying to get more sleep.

"Good morning," Vincent greets me when I come out of the room. He's cooking in the kitchen, filling the air with the savory scent of bacon.

I probably look like a tired kid as I shake my head no but might as well get this out of the way. "You should probably know that I'm not in the best mood when I wake up. I need my morning walk first. Then coffee. Then a good twenty minutes. You can save me some bacon though. I assume your neighborhood is safe to walk around this early?"

Vincent turns over a strip. "Noted, noted, and noted. And yes, the neighborhood is perfectly safe." I begin walking to the door, and he continues. "Just be careful when you pass Mr. Rivera's house. It's the last one before the stop sign. He used to be a clown and sometimes gets confused. Thinks he's running late for a children's party. If he comes running out in full gear, muttering about his little car being stolen, stand still like a tree and he won't even notice you're there."

Oh God.

I shudder hard. I hate clowns. And Vincent lives on a cul-de-sac, so it's not like I can walk the other way to avoid the house. I guess I could drive to one of my favorite parks or the golf course, which would only be about twenty minutes away.

I turn to Vincent, ready to ask if he can recommend somewhere nearby, only to see his shoulders shaking as he stands over the stove.

My right eye begins twitching. "You are not funny, Vincent!" I exclaim, barely containing the urge to stomp my foot like a child.

With the jig up, Vincent is free to let his laughter loose.

"Oh, but I am." He wipes tears from his eyes. "You should have seen the look on your face."

Now I do stomp to the door, and Vincent's deep laughter trails after me until I'm outside.

Unlike the man, his neighborhood is quiet. Peaceful. The type of place where young couples settle with hopes of growing their families and older couples wait for their adult kids to come home for a visit, arms open and eagerly awaiting hugs from their grandbabies.

As I wait to cross one of the streets, a man in a white SUV waves as he drives past. I'm so stunned, it doesn't dawn on me to wave back before he's gone. In apartments, unless you own the unit and live there for years, most people try to avoid leaving at the same time as their neighbors. Forget making eye contact. Neighbors being *neighborly* is something I'll have to get used to.

I walk toward a small park with a red jungle gym, slides, and swings. It's too early for anyone to be out playing, but I imagine it's the hot spot for toddler fun in the afternoons. A lady walking two German shepherds, coming from the opposite direction, smiles when we make eye contact.

"Good morning," she says.

This time I'm prepared and quickly respond, "Good morning." We keep going our separate ways, and I smile.

The fresh air has seeped into my lungs, and the sun has lightened the sky with streaks of orange by the time I make it back to Vincent's house. He's sitting at the kitchen table with his laptop out and his phone to his ear.

He moves the speaker away from his mouth and addresses me. "There's a plate in the microwave, and the coffee maker is filled with plenty of water."

"Thank you."

"Yes, that was her," Vincent says as I open the microwave.

I wasn't intending to listen to his conversation, but it's obvious he was talking about me. As I begin quietly moving around the kitchen, I keep one ear turned toward him.

I have to pull out two drawers before finding the utensils and three cabinets before coming upon the coffee mugs.

"You don't need to talk to her now," Vincent says to the phone. "You'll talk to her when you meet her . . . When? When we come down on the twenty-first."

I can't make out the words, but an excited female voice blasts from the phone as Vincent pulls it away from his ear. That answers my question about who he's speaking to.

I move to the sleek coffee maker and stand there for a minute. It looks like one of those machines that can give you cappuccinos, lattes, and other fancy drinks my dad would scoff at. Which button will make a simple black brew?

"I'll give you a call later, Mom. I need to help Amerie before she spills coffee all over my floor . . . Yes, I said we're coming . . . Love you too." He rises from the table and comes to stand next to me. "Do you want to add any syrup or creamer?"

Next to the coffee maker is a half-empty bottle of caramel syrup. As sweet as Vincent took his coffee at Moon Bean, I wouldn't be surprised if he goes through one in a week.

I give him the side-eye for that quip about me spilling coffee and shake my head no. "All I need is cinnamon, if you have it."

Vincent takes the cup from my hand, his fingers brushing mine, and he sets it under a silver nozzle. The machine barely makes any noise before coffee begins spouting out.

Vincent remains standing next to me as we watch the cup fill to the brim in silence. When I left for my walk, he had on flannel pajamas and a white crewneck. Now he's wearing dark jeans and a red sweater, smelling like fresh soap. I turn slightly away, aware that after my walk I probably smell like outside.

"Your mom must be pretty happy that she'll see you on her birthday," I say, scooting over an inch.

Vincent nods. "That, and she's beyond excited to meet my girlfriend."

"That explains why I heard what sounded like her speaking in tongues when you told her we were both coming."

The side of his mouth twitches.

The coffee stops, and before I can grab the cup, Vincent opens the cabinet above, his side once again brushing against me, and he hands me a glass jar of cinnamon.

"Thank you," I say.

I take my plate and coffee to the table and eat while Vincent goes back to his computer. When I take a sip of coffee, I almost fall out of my chair.

"Vincent!" I exclaim, and he snaps his eyes to me. "You mean to tell me you have this glorious coffee machine at home, and you still stop at Moon Bean on the regular?"

He quirks an eyebrow. "You like it?"

"Like it? I've decided that when this whole thing is over"—I gesture between us—"I'm actually taking your coffee machine with me and we're getting married."

"Who says I'll let you leave?"

I roll my eyes at him and go back to my food. Fork in one hand and phone in the other, I navigate to the list I worked on last night and text it to Vincent.

His phone vibrates beside him, and he picks it up, then looks at me with a puzzled frown. "What's this?"

"Important facts you need to know about me so we can make this act convincing."

"I thought one of the points of you moving in was so we

could get to know each other better organically. Not through lists."

Yes, that was one of the advantages to moving in. However, once I unpacked and was in the room by myself, I heard Vincent moving around upstairs in his office, and I'm not ashamed to say the thought of actually spending time with him made me . . . nervous.

Okay, maybe I am a *little* ashamed to admit it.

I'm just going to chalk it up to the fact that he likes to try to annoy me. Case in point, his joke about the clown. So yes, lists are a better way to go. But is it my imagination, or does he seem disappointed?

"I'm sure we'll get to that point," I say. "But this is a good start, don't you think?"

He studies the list for a few moments, then looks at me with a glint of teasing in his eyes. "You hate clowns?"

"Obviously."

He chuckles. "You also hate roller coasters and heights. You don't like seafood. Ironic since you practically live on the Gulf. But peanut butter and jelly sandwiches are your comfort food?"

I shrug. "My dad works for a bread distributor. When I was younger and he was a factory worker there, he'd bring fresh loaves home and make the best sandwiches. The secret is to add butter."

"Butter to PB and J?"

"Don't knock it until you try it."

"I'll guess I'll take your word for it." He continues reading, and I take a sip of the coffee. "Your favorite color is gold. Classy. You're allergic to cats and dogs." He frowns.

"Is that a problem?"

"My youngest sister, Brianna, just got a goldendoodle. I'm sure she'll bring it to the cabin with her."

"Oh, aren't those a hypoallergenic breed?"

When Gina was on the hunt for a pet, she initially set out to get a goldendoodle so I wouldn't be miserable when I went to her apartment. That was until she saw the price tag from a local breeder. She ended up adopting Mack from the shelter instead after I continuously assured her I wouldn't take offense and that we could still hang out at my place.

Vincent shakes his head. "No dog is truly hypoallergenic. Yes, some breeds shed less than others, but I don't want you to be miserable while we're there. Do you have medicine for your allergies?"

"Yes."

"Good. Make sure to bring it."

I bite back a sharp comeback about being able to take care of myself. Not that my parents were neglectful, but I found it hard to complain about runny noses or headaches when it was nothing compared to what my mom went through. But since Vincent's heart is in the right place, I hold my tongue.

"Noted," I say. "Now, as you can see, I'm an open book. Why don't you think of the things that matter most about yourself and send me a list as well. We have, what, two weeks before your mom's birthday? That'll give me time to study—"

"Whoa." He looks up from my list again and cuts me off, then regards me with wide, incredulous eyes. "You've lived in Houston almost your whole life, and you've never been to the Space Center?"

I narrow my eyes at him. "Are you going to have something to say about everything I've written? I'm sure it's a cardinal sin to you, but it's not that serious. I lived in San Antonio for a few years, and I'm guessing that's when the majority of the field trips happened. I came back for high school and wasn't in any of those sciencey clubs that visited often."

Vincent obviously can't wrap his mind around the fact because he doesn't let up. "And you were never curious about going yourself? And let me guess, when you were in San Antonio, you didn't visit the Alamo either, did you?" He shakes his head. "I don't need the answer to that."

"Good, because you won't like it."

"That's it. I'm taking you there."

I eye him up and down. "To the Alamo?"

He lets out an exasperated sigh. "No. To the Space Center. Today."

"Vincent, you can't be serious," I sputter. "For one, it's the weekend, so I'm sure it'll be packed. If I recall correctly, you hate crowds. And two, you're working."

"You remembered I hate crowds. See, we're getting to know each other better already. We don't need these lists. Okay, okay." He laughs when I cross my arms and glare. "But in all seriousness, do you think my family is going to believe we've been together for months and I've never taken you there? Consider this part of the getting-to-know-me phase."

CHAPTER ELEVEN

I tilt my head for a better look at a model of an old-school space suit that looks like it was inspired by the Tin Man from *The Wiz*. "So this is where it all began, huh?"

As we walk through the Space Center's exhibit, the uniforms become more modern until we stop at a blue suit I remember Vincent wearing on his NASA biography page.

I lean into him. "Do I get any special behind-the-scenes access? Can we see Mission Control? Oh, I want to see your spaceship! And I'm not talking about that mock ship we passed through earlier. I want to see the real thing. Where y'all eat. Sleep. The kitchen."

Vincent massages the bridge of his nose, and I swear he utters "Bruh" under his breath. "Amerie, let's get one thing straight—this isn't *Star Trek*. It's a space shuttle, or spacecraft. It's used to efficiently shuttle people to and from Earth."

"*Efficiently*," I mock. "Sounds fun." It actually sounds horrifying, but who am I to tell people how to live their lives?

I stop in front of a large framed picture of the *Columbia* shuttle. "How fast do these things go, anyway?"

Vincent shifts beside me, and for the third time today his body brushes up against mine. I ignore the tingles.

"In the span of eight and a half minutes, spacecraft go from zero to about eighteen thousand miles per hour and must maintain that speed to keep from falling back into Earth's orbit."

"I don't know what's more amazing: the fact that we have the capability to make something that sophisticated or that people willingly travel at those speeds, stuck in close quarters with strangers."

"We're really not strangers." Vincent shrugs. "These are people I've been learning alongside for years. We're more like family. We're all working with a common goal in mind and have to rely on one another to make our mission successful. Let's check this out."

He leads me to an area with a line of people, and my stomach tightens when I see the large white dome ahead. "What is this for?"

"Well, you got a crash course in space shuttles, now it's time for your very own space walk. It's virtual reality."

His eyes gleam like he's about to show me one of his favorite toys, but I bite down on my lip and look away. "Oh."

Vincent bumps me with his elbow for contact number four. "What's wrong?"

"Nothing's wrong . . ." I reach for my necklace. "But aren't these things more like roller coasters? I've seen those videos of people falling when it gets a little too real."

"Now I know another thing about my Mimi. She likes parties but doesn't like to live on the edge."

"*Your* Mimi?"

He looks away like he's momentarily embarrassed, then hits me with a panty-dropping smile that sends my heart pumping way too hard. I hear a woman's gasp somewhere behind me and wonder if she's just seen an awe-inspiring space exhibit or Vincent's grin.

"You're my Mimi for the next few months, right?" he says.

"Next person," the attendant says.

"It's your turn." Vincent pushes me forward before I can protest.

"My turn? What about you?"

"I'll be right here watching and talking you through it." He points at a curved monitor, which I realize will show what I'm doing. Right next to the monitor is a sign that warns people the experience may cause severe disorientation. I cut a glare at him.

"Don't worry. You've got this."

Well, I'm not about to back down now, not with an audience around. I step into a large white box and walk to the small black circle that indicates my station. Before covering my eyes with the freshly sanitized boxy goggles, I turn to Vincent and, true to his word, he's behind me, only inches away. "I can't believe I let you bring me here." I huff out a puff of air and put the headgear on.

My goggles turn on, and the first thing that pops up is another ominous warning about severe disorientation. I swallow. Then the screen turns on and I'm in a bright white room.

"Welcome to Gateway,*"* an ominous voice says in my ears.

I'm onboard the command module that orbits the moon. My mission is to go to the moon's south pole and extract ice. Sounds simple enough.

After getting instructions on squeezing my hands to grab items, it's time to climb the rungs and get into the vehicle that will shuttle me to the moon's surface. The movements are intuitive.

"It feels like I'm really here," I say, swiveling my head around to explore the small craft. I reach a small window and peer out into an endless dark void. While I know it's nothing but a convincing simulation, my stomach immediately rejects what my brain knows, and I jerk forward on a gag. "Nope." I shake my head, ready to take the goggles off and call it a day.

"You got this," Vincent says, and gives me an encouraging pat on the back.

I most certainly do not. But I close my eyes and breathe in deeply until my stomach settles. "Okay, I got this."

I make it through a small hatch and glide to a shuttle that will transport me down to the moon. The moon landing is easy and painless, and I think I'm starting to get the hang of this. I'm surrounded by shades of gray on rough terrain. I look up, and I'm met with a glorious view of Earth. It's a half sphere of glowing blue and white on the horizon, and farther than I imagined it would be. The whole moon lacks any clouds or sound. It's eerily quiet.

"Let's get to work," the voice urges. *"Take the drill from your toolbox and use it to break the ice."*

Apparently I have a toolbox, which pops up to my right. I squeeze my hand over the lock to open it. A silver drill lies there, but before I reach for it, it floats away. "Oh no!" All I can do is watch helplessly as it gets smaller and smaller.

Vincent chuckles behind me, and as I swat him away, an alarm begins going off.

"It looks like we've got space debris coming our way. Hurry and get to the shuttle!"

My heart hammers in my chest as I once again can't get my body to reconcile the fact that all of this is fake. It's a race to get back to my shuttle, but everything is moving so slowly. Damn the moon's weak gravity.

"Try leaping," Vincent says.

I do what he says, but just when it feels like I'll make it back to the shuttle in one piece, chunks of space debris begin hammering down.

I jump back, and Vincent's right there, in actual reality. "Whoa," he soothes. "You're okay."

I don't believe him for a second. I grab his arm and squeeze my eyes shut while the commander continues railing in my ear and particles fall from the sky. I guess eventually my mission is deemed a failure or I die or something, because the screen goes black.

And this is exactly why I could never be an astronaut.

Vincent pries my fingers off him and takes off my gloves, then goggles. I look to him as I escape the box of doom. While he clearly feels sorry for me, as he should for sending me in there, he also looks seconds away from laughing.

I hit him with my frostiest glare until his smirk disappears, but when a smile cracks through, I stomp away from him.

"Where are you going?" he asks, easily catching up with me.

"To the restroom."

He hangs back by the gift shop as I walk into the women's bathroom. I don't even need to go, but I wash my hands, then move to the paper towel dispenser. After drying my hands, I put the damp, rough paper against the back of my neck and sigh. Why does it feel like my failed mission is some sort of bad omen for this act with Vincent? All these doubts are creeping up again. What if I get in front of his parents and they ask me the kind of questions his girlfriend should know about space, and when I don't, they instantly peg me as an imposter. Then I'll have no choice but to come clean.

"Excuse me," a lady with dripping hands says, interrupting my doomsday thoughts.

"Sorry." I instantly move from in front of the dispenser and throw my paper towel away before leaving.

Vincent waits for me in the same spot where I left him, a respectable distance away from the restrooms. No smirks or laugh lines adorn his face. Instead he looks at me with the most contrite eyes that tell me he's sorry for laughing earlier. He looks so pitiful that now I want to laugh.

As I approach, he presents a stuffed animal from behind his back. It's the cutest round teddy bear wearing a white space suit and plastic helmet.

"What's this?" I ask.

"I couldn't let you leave here with only a sour stomach, now, could I?"

I don't hesitate in reaching for the toy. Maybe it's the little kid in me who never had extra money for cute mementos from school field trips or it's simply that I love gifts in all shapes and sizes, but just like that, I forget about my worries from minutes prior.

After testing the bear's softness, I hug it to my chest. "Thank you."

He looks pleased as he smiles down at me. "You're welcome. And now I think it's time to feed you."

Gifts and food? Hell, be still my heart.

———

THE SHOCK HAS WORN OFF BY THE TIME WE GET TO THE BOARDWALK.

Vincent and I sit on a wooden bench facing Clear Lake, where boats move across the water, leaving trails of upturned waves in their wake.

"So do you think you're ready to take astronaut training?" Vincent says.

I set my new stuffed bear down beside me and snort. "Even if someone offered me Bezos amounts of money, I would not go into space. I like it fine enough down here, thank you very much."

I look up at the sky and briefly imagine what hurtling thousands of miles per hour above the earth right now would be like. It all seems so inconceivable.

"So have you always been a daredevil, and becoming an astronaut was like the ultimate level you had to achieve?"

Vincent chuckles. "I've always wanted to make a difference. Life is too short not to give it your all. After I finished school, I got into teaching, and that was fun. Then I did Search and Rescue. Neither of those fulfilled me like exploring space has. I may not be directly impacting lives, but I am impacting the future and laying the foundation for us to make a home in deep space."

"What was it like in space? I know I did the virtual reality, but tell me through your eyes."

He looks toward the sky while he thinks. "It's nothing short of amazing. Looking out the window and floating above Earth helps you appreciate life. My favorite moments happened during space walks. I'd get to sit on top of the ISS, turn off the lights on my helmet, and gaze into infinity. There's nothing comparable."

I want to close my eyes to experience the picture Vincent paints, but then I'd miss the way his face transforms and his eyes shine with wonder. It's so evident that he's found something to be passionate about in a way most people never will.

"You are very fortunate to be living your dream," I say, and I know my voice doesn't disguise the wistfulness I feel.

"But you are living your dream now, right? Working on your own business."

"Not yet. I'm chasing the high that came with the first event I planned by myself. My client was throwing a surprise party for her husband's fiftieth birthday. There was gold and black everywhere, and it looked like he was having the best day of his life. It was so gratifying to see all the planning and hard work pay off. I can't wait until I see that again."

"Is that your ultimate goal?"

If anyone else had asked, I might have left it at that. But being here with Vincent, knowing he's not judging and is truly curious, I shake my head. "Not quite. It was awful being let go from my job after so long. Even worse that I'd given my all and had planned on staying there forever. I went from having purpose in each new day to now having no idea what to expect from one day to the next. I guess my ultimate goal is stability. That will include not only my business being successful but a real home as well." I smile at him. "Thanks to you being gracious enough to let me take over for a few months, I think I'll get there eventually. I must admit though, I still feel bad for kicking you out of your room."

"You do?" He lifts an eyebrow skeptically.

Try as I might, I can't keep a straight face. "Sorry, but I really don't. Let me tell you something. I've lived in countless apartments, but I've never gotten such a strong urge to cry as I did when I stepped into your guest room. I think you need some yellow police tape barricading the door."

"Ouch." Vincent grimaces. "Tell me how you really feel."

"You know what? I'm going to give the room a makeover for you. I mean, if you want me to."

"That would be great. I haven't been able to put as much time into the house as I'd like, so this would be a great help."

I nod, satisfied. It will be my own little pet project.

We continue to eat in silence, and Vincent finishes before me. He crumples his trash into a ball and places it in the brown takeout bag, then picks up my astronaut bear for inspection. "So you moved around a lot? Why is that?"

"Because of my mom's condition, medical bills have always been something my parents had to deal with, which always left us tight on money. Most of the apartments we moved to were on a month-to-month lease, and rent usually went up after a while, so we'd find another apartment in our budget." I close my eyes and relax against the bench. Salty wind from the Gulf hits my face, while memories of getting home from school only to be told to start packing my room run through my mind.

"It must have been hard to get settled in if you were constantly moving."

"I don't want it to sound like I was raised without any sort of structure. No matter where we were, my mom made sure I went to bed at the same time and had balanced meals. My furniture was always arranged the same way, so the rooms all looked and felt like mine. They tried to find new places within the same school district, though that wasn't always possible. But you know . . ." I shrug, hoping it doesn't sound like I'm ungrateful for what my parents were able to provide. "Kids adapt. As long as my mom was healthy, I was happy. I just really wanted her to not be in pain, so I tried to make their lives as easy as possible."

"What, no sneaking out or school fights?"

"Not even once. I guess you could say I was one of those kids who never went through a rebellious stage, contrary to what my name means." I open one eye and use it to shoot Vincent a dirty look before settling back down. "No, I take that back. I did have one act of rebellion throughout my childhood."

Sitting up straight, I open both eyes now to look at Vincent, and lose my breath. He's staring at me with such an intensity, those topaz eyes sparkling so much I want to ask if he was just staring into the sun. More than that, I want to ask what he's thinking when he looks at me. But then he blinks, and his expression is mere curiosity.

"What was your act of rebellion?" he says.

It takes a good ten seconds for me to remember what we were talking about.

"Each time before we'd move, I would sign my name somewhere in the apartment. It was usually inside a closet, but sometimes under a kitchen cabinet. Once I signed my name on one of the blinds slats. Just something to say 'Amerie was here.'"

"Ah, a little vandalism. I like it."

"Stop it!" I laugh. "I wasn't a vandal, I was just . . ."

"A vandal?" he finishes when I can't even come up with an empty excuse.

I shake my head. "Fine. Maybe just a little bit of one."

His dimples are out now, and it feels good to be the cause.

"And where will you sign in my house?" he asks.

I wiggle my eyebrows at him. "I only sign when I leave. And once I do, I don't think you'll find it."

CHAPTER TWELVE

I stand up and pop my knuckles. After spending hours working on my inventory of centerpieces, bending wire and wrapping floral tape around stems, my hands are beginning to cramp. I'm almost done with my last piece, so it only figures I'd run out of tape.

Vincent didn't warn me to steer clear of his office, so now is the perfect opportunity to snoop in there.

That is, now is the perfect opportunity to see if he has any tape I can use.

My footsteps are light against the carpeted steps as I walk up to the landing. Vincent's office takes up the whole second floor, with no other rooms or doors attached. In another house, a space like this would probably be converted into a home theater or kids' play area. However, Vincent makes it work for his needs, and I realize two things.

First, Vincent must have spent all his energy decorating here rather than the rest of the house. It's the one place I'm finally getting a glimpse of the man who's made space exploration his life. The walls are still that generic eggshell but on one wall, like a tiny gallery, are large framed photos of the moon, a shot of what I can only assume is the Milky Way galaxy, and distant views of Earth. A telescope, a smaller version of the one sitting in the backyard, is stationed by a window, with a black cover draped over it. An astronaut's helmet rests on top of a black bookshelf. If I didn't know Vincent was an astronaut before, this room is a dead giveaway.

The next thing I realize is that Vincent is a plant dad. Next to the telescope, the largest monstera plant I've ever seen shoots up from a black pot. It's taller than me, with leaves spanning the length of my forearm. On Vincent's mahogany desk, a trio of small succulents perch on the edge, and other potted plants litter the floor, with various leaves and vines stretching toward the window. It could be my imagination, but the air in here feels crisper.

Remembering what I came for, I walk to the desk and scan the area for tape. I don't see any, but there is a lineup of Lego spaceman figures under the computer monitor. I reach for the pink one, inspecting the yellow face with a tiny smile. I wonder if Vincent uses them to reenact moon landings and space walks or if they're strictly for aesthetics.

When my phone pings with a message, I set the space person down and pull it from my pocket. Mom has sent a picture of a chocolate cookie baked in a personal pan with a scoop of ice cream on top. They must still be in Vegas and are obviously enjoying the food. My mouth waters as I reply.

Me: That looks positively sinnnnnful.

I smile once the message is sent. See? Gina isn't the only one who can do fun wordplay. Mom appreciates my humor and sends back a laughing emoji. Next, she sends me a picture of Dad's colossal steak that looks like it could have tipped over Fred Flintstone's car. Trust Dad to get an extra heaping of protein while Mom goes straight for dessert. After I send off a series of surprised emojis and a gif of Fred Flintstone wiping his mouth with a napkin, I make my way to the leather couch and continue sifting through the other pictures they've sent me.

Browsing pictures turns into checking my social media and e-mail, and soon enough, I'm kicking off my house shoes and curling against the armrest. I'll say this about Vincent, he knows how to pick comfortable furniture. I'd only meant to find some tape, but since the cushions envelop me, practically begging me to stay awhile, I settle in even more and pull up my Kindle app.

I pick one of the many books from my TBR list, but my eyes get droopy by the second chapter. It won't hurt to spare a little more time away from work, so I close my eyes and set an internal alarm for ten minutes.

On Vincent's couch, I'm surrounded by his scent, so it's no surprise that my dreams drift to him.

He comes upstairs, surprised to find me here of all places. I've overtaken not only his bedroom but now his office. He debates what to do about me as he loosens his navy tie, unfastens his shiny cuff links, and folds up his sleeves. After glancing at me a few more moments, he shakes his head and goes to his chair. Immediately, his eyes fall on the pink space person. He gently pushes it back in line with its comrades, then starts up his computer, even though I'm sure he must have put in countless hours working already. It all feels natural, me being in his space as he goes about his regular routine.

My mind is nothing if not efficient. After ten minutes, I open my eyes. They almost pop out of their sockets when I see Vincent really is sitting at his desk. Unlike Dream Vincent, his navy blazer is on, though his tie has been completely removed.

Should I just lie here until he leaves? What if he never leaves? I guess I'll become part of the couch.

After a few more moments of mentally kicking myself for falling asleep and cursing Vincent for coming back early, I ease my feet back to the floor and sit up.

Vincent notices my movements and looks away from his screen to me. The heat on my neck turns up a thousand degrees as we stare at each other for what feels like eons.

Finally, I roll my eyes and huff out a sigh. If he's going to have something to say, he needs to hurry up so I can get back to work.

"I was looking for some tape," I offer as an explanation for why I'm here. What I don't have is an explanation for why I decided his couch made the perfect napping spot, but if he's upset, he doesn't show it.

His eyes light up with laughter as he opens a desk drawer and flaunts a packet of clear tape. Gritting my teeth, I stand up and cross the room.

"You snore," he says when I'm in front of him.

I gasp. "I have never."

"You have and you do. I could hardly concentrate with all the racket."

"Yeah? Well, you're a plant daddy," I counter. I'd meant that to come out as an insult, but by the confused yet pleased smirk Vincent sports, it didn't give nearly what it was supposed to.

Not giving him the chance to harp on me basically calling him Daddy, I snatch the tape from his grip and head to the stairs, but stop before I make it to the landing. I won't call it curiosity about the man I just discovered more about in the seconds it took my eyes to sweep across his office than a whole tour of the downstairs portion did, but . . . okay, I am intrigued. And it's not like the flower arrangement is going anywhere.

"I take it these will need to be watered while you're away?" I gesture at the plants by the window.

"Yes. Want me to tell you about them now?"

At my nod, Vincent rises from his chair. In a very Dream Vincent–like move, he takes off his jacket, hanging it on the back of the chair, and folds up his sleeves before moving to the front of his desk, where the succulents are. "All of my plants are pretty easy. These only need water about every other week, once the soil is dry."

I walk farther into the room as he points at the different pots until finally we're standing in front of the monstera together.

"This is another one that only needs water once the soil is dry. You should be able to tell by a glance, but you can also feel the top."

"You've taken such great care of your babies. What if I kill them?" I reach for my necklace. "You know what? Maybe you should just call someone to come care for them."

I can't help but imagine Vincent coming home after his mission to a room full of sad-looking pots. Right now it's feeling like this will be a repeat of my failed NASA VR exercise. Only this time, plant lives are on the line. I don't want to let Vincent down.

"How about this," he offers. "For the next few months, I'll walk you through the watering schedule. That way, when I'm gone, we'll both feel confident that Gladys and Billie Jean are in good hands."

I bend down to push at the top of the soil. It's moist and gives easily. When I turn my finger over, a small layer of dirt coats the pad.

Vincent takes my hand in his, wiping my finger with his thumb before I can do anything. "I watered Billie Jean over the weekend. She'll be good for at least another week."

Part of me wants to laugh at how silly it is for us to be standing less than an arm's length away, with a huge leaf hanging between us, as Vincent casually drops the ridiculous name of his plant. But all I can focus on is the tingle his thumb left like an imprint on my finger.

I fold my hands together and clear my throat. "If this is Billie Jean, I take it that's Gladys?" I point to a white hanging pot with vibrant vines spilling out. When Vincent nods, I jerk my head to the succulents. "The Pips?"

He folds his arms across his chest and shakes his head in disapproval. "Of course not. They're Neil Armstrong, Sally Ride, and Buzz Aldrin."

I thought the dessert my mom texted me was sinful, but the way Vincent's forearms look is downright devious. And the way his biceps strain against his shirt—treacherous. Vincent is a whole banquet of temptation.

"What do you think?" Vincent says, regaining my attention.

I snap my eyes up to his face and hope he doesn't realize I was three seconds away from salivating over him. "Think about what?"

"Lasagna for dinner? I have a little more work to finish up and then I can pop some in the oven."

Eating lasagna is the last thing I want right now. Eating *him* up though . . .

And it's that exact thought that pushes me back to the stairs. "Thanks, but I don't think I'll be hungry for dinner. Don't worry about me."

Without another word, I run downstairs.

———

I SKIP DINNER, DECIDING INSTEAD TO WORK ON MY WEBSITE. IT'S SO plain. I won't be able to use pictures of events I did with

Jacob and Johnson. I'll have to build my portfolio up as quickly as I can. The baby shower will help, but I need more.

In the meantime, I get lost in my work until I get a phone notification showing I have only 15 percent battery left. I didn't realize how late it was, but it's getting close to midnight. It's a familiar comfort realizing I've gotten lost in the zone of planning and pinning after so long, but now my mouth feels as dry as cotton.

I get up, hoping I won't disturb Vincent from his sleep as I walk to the kitchen for a bottle of water. Once I round the corner, I realize I didn't need to worry. Vincent is standing in the kitchen in nothing but pajama pants.

Gray pajama pants.

My lungs fight to work as I stare at his bare chest. Without a shirt on, he clearly has strong, lean muscles. I'm looking at him in Ultra HD, and the view is glorious.

I lick my dry lips. "W-what are you doing up?" Not that I have the right to ask. It's his house, after all.

"I was thirsty." He holds up a glass that's nearly empty, though I can see remnants of milk inside.

Milk. It sure does do a body good. And I still can't take my eyes off his chest.

He sets the glass next to the sink and moves closer to me. "Did you need something, Amerie?"

Do I need something? Like to trace my hands all over his body? Yes, I need that.

"Amerie?"

"Hmm?" I jerk my gaze up. Vincent's jaw is covered in stubble, since the day is way past over and he needs to shave. His eyes, hooded with sleep—no, *lust*—travel down my legs, and he swallows.

It occurs to me that I'm wearing nothing but an old college shirt that barely hits my thighs. At any other time I'd be beyond embarrassed for someone to see me in this tattered shirt, but embarrassed is the last thing I feel with Vincent's burning gaze on me.

What would he do if I closed the distance between us, stood on my tiptoes, and crushed my lips to his? Could my one small step lead to one giant leap for Vincent and me? Judging by the intense attraction, the invisible yet present force of gravity drawing us into each other, I'd say yes. And who am I to fight against the laws of physics?

Vincent licks his lips and his right hand flexes. I think he might be the one to make the first move by reaching for me. I hold my breath, waiting for him to do just that. First, he closes his eyes and takes a deep breath. When he opens them, he begins backing away.

Wait, *away*? Yes. It's inconceivable, but that is what he's doing. I blink a few times to get my brain working again. To remember that boxing him in and demanding he take me on the counter is a bad, bad idea. To remember that Vincent and I have a deal and my stay is temporary.

After a few gulps of oxygen, I'm thinking coherently enough to function. I clear my throat. "I just needed some water."

I grab a cold bottle of water from the fridge, mindful of him watching my every move.

"Good night," I say, and for the second time tonight, bolt to safety.

I close the door and chug the water like I'm in the desert, dying of thirst. When that does nothing to cool my simmering blood, I stop by the top drawer of the nightstand on my way to take a nice, long shower.

CHAPTER THIRTEEN

From the comfort of the passenger's seat of Vincent's truck, I watch as cars pull in and out of the gas station. There's the *clink* of a gas nozzle being replaced, and then Vincent appears at the driver's-side window, peering at me through aviator shades. "Do you need anything from inside?" He tosses his keys in the air and catches them with one hand.

I shake my head while keeping my eyes glued to my phone. Once we hit the highway, I plan to tug my silk-lined beanie down far enough to cover my eyes and take a nap.

"Do you need to come in and use the restroom or anything?" he presses.

It's common sense to handle your business before going on a long road trip. Not to mention, we're less than two miles away from the house. Of course I don't need to use the restroom. I sigh and shake my head no once again.

"I'll be right back, then." Vincent pushes off the window and walks toward the front of the store.

It's only then that I raise my head to watch him walk away. And what a walk it is. Even my mom would have to admit it rivals the likes of Denzel's. His steps are easy and sure, with a quiet confidence.

I keep watching as he first holds the door open for a

man with a case of beer under each arm, then disappears inside. Obviously, Vincent's trip out of town for training wasn't enough of a breather.

I've made it a point not to think of Vincent and his sudden aloofness, or our almost kiss. Then today, Thursday morning, he came home as promised.

He greeted me with his affable smile and quick teasing, appearing so composed and unaffected. Like he hasn't given a second's thought to our kitchen rendezvous, while the first thing I did was zero in on his lips and wonder if they'd be as soft as they were on New Year's Eve. Once I realized the direction my thoughts had taken, I was mad at myself and snapped a quick hello before hiding in the bedroom. Essentially keeping him from his closet and access to the master bath.

Part of me hopes he'll lash out at some point and say something rude or disrespectful. Anything to help me get rid of this attraction. But not Vincent. He won't allow himself to be fazed by my petulance.

He knocked on the door and said he'd be ready to load my bags when they were packed.

As much as I appreciate a man who can put up with the worst of my moods, why can't he just be predictable?

Two minutes after walking inside, Vincent comes back to the car, pausing at the window. "In case you change your mind and need a snack later."

I jump when a white plastic bag lands in my lap. Before I can say anything, Vincent is gone again, reaching for the complimentary squeegee on the side of the fuel pump. While he meticulously cleans the front and back windows, I open the bag and find two Snickers Almond bars. My favorite candy.

I stare at the treats and twist my lips as guilt stabs at

me. Damn it. Why am I fighting so hard to box Vincent out? We are supposed to be partners.

Have I always been this way? Desperate to keep myself closed off from people who just want to help? Growing up, I always made it a point not to place any more burdens on my parents than they already had, so I guess naturally that's extended to other people. I should probably talk to a professional about it.

At the very least, I need to stop being so prickly with Vincent. I need him, and he needs me. I can ignore the attraction I feel toward him while we get through this week with his family.

I tie the handles of the bag into a loose knot and lay it back in my lap as Vincent steps up into the truck. "Thank you for the candy, Vincent. You really didn't have to get me two."

"I know you already ate lunch, and we should make it to the cabin before dinner, but we can't have you all hungry and mean while we're on the road." He winks at me and starts the engine. "And one's for me. I love Snickers."

He has good taste in candy, and I *can* be mean when I'm hungry, so I'll let his comment slide.

I take my beanie off. "So, let me make sure I remember everything correctly. This cabin we're going to was actually your childhood home?"

"Yes. We're from a small town called Bliss, not to be confused with Fort Bliss. It's close to Garner State Park. Have you ever been kayaking out there on the Frio River?"

"I've never been there or been kayaking."

"I'll have to take you one day. I don't think we'll have time this visit, but maybe next year when I get back."

When he gets back? Our deal will be long done by then. I won't read too much into his comment, however. Maybe

Vincent is the type of person who makes hypothetical plans. Like how you might run into an old friend from school and, after making small talk, express how good it would be to catch up over coffee, knowing it will never come to pass.

Vincent continues. "Once my siblings and I graduated and moved to different cities, my parents packed up and moved to Houston. Mom's dad built the cabin though, so they've kept it and still go out there for regular visits."

"Let me make sure I have everything correct. Your mom's name is Cheryl and your dad is William. You have two siblings, and you're the oldest." I look at Vincent, and he frowns slightly, opening his mouth before he shuts it and nods. "Camille owns an OB-GYN clinic with your mom. Brianna is the youngest. She's a guidance counselor in Dallas, and she'll be there with her dog." I mentally recall the list he sent to me after much prodding and a small threat to box up his coffee machine while he was gone.

"Right," Vincent says. "That reminds me, did you bring your allergy medicine?"

"Yes, dear." I coat my voice with mock sugar and obedience. I smile when Vincent rolls his eyes before merging onto the highway.

Ooh, did I finally hit on something I can use to get under his skin? Are cringeworthy nicknames his repellant?

I place my elbow on the armrest between us and lean in close. "We should have nicknames for each other, shouldn't we? That way your family really gets the hint that this is all very serious. What should I call you? Hmm, let me think." I squint. "How about honey bun? Or Vincey-poo?"

Instead of cringing, the infuriating man smiles. "I'm glad you're finally warming up to the idea of nicknames. Call me whatever you want." He looks thoughtful as he strokes his chin. "I do like Mimi for you, but I think bae would work too. That's what the youngsters are still saying these days, right, bae?"

"The fact that you used 'bae' and 'youngsters' in the same breath should already tell you that's not happening."

"Okay, okay. How about wifey? Baby girl? *My precious?*" He says the last in his best Gollum voice.

I shift back and cross my arms. "I think you're done."

He laughs and reaches over to squeeze my thigh. I swallow hard, glad to be sitting down. Otherwise, it would be evident how his touch has me weak at the knees.

He puts both hands on the steering wheel to switch lanes, and I look out the window. This is going to be a long visit.

———

I DECIDE TO STAY AWAKE FOR THE DRIVE. VINCENT TURNS ON A PLAY-list of smooth jazz, and I sit back and watch as the scenery changes from flat roads to acres of green farmland dotted with cattle and goats to steep rolling hills as we venture deep into the heart of Hill Country.

"Are you doing okay over there?" Vincent says.

I'm holding on to the armrest for dear life. At my high-pitched "Mm-hmm," Vincent quickly glances at me, and it's all I can do not to yell at him to keep his eyes on the road. No way he missed the sign that reads CAUTION, FALLEN ROCKS.

We're passing through hills—though they look more like mountains—going around some of the steepest curves I've ever seen. Limestone cliffs line one side of the road— Vincent's side—while nothing but a short, metal guardrail separates me from a long tumble down.

"So you're serious about that scared of heights thing, huh?" Vincent says, but I don't respond.

I don't have time for his nonsense when my heart is trying to leap out of my chest. Is this what I missed out on by not traveling as a kid? If so, I'm not mad at my parents at all.

I close my eyes and try to talk myself out of a full-blown panic attack.

Vincent is an astronaut capable of navigating spacecraft and helicopters. He can certainly drive this truck around a few crazy roads.

Blessedly, we come out of the latest curve; however, I see that while the road may be straight, there are still many dips and hills we have to pass over. My stomach can't take this. I turn toward the window and try not to throw up all over Vincent's shiny dashboard.

Vincent reaches over and pulls at the hand I have wrapped around the armrest in a death grip. "It's better to focus on other things instead of how scared you are," he says gently. "Squeeze my hand and count to ten. It'll help, I promise."

Right, it'll help. Just like he said the virtual reality experience wouldn't be scary. But what else can I do at this point but trust him?

Slowly, I let go of the armrest and put my hand in his. His is so much larger than mine, but I squeeze for all I'm worth, counting to ten and taking slow breaths. It does seem to help.

I loosen my hold on him, but my stomach lurches when we go down another steep dip.

"You're doing good," Vincent says. "Keep counting."

I squeeze again, this time counting and concentrating on the smooth texture of the back of his hand compared to the rougher part of his palm. It's warm, and quite secure. I have a mind to thank him, but in the middle of my sixth round of counting, I doze off.

What feels like the blink of an eye later, I'm awoken to Vincent shaking my shoulder.

"Amerie, wake up."

I open my eyes. The first thing I notice—and am instantly thankful for—is that the car is stationary. We're surrounded by a canopy of green trees, and through branches I see the sky is quickly darkening.

"We're here," he says. "You made it."

"We're here?" I repeat. At his nod, I close my eyes and let my head fall against the headrest with my hands over my heart. "Thank you, Lord."

"Remind me to get you some antianxiety pills for next time."

Next time? Yeah, that's not happening.

I open my eyes to tell him just that, but stop at the sight before me. "I thought you said we were going to your family's cabin?"

Vincent gestures forward. "Yeah. We're here."

"But that's not a cabin."

"Yes, it is." He shrugs. "At least, that's what we've always called it. See the siding and the deck? It's all wood."

"This looked a lot different in my head," I murmur.

I pictured those cute little cabins a kid might draw with two windows on each side of a wooden door, large logs holding up the frame, and a triangle roof. This is . . . not it.

While it's technically made of long logs, it's a two-story home with a large deck winding around the second floor. Floor-to-ceiling windows give it a clean modern look, and the open curtains bathe the front porch and green shrubs in a picturesque glow.

Vincent has parked beside an old red pickup truck, and I wonder how long he's been sitting out here to let me sleep.

"Should we go in?" I ask.

"Yeah." Vincent lets out a heavy breath, then opens his door.

I follow suit and meet him at the bed of the truck. It's once again a game of speed when I reach for my overnight bag, but Vincent grabs it first and slings it over his shoulder before reaching for his own. Again, he heaves a sigh before turning away.

We walk toward the front door, and I'm reminded of how tense he was when we got to the New Year's Eve party. His jaw is set in a tight line and his shoulders are stiff. It looks like he's walking toward his doom, not about to see his family.

Once we approach the wooden steps, I wrap my hand around his forearm in a show of support so he knows I've got his back this week.

Vincent looks down at me in surprise, then a smile helps to relax some of the strain around his eyes.

"My first time meeting the family," I say as brightly as I can. "Do you think they'll like me?"

He covers my arm with his hand. "They'll fall for you as quickly as I did."

I know his words are fake, just like mine were, but my heart jumps into my throat.

We face the door, but it swings open before we can knock.

"Vincent's here!" A woman who must be Vincent's mom lets loose a joyous laugh before throwing herself out the house.

I let go of Vincent and step to the side as his mom wraps him in a fierce hug. "You're finally here." After getting her fill, she steps back and wipes a tear away.

I'm caught off guard when she turns her attention to me.

The woman inspecting me, Mrs. Rogers, is beautiful. She's in her midfifties, though I never would have guessed if Vincent hadn't told me beforehand. Her brown skin has a bright, youthful glow, and her arms have more definition than mine. She looks like she could be Vincent's slightly older sister, and I can't help but compare her to my mom, who seems to age with each hospital visit. A knot of sorrow pinches my chest.

"Finally, the woman my son's been hiding away from me," Mrs. Rogers says.

"Momma," Vincent says. "This is Amerie."

I blink, and like a light switch, I flip on my best smile while holding out my hand. "It's nice to meet you, Mrs. Rogers."

My outstretched hand gets ignored, and instead Mrs. Rogers pulls me into a hug. "I'm so glad to meet you," she says, rubbing my back.

"At least let them come inside where it's warm before you start hugging everyone to death," a deep voice says.

Mrs. Rogers steps back with her hands clasped so tightly I figure she's trying to hold back from reaching out to Vincent again as we walk through the doorway.

Once we step inside, I take a look at my new surroundings. Now *this* is a home.

Pictures on the walls, tailored curtains, pieces of furniture that look both used and cared for. I know without a doubt that love not only grows here but is embedded into the very soil this house was built upon and has seeped into the life of each occupant. That laughter has climbed up the walls like a vine, entwining each surface with memories and stories. Even if they decided to empty the place, the love would still be as tangible a presence as the warmth blasting from the fireplace.

"We're so glad you could make it."

I turn to find Vincent's dad embracing him in a hug full

of hearty slaps on the back. He's as tall and broad shouldered as Vincent, with light brown skin. His hair is more salt than pepper, but he's the embodiment of the notion that some men look better as they age. I see Vincent inherited his dad's nose, strong jawline, and good looks.

Mr. Rogers then turns to me and holds out his hand. "Amerie, it's nice to finally meet you."

Camille walks into the large living room with a glass of ice water. "Look who made it to two functions in a row. I'm proud of you, Vince. Let's see if you can keep it up."

Vincent rolls his eyes but doesn't respond to his sister. "Momma, I want to get Amerie and me settled in. We had a long drive."

"Of course." Mrs. Rogers turns to me. "Vincent told us about your allergies, so we put you two in the guesthouse out back. But don't let that make you feel unwelcome. You're free to come over here to the big house anytime, of course."

"That sounds perfect," I say. In fact, it's the best thing I've heard all day. I'll have somewhere I can relax so I won't have to pretend this whole trip.

"That'll be fine, Momma. Thank you." Vincent uses his free hand to steer me to the back of the house and out a glass door.

The guesthouse is really more of a large room. It fits a queen-size bed and has a mounted TV, a portable heater plugged into the corner, and a small restroom. It's cute and homey. And my eyes keep snagging on the bed.

There's no getting around it. I'll be sharing it with Vincent.

I watch him shut the wooden door and sigh. If he keeps this up, he'll pass out from oxygen overload.

"The drive didn't hit you that hard, did it?" I ask.

Vincent doesn't answer. Instead, he sets our bags by the

door and moves to sit on the bed. The bed we'll be sharing in a few hours, but it's best not to dwell on that fact for now.

"Hey, what's up?" I say softly.

"I haven't been out here in years. It's a lot to take in right now."

"How many years?"

Vincent blows out a breath while running a hand over his head. "Eight."

I try not to let the shock show on my face. I can't imagine staying away from a home like this for eight whole years. I get that his parents now live in Houston, and this is more of a vacation home, but still.

I wish I had a place like this to call my home. So much so, it almost hurts to breathe.

When people ask where I'm from, it's easy to proclaim Houston, but there's no evidence. There's no single address imprinted in my mind or funny stories I can tell about the neighborhood kids racing home before the streetlights came on. Just impressions of different apartment buildings with different stairways and concrete steps.

I push past the homesickness for a home I've never had and move to sit by Vincent on the bed, leaving a good six inches between us. "Your mom seemed really happy to see you. She seems sweet too. I don't think these next few days will be so bad."

Vincent snorts. "Remember those famous last words for me, okay?"

"Come on, we've got this. And, with your doting girlfriend demanding a lot of your attention, I think we'll be able to keep the pressure off you this week."

His eyes rove over my face, lingering on my lips before he looks away. "There is that." He takes one more deep breath and stands up. "Do you think you can handle dinner in the house? I think we've got twenty minutes, tops, before anyone comes knocking at the door."

"Sure. I just need to get out of these travel clothes."

I grab a top and jeans from my bag, as well as my phone, then go into the tiny bathroom. I turn on the phone's screen and see a missed call from my mom. I always try to answer or call her back right away, but this call is from four hours ago. My stomach tightens as I worry something might be wrong until I see she also sent a text.

> **Mom: Everything's fine, I was just calling to catch up. Your dad and I are on the road again. We're heading to Yellowstone!**

My shoulders relax on a long exhale. I'm relieved to know she's fine, but now I'm debating whether I should return her call now or later. I don't want to dodge my parents' attempts to get ahold of me, but it's hard to stomach the thought of talking to them right now and pretending that nothing has changed in my life.

As overjoyed as Vincent's mom was to see him, I have no doubt she can be a handful. But I also saw how genuinely happy Vincent was as she embraced him. When it comes down to it, there's nothing like a mother's love.

I send mine a text.

> **Me: I'm taking on a lot of work and won't be able to get to my phone much in the next week. Text to keep me updated though. Love you.**

CHAPTER FOURTEEN

Mrs. Rogers sits at the family table, sporting the biggest grin as she watches Vincent shove a bite of mac and cheese into his mouth. If I weren't pretending to be equally besotted, I'd be alternating between laughing and gagging at the display.

"This food is so good, Mrs. Rogers," I say.

She finally takes her eyes off her son. "Thank you, dear. Food is my love language. And please, call me Cheryl." Her eyes bounce from Vincent to me, taking on a dreamy quality. "Or Mom."

The food goes down like a rock in my throat. "Thanks . . . Cheryl."

Mr. Rogers chuckles. "Come on, Cheryl. Try not to scare the woman away."

Mrs. Rogers looks around like she has no idea what he's talking about, and I bite down on my lip to keep from laughing. I almost lose it when I look at Vincent and he has a pained look on his face.

When I go back to my food, I hear the front door open and close, followed by the jangling of metal and a woman's "Down, Sheba!" Seconds later, Vincent's youngest sister comes into view.

The first thing I notice is her hair: waist-length caramel-colored braids. With her faded Baylor University sweat-shirt, she looks like she's just starting her college career instead of having already graduated. Her deep brown eyes light up when they land on Vincent. "You made it!"

Vincent stands up to hug Brianna before introducing her to me. As I rise from the chair to shake her hand, two furry paws land on my thighs, and I look down into the cutest, furriest curly-haired face.

"Hi, sweetheart," I coo while keeping my arms up.

Brianna gently pulls at her dog's jewel-studded collar. "Down, Sheba. Down. Sit. Good girl." She looks at me. "Sorry about that. Her training has been coming along well, but now we're working on socialization and getting her to listen with distractions around."

"It's okay," I say, but Vincent takes ahold of my elbow and pulls me back a step.

"She's actually allergic to dogs," he says.

Brianna's eyes go big. "Oh, shoot. Sorry, I forgot."

I cut my eyes to Vincent, who's now frowning at Sheba as she sniffs my ankles. "No, really, it's okay. I already took some allergy medicine when we got here, so I'm sure it won't be an issue."

"No, you can't be sure it won't be an issue," Vincent presses.

Hoo boy. Not even two hours into the visit, and he's already trying to make it hard for me to maintain the facade.

"Well, I know my body, and I know I can handle being around a dog for three minutes," I say through clenched teeth.

"Come on, Vince," Camille pipes in. "Don't give your woman a hard time now. She's still trying to make up her mind about you. You'll send her running to the hills with that know-it-all attitude."

I actually won't be running anywhere near those hills we drove through. All the same, I send a thankful smile to Camille, then a triumphant smirk to Vincent.

Vincent casts a sullen glance at Mrs. Rogers. "Momma, tell Camille to leave me alone."

Mrs. Rogers shakes her head. "Can you two go five minutes without trying to give me a headache? You've barely seen each other in years, and you're already getting started."

They both look quelled, but when Mrs. Rogers goes to put her plate in the sink, Vincent makes a funny face at Camille.

Mrs. Rogers gives him a warning look when she turns back around. "Let's go sit for a while."

We all march to the living room, with Camille punching Vincent in the arm as she passes him.

"Ouch," he hisses, and I hold back laughter as he rubs his arm.

I have to admit, the pout that adorns his full lips is equal parts pitiful and adorable, and I'm smiling at him as we sit down on one end of the large wheat-colored sectional.

I'm content to listen and observe as the family catches up with each other's lives. Brianna is thinking of continuing her education so she can become a principal. Camille has been considering opening up another practice in one of the more underserved areas of Houston. I think it's an admirable idea, but can't help but notice Lance doesn't seem too thrilled when she mentions it.

"So what do you do, Amerie?" Mrs. Rogers says.

Her voice holds only curiosity, but it feels like I'm being inspected under a microscope. I already decided to tell the truth, like I did when I met Camille and Lance. Well, as much of the truth as one can divulge when presenting themselves as another's fake girlfriend.

"I'm an event planner. I've been in the business for years but took some time off when my mom got sick. I'm back now and just recently branched out on my own." I hadn't meant to bring up my mom, but the words just slipped out.

"I hope your mom is doing better?"

I nod. "It was a rough time, but she is doing better. Significantly."

Vincent moves his arm behind me on the couch. We're not touching, but it would be so easy to fall against the comfort he seems willing to offer.

"I'm so glad to hear that," Mrs. Rogers says. "I look forward to meeting her one day."

While I have no doubt Mrs. Rogers would adore my mom, I just smile and nod, knowing a meeting between the two will never come to pass. For some reason, the thought is a little disheartening. I think Mom would like Mrs. Rogers too.

"One of my girlfriends recently posted pictures of a luxury picnic that her boyfriend set up when he asked her to marry him," Brianna says. "It was so adorable. Is that something you do?"

I perk up and lean forward. "I love planning luxury picnics. They're perfect for engagements. Anniversaries and dates too. Anything, really. It's amazing what you can do with a tent and a handful of blankets. I have a whole Pinterest board dedicated to them." When I sit back, my neck lands on Vincent's arm, and I'm all too aware of the heat radiating off him.

"What are luxury picnics?" Vincent says.

What we should have done instead of going to NASA for that virtual space walk.

"It's your ordinary picnic, but so much more," I say. "I love doing mine with tents, but regular blankets work well too. You can use low wooden tables so you aren't eating on the ground. And you can't have too many pillows."

I swear his eyes have glazed over.

"Maybe Amerie should plan the vow renewal, Momma," Camille says. She's sitting on the other end of the couch, reclining on Lance like he's a large pillow.

Mrs. Rogers smiles, but it quickly turns into a frown when she looks at Vincent. "It's a shame my son won't be able to make it."

Uh-oh. There's a shift in the air, and I hear Vincent let out a sigh. Is this the dreaded part where Mrs. Rogers begins bemoaning Vincent's impending takeoff? I try to think of how to steer the conversation in a different direction.

"A vow renewal? How many years will you two be celebrating?" I ask. Vow renewal ceremonies are a lot like weddings, but I make myself ask the question anyway.

Mr. Rogers is the one to answer. "Thirty-five years, but it feels like we just got married yesterday." He's a charmer.

Mrs. Rogers still doesn't look happy, but her eyes soften as her husband places a soft kiss on her hand.

"Dance with me," Mr. Rogers says to his wife. "Alexa, play our song."

As the first notes of "Always" by Atlantic Starr begin playing from a small speaker above the fireplace, Mr. Rogers stands up, pulling Mrs. Rogers with him. Soon after, Lance and Camille join them.

"I can see where this is headed," Brianna grumbles. "Let's go, Sheba. We'll see y'all in the morning." She leads Sheba upstairs.

I wonder how many times this exact scenario has played out—Mr. and Mrs. Rogers dancing in front of the glowing fireplace in their beautiful home, happy and in love. The intimacy of the moment should make me feel out of place.

Here I am, a stranger intruding on their special moment. Instead I'm sitting here, snug as a bug, with Vincent beside me.

The mantel above the fireplace is crowded with framed photos of Vincent and his sisters when they were younger. They spill over to the wall, where I see a picture of Camille with a rounder, softer face and braces as she poses with a tennis racket. One photo catches my eye. Initially, I thought it was a teenage version of Vincent, but upon closer inspection I see that the boy's lips are a tad wider and his eyebrows are a different shape. And now I realize there are more pictures of him sprinkled in with the rest of the family.

"Do you have a brother?" I say quietly.

Vincent briefly glances at the wall, then away. "Yeah."

I raise my eyebrows, waiting for him to explain why he didn't tell me he had a brother before, but he remains silent. "Well, is he coming too?"

"No. He, um, passed away some years ago."

"Oh, Vincent. I'm so sorry."

"Yeah, it happened a long time ago. Do you want to dance?"

No, I don't want to dance. I want Vincent to elaborate more on the bomb he just dropped—why has he never mentioned a brother? And what happened to him? I'm trying not to feel hurt, but if we're supposed to be partners this week, with me working to impress his family, why would he keep this from me?

Each question must be clear across my face, but Vincent turns to me, his eyes pleading that I not push him on this. The hurt and irritation at being left in the dark fade, and what I feel for him is deep sorrow. I'm not entitled to the pain he's no doubt been through, and he doesn't owe me any explanations. But I do owe him my cooperation, so I nod and take his hand as he stands up.

Mr. Rogers tells Alexa to play the song again as Vincent places his hands on my waist. As we sway in silence with the other two couples, it no longer feels so cozy. Vincent has withdrawn into himself and seems a million miles away. The loss must have been unimaginable, and I wonder if there's more to why Vincent doesn't enjoy coming home.

WE ALL CALL IT AN EARLY NIGHT TO GET READY FOR TOMORROW'S activity of a morning hike. Once Vincent and I return to the guesthouse, the first thing my eyes land on is the bed.

"You can have the shower first," Vincent says. He still seems to be in some kind of mood. Not exactly gloomy, but more subdued than I've seen him. Maybe even a little lost.

It's a feeling I'm all too familiar with, and even though he's a grown-ass man, I'm filled with the urge to reach out and hold him until he finds his way back. I hold myself in check though, instead moving to my bag as I wonder where that came from. Hold him? I don't hold men.

I find my pajamas, a long-sleeve cotton shirt and lounge pants, then take a shower. Trying to be considerate of not using all the hot water, I'm out ten minutes later.

Vincent takes his turn next. While he's in the bathroom, I set myself up on the left side of the bed. After my nap in the car, I'm not quite ready to fall asleep yet, so I sit up with my back against the headboard. After smoothing the blanket over my legs, trying to get comfortable, my eyes are drawn to the spot Vincent will soon occupy. Judging where the middle is, I use the side of my hand to make a faint imprint of separation and frown. No, that will still be too close. I scoot more toward the edge. But what if I fall off the bed while I'm sleeping?

This is ridiculous. I shake my head and move back.

There's no reason to be so apprehensive. This is a bed. Sure, there are multiple activities one can partake of in it; however, we are adults and will be using it for sleeping.

I make a conscious effort to put the awkwardness of the moment out of my mind, and by the time Vincent shuts off the water, I'm scrolling away on my phone.

Then he opens the door.

Steam carrying the masculine scent of his soap hits me before he takes one step into the room. Notes of cedarwood float in the air, but I swear it must also be infused with some kind of pheromone, because it sends all my senses on alert, feeding me an image of lounging naked, with Vincent's arms wrapped around me, after a luxury picnic. Or maybe it's the sight of Vincent with a white tee clinging to his muscles and those damn gray pajama pants hanging low on his hips.

Lord, are those the only ones he owns? He couldn't pack some flannel or dingy fleece pajamas? Or one of those adult onesies that have a flap on the butt? On second thought, imagining Vincent's butt is not helpful.

We make eye contact, and I flash a quick smile before going back to my phone. Hopefully he doesn't realize that my eyes aren't processing a thing as I stare at the screen, because for the life of me I have no idea what I'm looking at.

Vincent moves about the room. First he turns on the heater. It sputters to life, and I wonder how effective it will be overnight. He goes on to rummage in his suitcase and ensures the front door is locked before coming toward the bed. I hold my breath as the bed dips from the shift of weight as he settles in. It seems much smaller with two bodies in it. Vincent is so close our elbows will probably touch if either of us moves.

So close Vincent could reach out and squeeze my thigh like he's fond of doing in the car. Only now, in bed, he'd be able to let his hand linger. Or slide higher. I swallow hard.

"So it's going pretty well so far, don't you think?" I say with forced normalcy. Like all kinds of naughty thoughts aren't doing leaps and sprints through my mind.

Vincent mimics my pose, sitting against the headboard with his phone in hand. He turns his head toward me. "It was a good start. One day down with six to go."

His normally smooth face sports a nice five-o'clock shadow, and for the second time tonight my hand itches with the need to reach out and touch him.

"You didn't shave today," I remark stupidly.

Vincent runs his hand along his jaw and looks at me like he's pleased. "Noticed that, did you?"

"I was just wondering if you're turning into a lumber-jack now that we're out in the country for a bit." Nice save.

His laugh is soft. "Maybe I will."

I go back to my phone. At least he doesn't seem so sad anymore.

When he shifts, he rests his right hand down in the space between us. It's dangerously close to my thigh, and all those images I managed to suppress come dancing back up like they're in line for a soul train. In my head, a miniature Amerie dances down the middle, shaking her hips while beckoning Vincent forward with a sensual curl of her finger.

I catch myself just as I begin inching my leg closer to his hand. What is going on here?

"Is there a full moon tonight?" I ask. That would explain why I can't get ahold of my libido around him.

"Uh…" Vincent turns his head to me, eyebrows pinched. "No. It's a waning crescent."

I blink, having no idea what that means. "Well, how many days is it until the full moon?"

"Twenty-one." He studies me and tilts his head to the side. "Why do you ask?"

"Just curious."

If it's not the moon, it must be that the long, stressful drive has gotten to me. What I need is a rest. In the morning, I'll be back on my game and not thinking of all the things I'd be doing with Vincent right now if our relationship were real.

Abruptly, I place my phone on the nightstand and turn off the small lamp. "Well, good night."

"Good night," Vincent says after a moment of hesitation.

He's probably wondering why I'm acting so erratically, but it can't be helped. I turn to the wall—away from Vincent—and close my eyes.

It's ages before I finally fall asleep.

CHAPTER FIFTEEN

What I hated most about moving as a kid were the first few days of disorientation from waking up in a new room. A sense of knowing, before I even opened my eyes, that something wasn't quite right. That the sounds filtering in through the window were coming from the wrong side, or the hum of the ceiling fan was off pitch.

So when I wake up after a restless night, the first thing I notice is that the suburban noise of cars and buses passing outside is absent. The second thing is the hard body I'm plastered to.

My eyes pop open, and I find my face burrowed into the back of Vincent's neck. Good Lord.

There was plenty of space between us last night, but I guess at some point I must have turned over, and now here I lay, wrapped around him as tight as an anaconda, with my breasts smashed against his back and a thigh thrown over his hip.

What I need to do is keep a cool head. Hyperventilating will only wake Vincent up, and he'll feel how close I've gotten. Probably think it's on purpose too. It's one thing to fall asleep on the couch in his office, but to sleep glued to him? Yeah, he'd never let me live that down.

A little voice in my head, which sounds a lot like Gina, tells me to enjoy this wake-up call. My body is quite comfortable with him under it. Why ruin the moment when Vincent is quiet for once?

Gina is such a bad influence. With even breaths, I slowly move my leg to extricate myself as calmly as possible. Then I realize it's sandwiched between Vincent's hip and arm. With the slight movement, his hand flexes and his fingers move along the outside of my leg. At the same time, something nudges against my calf. It's hard and growing bigger by the second.

I swallow. Vincent—*all* of Vincent—is waking up. I ignore the pulse of heat rushing through me and yank my leg back. I scoot back to my half of the bed, stopping before I roll off the edge.

My sudden movement causes Vincent to jerk awake and he faces me with wide, bleary eyes. "Everything okay?"

"Everything's great." I look down and quickly cross my arms over my hardened nipples.

Vincent yawns and stretches before grabbing his phone and checking the time. When he speaks, his voice still has a layer of sleep over it that gives his deep timbre some extra rumble. "That internal clock of yours is on point. In another five minutes my alarm was set to go off."

What I get out of that is, I could have enjoyed the warmth of his body for a few more minutes. What a shame.

"I'm a fine-tuned machine," I say. "It was the plan to leave early for the hike, right?"

"Yup." Vincent stretches again. I can't help but appreciate the up-close-and-personal view of his biceps flexing, but quickly avert my gaze when he turns to me. "We'll eat breakfast first, then head out while the sun is still low."

"Sounds good to me."

I'm in a better mood now than I am most mornings, looking forward to the planned hike with everyone. Vincent told me how his mom, having grown up in this town, taught them how to navigate trails as they were growing up. Before moving to Houston, she volunteered as a trail guide at Garner State Park in her free time. And even now, she comes back regularly throughout the year for a dose of fresh air and weekends spent outdoors. Her birthday wish was to spend a few days hiking with her children.

I tie my shoes and stand in front of the dresser mirror. I have on black joggers, a long-sleeve blue shirt, and a fleece jacket. After putting my hair in a high puff and covering my ears with a white knitted headband my mom made, I put my gloves on.

Vincent wears khaki cargo pants with a long-sleeve shirt, a vest, and a gray scarf. He kneels on the ground next to his open backpack, filling it with two large canteens of water that add to the reservoir in the front pocket, a first aid kit, granola bars, apples, rain ponchos, sunscreen, and a pocketknife.

"How long do you think we'll be gone?" I ask, looking at everything.

"Better to be prepared than be sorry."

I shrug. He must know what he's talking about, and he's carrying everything, so I won't complain.

When Vincent stands up, he inspects my outfit, starting at my head and going all the way down to my toes, and frowns.

I place my hands on my hips. "What?"

"Where are your hiking boots?"

Vincent told me to get some shoes specifically made for hiking. Or should I say, *suggested*. I considered his suggestion, but ultimately couldn't justify the expense when I won't be wearing them on a daily basis. It's not like we'll be climbing up those large hills. I made Vincent promise me that.

I look down at my old arch-supporting walking shoes and wiggle my toes. "These are all I have."

"What size do you wear?"

"My size," I say, laughing when Vincent's jaw ticks. "Okay, fine. I wear an eight and a half."

Vincent shakes his head and picks up his backpack, swinging it on. It should look ridiculous, him wearing the large pack. No doubt *I* would look like Frodo about to embark on a grand adventure if I had my own. Instead, Vincent looks large and in charge. A man on a mission.

Am I really going weak at the knees over Vincent right now?

Blessedly unaware of my thoughts, Vincent frowns. "Your feet are too big to fit my mom's or sisters' shoes."

"My feet are average size."

He smirks. "I didn't state otherwise."

"It was implied by your tone."

"Just watch your step out there. We're taking a pretty easy trail today, but some of the inclines and declines can be steep, with loose rocks."

"I'm sure I'll be fine."

He looks at my feet skeptically but doesn't argue. "Let's go wait for everyone outside."

———

I SUCK IN A LUNGFUL OF THE COLD, CRISP AIR. EVERYONE EXCEPT VINcent's parents is outside on the back deck. Even Sheba is here, sniffing as far as her leash will allow.

"Have you done much hiking before, Amerie?" Camille asks as Vincent and I approach.

"I can't say that I have. Back home I like to walk in the mornings, but always on sidewalks."

"Welcome to your first Rogers Family Hike," Lance says with a resigned sigh.

"Look at my tough man." Camille squeezes Lance's arms. "He's sailed oceans and seen combat, but the thought of crossing paths with a wild hog terrifies him."

I make no attempt to erase the accusation from my tone as I glare at Vincent. "Y'all have wild hogs out here?" Nope. I want to go back to Houston.

"Don't worry," Brianna says. "Vincent and Sheba will protect us."

"There are wild hogs, but attacks on humans are uncommon," Vincent says with a pointed look at Camille. He looks at me and huffs before removing his scarf to instead wrap it around me in two loops. "But Bri's right. I'll protect you. You've got nothing to worry about."

This must be part of the show. Fawn on me in front of the family like any other boyfriend would, especially when their girlfriend is under duress. Should his gentle shoulder kneading and calm aura help dull the rising panic at the thought of coming in contact with an animal the size of a boulder? Hell, no. But somehow, here I am, breathing steadily and not racing to the guesthouse to pack my bags.

I touch the scarf while looking up at Vincent. It's warm from his body heat, and the scent of his face lotion wafts up to me. "Thank you."

"How stylish is that?" Mrs. Rogers says. She steps out the back door, with Mr. Rogers right behind her. She makes a show of trying to style her own scarf in the same simple fashion before giving up. "Vincent, can you come give me a hand with this?"

I stifle a smile when Camille looks at me and rolls her

eyes. We both know full well Mrs. Rogers's helpless act is a ploy to get her son to dote on her. And it works. Even my weary heart can barely take it when Vincent towers over her and ties her scarf before leaving a kiss on her cheek.

We begin the hike by heading toward the line of trees behind the guesthouse. Vincent's parents take the lead, followed by Vincent and me, Brianna and Sheba, then Lance and Camille.

Green grass quickly gives way to a worn dirt trail, then there's nothing but white stone and loose rock as we venture farther from the cabin. From our fantastically low vantage point, I'm in awe of the many hills in the distance that make a mosaic of greens and browns. As we approach some low bushes and cactuses, I glance back to check on Sheba and hope she's staying clear of the sharp spines. What I see, however, is Vincent staring at my ass. Intently. So focused, it takes him a few seconds to realize I've turned around. Once he does, he blinks hard, as if coming out of a trance, then meets my gaze before looking off into the distance.

After waking up draped over him this morning and going gaga again when we were getting ready, it's a nice ego boost to see he's attracted to me even if he's good at hiding it. And as I face forward again, I may be adding some extra sway to my hips.

"Potty break," Brianna announces after a while.

Everyone pauses for water while Sheba sniffs and circles around to do her thing. After I hand my canteen back to Vincent, I'm drawn to a patch of yellow flowers growing beside an old rotting log. It's a splash of life against the otherwise monotonous white terrain and sparse tufts of dormant grass.

"Daffodils," I say, pointing at them as Vincent comes to stand next to me.

He smiles at me before squatting down to pluck one. "Maybe you should have been a botanist." He straightens up, twisting it by the stem with his long fingers as he faces me. "You know, these begin sprouting around springtime and are said to represent rebirth and new beginnings."

New beginnings. I like the sound of that. It makes everything seem possible. Like it's possible that my business will thrive. That the secrets I've held back from my parents will be worthwhile as I pick up the pieces of my life. That the days of uncertainty over where I'll live next and all the lies will once and for all be a thing of the past.

Standing here with Vincent now, I realize how glad I am for that fateful day in the café.

Thank you for teaming up with me. For giving me this time to get my head on straight and ensure my parents enjoy the best of whatever time they have left together is what I want to say. My whole body tenses as I fight the sudden compulsion to slide my hands up Vincent's broad chest and hold on for all I'm worth. This can't be good for my health. Neither is the fact that I'm standing here with his scarf keeping my neck warm, inhaling Vincent's scent with every breath, and the memory of waking up pressed against him has yet to leave the forefront of my mind.

I glance to the sky, knowing full well that even if there were a full moon driving my reaction to him, I wouldn't be able to see its glow now that the sun is out. But breaking our eye contact does have the added benefit of allowing me to catch a breath, so when I glance back at Vincent my emotions are firmly contained and what comes out of my mouth is "You are just a well of knowledge."

"Knowledge is power," he responds.

With the flower still in his hand, he twists it one more time before reaching up to place it in my hair. I'm taken aback by the unexpected movement, and my eyes go wide while Vincent smiles at his handiwork.

"I'd use more to make you a proper crown, but we try not to take from Mother Nature too much." His eyes roam over my face and hair. "Not that beauty like yours needs much adornment."

I know it's all an act. I know this. But damn. Be still my heart. Vincent hits every cue and knows all the right words. Not only does he call me beautiful, but with his eyes reflecting nothing but sincerity, I feel it. Now it's really too much. A brush against my leg gives me the excuse to look away.

Sheba, having done her business, has just passed by me and now inspects the flowers. She sniffs one then sneezes and growls at it.

"Smart pup," Vincent says. "They're poisonous if eaten."

"Come here, Sheba," Brianna calls. "We don't need any accidents this weekend."

Like he's a magnet I'm fighting to pull away from, I can't help but sneak another glance at Vincent. His expression is once again concealed behind his usual easygoing demeanor, carrying none of the intense weight from moments before. He picks up a long stick near his foot, tests its sturdiness by striking one end against the ground, and grins at me.

Men and their tools.

"I bet you just loved it out here when you were a kid," I say. "What with all the rocks and plants."

"Oh yeah," Mrs. Rogers says, coming to stand with us. "When they were younger, Vincent and Octavius would explore all around here from sunup to sundown. There was some explorer they always pretended to be—Joe Buckworth, I believe."

"James Beckwourth," Vincent corrects. His gaze is back

on the daffodils, though a faraway look dims his eyes, and I realize Octavius must be his brother's name.

Mrs. Rogers snaps her fingers. "That's right." She lets out a low laugh and looks at me. "You should've seen them. Always coming home with rocks or new walking sticks. All rare and special, of course. Vincent, do you remember when you two nursed that bird with a broken wing? Camille ran around screaming bloody murder when that thing started flying around, while y'all tried catching it with a pillowcase. Of course, Brianna had to copy her big sister, so she started screaming too."

A hectic scene plays out in my mind of a young Vincent and his siblings running around their beautiful home, complete with yelling and floating feathers. I can only imagine the messy aftermath of such an event. It would have been a world away from my solo childhood of quietly playing with Barbies in the aged dollhouse one of our old neighbors had gifted me.

"You and Tay always were my adventurous ones," Mrs. Rogers says, smoothing the sleeve of Vincent's right arm. "Come on. Let's go to the creek."

Before taking off, she looks at me with a gleam in her eye and a smile that grows when she sees the flower Vincent placed in my hair.

The creek isn't so much a body of water as it is a dried-up mass of rock, split with hundreds of cracks from years of erosion, descending into a small, damp valley. To me, it looks like a close-up in a commercial for dry skin, but Vincent seems to hum with energy as we step down onto the outer edges of the creek bed.

"What's the story behind this creek?" I ask him.

"It doesn't look like much now, but come the first good rains of spring, it's a nice little spot. This is where I learned to skip rocks. Can you do it?" He doesn't look surprised when I shake my head no. "We'll have to come back in the fall. I'll teach you."

"Good idea, Vince," Mrs. Rogers says, stepping over a small crevice in the ground to come stand near Vincent and me. "You *must* bring Amerie back to see the creek. We'll all make a weekend of it. We'll do that and the wine train."

Given how excited Mrs. Rogers is at the thought of Vincent coming back, and the fact that the bargain between Vincent and me will be well over by the time he's able to visit again, I should let the topic drop. However, the event planner in me has her curiosity piqued.

"I've heard of the wine train, but have never experienced one. Can you tell me about it?" I ask her.

She graces me with a pleased smile. "Of course. The wine train isn't here, but the next town over. Camille, Brianna, and I went last year. We rode in a restored Victorian car all around the countryside for three hours. They had plenty of wines for tasting, but nothing compared to the food. I had the best pumpkin bisque soup of my life."

"Ooh, are you telling her about the wine train?" Camille asks, then takes a sip from her water bottle. "Have you ever had a peach-and-fig salad? So, so good."

"Now that you're family, you'll have to come on some of these girls' trips with us," Mrs. Rogers says. "Vincent can find something to do with his dad. Both of them say my trips are too boring and soft anyway." She waves her hand negligently.

I nod while inwardly cringing. I knew I should have let the topic die down. It's touching that Mrs. Rogers would so willingly label me as one of her own, but now guilt stabs at me for this act she's clearly eager to buy into. How quickly would she rescind her offer if she knew there would be no more visits from Vincent with me in tow because there *is* no Vincent and me?

I want to gauge how Vincent feels about her future plans, but when I turn around, he's not there. Maybe his mom was right that he has no interest in wine trains, because he's standing in the middle of the empty creek with Lance.

The sun shines directly on Lance, with a bright beam reflecting off the corner of his glasses, making him squint as his hands move animatedly. Vincent's face is little more than a shadow with the light directly behind him, but I see his strong profile and the flash of white teeth as he starts laughing at whatever Lance says. It's a full, hearty bellow with no pretenses, holding nothing back. The kind of laugh you let loose only around those you feel truly comfortable with, not caring if they see your face at an unflattering angle or have a wide-open view of your tonsils. The kind of laugh that almost makes me wish I were a stand-up comedian capable of delivering funny one-liners at will so I could have him cracking up until he loses his breath.

"You know, they make for great romantic dates too," Mrs. Rogers says.

I turn back to her, and it takes me a moment to remember that we were talking about wine trains. The smile she flaunts like a proud momma bear, however, tells me she's more than pleased with my getting off track and staring at Vincent. My face heats, and if it were someone else— say, for example, Gina—regarding me in the same way, I'd without a doubt tell her it wasn't what it looked like. I'm not obsessed with him or anything. I just haven't heard him laugh so loud before. And of course I wouldn't dream of becoming a comedian to hear it again. That was silly hypothetical thinking.

But this is Mrs. Rogers, and I am here to get her to believe everything *she* thinks I feel for Vincent is real. So I smile and nod. "The whole thing sounds delightful."

As Mrs. Rogers and Camille walk around to get reacquainted with their creek, I hang out by myself, unsure of what exactly to do. Vincent seems to be having a good time and doesn't need any interference from me. He and Lance are now tossing small rocks, in what I can only assume is an imitation of skipping rocks on water, while a few feet away, Mr. Rogers holds Sheba's leash so Brianna can wrap her braids into a large bun on top of her head.

Vincent may have been wary of coming to spend the week with his family, but there's no doubt in my mind how much they all love and enjoy being around one another. Even though I have my mom and dad, who I love above all, watching everyone here interact so seamlessly makes me wish for a big family to go along with a big home.

I let myself imagine that I really am becoming a part of their family. Just for a minute. That Vincent and I really did come together after some whirlwind romance and this is only the first of many trips we plan to take out here, spending fun-filled weekends at his childhood home.

"Look!" Brianna says, and I'm snatched from my daydream. She's pointing at something in the distance, but everyone is huddled in a line, staring across the creek, and I'm too far away to see.

I'm content to let them have their family time and not worry about whatever I'm missing out on until Camille speaks up. "Where's Amerie?"

Six heads swivel around, but it's Vincent who spots me right away. He seems surprised that I'm off by myself and immediately comes to me. "What are you doing all the way over here? Come on, I want you to see this," he says with his hand out.

I look at Vincent, then at everyone behind him waiting to include me in the sight, and place my hand in his, ignoring how my heart lurches at our contact.

When we join everyone, I look in the direction I think they're staring, but all I see is overgrown grass. "What am I looking for?"

"It's straight ahead," Vincent says.

I scan the area again. "What's straight ahead?"

"Right there." Brianna gestures with her hand. "You see it?"

"No. I don't see anything."

"You don't see that thing right in front of your face?" Vincent questions.

I grit my teeth. "The only thing right in front of my face is air, which, last time I checked, was invisible. Just tell me what to look for."

"It's right there," Camille chimes in, as if it's so obvious.

The only thing stopping me from going back to my tree and letting them watch whatever it is that apparently only people in this family can see is the fact that Vincent hasn't let go of my hand. And I haven't pulled away.

"Follow my finger," Mr. Rogers says, his deep voice encouraging.

At least someone is trying to be helpful. I do as he requests, imagining a laser shining from his extended pointer finger, and move my chin a few degrees to the right. When I finally see a small animal with dark striped fur strutting around, I gasp. "Is that . . . ?" I trail off.

"A wild hog," Lance finishes.

At the strained sound of his voice, I turn to my left where Lance stands behind Camille. Or more like hides behind her.

"A piglet," Camille corrects, shaking her head.

I hold in a smile and turn back to the piglet. Two more

come out to join the first, all weaving through the grass with their adorable skinny legs and big bellies. As cute as they are, the momma is right on their heels to keep them safe, and *cute* is not a word I'd use to describe her. She's got a stocky body, coarse hair, and small tusks. I more than understand Lance's trepidation, and my heart begins to thud hard against my chest.

"Should we be standing here?" I whisper, not wanting her to hear me. "Won't she smell our food or get mad at us for being too close to her babies?"

It's not like there's a body of water here to ensure she doesn't come charging at us.

"It's okay," Mrs. Rogers says confidently. "See, they're already moving on. Momma's probably just bringing her babies out for a little grass to munch on. All moms love to feed their kids."

It's not that I don't believe the expertise of the woman who's likely come across dozens of wild animals versus my zero interactions, but I wait until the wild hogs are a good distance away and Lance no longer has a death grip on his wife's arms before I relax.

Vincent squeezes my hand. "You good?"

I nod. "Yeah. I'm good."

"Okay." He squeezes my hand one more time before letting go.

I stand there for a second, letting my arm hang awkwardly, unsure of what to do at the sudden loss of his warmth. Mentally kicking myself for feeling this way.

Vincent takes a few steps to where his family is now gathered and digging in their packs, but stops and turns to me. "Are you waiting for the hogs to come back so you can pet them? Look at you, growing braver already."

I roll my eyes, though part of me is glad to have him

say something annoying to lighten the mood. "You know I'm not."

"Then let's go sit with everyone." He reaches for my hand again, but this time I sidestep him. Vincent is right on my heels with an annoying chuckle.

"I still want to keep it light this first day," Mrs. Rogers says. "So we'll fuel up, make it to the field, then turn back."

"You can sit here by me, Amerie," Camille says. "I already checked that there's no ants."

I send her a thankful smile before sitting down, and Vincent follows suit, sitting next to me.

"Granola bar or apple?" he asks.

He's too close to my face, but I can't very well pull away. "The granola bar sounds good."

He hands me a bar with a picture of a bear on the wrapper along with my canteen.

"Did Vince ever tell you how he used to jump out of trees while pretending to be a squirrel?" Camille says with an evil grin.

"A squirrel?" Vincent is clearly outraged. "I was a ninja. You know that, Cami."

Camille shrugs and scoops a handful of trail mix into her mouth.

Vincent glares at her, then looks to me to plead his case. "I was a ninja."

I pat his knee. "Sure you were."

Their back-and-forth continues. I know it's likely to continue for the rest of the trip, but I'm so amused that I don't mind one bit. When Vincent pleads with me to agree with him again, ensuring I'm not left out of their conversation, I inwardly smile. It's all so Hallmark and fun. I think I'll pretend it's all real for a little while longer.

CHAPTER SIXTEEN

There will come a day, when I'm in my own bed in my own home, when I'll wake up to a feeling of peace like I've never known. There will be no grogginess, no disorientation, no dread for what lies ahead. Just a slow and soft emergence into consciousness as I greet the morning.

Today, however, is not that day.

I lightly flex my fingers, giving Vincent's biceps the barest squeeze. As toned as he is, there's barely any give. Not on his arm, nor on the chest where I rest my head as I cling to him like a favorite stuffed animal. Bonnie the Bunny was my favorite stuffy's name. She had big floppy ears and a white stain on her belly that stood out against her faded golden fur. I'd accidentally sprayed her with Windex while cleaning one of my old rooms before a big move. Stained or not, she was so soft. Not like Vincent, who's all hard, lean muscles. Bonnie also wasn't as warm as Vincent. And with the cold air at my back, it's no wonder I sought out his warmth again.

My eyes feel heavy when I open them. The room is pitch black, and all I hear is the stillness of the country. Being a city girl, I never would have thought a dark, silent morning would be peaceful, but maybe soft mornings aren't only reserved for your own bed. With no idea what time it is and when the alarm will go off, I shut my eyes.

"Amerie."

I feel a warm caress against my back and stir. "Hmm?"

"It's time to get up," Vincent says. He runs his large palm down my back again, and it feels so good, I arch into him.

When I hear his sharp intake of breath as my knee pushes against the physical evidence that he just woke up, I freeze.

I remove my leg and loosen the hold I have on his side. After I sit up, it takes a good minute to find the courage to meet his gaze, and even then I hold it for only a moment before looking away. "Sorry. I think I just gravitated to the warmest thing I could find overnight."

Vincent sits up against the headboard. "It's okay."

Unlike yesterday morning, his voice doesn't sound raspy in the slightest, and his eyes are bright and clear. Just how long was he awake, lying under me, before he woke me up? Was he simply being thoughtful and letting me sleep once he realized he was trapped? Or did he enjoy me being pressed to him as much as I did and was loath to stop it?

"You were keeping me warm too," he adds, and the words are an espresso shot straight to my groin.

I bite down on my bottom lip, and Vincent's eyes focus on my mouth. His gaze continues to lower, sweeping to my chest, then back to my lips. He swallows before averting his gaze far away from me, and I know it's time to go back to our normal status quo. The one where we decide all these little heated moments are just that—fleeting and of no consequence. We're here to play the happy couple in front of Vincent's family only.

But man, if I had the ability to time travel, I would be an

absolute menace. Back I'd go to the moment before I sat up and Vincent and I remembered that waking up in each other's arms isn't part of the deal—and I'd keep going back to that moment over and over again.

Vincent is the first to slide out of bed and head to the restroom. "I'm going to check in at the house, then I'll be back," he says when he comes out, hardly daring to look at me.

I shake off the tension and slip into my fleece-lined leggings when he's gone. I pair them with thick socks, one of those long-sleeve shirts that keeps you warm while wicking moisture, and my jacket.

By the time Vincent returns, I'm sitting on the bed, going through text messages from my parents and Gina. Mom and Dad sent me pictures of their drive through Wyoming. Gina has sent me about a million TikTok videos with requests for an update. I send her a thumbs-up, knowing full well the vagueness will annoy her, but it's not like I have anything juicy to share.

"My mom made some tacos," Vincent says. "I'm pretty sure your list didn't mention anything about not liking chorizo and eggs, right?"

I wasn't hungry before, but at the word *tacos* I sit up straight. "Are you kidding? I love chorizo and eggs. I told you we had a short stint where we lived in San Antonio, right? I don't remember much from the city, but I do remember the tacos."

He hands me a foil-wrapped taco before sitting a few feet away on the bed.

"Why do I get the impression that living with your mom was like living full-time on a cruise with an all-you-can-eat buffet?" I ask after my first bite. "If I keep eating like this all week, my leggings will be the only thing I'll be able to fit into for a while."

He frowns. "Would wearing only leggings be a bad thing? It's not like they look bad on you."

How can he compliment me so nonchalantly while making my heart race?

When I don't respond, he looks at me with a slow grin, and I realize he knows exactly what he's doing. It makes my pulse pound all the more, so I ignore him and direct all my focus on the delicious taco.

"We're hiking to a cave today," Vincent says when he's done eating.

My enthusiasm for eating the taco dies as my stomach begins to feel queasy. "A cave?"

I might have thought twice before agreeing to this trip if I'd known all Vincent's family members were adrenaline seekers. I still would've come, but I would have been at least a little more mentally prepared. And while I may be with a group of experienced experts, it's a damn cave, where bats and who knows what else make their home.

"Yes, a cave," he says. "We used to go all the time. It's not that deep, and it gets a lot of visitors, so the animals stay away."

"I don't know, Vincent. Maybe you and your family should go and I'll sit this one out."

He sets my unfinished taco by the lamp and pulls me up so I'm standing, and I don't resist. "If I'm going to keep my mom off my back, I need you out there with me. You'll be fine," Vincent assures me.

I know when he says he needs me, he doesn't actually mean me, but rather his fake girlfriend. Still, his declaration halts the words in my throat, and pleasure curls around my spine. Where did this reluctance to say no to him come from? I need to find out and nip it in the bud. But until I do, all I can do is shrug. "I guess we're going to a cave."

WE'RE ABOUT FIFTEEN MINUTES INTO THE HIKE, AND VINCENT AND I have been glaring at each other nonstop. Actually, I've been glaring at him while his focus has been on my shoes. And in all fairness, I have slipped three times.

I do my best to follow Camille's steps, but the rugged trail we're on today is full of loose rocks, and my shoes don't have a huge amount of traction. I can see why Vincent may be a little upset and probably thinking *I told you so* about me bringing hiking boots, but how was I supposed to know we'd be out here doing extreme sports? It seems like yesterday's hike was an appetizer and this is the real deal. I'm out of my wheelhouse and highly annoyed.

After I step over a raised tree root, my foot slips on the rock I land on, and I lose my balance. Vincent grabs my upper arm to help steady me. I would've appreciated the gesture if he hadn't also huffed out a breath. Instead, my irritation is kicked up a notch, and I wrench my arm from his hand while shooting another glare at him.

"Do y'all remember this?" Mrs. Rogers calls from the head of the group.

We all make it to where she's facing a stone as tall as I am.

"Aww, I should have brought some paint with me," Brianna says.

"What's the story here?" I ask Vincent. I'm still annoyed with him, but also curious.

"On our way to the cave, we used to stop here and pretend that it was a door to some magical land. Bri convinced

Mom to let us paint it one day, and each time it would rain around here she would beg to come back to fix what the water had wiped away."

"Let's get a picture of the siblings!" Brianna suggests.

After a little coaxing, Vincent and Camille join her at the rock. Rather than hand Sheba off, Brianna puts the leash under her foot, then pulls her siblings tight to her.

They all look so different. Vincent, tall, dark, and handsome, with his jaw that's all hard angles. Camille, with her brown complexion a little darker than the others and an air of competence. And Brianna, so lovely with dimples on each cheek that fit perfectly with her baby face. When they smile, they all have the same crinkle to their eyes, and the resemblance is unmistakable.

"Look at my babies," Mrs. Rogers says when she's taken at least ten photos of them. "My heart is so full. I'm so glad to have all of my kids home, if only for a little while."

As soon as she says the words, her body stiffens and her eyes immediately pool with grief. My guess is she's thinking of her one son who isn't here.

She looks at each of her kids, stopping at Vincent as her mouth thins.

"Momma." The plea is soft but evident in Vincent's voice. As if he feels the tangible shift in the air, and her turn of mood could be as predictable as the sun rising in the east. And maybe for him it is.

Mrs. Rogers shakes her head. "Sometimes I just wonder, if we'd raised you all in the city instead, whether things would have been different. If we could've kept you safe that way."

"Enough, Momma." This time Vincent's voice is firm. He lets out a controlled exhale and pushes away from the rock. "Let's keep going." He takes off, back on the trail.

The phone Mrs. Rogers used to take pictures of her kids is now held loosely in her hand, and Mr. Rogers puts an arm around her slumped shoulders as he speaks low in her ear where no one else can hear. Camille looks at her mom, then sighs and shakes her head after Vincent. Only Lance meets my gaze, and I know we're both in unspoken agreement that what has so far been a joyous occasion has taken a turn.

I watch Vincent, my heart clenching as the distance between us grows wider and wider. I may have been annoyed with him earlier, but his dejected walk causes all my annoyance to fade. Before he can get too far ahead, I call after him, "Vincent, wait!" I start down the trail, then begin jogging when he doesn't stop.

"Sheba, no! Heel!"

I slow when I hear Brianna calling after her dog, turning to see the golden ball of fur has gotten free and is bounding toward me. With my attention diverted, my foot catches on the edge of a large rock.

In the second it takes me to hit the ground, it crosses my mind how lucky I am to have on gloves. At least my hands won't get all scraped up. Once I'm on the cold, hard ground, I only have time to pick up my face before Sheba is on me.

She's not heavy, but I'm pinned, trying to cover my face as she assaults me with kisses. She manages to get in a few good licks to my cheek before she's removed. I uncover my face to see Vincent standing by me, holding Sheba by her collar.

Brianna scrambles to us and grabs Sheba's leash from the ground. "I'm so sorry, Amerie. Are you okay?"

"I'm fine," I say, pushing to my elbows.

"You do know if you can't control your dog, you probably shouldn't have one," Vincent growls at Brianna.

"Vincent, I said I'm fine," I say more firmly, mostly for Brianna's benefit. I can tell she feels bad about Sheba getting loose, and Vincent isn't making the situation easier for anyone. "I'm the one who made the mistake of running and setting off her little wolf instincts."

"All the more reason to keep control over your pets. You're lucky she only licked you."

Sheba is whining and trying to get to me while Brianna struggles to pull her even farther away.

"Well, instead of standing there and looming over me, maybe you should help me up so I don't look so tempting anymore."

Armed with a deep scowl, Vincent grabs my outstretched hands and gently pulls me up. I stand and immediately wince as what feels like lightning strikes my right ankle.

"What's wrong?" Vincent says.

"I think I hurt my ankle when I fell."

"Can you walk on it?"

"Hold on. I need a minute." I breathe in and out through my mouth, hoping I've just banged myself up on the rock and, with enough time, the shock of pain will ease. But when I try to step again, the blinding ache only intensifies. "Okay, I don't think I'm going to be able to walk."

"I'm taking you back to the cabin." Vincent's tone brooks no argument.

"Do you need help moving her?" Lance asks.

Vincent doesn't answer. I'm not sure if he even heard a word Lance said. He seems laser focused on my leg, as if he can see through the pants and straight to my bone.

"Let's go ahead and turn around," Mrs. Rogers says. "I don't want y'all walking all the way back by yourselves."

Since Vincent isn't talking, I'm the one to speak up. "Please, don't let this ruin the hike. You all should stay out here and keep going." There's no use in everyone calling it an early day.

After a bit of back-and-forth, they agree to go on while Vincent and I turn around.

"It'll be too hard trying to navigate over the rocks on one foot. I need to pick you up," Vincent warns.

Pick me up? He'd have to carry me for at least twenty minutes. Without dropping me on the rocks. And with the way my body's been reacting to him, I'm doubly pressed to find my own way back.

As I'm searching for some kind of stick like the one Vincent found yesterday, he presses, saying "Amerie" in a low, thinly controlled voice.

We both know I'm only stalling the inevitable, so I let my shoulders fall in defeat and nod.

Vincent doesn't waste any time. He scoops me up with one arm behind my back and the other under my knees, and as we begin the trek back, I look over his shoulder and wave bye to the group of concerned faces.

Vincent sticks to flat areas as much as possible, while I hold on to his neck, stiff as a board. I didn't want to make a scene in front of his family, but everything in me screams to demand he put me down so I can walk.

If he wants to carry my luggage, I'll overstuff bags until he can barely walk. But my precious life is in his hands, and I don't trust that he won't slip and fall.

As we come upon a rough part of the path, packed densely with rocks, Vincent strikes a large one and thrusts forward. I take in a sharp breath when my good foot bumps into the other and it feels like lava is being poured on my ankle. I can't help it as I turn into Vincent's chest and will the pain away.

"Sorry," he says, slowing his pace.

"So you've done this often, right?" I need to take my mind off the throbbing. "How many people did you have to carry out when you did Search and Rescue?"

"Carry like this? Not many." Vincent's voice is slightly labored, and the muscles of his face are strained. "We were usually strapping people to gurneys and loading them onto a helicopter."

"So what you're saying is I get special treatment."

His features relax minutely. "I guess you could say that." He trips over another rock, this time holding me steady to his chest, then comes to a complete stop. "I'm sorry, Amerie."

"For what? You didn't put all these rocks here."

"I knew those shoes didn't have enough traction. If I had waited for everyone, I could've made sure you knew the rocks were loose."

"Then you would have been right by me when I busted my ass rather than ten feet away."

His lips twitch like he wants to laugh but is obviously holding back. Then all traces of a smile completely disappear and he looks more miserable than before, so I brush my hand along his chin. He didn't shave again, and I'm kind of digging this grizzled look.

"No. I would have been there, holding you up to make sure you didn't fall."

"Vincent, seriously, you can't control everything. It was an accident. Use that big brain to go over the word's definition. I'm not placing any blame on you, and I won't allow you to accept it all either."

His mouth tightens like he wants to argue more, but he remains quiet and starts walking again. I let my hand linger for a moment before pulling away and do my best to relax into his hold. We're almost to the guesthouse now, approaching the wall of trees that marks their property.

Vincent still looks tense, and I think of the conversation with his mom that led us to this path. "Will you tell me about your brother?" I ask quietly.

He continues walking, and I think he won't answer until he lets out a deep breath. "He was my best friend. We did almost everything together and used to spend so much time out here exploring. These woods aren't the same without him." He clears his throat and swallows, and I know that's all I'll get out of him.

I lay my head on his chest. Almost losing my mom just about did me in, and I still haven't quite recovered. I can't imagine the pain Vincent has gone through, and I instantly regret bringing it up. "I'm sorry you lost him."

When we make it inside the guesthouse, Vincent carefully sets me on the bed. He's in efficient mode as he unties my shoe and slowly pulls it off, then grabs the pillow he slept on to prop my foot up.

He pulls off my sock and frowns once he realizes my leggings actually close over my toes like stockings. "I can't examine your ankle with these in the way. Do you want me to cut them?"

I gasp and clutch my chest. Cut the leggings Gina gave me two Christmases ago? I shake my head adamantly. "Never."

Vincent tries staring me down before shaking his head and throwing his hands up. "We'll have to take them off, then."

"Fine," I throw back.

This is fine. I'm injured; he needs to assess the damage. He's seen plenty of legs, and it's not like I've ever had an issue showing mine in shorts or swimsuits.

There is absolutely no reason my heart should be racing this fast.

I bite my lip as I grab my leggings, but the small movement of lifting my hips causes more pain.

"I'll help you," Vincent says.

He reaches for the waistband of my pants and tugs them over my hips, exposing my flesh-colored panties. I love them because I don't have to worry about my underwear showing through clothes, but upon first glance, it does look like I'm bare. Evidently it does not escape Vincent's notice. I swear he stops breathing for a moment before he meets my gaze, and electricity arcs between us.

His throat bobs in a swallow, and he bends his head back down.

He continues his task, and I track his movements as the warmth from his knuckles sears my bare skin like hot coals.

Once the leggings are fully off, Vincent races to grab a spare sheet from the dresser and practically throws it at me. I'd be offended if it weren't for the bulge in his pants that makes it evident how affected he is right now.

He sits at the foot of the bed. "Brace yourself." Taking my ankle into his hands, he rotates it, and all the heat I felt moments earlier is nothing but a memory.

I cover my mouth to stifle a scream and a whole slew of cuss words.

Vincent places my foot back on the pillow and actually smiles. "Good news. It's not broken."

"How can you tell?" I pant.

"Search and Rescue personnel, remember? And I'm our crew's medical officer."

"I think Gina was right and you are a male Barbie." I think the pain is making me delirious.

"Wouldn't that be Ken?"

"Are you a beach bum?"

Vincent shakes his head. "Like I was saying. It's not broken, but you have a pretty good sprain. We'll have you take it easy the next few days, and you'll be back on your feet before you know it."

My ankle is swollen to twice its usual size, but everything is straight and intact, so I decide to take Vincent at his word. "Okay. Sounds good."

I watch him go to the bathroom and come back with a small towel.

"What's that for?" I ask.

"It's to clean your face. Sheba licked all over you."

"Good idea." I reach for the towel, but Vincent keeps it in a tight grip.

"May I?" he says.

Touched, I nod and allow him to lift my chin up. I immediately shut my eyes as he begins dabbing at my cheeks.

"Does your face itch?" he asks.

"No, I feel great. Well, apart from the feeling that someone's beating at my ankle with a hammer."

He lets out an amused sound from the back of his throat. "You're kind of a wuss when it comes to pain, huh?"

"Not all of us grew up falling out of trees and scraping our knees." I let myself relax as he moves from one cheek to the other, so gentle and attentive. "I never wanted to make my parents worry, so I guess I was pretty careful as a child."

"I can tell. I didn't see one scar on your legs."

How good of a look did he get? Did he like what he saw? The thought makes me squeeze my thighs together.

"I'm all done," he says, finishing with a swipe along my chin, but I keep my eyes closed. I hear the thread of need layered within his husky timbre, feel the stir of his breath against my damp skin. I'm scared of what I'll see if I meet his gaze. Or more like what will be reflected from my own eyes. This is a dangerous game we're playing when we both know our time together is temporary.

When his hand drops and his footsteps move away, I garner the courage to open my eyes and find him digging through his backpack.

"Let's get you some medicine to help manage your pain," Vincent says.

"Yes, Doctor."

After I take two small pills, Vincent walks to the door. "I'm going to get some ice to wrap you up. Do you need anything from the house? I can make you a sandwich."

"No, thanks. Just the ice will be perfect, Vincent. Thank you."

When everyone comes back from the hike, Brianna stops by to once again apologize, and with Sheba under Vincent's watchful glare, I assure her I'm okay.

Later in the afternoon, I'm able to convince Vincent to have lunch inside with his family while I take a nap without his hovering. Once he's gone, I decide to check in with Gina.

"Tell me everything," she says as soon as she pops up on the screen. She's sitting on her red couch with Dog Mack in her lap.

"Hi, Mack," I sing. "Is Mommy giving you enough yummy treats?"

He sniffs and whines at the phone.

Gina pushes him away, frowning at me. "Tell Auntie Mimi to spill the tea before Mommy decides to drive up there and see for herself."

I imagine her trying to navigate the scary hills, then going off on me once she makes it here, and I laugh.

Gina's face jostles like she's just dropped the phone. "Whoa, Mimi, what's got you smiling like that? Or I guess I should say *who*? I take it you and Mr. Astronaut are getting along?" She wiggles her eyebrows.

I purse my lips. "What are you talking about?"

"You know exactly what I'm talking about. What is going on between you and ol' boy?"

"Can't you ever just say Vincent? It's always Mr. Sexy, or Mr. Astronaut, or a variation of the two. And nothing is going on between us. Vincent and I are just . . . friends."

I lean back against the headboard at the realization. I can't remember the last time I gave that title to anyone other than Gina and meant it. Sure, I've had colleagues I was *friendly* with, but obviously those relationships didn't survive me leaving Jacob and Johnson. Somehow Vincent has gone from daily annoyance to partner to helpful friend. It almost feels like I should be calling my mom up, telling her how her little girl made a new friend at school. A sweet friend who's fretted over me—carrying me all the way back to the cabin and making sure I haven't so much as breathed in discomfort—but friend, nonetheless.

"I'm glad you're warming up to him," Gina says. "How's the visit with his family going? Are they buying the whole couple thing? Don't leave out a single detail."

I laugh again at her eagerness. "Simmer down. I think it's going well. We've gotten through two days and two hikes. Actually, one hike. The other one was a bust." I tell her about the fall and my ankle.

"I can't believe he carried you all the way back. Mr. Space Cowboy is a sweetheart." She waits for me to acknowledge her new nickname, but I roll my eyes.

"Yeah, yeah. How are things going back home?"

"Oh, you know, trying not to drink myself into oblivion before we go see Mack's mom this weekend for their monthly family dinner."

I hear the door of the house close. "You'll survive. I know it. I have to let you go though. Vincent's heading back."

"Okay. Keep me posted on your sexy astronaut and do all the things I would!"

If she only knew how close I truly am to doing just that. I put my phone down and try to ignore the way my heart leaps as Vincent walks through the door.

CHAPTER SEVENTEEN

A re you sure I can't come?" I say, pouting, with my arms folded across my chest, while Vincent laces his boots.

He continued waiting on me hand and foot throughout the evening and morning. So much so, I'm positive that if I had only hinted at a taste for grapes, he'd have gladly hand-fed them to me straight from the vine.

Admittedly, it was fun playing patient for a while, but I've been confined to the bed coming up on twenty-four hours now. I need to move and get some fresh air. An open window can only do so much.

I woke up this morning and realized Vincent was right about it being only a minor sprain, as evidenced by the fact that my foot no longer resembles a baby hippo. I convinced him he didn't need to stay by my side all morning. Then once he began getting ready, I oh-so-casually mentioned that I was ready to accompany everyone as well. He wasn't having it.

He stands up and drapes his scarf over his neck. "No, Amerie. You still need to stay off that ankle."

"Can't you just give me a piggyback ride? You're strong. Put those muscles to good use. Besides, you said yourself it's not a serious sprain." I rotate my ankle and only wince a little.

"It's not serious, but you don't need to agitate it unnecessarily. A morning of hiking won't do you any favors."

"Piggyback ride," I repeat. I mean, at this point I'm simply arguing on the principle that I'm unhappy at being kept inside.

"Right," Vincent says. "That way I can collapse from exhaustion due to the extra weight."

I narrow my eyes at him.

"Not that it would be a lot of weight," he adds. He leans against the dresser and crosses his arms. "Amerie, if you need me to stay here, I'm happy to do so. To be honest, I'd rather make sure you and your ankle are taken care of."

I will not let his obvious concern make me blush.

I wave my hand. "No, you go. I'll be fine here."

"Okay. We won't be gone too long. And I'll tell you what. Later today, I'll use my big, strong, manly, well-defined—"

"Is this going somewhere?"

"—muscles—"

"Really, Vincent?"

"And carry you to the car for a ride around the town." He winks. "Now, do you have everything you need?"

A ride around does sound nice. I sweep my hand to encompass the bed. "I've got my throne, laptop, and breakfast taco. I'll be fine."

Vincent nods and hefts his backpack. If I were his real girlfriend, he'd walk over so I could send him off with a proper goodbye kiss.

I blink. Why did that image pop into my head? It was one thing to wake up curled around him when I was unconscious. Because yes, I woke plastered to his back again, bum ankle and all, and moved before he woke up. But the desire to kiss him while I'm fully awake is out of hand. I really need fresh air. Barring that, I at least need to not be breathing in the air laced with his scent.

"Okay, bye. Have fun," I say quickly.

Vincent looks at me funny but walks to the door. "I'll be back in two hours, tops."

"*I'LL BE BACK IN TWO HOURS,*" I MOCK, DOING A FANTASTIC IMPRESSION of Vincent. There's nobody here to tell me otherwise, since I'm still alone.

It's three hours later, and Vincent hasn't returned. It wouldn't be so bad if I were in the comfort of a familiar place like Moon Bean, where I could people-watch out the window, or Vincent's house, where I'd be surrounded by the comfort of my belongings. But no, I'm cooped up in a large room where the only company is my computer.

I worked on my website, then decided to torture myself by going to the Jacob and Johnson website. They still have pictures of events I planned posted in their galleries. Pictures I can't use, even though I'm the one who put in hundreds of hours of work.

I also tried calling my parents, but the call went straight to voice mail. My conscience volleys back and forth between being glad no one picked up and being worried. I know Mom must be fine; they would reach out to me if there were some kind of emergency. But I want to hear her voice myself and not rely on the text messages we've been exchanging. On the other hand, if I do speak to them, no doubt they'll have questions about where I am and who I'm with. And I can't tell them the truth.

Now, with nothing to do, I stare up at the ceiling, boredom driving me to connect dots like constellations while my computer sits on my chest.

A knock comes at the door, and I eagerly sit up. "Come in."

Camille is the one to enter. It must have been a good hike. Her fine, curly hair has puffed up around the edges, and she has an empty water bottle attached to a fanny pack at her waist.

She leans against the closed door. "Vincent wanted you to know he'll be a little longer than expected. He said you get antsy if y'all are apart for too long."

I open my mouth to immediately set the record straight: I get antsy for no man. But at the last second, I remember I'm supposed to be playing this relationship up. A doting girlfriend would want to spend every second with her boo. Gag.

It feels like my mouth is full of hot gumbo, but I manage a smile. "Thanks for the heads-up."

Camille watches me closely, then erupts in laughter. "Yeah, your expression pretty much mirrored mine."

My shoulders sag in relief, and I join her.

"What are you working on?" Camille asks when her giggles die down.

"Nothing now. I was just looking at some old photos of events I did."

"Do you mind if I take a peek? I've been curious about your work."

"Sure." I turn the laptop so Camille has easy access to the screen as she sits on the side of the bed. "These are actually from the old firm I worked with, but I was the main coordinator."

She points to a picture full of bold colors. "What kind of event is that one for?"

"It was a birthday party. My client's theme was Arabian Nights."

"Wow, it looks stunning. You really put my little New Year's Eve party to shame."

"No, Camille. You threw a lovely party." Still, I can't fight my smile. I love when people take pleasure in my work, and the Arabian Nights party was one of my favorites. My client, Salima, wanted a lot of purples, teals, and golds, and I delivered. My favorite element from the setup had been the centerpieces. Fresh royal jasmine bloomed from gold birdcages surrounded by traditional Moroccan candles.

Salima had been ecstatic when she'd walked into the finished hotel ballroom, and I'd been right there with her.

"You know," Camille says. "I really would love to hire you to plan Mom and Dad's vow renewal. Brianna and I were supposed to do it together, but it's hard coordinating while she's in Dallas and I'm delivering babies. Vincent and I live in the same city, but I already know he won't help. It's hard enough getting ahold of him now." She's got the same disappointed expression I saw when we went hiking yesterday and Vincent walked away. "Only thing is, it's in three months. Is that too little notice? We sent out save the date cards, but don't even have a venue booked yet."

I lick my suddenly dry lips. She wants me to plan the vow renewal? There are so many reasons I shouldn't. One, vow renewals are a lot like weddings. Usually they're not quite as spectacular, but they may as well be termed Weddings 2.0. With no team to rely on for planning or backup, if I do this for Mr. and Mrs. Rogers and something goes wrong, there goes my reputation. Again. Two, how can I accept this job knowing that I'm not the person Camille thinks I am? It's morally wrong. As bomb as my work is, for all I know, she's offering me the job only because I'm her brother's girlfriend.

But can I turn down the job? I already know the answer to that. A resounding no.

I meet Camille's hopeful eyes and smile. "I can pull it off in three months. I've planned military weddings in three weeks."

"Great! Why don't you go ahead and draw up the contract so we can get started?"

"I'll have it ready for you tomorrow."

Once Camille leaves, I stare at the closed door, wanting to call her back and say I changed my mind. What did I just get myself into? I'm supposed to be here supporting Vincent, not making future plans to get more involved with his family. What if this bargain between Vincent and me doesn't even work out and I'm forced to back out of the ceremony at the last minute? I'd have to legally change my name if I wanted to work in Houston again.

The bed bounces as I flop back.

Twenty minutes later, I jump when a loud crack splits the air. Heart hammering, I try to imagine where a small explosion may have occurred. Is there a fire department nearby? Who the hell is going to come get me?

Then it happens again, and again, becoming methodical. Careful not to move too quickly and hurt my ankle, I turn to look out the window behind the headboard. What I see is a sight.

Vincent is chopping wood. With heat from the afternoon sun, temperatures must be in the midsixties now. He's removed his vest, but still wears a black shirt with the sleeves rolled up to his elbows. As he brings the axe over his head and down in perfect form, my heart takes off for a whole new reason.

Without hesitation, I take a picture of him and send it off to Gina. I'm not surprised when she instantly replies.

Gina: I think he missed the memo that wood chopping
is 100x sexier without a shirt. Or at the very least,
plaid. But still, get it, Zaddy!

I roll my eyes at the line of sweat emojis and set my
phone down. Now that I've sent the message, I feel a bit ridiculous. Gina will never let me live that one down. I'll
never let myself live it down. I am officially out of my mind.

Or it's a case of cabin fever. That makes more sense. I
need to get out of this room. Vincent said we'd go for a ride
later, but who knows how many more hours that will be.

There's a moment of silence from the steady chopping,
so I look out the window to determine whether Vincent is
done with his chore or taking a short break. There he is,
grabbing a stack of chopped wood and walking out of sight
to the front of the house.

Mrs. Rogers is outside, placing a pizza in a brick oven,
and Brianna is sprawling in one of their many lawn chairs,
reading a book. This is my chance.

I move my legs to the edge of the bed and test my ankle.
I remember how, as a kid, I used to get jealous whenever a
fellow classmate would break an arm or leg, and everyone
would sign their cast. I thought they looked so cool and
wanted one for myself. Thank God that wish never came to
pass. This being injured thing is not it.

I take a deep breath and hoist myself up. After the first
few hobbling steps toward the door, it really isn't that bad.
With one shoe on and the afflicted foot and ankle in a sock,
I play a grueling game of one-footed hopscotch to make it
to the back deck.

Mrs. Rogers and Brianna watch me with twin looks of
bemusement, like they can't believe I'm crazy enough to be
hopping through the yard, yet they're ready to come help if

I fall and bust my ass. But I make it up the three steps to the wooden deck and use the last of my energy to fall into an empty chair. I smile at the ladies in triumph, even Sheba, who lies under Brianna's chair while regarding me with the saddest of eyes, as if to say sorry.

"Uh-oh," Brianna says. "Vincent's not going to be happy to see you out here."

Vincent and Brianna are five years apart, so I have to imagine he played not only a brotherly role but a fatherly one as well while they were growing up. Maybe the thought of Vincent being upset causes Brianna a bit of trepidation, but not me.

I shrug. "Well, too bad, so sad for him. *He* wasn't the one confined to the guesthouse all day, so he can stay mad." I see Mrs. Rogers watching me and wince. I need to tone down the snark, lest Mrs. Rogers think her son is with someone intent on causing him stress. "It's a lovely room, Mrs. Rogers. I just needed some fresh air."

Mrs. Rogers grins as she takes her seat. "It's Cheryl, remember? And I'm not bothered in the least that you needed to get out of there. In fact, I'm glad you joined us. We get to chat, and it'll do Vince some good to realize he can't make everyone do what he wants."

Speaking of the man, Vincent comes around the corner of the house. When he sees me posted in my new favorite chair, he stops in his tracks.

Brianna shifts to a more comfortable position in her seat. "Where's my popcorn?"

"Hush," Mrs. Rogers says.

Vincent and I are locked in a stare-down. By the set of his jaw and straight line of his brows, I know he isn't happy to see me out here. But the only way he'll get me back inside is by hauling me kicking and screaming.

He'd better not try it.

I tense as he stomps my way, stopping to loom inches above me. "You're supposed to keep that elevated."

He grabs an empty chair and, far from gently, sets it down in front of me. When he then turns to face me, I straighten, daring him to try to manhandle me in the same manner. But Vincent slowly and deliberately reaches for my right leg and places it on the chair. Gently, he sweeps his hand from my calf to my ankle.

Through my leggings and the tough material of Vincent's gloves, I can't feel the heat from his hand. Still, warmth spreads through me as if he's touched my bare skin, melting away all hostility.

"Did you hurt yourself getting out here?" he asks quietly. Oh Lord, his irises are doing that shining thing again that makes me want to drown in them.

I shake my head and respond in the same low tone. "Not too bad."

"Let me know when you want to go back inside, and I'll help you."

"Okay," I say, and that's it. No scoffing or proclaiming how I'm an independent woman who can manage to get back inside the same way I came. I'm hypnotized by his eyes and as docile as a lamb.

"Okay." He nods once and backs away.

I watch as he gathers more bundles of wood, then glance toward Mrs. Rogers and Brianna once he disappears around the side of the house. It's evident the two women have been staring at me as long as I was at Vincent. I reach for my necklace. "What?"

Brianna smiles but remains silent, while Mrs. Rogers places a hand over her heart. "I love seeing him so smitten with you."

I can't argue with that. Not that I think Vincent is smitten with me. Obviously, we're both playing the part while his mom is right here. Sure, he's got this thing going on where safety is really important to him, and he's probably mad I ventured out of the bed. But his look and touch, while convincing, were fake.

Fake. Fake. Fake.

I can't let myself forget, or my mind will get the same mixed signals my body obviously has.

"That's a beautiful necklace, Amerie," Mrs. Rogers says, snapping me out of my haze.

I raise my hand to the necklace again. It's been a staple in my wardrobe for years. It's gold, with a short chain so the diamond pendant rests at my clavicle. "Thank you. It actually used to be my mom's. My dad gave it to her before I was born, and I loved it so much as a girl, I'd always ask to wear it. She gifted it to me when I graduated high school."

My mom doesn't have a lot of jewelry, so it meant the world to me when she entrusted me with her necklace. It's also a constant reminder of how much my parents love me and are willing to give up for me.

"It's an heirloom?" Mrs. Rogers says. "You've done a beautiful job caring for it. And it sounds like you and your mom are close."

"We are, very. I'm an only child, so my parents were all I had growing up."

Soon enough, the other family members come outside. Camille joins us while Lance and Mr. Rogers go inspect Vincent's handiwork.

"It's official," Camille announces. "Amerie's going to plan the ceremony."

I breathe easier when Mrs. Rogers smiles and Brianna appears relieved. Part of me was worried they might feel like I was stepping on their toes, even though Camille came to me. Plans are made to form a group chat so everyone can keep up to date, then Camille begins asking me questions about the process and other past events I've done.

"I think it would be really cool to have the ceremony on a yacht," Brianna says. "Have you done one of those before?"

Gina and I tried one of those restaurants on a boat before, and I threw up twice before appetizers had been served. Me and moving water are not friends.

"I have not," I say, trying not to grimace at the memory. "If we don't do the ceremony on a yacht, there are so many stunning places around Houston. I'll find you all the perfect spot." I flash my most reassuring smile.

"You and Vincent both seem very passionate about your jobs," Mrs. Rogers says. "No wonder you two get along so well."

"I do love what I do, and I know Vincent does as well."

She nods and smiles, but it doesn't reach her eyes. My nerves ratchet up. Did I do something wrong by agreeing with her?

Mrs. Rogers then looks at Vincent, who is once again chopping what seems to be a never-ending supply of wood. "I don't know how you do it, Amerie."

"Excuse me?"

"How do you deal with the fact Vincent is about to launch off into deep space, with no assurances he'll be back?"

Oh boy.

I bite my lip and carefully consider my next words. "I'm worried, of course, but this is the life Vincent wants."

When I think of our trip to the Space Center, I don't think about how scared I was in the virtual space walk.

Well, mostly not, anyway. I think of how excited Vincent was to walk me through the shuttle and the Mars exhibit. And how alive he looked while talking about his time on the International Space Station.

"I just wish he would find a different job. He could be anything he wants. An accountant, an engineer, a doctor. He was brilliant as a professor. Why an astronaut?"

It's plain to see how distressed Mrs. Rogers is, and I feel for her, but my heart goes out to Vincent. He's got his high-profile career and a good head on his shoulders, but he doesn't have support at home. I don't count, since my position in his life is only temporary. How amazing would it be for him if his mom could show her support of his choices?

"I haven't known Vincent very long," I say, but immediately realize my blunder. "I mean, as long as you. Obviously." I cough into my hand. "But he loves what he does. He's so excited for this opportunity to go into space and help advance science, even knowing the risks."

Mrs. Rogers shakes her head. "He's going to end up just like his brother, and he doesn't care what that will do to us."

"Momma, you're getting yourself too worked up," Brianna says. "Vincent is not going to end up like Tay." But Mrs. Rogers doesn't look convinced.

Is everyone in this family convinced something bad will happen to Vincent on his mission? I want to shake them all and tell them to have faith.

"I can't imagine the pain you've all felt after losing someone you love. And I know as someone without kids, my words may not hold a lot of weight. But I think it's pretty clear Vincent is set on this course. You may not agree with it, but if you don't support him, you might lose him."

Mrs. Rogers stares at me without emotion, then wordlessly gets up and takes the pizza from the oven. She cuts it and places her hands on her hips and heaves a sigh. "Food's ready," she calls loud enough for the men to hear.

"This smells good, Momma," Vincent says. He grabs a plate and turns to me. "Do you want one or two slices?"

"I'll take two, please."

We all sit and eat, but my stomach ties itself up in knots when I realize Mrs. Rogers is avoiding looking at me. I really should have kept my mouth shut. In the moment, all I wanted was for Mrs. Rogers to realize the strain she's placing on her relationship with Vincent, but I may have done more harm than good.

"You see all those trees behind the guesthouse?" Vincent asks. Instead of sitting like everyone else, he's standing behind my chair and leaning down close to my ear. "Most of them are pecan trees. Every October we used to pick up buckets and buckets full of pecans."

I tilt my head back to look at him. "What did y'all do with them all?"

"A lot we gave to neighbors. Some we shelled and toasted ourselves to make pies."

"I'm sorry, but did I just hear you say 'we'?" Camille says, and turns to Brianna. "If I'm not mistaken, wasn't he the one always missing when it was time to take the shells off, but suddenly around when Momma took a pie from the oven?"

Brianna nodded. "I'm pretty sure that's how I remember it."

"Yup. We all know how Vincent can't stand to be around for the hard stuff." Now the teasing is gone from her tone, and Vincent grows quiet behind me. It doesn't sound like they're talking about pecans anymore.

"Camille," Mr. Rogers admonishes.

Camille shrugs one shoulder and continues eating her food.

I lean my head back until it's resting on the chair so I can see Vincent. "So, no shelling pecans, huh? You mean there's something you're not perfect at?"

Brianna snickers.

"Working pecans isn't the only thing," Lance says. "Have you ever seen him out on the basketball court? Man is straight garbage."

"See what you did?" I can't see his face, but by his tone I imagine Vincent is pouting at Camille. "Got me out here revealing my secrets."

"But was it a secret, Vincent?" I ask. "Really?"

Everyone laughs, even Vincent, whose low bass rolls through me. As I pick my head back up, he places a hand on the back of my neck and begins massaging. Camille has thawed too as she laughs around a bite of food. The only one not happy is Mrs. Rogers. She stares at her plate with a furrow between her brows, refusing everyone's attempts to engage with her.

It's very possible that I've caused the woman to hate me. Is this how uncomfortable Gina feels when she visits Mack's family? I know it shouldn't matter what Mrs. Rogers thinks of me since, in the long run, we won't be in each other's lives. But for some reason, it does.

Vincent's hand is still on me, still massaging, and it feels wonderful. Once I've managed to get all my pizza down, he leans close to my ear. "Ready to head in?"

I sigh and nod. I was enjoying hanging outside, but maybe if I make myself scarce, Mrs. Rogers will cheer up. It is her birthday celebration, after all.

Vincent comes around to pick me up from the chair. It's actually not so bad being carried around this time. His hold is secure under my knees and back, and I relax against his chest, knowing he won't let me fall. Once we're inside, he sets me down on the bed and removes my one shoe.

"Are you happy now that you went against doctor's orders?"

I grace him with a toothy grin. "Of course. When said doctor gives unreasonable orders, they have to be disobeyed."

My shoe is off, and Vincent is looking at me with the same intensity as that night in his kitchen. A night that's been seared into my brain and inducted into my core memories. And Lord help me, but I want to reenact that moment, this time giving us both the satisfying ending our bodies crave.

Our gazes hold as he stands and grabs my waist, helping me scoot to the top of the bed while I brace my hands on his arms.

I impulsively reach for his hand before he can back away. "You look tired. You should lie down."

He looks down at our hands for a long moment, and I have no idea what's going on in his head. "I need to take off my shoes," he finally says, slipping his hand free and making his way to the dresser, where he slips free from his boots.

When he comes back to the bed, he sits at the foot, and I almost have to laugh. I'm pretty sure he got the message that I was implying he lie down with me, but here he is doing the most to keep his distance now that we're alone. I guess everything outside really was an act for his family. Either that or he's set on maintaining our boundaries. If I were as smart as him, I'd be thanking him and not lamenting that he's not up here holding me. And that just goes to show how out of my mind I am. I lean my head against the headboard and close my eyes.

"My family likes you," Vincent says. "Don't be surprised if Camille starts calling you up every weekend for coffee to exchange insults about me."

I crack one eye open and look at him. The idea of airing my grievances or insulting him doesn't seem as fun as it would have a few weeks ago. "I don't think you have to worry about that," I say softly. "Anyway, I'm not sure if all of your family likes me. Actually, there's a tiny chance I've made things more difficult with your mom." I hold my thumb and index finger close together.

"What happened?"

"She was talking about you putting your life at risk and all the other things you could be doing, and in not so many words I said her lack of support was driving you away." I sigh. "I'm sorry. I know it wasn't my place to get between you two, but . . ." I don't know how to finish the sentence. Tell him that I want his mom to acknowledge the sacrifice he's making? To realize it takes a special human being to take all the risks he's willing to in hopes of forging a better future? I already feel foolish after trying to get him to lie down with me. I need to hold on to my self-preservation before all my defenses against him are gone.

Vincent rubs the back of his neck. "A lot of the decisions I've made in life haven't been easy for my mom. This one especially. But thank you for trying to make her see things from my point of view. It's crazy that I've only known you for such a short amount of time, but you understand me more than she has in over thirty years."

"I think she really does want what's best for you, but a lot of her concern comes from the fear that you'll end up like your brother."

The words leave my lips, and Vincent looks like I've ripped a sledgehammer through his heart. I brace myself for him to shut me out like he did his mom on the hike. But he surprises me.

"My brother died in a helicopter crash," he says quietly. "A crash that should have been prevented. We always used to fly together, or at the very least, check each other's aircraft before we left. Even though he was my big brother, I looked out for him in a lot of ways because he was often impatient and rushed things." He shifts so he's on his back, staring at the ceiling. "The morning he was flying out, I got there a little later than usual. Right as I was about to do a walk around, I got a call from my fiancée."

While I'm positive I make no outward response, the word *fiancée* jolts through me, and I'm assaulted by a slither of jealousy I have to immediately wrangle in. A large part of me is dismayed that Vincent is only now telling me he was engaged before, though I know the revelation shouldn't surprise me. He's had enough time to finish school and explore multiple careers before ever meeting me. Of course he would have had his future planned out with some woman once upon a time. Yet, as I'm learning about his life growing up here, learning about the brother he lost, learning about the fiancée he must have loved, I want to know even more.

"I don't even remember what the call was about. But I answered it. When we hung up, Tay said everything was good to go, and we made plans to meet up the next day. Then I got a call from my dad that the helicopter went down and Tay was gone." He covers his face with both hands like he can't bear to think about that day. "There's this tightening in my gut that's been there since the second I got the news. And when I'm here, back home, surrounded by all our best memories, it's like I'm being crushed from the inside out over and over again."

Oh, Vincent. My soul aches for him and the grief he's gone through. That tightening is all too familiar; it's there when I think of losing my mom. As scary and anxiety-inducing as it is to me, he's lived with it nonstop. His whole family has.

I can't hold back. I inch toward him and wrap my arms around his middle, laying my head on his shoulder to offer whatever comfort I can. "I'm so sorry." They're the only words I have, and they feel vastly inadequate for the heartache I know he's suffered through.

"I honestly don't know if my checking the helicopter would have made a difference, and I never will. But I can live every day in part to honor him and the spirit for adventure we always shared, even if it breaks my mom's heart."

We don't say anything else. We lie on the bed with only the sputtering of the heater to ensure we're not in total silence. As the seconds tick by, little by little, Vincent's body relaxes, and I realize that sometimes more words aren't necessary. He hugs me back, circling his arms around my back to pull me closer, and I don't hold in the exhale that must give away how much I need this embrace, too. I don't block out the invasive thoughts in the back of my mind saying how right this feels. But when there's a knock at the door and Vincent draws away to answer it, I do mourn the loss of his warmth.

"Can we take a walk?" Mrs. Rogers's voice says. She sounds upset.

Vincent's shoulders rise up in a sigh. "Sure."

After the closeness we just shared, I try not to let it get to me that he leaves without even glancing in my direction. Groaning, I flop back on the bed and stare up at the ceiling. What in the world am I doing? So far, all I've managed to do is get hurt, piss off Vincent's mom, and make him relive what had to have been the worst day of his life. He doesn't deserve any of this. I wish I could take back the last ten minutes.

I close my eyes, unable to shake the feeling that I'm the worst person in the world. Without meaning to, I must doze off, because when I open my eyes again, it's darker outside, and Vincent is pacing in front of the door.

I rise to my elbows. "What's wrong? Does your mom want me to leave?" I wouldn't be surprised if she did, though the thought of leaving now has my stomach in knots.

"No," Vincent says, and I let out a slow breath. He stops pacing and looks at me. "She gave me my grandmother's ring. She wants me to propose to you."

CHAPTER EIGHTEEN

Vincent resumes his pacing, showing all the agitation of a cornered bear. "Look, you don't have to say yes. Mom's out of her mind to even suggest it."

If I wasn't so stunned, I'd be agreeing with him. But my pulse is racing a million miles an hour and my stomach is cramping up. Vincent can't mean put-a-ring-on-it propose or meet-me-at-the-altar-in-your-white-dress propose and surely not spend-my-life-with-you propose, can he? A hundred images of a hundred ways Vincent might drop to one knee zoom through my mind, and I grit my teeth to force them to stop. There's no time for ridiculous daydreams when what I need are answers.

I slowly make my way to him, stopping an arm's length away so he doesn't bulldoze right over me as he treks from wall to wall. "Vincent, please calm down and tell me exactly what happened."

Thankfully, he's not so far gone that he doesn't hear me. He stops in front of me and lets out a deep breath. "From what she's seen, my mom thinks we're perfect for each other. During her birthday dinner tomorrow night, she wants me to propose to you in front of everyone."

Now it's time for me to freak out. Balanced on my good foot, I almost fall over.

Vincent steadies me, holding on to my waist. Our eyes lock together, and I imagine we're both trying to make sense of the new curveball that's just been thrown into our already tenuous game.

"You should sit down," Vincent says after a few heart-stopping moments.

I lean on him for the few steps it takes to reach the bed. "She wants you to propose at her birthday dinner? But she has to know that won't stop you from going on your mission, right?"

"Amerie, I wish I could tell you what's running through her mind. I made it clear my mission is my top priority. She said you helped her realize there's no backing out, and that's why you're such a good match for me."

I take comfort in the fact that Mrs. Rogers doesn't hate me after all. But for her to now insist that Vincent propose is . . . ridiculous. There's no other word I can think of.

Vincent is back to pacing. "This isn't what you signed up for. I won't propose in front of everyone. When we get back to Houston, I'll tell her that we talked about it and broke up after realizing we want different things." He nods to himself. "And don't worry, I'm not kicking you out. You have a home as long as you need it."

Vincent's words don't sit right with me, though at this moment I won't examine how my feelings for him are changing. Right now, it's enough to know in my gut I hate this new idea of his. And there's also his parents' ceremony.

"Us breaking up might complicate things. Your sister asked me to plan your parents' vow renewal, and I said yes." I grimace. I knew I should have told Camille I had to think about it. At the very least, I should have gotten the okay from Vincent first. "Plus, the whole reason I'm here is to get your mom off your back as you prepare for your mission. Do you think that will happen if you tell her it's over between us and she thinks you're nursing a broken heart?"

Vincent doesn't answer. After a few more laps to the wall and back, he finally sits on the bed and pulls a ring box from his pocket. As he opens and closes it a few times, I get a quick glimpse of the gold ring inside.

I'm the one to break the silence. "It's a family heirloom."

"It is."

I touch my necklace. "Your mom commented on my necklace, and I told her how it belonged to my mom. She seemed impressed by how well I've taken care of it."

I don't know if I'm really expecting a reaction, but part of me wonders if Mrs. Rogers's actions are somehow my fault. She fell for my front of having my life all figured out, combined with being responsible, and decided I'm it for Vincent.

For his part, Vincent looks at me with another one of his unreadable expressions before turning away.

"My dad told me how his dad, Grandpa Joseph, worked for the railroads. The day he met my grandma, he knew she was the one and began saving up for an engagement ring. It still took him six months to work up the courage to ask her out. After the third date, he sold his car because he couldn't wait any longer." He opens the box, and this time I get a better look at the single diamond set with gold roses on each side. "On their fourth date, he proposed."

"Fourth? He didn't waste any time."

"No, he didn't. My dad was the same way. He knew my mom was the one from the moment he saw her at Texas Southern University. It took a little while for her to agree to go out with him, but eventually they started dating and were engaged by the end of sophomore year. My grandma passed this ring down to my mom."

"It's really special, Vincent."

He blows out a breath. "This isn't how everything is supposed to happen."

It sounds like he's talking more to himself than to me, but still, his words hit me. That ring represents generations of love, and Vincent deserves to give it to someone he's fallen madly in love with. Not an imposter like me.

I study his profile as he continues to stare at the ring. And there it is, that pull to hug him again. But imagining him in a different scenario where he's happy to be able to pass the ring to someone he loves keeps me rooted in my spot and makes me want to throw up. I'm a damn mess.

"This doesn't have to go any further," I say. "I'm here to make things easier on you, and I realize so far, I've missed the mark. Like you gave me your word that I could live in your house, I gave mine as well. Tell me what you need as far as your mom goes. Whether it's continuing as we are now or packing up and leaving tonight."

Vincent's head jerks to me. "I don't want you to go anywhere."

I'm taken aback by how quickly he shifts gears from helpless to fierce.

"Amerie, it may not feel like much to you, but you just being by my side has made a difference. I don't want you to leave," he reiterates, and I can't do anything but believe him. "My mom just caught me off guard. No one will ever be able to say she's predictable, I'll give her that. If you're willing to stick it out here a few more days, I'll count my lucky stars." He takes my hand in his, running his thumb along my knuckles.

Sirens are blaring in my head that things between us are getting too muddy, but I send him a small smile. "Well, looks like you're still stuck with me. Lucky you."

"Lucky me."

CHAPTER NINETEEN

"Y ou okay?" Vincent asks.

After responding with a heart emoji to the picture my mom sent of Dad standing in front of a waterfall at Yellowstone Park, I put my phone to sleep and glance at Vincent. "I'm good."

We're in his truck, following his family to a Brazilian steak house for his mom's birthday dinner.

I know I've been more distant than usual. We still have two days here before we go home to Houston, but it feels like the whole situation is raveling out of control. Our fake relationship. Vincent's mom urging him to propose. How panic overtook me when I imagined him calling off our bargain. I spent half the day trying to deny the truth until I gave myself a headache—I want to be here with Vincent.

But that's crazy, right? To go from being somewhat physically attracted (okay, maybe more than *somewhat*) to having a full-blown crush on a guy I know will be leaving soon. Insanity.

"Are you sure you're okay?" he says.

"I'm great," I say. "So, your aunt is meeting us there? Does she live close by?"

"She lives in Fort Worth, so it's a good drive, but she and my mom try to see each other often. My sisters and I love her. She's child free, so she always spoiled us when we were kids."

It's not long before we arrive at an upscale black-brick restaurant. It's way more than I expect for a small town, and I'm excited to try the food.

"I'll come around," Vincent says once we park.

"We probably should have invested in some crutches so you don't have to help me get everywhere," I say as he helps me down and I wrap my arm around his elbow.

The ankle's swelling is hardly noticeable now. I was able to put on two shoes with little discomfort, though Vincent complained as we were leaving that if he had his way I would spend another day in bed. My mind absolutely did *not* drift to thoughts of staying in bed with him.

He takes on more of my weight as we step onto the curb. "What, and have me miss out on being close to you like this?"

I fight a smile and roll my eyes. I'm getting used to how he likes to flirt when he's in a playful mood.

The family is seated right away in the back of the restaurant. I sit next to Vincent with Camille and Lance on my left. Brianna and Mr. Rogers are across from us, and the birthday queen is perched at the head of our long table that still has room for one more. Since breakfast, Mrs. Rogers has been glancing between Vincent and me with eyes full of hope and expectation, so I do my best to avoid her direct gaze as we all settle in. I don't want to witness her inevitable disappointment when she realizes Vincent won't be proposing tonight. If I feel pressured by her wish, I can only imagine how much weight is on Vincent's shoulders.

Not that he shows it. After everyone places orders for drinks and appetizers, he relaxes with his arm around the back of my chair. Each time I move, his fingers brush my arm or shoulder.

"I wonder when Aunt Shelly will get here," Brianna says. Her eyes follow a waiter dressed in all black as he walks around with a sizzling rack of lamb on a metal skewer.

"Oh, I'm sure she'll be here by the time we're full and ready to leave," Mr. Rogers says.

Mrs. Rogers places her phone in her purse and spears him with a sharp glance.

"What?" Mr. Rogers says.

"You know what. Can we have one get-together where you don't go at it like bickering animals? I want to enjoy my birthday." Her eyes slide to Vincent and me as she sings, "I have a feeling it's going to be the best one yet."

Oh Lord.

I lean a little farther back in my chair so I'm hidden behind Vincent's body.

"You act like I'm lying," Mr. Rogers continues. "Your sister couldn't be on time to save her life. Can you imagine a doctor constantly running on BP Time? You get there at eight, but they don't show up until nine." He shakes his head. "Couldn't be me."

"Will, stop it!" Mrs. Rogers whacks his shoulder, but that doesn't stop her from laughing as she continues. "Shelly does not run on Black People's Time. She gives her patients the time and attention they deserve, so yes, sometimes she's a bit behind."

"Sometimes," Mr. Rogers says with an unconvinced grunt, and I can't help my quiet chuckle.

Mr. Rogers has been quiet around me these past few days, but now I see he's actually a hoot. He's probably the reason Vincent thinks he's so funny.

As appetizers arrive, a woman's boisterous laugh comes from the front of the restaurant.

"Auntie's here," Camille announces.

I turn around and see the hostess leading a woman who looks almost identical to Mrs. Rogers, save for her beautiful long locs, to our table.

"Is she your mom's twin?" I ask Vincent.

"No, but they're only thirteen months apart."

"Happy birthday, little sister," Shelly says when she's still three tables away.

Damn, if someone announced it was my birthday in a room full of strangers, I'd die of embarrassment. There's a reason why, as much as I love parties, I prefer to plan and remain behind the scenes. But Mrs. Rogers and I are not the same. Mrs. Rogers looks every bit the regal queen accepting her subjects' adulation as her sister comes closer.

Mrs. Rogers stands up and embraces Shelly in a hug full of laughs. Shelly then goes around the table greeting everyone.

Vincent stands when she gets to him. "It's good to see you, Auntie."

"I swear you get more handsome with each passing year," she says, and Vincent beams at the compliment.

He places a hand on my shoulder. "This is my girlfriend, Amerie. She sprained her ankle so she can't get up."

I shake off his hand and stand just well enough. "Actually, I'm doing a lot better. It's nice to meet you."

Shelly's eyes twinkle as Vincent sighs. "I'm so happy to meet you, Amerie. Welcome to the family."

Shelly sits across from me, next to Mrs. Rogers. Her eyes light up when they land on the platter of oysters Mr. Rogers ordered. "Oh, yum!"

Mr. Rogers frowns as Shelly places one oyster on her small plate but doesn't say anything. I guess he's on his best behavior at his wife's request.

Shelly, however, isn't playing by the same rules. She

shoots Mr. Rogers a sly look before saying, "Anyone else want one? Amerie?"

I shake my head no.

"My Mimi isn't a big fan of seafood," Vincent says, quoting from the list I sent him weeks ago.

Though it shouldn't, my stomach dips. He hasn't called me *his* Mimi since our visit to the Space Center, and then he was teasing. Now the name rolls easily off his lips.

"Anyone else?" Shelly says. "Camille? Lance?" When no one takes her up on the offer, she shrugs. "Suit yourselves."

"Now, that is enough," Mr. Rogers finally explodes as Shelly loads two more oysters onto her plate.

"What?"

It's like I'm watching a scene from the iconic show *Martin*.

"Are you enjoying yourself?" Vincent asks me.

I ignore the goose bumps his rumbly voice causes and nod. "I am. I don't have a large extended family. It was always just my parents and me, so our dinners were never this lively."

"Lucky you. Can you imagine the kind of looks people would throw our way whenever we went out to eat in a group like this? Shelly and Mom can get rowdy. It felt like doing the walk of shame leaving the restaurant. Every Sunday." A pained look crosses his face.

"I swear," Mrs. Rogers says exasperatedly when Shelly smacks Mr. Rogers's hand as he tries to reclaim an oyster from her plate. "You two are worse than Vincent and Camille used to be, and you're twice their age."

"Oh, I don't know about that, Momma," Camille says. "Vincent was pretty horrible to me when we were kids. Vince, remember when you and Tay used to act like I was invisible, and you didn't know where my voice was coming from? It was cute when I was seven, but so annoying when I was twelve. At least Lance never joined in with y'all."

Vincent frowns and looks around. "Mimi, did you see where my sister went? I could've sworn I saw her sit by you earlier." He makes a show of looking down the table. "Lance, where is Cami?"

"Amerie, count yourself lucky you're only his girlfriend and can walk away from his foolishness at any time," Camille says.

I turn to Vincent. "You're right. She was here earlier, but now she's gone. I hope she comes back before we're ready to start eating."

"Woooooow." Camille stretches out the word. "You actually found someone willing to go along with your absurd sense of humor. Well done, Vince."

Breaking character, I turn to Camille. "I'm so sorry, but I had to. I'm an only child, so I never got to tease any siblings when I was younger."

Camille shakes her head. "I guess Momma was right about you two being perfect for each other."

I force my smile to remain. This family sure loves throwing around that phrase.

When I look at Vincent, his grin is wide, and my heart does a flip-flop.

Shelly lets out an appreciative sigh. "Young love. We love to see it."

We're finally ready to eat, so we flip over the little round cards from red to green. Instantly, waiters carrying side dishes swarm our table. When they leave, large servings of rice, fried bananas, and potato salad are right in front of me in elegant silver dishes. Another set of waiters comes to offer portions of filet mignon, ribs, and steak, just to name a few.

Vincent digs into his flank steak, taking a hearty mouthful. When he catches me staring, he holds his fork out to me. "Want to try a piece?"

I shake my head no and look at my own overflowing plate. The first thing I pick at is the potato salad. It looks a little different from what my mom makes. The chopped up boiled eggs and dill pickles are missing. Instead, this Brazilian style has small pieces of carrots and flakes of parsley. I take a small taste test, then sit straighter. The flavors are simple, but so smooth and savory I immediately go for another, bigger bite.

After a while, I lean back in my chair, stuffed, while Vincent waves a forkful of Brazilian flan under my nose.

"Just one bite," he encourages. "It'll be the best thing you try all night."

It does smell good. He even swirled the piece around in caramel sauce, so it's extra coated, and he offers it with a decadent dollop of whipped cream.

"Fine." I open my mouth and Vincent slides the fork in. I close my eyes, enjoying how the creamy treat melts in my mouth. It was so light and airy I didn't even have to chew. Once I swallow, I open my eyes, and what a mistake that is. Vincent is laser focused on my mouth. His intensity makes it difficult to breathe, and my nipples tighten.

"What do you think?" he says, not taking his gaze from my lips.

"Not bad." I try to make my voice sound normal and unaffected, but he's not making it easy. "I don't know if I'd say it was the best thing though. That potato salad was pretty b-bomb." I trip over the last word and swallow. This is ridiculous. He acts like he's never seen someone eat. "Why are you looking at me like that?"

"You have some of the cream on you." Vincent reaches out and uses his thumb to wipe the corner of my lip. His eyes flick to mine as he brings his thumb to his own mouth and licks it.

Hot damn. I almost groan aloud. *I* want to be his thumb. To feel his tongue glide over my skin with the same finesse. I can imagine it now.

"Vincent, are you ready for your mission?"

I almost jump out of my seat. My brain is so muddled by lust, I forgot we're at a restaurant surrounded by Vincent's family. Did he just try to seduce me on purpose? I know it's not my imagination how slowly his tongue moved, and that smolder was definitely turned up to the nth degree.

When Vincent turns in his chair to face his aunt, I want to knock away the hand that's once again resting on my shoulder. Having any part of him touch me right now is too much. My body is too wound up because of him. I reach for my water instead, hoping it will cool my heated blood.

"I am ready," Vincent says. "The whole team can't wait to get there and explore."

Shelly takes a sip of her red wine. "I can only imagine. You know, every chance I get, I brag to my patients about my amazing nephew and how he'll probably be one of the first people to colonize Mars."

Mrs. Rogers's fork clatters against her plate. "Don't you *dare* put that idea into his head."

Silence engulfs the table, and Shelly grimaces. "Sorry." She pushes her wine away even though it's mostly full.

Mrs. Rogers ignores her, instead looking at Vincent with accusation. "And I bet you'd just sign right up for that mission, wouldn't you? You'd leave us here, knowing it would be years before we saw you again. If we ever saw you again."

All eyes are on Vincent as we wait for his reaction, mine included. I know NASA has been training astronauts for life on Mars with yearlong simulations in which they're cut off from the rest of the world. Would Vincent volunteer for the same kind of training and subsequent mission if given the opportunity? If so, Mrs. Rogers is right: It would be years before any of us saw Vincent again.

"Momma," he says, "let's not do this here. I'm only going to the moon."

Now I frown. He didn't shoot down the possibility.

"Cheryl, let's open the gifts," Shelly says. "Don't you want to see what I got you? It's totally not another one of those luxurious robe-and-slippers sets that you love." It's obvious she's trying to redirect the conversation, but Mrs. Rogers is having none of it.

"I'll open them at home." She throws her napkin on the table.

As I watch Mrs. Rogers, I'm a mixed bag of emotions. On one hand, I understand her panic at the thought of Vincent someday blasting off to Mars. It's a small possibility, but not something we can totally rule out. Vincent certainly doesn't seem to want to. But on the other hand, it's his job. His passion. Vincent wants to explore. To boldly go where no one has gone before.

Am I really quoting *Star Trek*, now of all times?

"I just don't understand why you have to go to space at all," Mrs. Rogers says. "What happens if space debris or a meteorite damages the shuttle? You'll be up there with no help and no way to get home. Vincent, why won't you reconsider? There are so many things here on Earth to study if you want to make a difference."

Vincent runs his hand over his face. "Momma, would you give it a rest for one night? I'm doing this."

"You're going to leave us, just like Octavius!"

"Then that's a risk I'm willing to take," Vincent explodes, then closes his eyes. "I loved Tay and wish to God every day he was still here with us. And I love you all. But I can't live my life basing all my decisions on the fear of what might happen. Tay wouldn't want that for any of us." He looks at his mom. "I need you to accept that." I can practically hear his silent plea that his mom accept *him*.

I look at Mrs. Rogers. She doesn't say anything, and tears stream down her face while Mr. Rogers takes her hand. Then I make the mistake of looking at Vincent. His face a blank mask, he sits straight in his chair with his eyes on a fixed point on the wall. My heart breaks for him over and over again.

"Here, Cheryl." Shelly puts the present on the table again. "Let me see you open it now. I want to watch your reaction."

Mrs. Rogers ignores her.

"Momma, do you want to try my carrot cake?" Brianna says. "I bet it's better than your cheesecake."

Mrs. Rogers shakes her head.

And so it goes. Everyone around the table tries to lighten the mood and draw Mrs. Rogers out, but she won't be placated.

"Are you holding up okay?" I ask Vincent quietly.

The resigned, sorrowful look he gives me is a knife straight through my heart before he redirects his focus to the wall.

I need to do something to fix this. To build a bridge over the ever-widening gulf between Vincent and his mom. It's why I'm here.

Quietly, so only Vincent can hear, I hiss out a breath.

Now I've got his attention. "What's wrong?"

"It's my ankle. I think my shoes are too tight and cutting off the circulation. Can you loosen them up, please?"

As I predicted, Vincent slides his chair back and gets to his knee so he can reach my shoe.

I gasp and cover my mouth with both hands. "Are you serious?" I shriek.

Vincent's head shoots up and he looks at me with eyes wide in confusion.

The whole table has turned to us as Vincent looks from side to side. "Uh . . ."

"Of course I'll marry you!" I bend down and wrap my arms around Vincent's neck.

When I pull back, not only is Vincent's family clapping, so are the surrounding tables.

"Give her the ring," Mrs. Rogers insists, wiping her tears away, a huge smile spreading across her face.

Vincent blinks until the shock seems to wear off. He pats his pockets, then scratches the back of his neck. "No one's going to believe this, but I forgot it at the cabin. I was so excited to ask her to marry me, it must have slipped my mind. I'll give it to you when we get back, okay?"

"Sure."

Vincent picks himself up and sits back in his seat. All eyes are still on us, and all I can think to do is interlock our fingers and hold our joined hands up. More applause.

"Don't forget the kiss!" Brianna encourages.

Thanks, Brianna.

My pulse races and blood rushes to my ears, but I turn to Vincent. He lifts an eyebrow, which I take to mean, *What have you gotten me into this time?* before pressing his lips to mine in a kiss that lacks any of the same finesse of what we shared at the New Year's Eve party. I'm shaking. The hand Vincent has braced against my back trembles. If anyone looks close enough, I'm sure they'll see we're both a mess and realize something about this situation is off.

Or maybe our act is just that good. The restaurant erupts into more applause as we part, and all I can do is wonder, *What in the world have I just done?*

CHAPTER TWENTY

I'm not going to open my eyes today. Once I do, reality will be right there, staring me in the face.

The reality that I got engaged last night.

I flip over in bed and sigh. Then I frown and pat the other side of the bed and my hand hits cold sheets. Sitting up, I look around the room and toward the bathroom, noting the lights are off.

Where is Vincent?

I look around again, this time seeing a note on his pillow. He went into town and will be back with breakfast. I sink back into the pillows and let out a breath. Good, one less thing to face right away.

Our ride back from the restaurant was filled with silence while we both contemplated the night. At least, the scene replayed over and over in *my* mind, all the while I was wishing I had a time machine to undo what I'd done. Then, when we got back to the cabin, Vincent took a long shower, and I pretended to be asleep when he came out. I wasn't ready to talk to him then, and I'm not ready to talk to him now. And seeing as Vincent is now gone, maybe he's avoiding me as well. I try to ignore the lump of dread the thought gives form to.

What I need is a nice hot shower to help take my mind

off Vincent and engagements and this bizarre situation I've gotten myself into. Then, and only then, will I be ready to face the day. But when I step into the bathroom, I realize how hopeless the endeavor is. There is no tub, only a shower stall where Vincent placed a wooden stool for me to get cleaned up without putting pressure on my ankle. He did it without me having to ask, and I paid him back by making him propose.

My resolve to go ten minutes without thinking about Vincent is gone in less than five seconds, and my shower turns out to be anything *but* relaxing as questions swirl through my mind. Why does he always have to be so considerate of my needs? Where did he go? What if he doesn't come back?

Once I step out of the shower, my phone begins ringing. It's lying beside the sink, and I'm able to reach it before the call goes to voice mail.

"Hey, stranger" is Gina's chipper greeting. "I'm glad you picked up. You haven't sent me hourly updates."

"I got engaged last night," I blurt.

There's half a minute of silence from the other line.

"Come again?" Gina says. "I think the FBI agent that monitors my phone is trolling me. I could've sworn you said you were engaged."

I sigh as I look at myself in the mirror. Steam saturates the room, leaving my image blurred and fuzzy. Just like my mind. "We went to Vincent's mom's birthday dinner last night, and his aunt showed up," I begin, going all the way up to the fake proposal. When I'm done, I suck in a gulp of hot air and shake my head. "Girl, it was a mess."

"Wow," Gina says after a few moments of stunned silence. "You really are serious. You're engaged to Vincent. And before me."

She's using his real name, so I know she's realized the gravity of the situation.

"Fake engaged, if it makes a difference," I say.

"It really doesn't, Mimi. From what you're saying, it sounds to me like things are starting to get real between you two."

It's become too easy to lie. From my parents to my ex and Vincent's family, it seems like it's all I do. But when I open my mouth to tell Gina how wrong she is about my relationship with Vincent, the thick bitterness of this lie coats my tongue before a single syllable can form, and I remain silent.

"Are you sure the only thing you feel for him is friendliness?" she continues. "There's no butterflies when he smiles at you, and you didn't enjoy when he carried you after you hurt your ankle?"

Well, there have been a few tingles here and there. And I did enjoy being in his arms . . . and waking up plastered to him these few past days.

"And was it simply feeling sorry for him that led you to act last night? You've caught feelings, just admit it."

"We're just friends," I persist, but the argument sounds weak even to my own ears. Gina makes a hum of disapproval over the line and I sigh. "Fine. Maybe my feelings toward him have grown a little more than I anticipated."

"Go on."

"I mean, he still gets on my nerves. But he's really sweet too." He didn't have to carry me and feed me and let me have his room. I catch myself smiling in the mirror and immediately drop it. "Regardless of any feelings I may or may not be developing for him, we're not a real couple and we're not really engaged."

"Okay, Mimi. Where is Vincent now?"

"I woke up and he wasn't here. God, Gina, for all I know, he's furious that I just complicated everything and can't stand to be around me."

I'm glad Gina's calling instead of video chatting. Otherwise, she'd read my face and see clear as day how stressed I am at the thought that Vincent might be upset with me. If he is, it would be fully justified.

"I'm sure that's not the case," Gina soothes. "He doesn't seem like the type to run from his problems."

"If the roles were reversed and he'd suddenly proposed in front of *my* parents, I would have called an Uber and sent him on his merry lying way."

"You say that, but I don't think it's true. Sure, maybe when you first met him, but you've come a long way since then. I feel like I'm seeing more and more of the Amerie who isn't afraid to take risks."

"What? You know I hate risks."

"Well, the kind that don't run the chance of bodily harm. Can you honestly sit there and say your *friend* Vincent, Mr. Rocket, had nothing to do with that? Not to mention, I've never seen you go to bat for anyone other than me like you have for him."

I *did* hate seeing him upset by his mom's words.

I hear the door open and shut.

"He's back!" I scream-whisper.

"I'll let you go, then. At least keep me updated and let me know about the wedding before it happens."

I put my phone down and quickly get dressed. Today I'm wearing a dark purple sweater and black leggings. Lacking the mental fortitude to deal with my hair, I leave it alone and let the tight curls, softened by steam, frame my face and fall to my shoulders.

With a shaky breath, I step out of the bathroom.

I immediately spot Vincent, and while I shoot for easy, breezy confidence, my "Oh, hey" greeting comes out breathless.

Vincent's leaning against the dresser, looking at his phone. He places it in his pocket and offers me a small smile. "Hey, yourself."

Okay, he's not yelling or asking what on earth I was thinking last night. I'll take that as a good sign and try to act normal, and not like I'm ten seconds away from rushing back to the bathroom to relieve my churning stomach. "So, what's on the agenda for today? Another family hike?"

"I was thinking we'd go ahead and take that ride around town I promised. Are you up for that?"

My pulse jumps as he pushes off the dresser and starts walking to me. "Sure. Is everyone coming?"

"Just you and me." He stops in front of me, eyes roaming over my face. "I like your hair down."

I don't need a man to validate my hair choices. I don't need a man to validate my hair choices. I don't need a man to validate my hair choices.

My cheeks heat up from his compliment. "Thank you."

We stare at each other for what feels like forever before he speaks. "Why didn't you take the out, Amerie?"

I could have sat there in silence like everyone else until the tension eased and then continued with our original plan. But in the moment, I wanted Vincent to know someone saw him. That I see him.

"I needed to uphold my end of the bargain. It helped with your mom, right?"

He searches my eyes, then smirks as he runs his finger along the chain of my necklace. "Did you know when you're lying or nervous you touch this?"

0

Tiny goose bumps prickle along my chest, and I let go of the diamond. "I'm not lying. And I'm not nervous."

Vincent reaches for the hand I dropped, drawing it close. His eyes don't stray from mine as he slides something cold over my finger.

I look down and gasp at the sight of his grandmother's ring, now nestled snugly on my finger.

Vincent chuckles, and it feels like a caress against my ears. "Unless I'm mistaken, which I rarely am, it's customary to wear rings as a statement that you're taken. Is it not?"

"Yes. I mean, no." I blow out a breath. "I mean, we're not really engaged though."

He shrugs and steps back. The air between us is now too cold, and I instantly miss his warmth.

"Everyone will expect to see you wearing it," Vincent says. "We've got to keep up appearances, right?"

I slowly nod. "Right."

"Good." He crosses the room back to the dresser and picks up a brown paper bag and coffee cup. "Your food, as promised. I got you a croissant sandwich. How about you eat it on the way?"

"Okay, sure." I blink hard, trying to get the gears in my brain to turn faster, but the ring on my finger feels as heavy as a boulder, and Vincent's attention is throwing me off-kilter. "Where are we going?"

"Since it's our last full day here, I think it's time for a good ol' tour around town."

In some ways, Vincent's hometown is like any big city. It has a Starbucks and shopping plaza centered around a Target—new additions, which Vincent said weren't here when he was a kid. But the town has only one major highway flowing through it. If you miss the exit, it will be miles before you can turn around.

I frown as I look out the window and we pass a small, old building with the word MARKET painted in white letters. "Wait. I don't remember seeing all this when we first drove in."

Vincent holds his smile and avoids my gaze. "There's two ways to get here. You can go I-10 for a straight shot or take a few farm-to-market roads. I took the more scenic route. Why are you looking at me like that?"

"You must think everyone is an adrenaline junkie like you. That, or you were trying to kill me before we even got here."

"Nah, I like you too much for that." He winks. "But now that I know you're scared of a few curves in the road, I'll take the other way back. At least until we build up your tolerance."

I shake my head, but otherwise make no comment.

The first place Vincent takes me to is his old high school. He pulls up to the front entrance and slowly drives around the semicircle for parent pickups and drop-offs.

"I don't even recognize this place," he says. "There used to be gates here so we wouldn't leave the campus during lunch. Our tiny marching band used to practice on that side of the parking lot, but back then it was full of potholes."

I follow his finger to the left, where high wire fencing surrounds a section of the parking lot and clear white lines shine against black pavement. I turn to Vincent. "How were you in school? Did you play sports? Were you homecoming king?"

One side of his mouth tilts up. "I was in the math and

chess clubs, but otherwise I was pretty quiet and kept to myself most of high school."

"Quiet?"

He ignores me. "I guess you could say I was pretty nerdy." He narrows his eyes at me as I keep silent. "What, you don't find that hard to believe?"

I suppress a grin. "I mean, it was you who had to tell me all about the physics of coffee and creamer. What was it, velocity? No, that's the speed of something," I say, recalling a morning of him trying to convince me to add creamer to my coffee.

"Viscosity," he says with a frown.

"Right. How could I forget?" I run my hand over his forearm. "Don't look so upset. Didn't you hear? Nerds are in. Women are over the overbearing alpha. We want smart, emotionally available cinnamon rolls. If he knows his way around a science lab, it's on."

He turns so most of his body faces me. "I've got a science lab. A big one at that, where I get to examine all sorts of things."

"Now, I just know you are *not* using your science lab as a euphemism for your . . . ahem." I glance down at his lap.

Vincent clears his throat. "Of course not," he says quickly. "I'm just saying the Space Station is one big science lab." I hold in a laugh as he avoids eye contact, but he continues. "I have to admit, I'm stumped about cinnamon rolls, because I doubt you're referring to the food. And as far as sexy goes, what do you think?"

I slowly let my gaze roam over him, from his low haircut to that chin he still hasn't shaved, which goes to show that a rugged Vincent is just as devastatingly handsome as a tidy Vincent (not that the fact was ever in question), to well-honed biceps that make me want to drool to strong thighs and back up again.

I shrug one shoulder. "You're all right."

"Just all right?" He gestures at his body as if to say *Look at all this chocolate goodness.*

And while I could eat him all the way up, there he goes with his big head, doing the most to get under my skin. "A man's sexiness isn't determined by well-defined muscles or a polite country drawl. Not enough is said about a humble attitude." I look out the window, expecting some witty comeback. Instead, when I look back at him, I see his face is carefully blank as we begin driving away from the school.

I chew at my lip. Now I've hurt his feelings. When will I learn to rein in my snarkiness? And how can Vincent even need to ask about his appeal, when he's in league to compete for the title of Sexiest Man Alive. He may have been a nerd in school, but he's all alluring man now.

"Not that my opinion should matter to you, but do you want to know what I find sexy in a man?" I ask.

He glances at me curiously. "What?"

"I think it's sexy when a man helps a woman out in her quick, ill-conceived plans when he could so easily walk away. When a man puts the safety and comfort of his friend as a priority, even though he's under immeasurable stress. And"— unwittingly, my voice lowers an octave as I remember how good it felt to wake up pressed against him—"I am absolutely vain enough to think hard muscles and a cut jaw are some of the sexiest features a man can have."

By the time I'm done talking, pride practically rolls off him in waves. I'm positive that if he had on a polo, he would have popped the collar by now.

Then he looks at me, eyes scoring me up and down, and thoughts of Vincent wearing a polo, or any article of clothing for that matter, dissipate. I let out a slow exhale when he turns back to the road, willing the flames he ignited low in my stomach to cool. That weighted stare was loaded with hot promises, and I wonder if Vincent's prepared to deliver on them. I'm certainly prepared to collect.

THE NEXT STOP DOWN MEMORY LANE IS THE LOCAL LIBRARY. IT'S BIG-ger than I expected for a small town. It looks like a huge house, with red bricks on the front and white panels on the sides. It's naturally landscaped to blend in with the rural town, with large trees, wooden benches, and a dirt path that leads to a large playground.

"Now, this is just as I remember it," Vincent says. "Ready for story time?"

As it turns out, Vincent is leading story time. I sit in the back with the parents while he's in front of a colorful carpet full of children singing the alphabet song and shaking their wiggles out.

"They're so cute," a woman with pink hair and perfectly laid edges says to me. She holds a sleeping baby in a wrap attached to her front while she strokes its back. "I don't think I've seen you around before. Which one is yours?"

"I'm just in town for a short visit, but I brought that one with me today." I point at Vincent, laughing to myself.

The woman's eyebrows shoot up. "You're Vincent's fian-cée? Congratulations."

I blink at her. "Thank you."

"Small town." She shrugs. "News travels fast. My sister-in-law's cousin was one of the waitresses that helped y'all last night. After that proposal, she called us as soon as her shift was over and told us all about it."

Just when I thought I was over the panic of my hasty

decision, I come to find out the whole town knows. I hate to imagine what kind of fallout Vincent will face once our bargain is over and we've parted ways.

"May I see the ring?"

I lift my hand and the woman *ooh*s and *aah*s. "It's beautiful. You're one lucky lady. My brother graduated with Vincent. Back then they used to make fun of him for being quiet and respectful, which I always thought was dumb. But he never seemed to let it get to him, and by senior year they were all asking for his help to pass calculus. He's a great guy."

I face the front, where Vincent is now reading his book. He opens it toward the crowd, slowly moving it side to side so everyone can see the illustrated picture of a young boy waving to his parents through a tiny shuttle window as he blasts away from his backyard. Everyone is captivated, and I imagine all the kids will leave here today knowing big dreams are possible. By the time he gets to the part where the boy is on the moon, bounding over craters, I'm leaning forward on my elbows, entranced by Vincent's story and his presence. It's amazing. Before turning the page, he catches my eye and winks.

When story time is over, we drive by the old rec center, then stop at the small grocery store labeled MARKET I noticed earlier. Vincent grabs a bottle of red wine and a bouquet of roses, which I assume are for his mom. The checkout clerk congratulates Vincent on his upcoming mission *and* our engagement.

"You know," I say once we're back in the truck. "Those cozy books I read that are set in small towns do not exaggerate about how quickly news travels, huh?"

"Are you kidding me? Half the town probably knew about the engagement before we'd even left the restaurant."

I lean my elbow on the armrest and look up at Vincent. "Gotta love that small town camaraderie. So, are we heading back to the cabin? If your mom's making pizza again, the wine will make a great pairing."

Vincent turns his head toward me, and his eyes widen slightly like he's surprised at how close I am. His hand flexes on the steering wheel. "Not yet. I want to take you to one more place."

Going back in the direction of the cabin, he turns onto a rundown dirt road. The road gets bumpy as we drive over raised roots, and I reach for the grab handle. When Vincent stops the car, we're surrounded by nothing but trees.

Pursing my lips, I look around, then turn to him.

"Before you say anything," Vincent says. "No, I'm not lost. And no, I didn't bring you here to dispose of your body."

What, so he's a mind reader now?

"I used to love exploring and hiking when I was growing up, but this is where I used to come after the crash. When things got to be too much at home, I'd come here to think . . . and mourn. Sometimes yell. It was the only place that wasn't tied to memories of Tay." He reaches in the back seat and grabs the roses. "These are for you. Having you with me this week has made all of this bearable. Before you say you're just holding up your end of the bargain, know that for me, you went above and beyond anything I could have ever expected or hoped for. Ready?"

All I can do is clutch the roses to my chest and nod.

"Good. The ground is uneven, so I'll come around and help you out."

I brace myself for whatever awaits us as Vincent rounds the truck.

CHAPTER TWENTY-ONE

I plant one hand on Vincent's shoulder and use the other to hold the roses to my chest while he helps me slide down from the truck.

"Can you hold the wine too?" he asks.

I take it, and he opens the back passenger door, pulling out a cooler I didn't realize was back there before coming back to my side. As we walk forward, he keeps a firm yet gentle grip on my upper arm.

We're not quite in the deep, deep forest as I feared, and once we're through a small thicket of trees, I gasp at the sight before me.

"Now, I couldn't find any of those fancy tents like the pictures you pinned on such short notice, but I hope this will do," Vincent says.

So many thoughts race through my mind as we walk to the black dome tent. First, apparently Vincent was paying attention when Brianna asked me about luxury picnics. He even managed to find me on Pinterest. Second, he picked the most beautiful location.

We're on the shore of a large lake clearing. Behind us are the trees we've just come from, but directly across the lake is a tall rock cliff. It makes the area feel secluded and closed off, like we're in our own little world. I can see why Vincent would find solace here.

Inside the tent, a white sheet covers the floor. Two large teal pillows sandwich a low rectangular table, and more pillows are strewn about for decoration.

Vincent leads me to one of the teal pillows. "Your throne."

Once I sit down, he goes to the cooler, where he pulls out a white table runner and lays it across the table. Next come plastic plates and cups fine enough to resemble glass. He unwraps a cutting board loaded with sandwich halves, grapes, and cheese, and places it in the center.

"Wine, please."

I pass the bottle into his outstretched hand, and he finds a corkscrew from the cooler and opens it with a *pop*. After pouring a healthy amount in both glasses, he sits across from me and grins. "How'd I do?"

I rearrange the food to make room for my roses to lie in the middle. "Vincent, this is perfect. I really don't know what to say."

I'm the planner, so it's never bothered me to be the one setting up special dates and occasions. But to see this picnic Vincent has arranged is beyond anything I could have imagined. It's very possible my chest might burst from how much gratitude and affection I have for him right now.

"You can tell me you're hungry and that these peanut butter and jelly sandwiches won't go to waste," Vincent says.

"You made my favorite?"

He nods. "They've got butter, too."

I instantly reach for half a sandwich and take a bite. It's sweet and savory all at once, and a hundred childhood memories run through my mind.

After the first bite goes down, I let out a contented moan. "Oh my God, this is perfect." After two more bites, I open my eyes and realize Vincent is watching me. My ears blaze.

Something's shifted between us. The scale that's precariously balanced the weights of ignoring what we feel for each other and acting upon it has tipped in favor of action.

It happened after he slipped the ring on my finger this morning. There was an imperceptible change in the energy flowing between us, and I'm not quite sure what to make of it.

"Aren't you going to eat?" I ask. "I can't finish these all by myself."

Vincent looks less than thrilled as he reaches for one. "Camille was looking at me like I'd lost my mind this morning when I made these." He peels the two pieces of bread apart and inspects each side like he wasn't the one to make them in the first place.

"It seems like y'all had a great childhood, but I have to be real." I wash the peanut butter down with a sip of wine. "You were sorely deprived of the goodness of PB and J with butter. Now, stop playing with your food."

He slaps the pieces back together and takes a large bite, devouring more than half.

"So what do you think?" I ask.

He continues chewing, moving his head from side to side like he's evaluating each flavor element. "It's not half-bad," he finally says. "For the sake of my cholesterol levels, this isn't something I'd eat on the regular. But the butter adds a nice richness I hadn't realized was missing before."

"Dare I say that I've converted you?"

He finishes the piece, then flashes a grin. "I think that's a pretty good assumption."

I whoop and take another bite, glad to have led him to the light.

Vincent uses a pair of tongs that look so tiny in his hands. "Cheese?"

"Thank you." I reach for the slice he holds out and pop it in my mouth. It's a creamy Havarti, and I'm so surprised at how well it goes with peanut butter and jelly. "Be honest. Did you set this whole thing up yourself? Or did your sisters help you?"

"Lance helped me."

"You two must have a good relationship."

"Lance is actually my best friend, other than Tay. I've known him since I was a kid."

"Wow. So you two were buddies growing up and now he's married to your little sister. How did that happen?"

"After we lost Tay, I was away in California and not coming home much. He really stepped in to be there for Camille. I don't know all the particulars and don't want to know, but they got closer. One thing led to another, and now they're married. I couldn't have picked a better man for my sister if I tried." He picks up a grape and tosses it in his mouth. "He's so good, he won't ask me to spend more time with the family."

"What do you mean?"

"He's ready to start a family with Camille. But she thinks it's her responsibility to look after Mom and Dad. Lance would never come right out and say it, but if I was around more, maybe she wouldn't feel so burdened."

Now the small amount of hostility I sensed from Camille toward Vincent makes sense. And here Vincent is, ready to accept all the blame without even knowing if it's true.

"Or," I hedge, "maybe if you were around more, she'd find a different reason not to start a family yet. Have you actually talked to Camille about it, or is it all speculation on your end?" He doesn't respond, and I shrug. "But if you really feel like that's the reason, maybe once you return you can commit to being around your family more. It's obvious how much you all love each other."

"Will you be there to help me get through each visit?"

Our deal is supposed to be over and done with by the time Vincent returns from the moon, so my answer should be an obvious no. However, it's getting harder to envision the end of our agreement.

He stares at me patiently, but I don't answer. I throw a grape at his head instead, which he catches and pops into his mouth with a smile.

WE CONTINUE EATING AND TALKING ABOUT EVERY SUBJECT UNDER THE sun. I tell Vincent about trying to rein in a drunken bridesmaid who gave a twenty-two-minute toast oscillating between being ecstatic the bride had found her soulmate and being terrified her best friend was growing up without her. Vincent gives a replay of a Search and Rescue mission where his team searched two days for a missing hiker, only to find out they weren't missing at all but instead were part of the local search party. We talk about our time in college—I went to countless parties, while Vincent obviously took his studies very seriously—and finally the age-old debate of Marvel versus DC. There's one subject left untouched.

"So, I have to ask . . ." I move a piece of cheese on my plate from one side to the other, avoiding his gaze. "You were engaged before? What happened there?"

"Why? Mad you didn't call dibs first?"

I throw the cheese at him, and this time he doesn't catch it. It hits him square in the forehead.

"Hey!" He still eats it. When he's done, he sits there and stares at me instead of coughing up the information he knows I'm dying to hear.

I glare at him. "Do I need to throw more food at you?"

He laughs. "Fine. Yes, I was engaged." He reaches for one of the stray pillows and leans to the side, propping his elbow on it. His shirt rides up, showing a delicious glimpse of abs so hard they should be illegal. "We got engaged after I finished my engineering degree. But things changed after we lost Tay. Or I guess I changed."

His thoughts seem to turn inward, but he doesn't shut down like before. I hope it's a sign that talking about his brother more is becoming easier for him.

"While doing Search and Rescue I'd be gone for weeks at a time. Unreachable for days. Even when I had the opportunity to at least make a short phone call, I wouldn't."

"Because you were grieving?" I ask.

"Because it was my responsibility to save lives. My team and countless people needed me present with my head on straight. I couldn't afford to be distracted like I was when I should have been checking Tay's bird." He takes a deep breath. "But that meant I didn't think about her needs. When I returned to the apartment we shared after a three-week mission, all her stuff was gone."

Damn. It's got to hurt to have someone you love just up and leave. At the very least, it would be hard to trust that a future partner wouldn't do the same. And Vincent would probably place all the blame on his own shoulders, even when he was going through an incredibly difficult time.

"Since then, it's been increasingly difficult to let anyone in on a personal level. I tend to keep most details private," he says.

"You mean the man who barely gave me any info before showing up to meet his family doesn't like to divulge his secrets?"

He takes the teasing in stride and grimaces. "Yeah, sorry about that. For what it's worth, it's been easy to open up to you. And spending time out here with my family, with you . . . It makes me realize it's okay to let someone in, and I need to find some kind of balance between work and life."

"You deserve to find that balance. Your career and everything you're doing is amazing, but it's only a part of who you are. The whole of you needs to be nourished."

We lapse into comfortable silence, staring at each other. My curiosity about his past is almost satiated.

"Did she wear this engagement ring too?" I hold up my hand and wiggle my fingers.

"No," Vincent says, his voice soft. Dangerously soft. "Mom never offered it up when I was engaged to her, and I never asked about it."

Oh.

Way too many fuzzy thoughts and feelings are swarming through me, so I reach for the last sandwich half to avoid his eyes.

When Vincent checks his watch, I finally realize the sun has gone down. There's no lamp in the tent, so we've been chatting in the increasingly darkening interior for who knows how long.

"Is it time to head back now?" I ask, trying to hide the disappointment this interlude is over.

"If we do, you'll miss the best part." Vincent uses the flashlight on his phone to clear the table and place leftovers back in the cooler. "Now, I need you to stand up and close your eyes."

"Why?"

He massages the bridge of his nose. "I know you don't like surprises, but I promise we're not walking into a cave or a herd of wild boars, so would you just do it?"

I huff, but do as I'm asked, even going so far as covering my eyes with both hands since I'm feeling generous. My ears perk at the swish of Vincent's feet against the nylon floor as he gets closer before his hands land on my shoulders.

"Don't peek," he says in my ear and turns me around. "We're coming to the entrance, so duck your head."

As soon as we leave the tent's thin barrier, a rush of cool wind blows against my sweater. With the sun gone, it's significantly colder.

Vincent keeps walking until we move from grass to stone. "Okay, now open."

I eagerly drop my hands and look around. And around.

Did he want to show me the lake? I like how it looks. Nice, if a little lackluster. The crescent moon's reflection looks like something you might be able to swim to and grab hold of, and the wind makes tiny ripples dance along the surface.

"The lake looks pretty. This is the perfect place to come and meditate," I say.

He chuckles. "It is, but that's not what I brought you out here to see. Look up."

When I do, I see stars. Hundreds, no, thousands of them littering the sky like a blanket of twinkling fireflies.

For the second time that night, I gasp as my heart swells. "Vincent, this is beautiful. I've never seen so many stars in my life."

Each time I blink, another one seems to appear. How can there be so many?

"When I was little, I used to think stars were magical," I

say. "Even though you can only see a handful from the city. But right now, it feels like I'm witnessing a miracle. I have no idea how you ever managed to leave this."

"I've never regretted leaving the country for life in the city, except for moments like this. Nothing compares to the handiwork of the universe."

I think of how awed my mom sounded when she told me about seeing stars from the Grand Canyon. While I was happy for her, I didn't fully grasp the magnitude of how she felt. But at this moment, I feel like I'm sharing something special with her. Along with Vincent.

I reach for his hand as we study the night sky in silence.

"Tell me something," I say, barely above a whisper so I don't break the spell we seem to have fallen under.

"What is it you want to know?"

"Anything, really. Tell me your favorite fact about the universe."

Vincent is silent for a moment before shifting on his feet. "Generally speaking, the distance between most stars is so inconceivably vast that it's unlikely any two will ever collide. However, there are clumps of stars called globular clusters where this is not the case. Like there." He lifts our joined hands, pointing to an area in the sky. "Those are part of the Hercules constellation. They're crowded together much more tightly, so the chance of impact is increased."

"What happens if they crash into each other?" Not that I care. I just want to hear him talk. I'm enjoying the timbre of his deep voice and the easy cadence of his words.

I sway to the side, seeking his heat, pleased when he lets go of my hand to wrap his arms around my waist and continues speaking. "If the stars are going too fast when they collide, it's a big explosion, and in the end, all that's left are star bits. But if they move relatively slowly, they'll merge." His voice drops an octave and goose bumps race down my spine. "They'll create something much bigger and brighter than what they were on their own."

His words are stirring a deep longing in my soul.

More still, he's seducing me. It's a slow and steady seduction that's been building since that night in his kitchen. Maybe even before.

"Did you see that?" he says.

"See what?" Sights and sounds lost their meaning a long time ago.

"Keep watching. The show's just getting started."

I open my mouth to ask what he means, but a light streaks across the sky, gone as quickly as it came. I hold still and wait. Another burning streak appears, then another, until what look like dozens of tiny fireballs begin pelting the atmosphere. How long we stand under the starlit sky watching the meteor shower, I have no idea. It could be several minutes or hours.

Vincent's chin rests on top of my head as he speaks. "If you haven't already, it's perfectly acceptable to make your wish now."

Even at his sweetest he can't resist being a smart-ass. Still, I close my eyes, trying to form the desires of my heart into concrete words. I want my business to flourish, but I also want to always feel how I do in this very moment—content, cherished, happy. Like I'm right where I need to be, with who I'm meant to be with.

When I open my eyes, I turn around in Vincent's arms. "Thank you for bringing me out here."

He reaches a hand to cup my cheek, tracing the arch of my eyebrow with his thumb. Yearning shines through his eyes loud and clear. It's a look I've seen there before, but he's always been quick to eclipse it with a smirk or smart remark. This time, however, he doesn't veil his desire.

In turn, I study his face. I like how the light from the stars illuminates his dark skin. It scares me how with each passing day, I discover something new I like about him. With each passing hour, his gravity pulls me deeper and deeper into his orbit, and I don't know if I'll be able to escape even if I want to.

And right now, I don't want to.

My gaze focuses on his gorgeous lips. We've kissed. Twice now. Once at the New Year's Eve party, then at the birthday dinner. But those times were for show. No one is around now but us.

Glancing back up, I see Vincent's hooded eyes watching me, like he's waiting for me to make the first move.

My heart hammers in my chest as I stand on my tiptoes and slide my arms around the back of his neck, bringing his face down to mine.

Once our lips meet, time stops. Gravity is gone. We're standing in the center of the universe, and everything is spinning around us.

I knew my imagination didn't hype up how good our first kiss was. But this right here—this is everything. The softness of his lips as they move against mine. The taste of him as I sweep my tongue over his bottom lip. He tastes heavenly, like all the stars and galaxies I never knew existed.

We're in a fight to get closer to each other as his fingers tighten around my waist, and I push my body harder into him.

In what feels like too short a time, my recovering ankle gives out. I lose my balance, but Vincent is quick to steady me. He's always quick to steady me. He holds me tightly, with my head pressed against his muscled chest, and we both gasp for air.

"I need to get you back to the cabin," Vincent says, and I shake my head.

I don't want to go. I want to stay in his arms and feel his mouth on mine again. I want it more than I want my next breath.

Vincent unhooks my hands from around his neck and brings them to his mouth, blowing warm air onto my skin. "You're turning into ice out here."

It's only then that I realize how cold it is. A shiver races through me as the wind picks up, and Vincent leads me back to the truck. He helps me in, then turns the engine on and sets the heat to full blast.

"I need to get the tent. I'll be right back," he promises.

I swallow and nod silently. He shuts the door, and already the magical haze is dissipating. Gone is the allure of standing together under the stars, and I have to wonder whether the Vincent who comes back will be the responsible man who knows what a bad idea it is to let things between us go any further.

Vincent's silhouette emerges from the trees. He's moving fast. The tent is loaded on his back, and the cooler, table, and pillows are balanced in his arms. He places everything in the cab, then opens the door and jumps into his seat.

He rubs his palms together and holds them over the vent. "Are you warmer?"

"Yes." I remain facing straight ahead, knowing that disappointment for the turn of events is heavy in my tone.

I sneak a glance at him. He hasn't started driving yet. He's just gripping the steering wheel, and it looks like an internal war is raging within.

Finally, he heaves a deep sigh and drops his hands from the steering wheel. He looks at me with his jaw tight, like something is my fault. "I need to kiss you."

"Oh." Well then. "Okay."

His upper body shoots over the armrest and he sweeps me up in another mind-blowing kiss. All my thoughts and worries disappear into the ether, and I kiss him back with equal force.

I run my hands over his biceps while his travel under my shirt, sneaking up to cover and knead my breasts. The bite from his hands, still cold from being outside, both hurts and feels too good to withdraw from.

An actual squeal escapes me when he leans back into his seat, pulling me with him, up and over the armrest, and I land straddling his lap.

"Sorry," he pants. "I didn't hurt your ankle, did I?"

A bubble of laughter dances up from my chest, and I don't recognize this weightless, carefree feeling. But I relish it. And him. "No, it's perfect."

"Good." He grabs my hips and trails kisses along my neck, and all I can do is close my eyes and enjoy the sensations. I've wanted these hands and lips on me for too long. It all feels a little unreal.

Real or not, instinct takes over, and I start rocking back and forth, grinding our hips together. Vincent kisses his way back to my mouth and sweeps his tongue along my lips. I gladly open, giving him entrance. With our mouths entangled and bodies rocking, within moments I feel the building of a familiar, delicious pressure. And once I finally explode, I collapse onto Vincent's chest.

"What are you doing to me, woman?" Vincent rumbles deep in his chest.

What am I doing to him? Obviously he has it twisted.

I'm the one whose world is spinning off its axis. I fought my feelings for this man as valiantly as an angel fights off demons, and yet here I am. In his truck, sitting on his lap, in a postorgasmic haze.

I lift my head and kiss him. My desire for Vincent hasn't eased in the least, and that scares me like nothing else can.

CHAPTER TWENTY-TWO

It's my favorite time of day, early morning, while most of the world is still asleep, and today I get to enjoy it twisted around Vincent. We fell asleep with him spooning me, but now we're vice versa, as I've once again managed to pin him under my leg. However, unlike the previous mornings, there's no rush to roll away before he wakes up. This time I tighten my hold around him and burrow my face into the crook of his neck.

Last night was unexpected in the best way. From the picnic and stars to the way Vincent stared into my soul and said he needed to kiss me. And kiss me he did. So much my lips are still tingling hours later.

I lick my lips and can't hold back what I'm sure is a goofy-looking smile at the thought of how good his lips felt against mine. We didn't go past kissing, and not because I didn't try. Vincent was the one to hold back, and damn if his self-control isn't sexy and infuriating. Now that we've crossed the line, he has to know it only makes me that much hungrier to be with him.

When I press my face against him again, this time inhaling his scent of wood and spice, he begins to stir. He runs a hand along my calf as he says, "Good morning," and the gravel in his voice goes straight to my core.

"Good morning."

Soon it'll be time to drive back to Houston, where Vincent will immediately take off to catch a flight, but right now we're still in bed. And I want him.

I kiss the back of his neck and I feel a shudder move through him.

"Amerie," he says. Maybe even warns. Is it a warning that I'm turning him on? Because if so, I will not proceed with caution.

I kiss the same spot and run my hand from his bare chest to the top of his pajama pants. Before I can explore any farther, he turns over and moves so I'm on my back, pinned to the bed, with him looming over me. This is much, much better, and so hot. His bulge presses into me, and I tilt my hips up, seeking more pressure. Vincent crushes his lips to mine, and we're back to kissing and grinding.

Before we can get too carried away, however, the alarm on Vincent's phone blares throughout the room.

He moves to pull away, but I keep my grip tight on his shoulders.

"Mimi, we have to get ready to head out," he says against my lips. When I shake my head no, he half laughs, half groans, but his mouth is still on mine, and that's all that matters.

I bite his lower lip, then soothe the nip with my tongue, worried that I might have been too rough, but Vincent's hips bear down on mine even more, letting me know I need not be concerned.

The alarm goes off again and he sighs. "I have a flight to catch in six hours."

Flights are stupid. Who needs to fly when you can make out all day?

Vincent, that's who. Time to let him get back to his job, and I need to get back to my business.

Sighing, I release my hold, and he kisses me one more time before getting up.

Within an hour we're outside with Vincent's family while he plays a real-life form of Tetris as he loads our suitcases into the back seat. Well, suitcases plus the three coolers of food Mrs. Rogers gave us. While Vincent took me around town yesterday, she spent the day cooking food for her children. She did not exaggerate when she said food is her love language.

As we exchange final goodbyes, Mrs. Rogers envelops me in a tight hug. "I'm so glad you were able to join us. You are a beautiful woman, and my son has found his perfect match."

"I've already got our group chat started so we can keep in contact about the vow renewal," Camille says as she steps up next. "And I'll be sure to spread the word about you to my friends who are planning events."

I stand up taller. "Thank you so much."

She embraces me in a hug. "Thank *you* for getting Vincent out here to spend some time with us. These few days have meant the world to my mom. To all of us."

As I hug everyone, guilt, along with the wish I hadn't come here under false pretenses, gnaws at me. It's amazing that in such a short amount of time, I've come to care about each family member, and even more so that they've so eagerly opened their home and hearts to me. Vincent and I buckle in, and as we pull away from the cabin, part of me hopes I'll be back someday.

───────────

WHEN WE ARRIVE BACK IN HOUSTON, I PACE IN THE BEDROOM AS VINcent shaves in the master bath. He'll travel to Death Valley, where his team will train with new tools they'll be using during the mission.

During part of our long drive, he told me how the first astronauts to walk on the moon trained there. I sat there and listened, when what I really wanted to do was talk about our kiss—and more—and what it means for our bargain. We crossed a line there's no coming back from.

Vincent walks out of the restroom, and I mourn the loss of his growing beard. I clock each of his movements as he moves to the open suitcase on the bed and places a small brown grooming bag inside.

He zips the suitcase up and turns to me. "I'll be gone until at least next Friday."

He comes to where I am in the doorway and stops close enough to place his hand on my waist. It looks like he wants to say something more, so I raise my eyebrows, silently encouraging him. I'm all for him taking the lead in the conversation to see where his head is at.

Instead, he gives a self-deprecating shake of his head and drops a kiss on my cheek. "I'll see you when I get back."

Once Vincent leaves, I'm too wound up. There's so much left unsaid between us, I just know I'll be obsessing about everything while he's gone.

In the meantime, I start unpacking my suitcase and receive a voice note from Gina.

> **It's been two days and you have not responded to my texts. If you don't contact me today, I'm going to assume Astro Boy has you locked up and call the cops. Love you. Call me back!**

Gina has to be the most dramatic person I know, but I love her anyway. I send her a text letting her know I'm back in town and available to meet for brunch.

When I arrive at our favorite spot, Gina is all manic smiles, and I know she can't wait to get the tea.

"God, finally you're here," she says as I sit down. "Tell me all about it."

"I haven't even ordered yet."

"Girl, here." She slides her wineglass over to me. "Give me the full details. Quick, quick, quick." She punctuates each word with a snap.

I take a sip of the drink and let the fruity flavor dance on my tongue. It's a sparkling wine, nice and refreshing. "Is this the house Moscato? I don't think I've had it before."

When Gina growls, I laugh and finally delve into the picnic and meteor shower. Gina hangs on to my every word.

It's been so long since we've sat around with glasses of wine and chatted. Aside from morning coffee, we used to make it a point to meet at least once a month for a brunch where we'd set goals for one thing we hoped to accomplish in the following weeks. Just two queens lifting each other up. I've missed that.

"Aww, Mimi," Gina says, placing a hand over her heart. "That is so romantic. So, is he your boyfriend now? Like, *for real*?"

I twist my lips to the side. "We haven't discussed it. Everything happened so quickly, and now he's gone for over a week in training. I guess we're just playing it by ear." And I hate how wishy-washy that sounds.

"Do you want him to be your boyfriend?"

Leave it to Gina to come up with the hard questions.

"I don't know. I like him, but he'll be gone in less than two months, and it's not like we'll be able to visit each other. And this is only one mission. What if he decides to go to Mars next?" I sigh. "I want someone I can count on to be here. With me."

"I think we're still years from going to Mars. It's not like you'll be long distance forever. If you think about it, him being gone for six months is nothing in the long run. I'm serious. You've grown close to him, and your relationship has reached a point some never get to after years of dating."

It does feel like I've known Vincent for years rather than months. I certainly feel more of a connection to him than I did to Derrick, and in that relationship the goal had been to end up at the altar. "Yeah, but it's not all real. Or, at least, what we have was built on lies and deception. Do you really think there's hope for us?"

Gina smiles at me. "I really do think there's hope for you two. Remember, you've been lying to other people, not each other. And I don't think I've ever seen you this tied up over a man."

I look down and start playing with the ring on my finger, twisting it so the rose scrapes against my pinky. I don't know why I have it on. However Vincent and I define our relationship, one thing is certain—we're not really engaged. But when I was getting ready for brunch and had the opportunity to place the ring safely in my jewelry box, I opted to continue wearing it.

A flashback of the way Vincent looked at me as he slipped it on my finger makes my chest warm.

"Wait, is that the ring?" Gina reaches over the table, and I slide my hand forward so she can get a better look. She's practically going cross-eyed trying to inspect it. "This is beautiful. And I can't believe how well it fits you. I'm telling you, Mimi, it's fate."

People sure love throwing out words like *fate* and *meant to be* when it comes to Vincent and me.

A waiter comes by, and I'm able to place an order for my own drink. And just because he's been the topic of conversation, and *not* because I can't stop thinking about him, I pull out my phone to see if Vincent has sent me a text. He hasn't, and I am decidedly *not* disappointed.

"Well, you're all caught up on my tea," I say, placing my phone back in my purse. "Now tell me what's going on in your world." When I look back, I'm alarmed to see Gina trying to hold back tears. "What's wrong?"

She takes a deep breath and closes her eyes. "Over the weekend I pressed Mack about really moving forward in our relationship. We've talked about marriage periodically, and I thought we were both on the same page, you know? Well, he finally told me that he wants to propose."

"That's great news!" Or, at least, it should be. "So why are you crying?"

"His mom is refusing to give him her blessing. And his grandmother's ring."

Oh no.

My stomach drops, and I feel like the worst friend. Here I am showing off an heirloom that doesn't rightfully belong to me, while Gina's been sitting here in turmoil.

"I'm so sorry," I say.

"Don't be. It's not your fault that woman hates me."

That woman really is a piece of work.

"So what should I do? Break up with him? Try and get his mom to see how amazing I am? It's been over four years. I don't think I'll get through to her now. And at this point, I don't care if she never likes me."

When I slide the drink back to her side of the table, she

picks it up and guzzles half the glass. Then she sits back in her seat, arms crossed in a huff. I know she's hurting, but she looks so adorable. I don't see how Mack's mom has managed to set herself against her.

"What should I do?" Gina asks again. "And I want you to be honest. I know we have our rule about not speaking against each other's boyfriends, but I feel like my relationship with Mack is at a crossroads, and I don't know which path to take."

She's never given me cause to doubt that Mack is the one for her. In all the years they've dated, it's his mom that has been a thorn in their side. But, then again, he's allowed his mom to be that thorn, and Gina has been pricked too many times.

I sigh. "I think you should drop the rope with his mom. She's not worth the heartache. Then ask yourself why Mack is afraid to go against his mom, but he isn't scared of losing you. I've said it before, and I'll say it again: You are the prize. You are my baddie BFF, and as much as I like Mack, he needs to show he knows he's already got his trophy."

Gina's nostrils flare as she dabs at her eyes. "Everything about this situation is just messing with my head."

"Whatever you need, I'm here. If you need a place to crash, I don't think Vincent would have a problem with you coming by. If you need someone to roll up on Mack while he's at work to tell him he's a fool in front of all of his colleagues, I got you."

Gina's eyes go big. "Mimi! You are out of pocket, and I love you for it. But you don't need to cause a scene on my behalf. Yet." She pushes back her shoulders and sits up straight. "But you're right. I *am* the freakin' prize, and when Mack gets around his mom, he acts like he's lost his mind. I guess it's up to me to decide how much more of this I want to tolerate."

"You know I'm in your corner and will back up whatever you decide to do." She nods, and I pick up my drink and raise it in the air. "Now, I'm tired of talking about these boys. It's been too long since we've set some queen goals. I'll go first. This week I'm going to get a new client."

Gina's glass is nearly empty, but she raises it anyway. "This week, I'm going to let go of the things I can't control. And drink more water."

We clink our glasses together and drink on it.

CHAPTER TWENTY-THREE

I turn my car's AC to full blast and angle my face toward the vents, trying to find some kind of relief from the warm air. If one more thing goes wrong today, I think I'll lose it.

It started when I checked my post office box this morning and discovered that the business cards I ordered had my name misspelled. All five hundred. Worse still, *I* was the one to make the mistake when placing the order. How the hell does someone spell their own name wrong? Instead of *Amerie*, each card reads *Ameris*. Money down the drain.

After the post office, I called a prospective client looking to plan a family reunion. In the time between her filling out the contact form on my website last night and me calling her back this morning, she found someone else to book with. That someone else? Jacob and Johnson.

To top off this glorious day, Gina was supposed to come shopping with me to get supplies to make centerpieces for the baby shower this week but has been MIA for the past four days. I know she's alive only because she responded to my text and said she needed time alone. I know it's not time away from me she needs, but I can't help but feel tossed aside.

My phone starts ringing, and I wonder if it's her, but my heart does a sudden leap, hoping it may also be Vincent. It's taken some adjusting, getting used to not seeing him while he's in training. Not seeing or talking to him on the phone or through text. I want to hear his voice and complain about my day. But when I see my mom's picture on the screen, my shoulders deflate. I mentally chide myself, instantly feeling bad. It's been too long since I've spoken to her or my dad. We've still been communicating through texts, with them sending me updates and pictures, but now it's time to give them my full attention.

I swipe the green button to answer. "Hi, Mom."

"There's my Mimi. How is everything?"

At the sound of her voice, I close my eyes as sudden emotion washes over me. I didn't realize how much I missed hearing her soothing voice. It feels almost like an embrace lifting me up on this trying day.

"Everything is going great," I say.

"Are you sure? You don't sound so happy."

"It's just the humidity getting to me. I'm out running errands while it's been threatening to rain all day. You know how it is; feels like I'm breathing in nothing but water."

"I certainly do. Poor thing, you must be miserable down there."

"Yeah." I'm glad she buys my excuse. "You're heading for Minneapolis now, right? You get to enjoy a real season of spring and shop at the biggest mall in America? Maybe I need to come hang with you and Daddy for a while." With the day I'm having, the thought is more than appealing.

My mom chuckles. "Well, you know I've been missing my Mimi, but there's no need for you to come up here if you want to see us. After your dad finishes his business, we'll start heading down south for a quick visit home."

I almost hit my head on the steering wheel as I jerk forward. "Y'all are coming home?"

"It'll still be about a week from now, but the Watsons recently moved out, so we'll check on the house, and I need to meet with Dr. Allison. Now, before you ask," she gets out before I can say anything, "everything is fine. This is a routine checkup. And Daddy and I would love to catch up with you over lunch or dinner. Unless you'll be too busy like you've been too busy to answer your phone lately."

Her guilt trip works perfectly, and I grimace. "Of course I won't be too busy. I'd love to see you and Daddy. Just keep me posted on when you'll be here."

We hang up a few minutes later, and my heart races the whole ride home. My parents are coming back to town way earlier than I expected. I thought I'd have at least a few more months to get my life settled before they came back. What if they want to come by my apartment, which I no longer have? Or meet up with Derrick, who's no longer in my life?

My life isn't hanging in suspense now. I have a home to sleep in, and despite this week's setback, I believe I'm on my way to a successful business. Sure, I don't have the longest roster of clientele, but that will come with time. There's always the option to come clean about everything. I don't have to mention the hospital bill I paid off, but I could tell them about Vincent.

I blow out a breath. And what, exactly, will I tell my parents about Vincent? It's not like we're *together* together, like Gina asked me. Yes, we had our scorching make-out sessions, but after nearly a week of silence from him, it's obvious we were both caught up in the moment and driven by our mutual attraction to each other. Which is fine. It's for the best in the long run. Because if there's one thing I don't need, it's to be tied up over a man when I have my business to focus on.

So no, I will not be telling my parents about him.

Ten minutes later, I pull up to the house and see Vincent's truck is parked on the side of the street.

If he'd come home two days ago, I probably would have been delighted to see him back. But now, after the news from my parents, the realization that Vincent had all week to reach out to me and didn't, and the overall suckiness of today, I park and slam my car door. Inside, Vincent's black suitcase is dumped on the floor of the entryway right beside his shoes. I use my foot to push it out of the middle of the walkway and make my way to the bedroom to get changed. There, he's thrown his navy suit jacket on the bed instead of hanging it up. I ball up my fist, knowing I'm at my tipping point.

The sounds of footsteps and the rustling of fabric reach my ears, and I turn around as Vincent appears from the hallway.

Still clad in navy slacks and a black button-down, he leans against the doorframe, filling the space with his broad shoulders. Thick biceps stretch the smooth material of his shirt as he folds his arms over his chest before looking me up and down with enough heat blazing in his eyes that my toes would curl if I let them. I don't.

"I thought I heard you get in," he says with a lazy grin.

I cross my arms, but unlike him, I know my stance comes off as aggressive. "You know, there's no use in keeping nice things if you're not going to take care of them."

Vincent slowly straightens and looks at me blankly. "Uh..."

"I don't think it would have killed you to hang up your jacket or put the suitcase in the closet. And you do realize there's plenty of room in the driveway for both cars, so you don't have to block traffic with your monster truck, right?"

I tip my chin up as he huffs out a breath and stalks toward the bed. But instead of grabbing the jacket, Vincent reaches for my shoulders. Awareness jolts through me, licking up my arms like an electrical pulse as his hands slide down to squeeze my own, and while I frown, I don't pull away.

I fight to keep my voice steady, strong, and unaffected. I will not be undone by a simple touch. "What are you doing?"

Vincent raises my right hand and lays a soft kiss against my knuckles. He mirrors the action on my left hand, letting his lips linger over the ring I have yet to put away for safekeeping, and I feel the icicles around my heart melting. Then, pushing my curls from my face, he cups the back of my neck and murmurs over my mouth, "If you missed me, just say that."

My gasp of indignation turns into a sigh of pleasure as Vincent's warm lips cover mine, and I don't hesitate in pushing closer to him.

As much as I hate to acknowledge it, he's the missing piece I needed all week. The reason the sun's shine has been that much duller has a name and a face, and a horrible habit of slipping under my every defense. Vincent's arms ground me. He's warm and solid in every literal and figurative sense, and I can't think of a time when being in another man's embrace made me feel this good. He makes me feel needy. Greedy. Like I want to get close to him until the world stops.

Vincent breaks the kiss but keeps his forehead pinned to mine. "Better?"

I shake my head no. As much as I needed that moment

of connection, he will not pacify me with a measly kiss. Like he didn't just go off-grid for a whole week while I was left to wonder if he was thinking about me or regretting everything we did. "You didn't call or text."

"I know. I'm sorry, Mimi." He kisses the tip of my nose. "But I thought of you. Constantly."

With a scoff, I brace my hands on his chest and push him away from me. The bed is right behind him, so he lands sitting on the edge, then looks at me with his eyes wide. Good, I've surprised him. Hopefully even scared him a bit. I can take the same advice I gave Gina.

"That's all you have to say? 'Mimi, I missed you'?" My voice is a perfect imitation of his vapid apology as I watch him through narrowed eyes. "I don't understand what's going on here. When we spend time together, you're all in, but then you just go off and disappear. You have to focus on your mission. I get it, and I respect it. But I'm not an after-thought." The more I talk, the more I kick myself for letting down my guard, knowing full well where his priorities lie. He even told me with his own words how his relationship with his ex failed. Did I really expect him to change after a few kisses?

"You're right." He heaves a deep breath and reaches for my hips. "And I really am sorry."

The only reason I don't jerk from his hold is because I can clearly see remorse etched into his features. That, and those damn topaz eyes that pierce right through me.

"You're not an afterthought," he says. "You're the *only* thought. For weeks, you've lived rent-free not only in my house, but in my head. I'm having to work off muscle memory to finish tasks and read data three times before I can understand it, because I'm wondering what you're do-ing and if you'll be home when I get back. I'm obsessed."

"You . . . what?" I know he's been attracted to me, but obsessed? I have a hard time believing that.

"Even though I'm not on my A game, I've been afraid that if I give in to distractions, if I allow myself to pick up the phone just once to hear your voice, something will go horribly wrong."

I can see how much the confession costs him, and I feel myself softening toward him even more. "Vincent," I say on a sigh, wrapping my hands around the back of his neck to stroke his nape. "I was never trying to be a distraction. I just need to know that I'm not alone in this. But if it's too much, maybe I should leave?" I say quietly, and hold my breath. I don't want to play guessing games or emotionally manipulate him, but if he can't be where I am emotionally, I need to know. Even if it hurts.

His hold on my hips tightens. "No, Mimi. I want to figure out a way to balance both work and home. Because I don't just want these three months with you. I want forev—"

Before he can finish, before he can lay me bare with a declaration that will make me want to pledge my heart and soul in kind, I bend down and kiss him.

I'm panting when I pull away. "I swear, Vincent, you are driving me crazy. One minute you make me want to throw you to the ends of the universe, and the next I'm melting for you. I don't know what I'm supposed to do about that."

"Give me a chance, and you'll never have to doubt how I feel about you again." His eyes are soft as he grabs my right hand from behind his neck and places it over his chest. "You feel my heart? Sometimes, when you stand in front of me, it beats so hard that I swear you must be able to hear it."

I close my eyes and concentrate on the accelerated thumping under my hand. Moved beyond words, I place his hand on my own chest so he can feel how our heart-beats race in sync. Vincent smiles before pulling my head back to his.

All traces of my earlier hesitation and annoyance have melted away, and I fully give in to the kiss. My body sinks into his as he pulls me in so tight I can't breathe in without him exhaling.

My nipples tighten, my body aching for his touch, which, even now, proves better than any visit from my rocket and thoughts of him. "I spent too many sleepless nights imagining touching you like this," he says.

"That explains why you always look so tired." I giggle when he nips my collarbone and soothes it with a kiss.

He kisses his way from my neck to my ear and back again. "You taste so sweet, I don't want to stop."

"Then don't. Because I don't want you to."

He lifts his head, questions in his eyes as he scans my face.

"Make love to me, Vincent."

He swallows thickly. "Yes."

I step back and lift my shirt up and over my head. When I reach for the top of my pants, Vincent stops me with his hands on mine. "May I?" he says.

I nod, and like he did at the cabin, he takes care to gently slide my pants down. His large hands glide up my thighs, coming to rest on my ass where he kneads my flesh with his palm. "I've been wanting to take these off forever. They're like my nemesis. Did you know that?"

I blink back the lust-infused haze that seems to have settled over me like a cloud of stardust. "You don't like my pants?" He wouldn't be the first, but is this the time to bring it up?

"Make no mistake, I love the way they look. But I can't

help but feel jealous that a flimsy piece of cloth gets to hug all these curves instead of me."

"I paid top dollar for these. There's nothing flimsy about any of my leggings," I say breathlessly.

Kissing right below my belly button, Vincent slides my underwear down. "I wanted to be the one to get close to your skin. Tasting you."

My mouth opens on a voiceless moan as he parts my lower lips with his fingers and kisses my core. I grip his shoulders to keep from falling, not that I need to. Vincent's got me. He's always got me. His hands hold my hips steady, and I brace my foot on the bed to give him better access. He takes advantage, diving in as his tongue explores. Just absolutely destroying me.

When he stops and stands up, I almost cry from the sudden coldness the absence of his mouth leaves.

"Don't get all mad," he says. "We still have a while to go."

He reaches behind me to unclasp my bra, leaving me bare before him. "You are an absolute masterpiece."

His finger traces around one of my nipples, then the other, leaving a line of goose bumps. He keeps going, moving over my collarbone where my necklace lies, then to my chin and over my lips.

"Beautiful," he breathes, outlining the slope of my nose.

At this, I smile. "I like how you see me." But if we keep going like this, we'll never get to the good part. I capture his hand. "Now take off your clothes."

It takes him too long to work through all the buttons on his shirt, but he shrugs the shirt off his broad shoulders.

I run my hands down his flat stomach and tug on his belt. "Off."

He obliges, pulling his pants and boxer briefs off in one motion.

Hot damn. His body possesses the kind of perfection you have to let soak in while your brain catalogs each stroke of beauty. He bends down to scoop me up by the thighs, and I wrap my legs tight around his hips as we fall onto the bed.

"Do you have a condom?" I say in between kisses.

Vincent reaches for the nightstand, going for the top drawer. Moving to his knees, he opens the square packet and rolls the condom on. I open my legs wide as he covers me with his body, but he doesn't try to enter me. Infuriatingly, maddeningly, he lets his hand rove over my body, outlining the curve of my hips. Why can't he ever do the logical, predictable thing?

"Vincent." I try to communicate my urgency, but he hushes me with a kiss.

I'm a burning ball of pent-up energy, and as much as I hate to admit it, Vincent's waiting is turning me on even more.

He reaches back to the nightstand, tight biceps extending by my head, and this time he has my vibrator in his hand. I stifle a gasp while Vincent smirks.

He turns it on, and buzzing fills the silence. As he reaches between our bodies, I'm unable to look away from his hooded gaze. Once he presses the vibrator to my core, pleasure like I've never known causes my hips to lift and my toes to curl.

I cling to Vincent's arm as bursts of ecstasy shoot through me. His breath is ragged, chest expanding with each inhale, but he manages to keep his body still. It's obvious he's a man on a mission to please me. As much as I appreciate it, I can't be the only one falling apart.

I reach for his length and stroke up and down, even as the pressure at my center threatens to push me over the edge. It figures, the only man who drives me up the wall would also be the only one to see me coming absolutely undone. But I don't feel self-conscious in front of him because, in the words of the wise Janet Jackson, "that's the way love goes."

Wait, love? I can't feel that way about Vincent. It's too soon. We're still getting to know each other outside the pretense of a fake relationship. But as my release gets nearer and I look at his magnificent face, I can't deny the whispers of my heart.

I know Vincent is done with this waiting game when I pull him to me and he doesn't resist. He settles his hips over mine and slowly pushes in. I take hold of the vibrator, raising it so I can feel every lick of sensation as he moves in me. We both let out sighs of relief when he's seated fully.

I once again meet his gaze and see so many emotions, which I'm positive must mirror my own. He drives in and out, and I can't get over how good it feels. How well we fit together.

He crushes his lips to mine and I moan. We're both getting close. His fingertips are digging into my thigh, and I feel him swelling inside me as his thrusts pick up in speed and intensity.

It's driving him crazy being inside of me, and if my mouth weren't full of his tongue I'd be screaming *Yes!* Yes, this was worth the wait. Yes, this is worth whatever heartbreak may follow.

I put the vibrator back against me. The pulses combined with Vincent not only push me over the edge but send me soaring as a billion galaxies explode behind my eyes. Vincent is right behind me.

When he lies still above me and we're both breathing at a normal pace, I feel the rhythm of Vincent's heartbeat keeping time with mine. He starts to get up, but after waiting for this moment for so long, I don't want him going anywhere.

"I'm crushing you," he says when I tighten my legs to keep him in place.

"No, you're not. This is perfect."

He settles back down, kissing the side of my face, and I let my eyes drift closed.

I didn't let Vincent finish his words earlier, but his meaning was clear—he wants forever with me. This kind, brave, amazing man wants to forget our deal and keep me around. Emotion clogs my throat and I hold him tighter.

Can I do this? Give my heart to Vincent, who, as wonderful as he is, loves to live his life on the edge? Home for only a few months, then gone among the stars. It's not the future I envisioned, but my heart doesn't seem to care.

I angle my head to capture his lips with mine, sighing in satisfaction when he reciprocates and deepens the kiss. Moaning when he grabs a new condom and begins moving in me again.

I'm not sure what the future holds, but for once, I don't care. For Vincent, I'm willing to risk it all.

CHAPTER TWENTY-FOUR

Mmmm." The enticing smell of bacon pulls at me as I step inside from my morning walk.

Vincent was still sleeping when I left, looking thoroughly worked over with his legs twisted in the sheets, but now he's standing over the stove with a pair of tongs. I lean against the kitchen island and watch him cook, trying not to cringe while he butchers Luther Vandross. At least he looks good standing there shirtless. The muscles in his back move as he meticulously flips over four strips, managing not to get popped by grease. He's got a smattering of moles on his right shoulder blade I'm just now noticing, and my fingers itch to play connect-the-dots. Or maybe I could use my tongue and trace them like a constellation. There are so many parts of his body I haven't gotten the chance to explore. Yet.

Vincent catches me staring when he turns around and flashes a grin that does nothing to help bring my heart rate back to resting. "Breakfast?"

My stomach growls in answer as I nod. Between last night and my walk, I've worked up quite the appetite.

He goes back to the bacon, and I wash my hands before grabbing a mixing bowl from a lower cabinet to start on the eggs. After cracking, seasoning, and whisking together five, I glance at Vincent, and he makes no attempt to hide the fact he was checking out my ass. It's dangerous to be within touching distance when he looks at me like that. It makes me want to forget all about sustenance and hop back in bed.

"Stop it," I say.

"Stop what?"

"Looking at me like you're picturing me naked."

He takes his time sweeping me from head to toe, then smirks. "I am picturing you naked. And you were the one ogling my goodies first."

I roll my eyes and join Vincent at the stove, where he's just set a skillet to medium heat. He hands me a red rubber spatula before taking his pan to the counter. It's all seamless and methodical, like we've done this a hundred times.

Between folding and stirring the eggs, I watch as Vincent transfers the bacon to a plate lined with paper towels, then wipes down the pan.

"What's that smile for?" he asks.

"On the rare weekend my dad was off, he and Mom would make breakfast together." I take the eggs to the kitchen island, dividing our portions between the plates Vincent has laid out. "I guess cooking with you makes me think of good times. The only thing missing is the stereo blasting some old-school R and B."

"I got you." Vincent picks up the plates and begins belting out some Tyrese.

I hold up my hand. "Yeah, no. Immediately, no."

Vincent places a hand to his chest in mock offense. "You wound me, Mimi."

"Look, we've already established you can't be perfect at everything, and obviously singing isn't in your wheelhouse."

I walk to the coffee maker. After I set one cup under the nozzle to be filled, Vincent eases behind me and encircles my waist. His body is flush against my back.

"Surely I make up for the bad singing in other ways," he says huskily.

I swallow as his hand slips under my shirt and he caresses my stomach. "I'll admit you have a few things going for you. I've heard you're a pretty good teacher." He cups my breasts, and my nipples immediately come to attention from the heat of his hands seeping through the thin material of my sports bra. "You're pretty good with your hands. You healed my ankle well enough."

He pinches my nipples. "Go on."

My body is throbbing. How in the world can I want him again so soon? "Well, you do have a pretty big . . . science lab."

He chuckles. "Indeed, I do."

"Vincent." I half gasp, half groan when he takes my earlobe in his mouth. "I just came from outside. I'm sweaty and need to shower."

He doesn't heed my warning, so I'm not going to waste my breath protesting when what he's doing feels too good. His hand dips into my pants and under my panties, his thumb pressing down on me. I moan and throw my head back against his chest while his fingers work me over. If I could stand here and have him touch me like this for hours, I would. But within mere minutes, the pressure of an orgasm builds and explodes, and I'm falling apart in his arms.

Vincent doesn't let go, holding me close while I come down from the high. "Coffee's ready," he says after a while.

I straighten my shirt and turn around. Using Vincent's shoulders as leverage, I reach up and kiss him, then smirk.

"You mean *your* coffee's ready. I'm making a fresh cup for myself."

He grumbles but takes his coffee to the table while I prepare more. When we both finally sit in front of now cool plates, I find myself uncharacteristically shy. It's the morning after, followed by a welcome morning encore. What is there to be self-conscious about? I tip my chin up and meet his gaze.

"Good eggs," he remarks, looking way too proud for my liking.

I narrow my eyes, then shake my head. I'll let him have this moment. If a smug Vincent is the price for tasty bacon and an earth-shattering orgasm, I'll gladly pay it.

MY MOOD IS SO HIGH I MUST BE TAKING UP ALL THE SPACE ON CLOUD nine as I watch the baby shower wrap up.

My first event. I did it.

The mom-to-be glows in her baby-blue gown as her friends and family hug her on their way out.

"Make sure you take one of the centerpieces," Ms. Katrina shouts across the room at a guest daring to leave empty-handed. Another reason I love Ms. Katrina—she knows how to clear a table. She's of the mind that centerpieces should be taken home for the guests to remember how much fun they had. In this case, the guests get to take home vintage tan teddy bears wearing white suspenders, which were placed in a wicker basket with mini blue, gold, and white balloons. It took hours to get the bears positioned correctly to look like they're in hot-air balloons, but seeing everyone's reactions when they saw them made it more than worth it.

While Ms. Katrina gets her daughter and all the presents loaded up, I send Vincent a quick message, letting him know the event went off without a hitch. I see he replied to the picture I sent of the initial setup with a simple brown thumbs-up. Where normally I would read into this as an act of vague interest, I know it's not Vincent's intent. He probably sent the message when he was on a quick break. It's enough to know that I'm on his mind, as evidenced by the times he's FaceTimed me whenever he takes a break while still clad in his training uniform, or the random Almond Snickers bars I find in my car when I head out for the day.

Ms. Katrina waves at me to let me know she's leaving, and all that's left is taking care of the balloon arches and stacking the chairs. I grab a pair of scissors from my bag and head to a window.

Some people like to stab the balloons and rush through takedown, but not me. For one, I hate the sound of a balloon popping. Even when I know it's coming, it scares me every time. Instead, I snip it at the neck. It easily deflates, just how I imagine Jacob's ego will deflate when, a year from now, he's crying himself to sleep for letting me go.

"Why are you smiling all demented-like?"

I jump and spin at the sound of Gina's voice.

"I could see your reflection in the glass," she says. "Let me guess, you were imagining Jacob's head on the balloon?"

"No." I tilt my head up and sniff. "But you're close. Fancy seeing you here."

When she didn't show up to help me shop or get the centerpieces ready, I didn't expect her to come for the teardown. Now here she stands, though quite subdued with her hands behind her back. I want to both hug her and cuss her out for her disappearing act, so I stay silent.

Gina sighs. "I'm sorry I've been out of touch. This mess

with Mack and his mom really got to me, you know? I went to stay with my sister in Corpus and kept my phone off so I wouldn't be tempted to easily forgive him and wash everything under the bridge."

Wow. Gina didn't even tell me where she was going.

"And are you feeling better now?" I say as pleasantly as I can manage through the hurt.

"Come on, don't look at me like that."

"Like what?"

"Like I hurt your feelings. I just needed to get away."

"It's fine, and my feelings aren't hurt. You needed space, so I'm not going to sit up here and jump down your throat for going AWOL." I turn back to the window and stab a gold balloon. I jump at the sound. Barely. Then I take the scissors to a blue one in the same manner. This actually isn't so bad. After ramming my scissors through another gold balloon with enough momentum to strike the one behind it like an arrow shot from a bow, I spin back around to face her. "I just find it funny that you went to see your sister, whom you barely tolerate since all y'all do is fight like cats and dogs, instead of reaching out to me."

"Mimi—"

"I get you have a lot on your mind with Mack, but you've always been there for me when I've gone through relationship troubles or health issues with my mom. I just wish you would let me do the same for you."

And just like that, I'm halfway done with the garland.

We're silent for a while before Gina finally says, "You're right, you know. I should have gone to you instead of my sister. By the second night with her, she was already driving me mad. She wanted me to deep clean her carpets as repayment for staying on an air mattress that leaked so bad I had to pump it at least three times each night."

I huff out a puff of air and turn around. "I won't say you deserved it by knowingly putting yourself at her mercy, but . . ."

"Yeah, yeah." Gina rolls her eyes. "I deserved it."

We both laugh, and in the span of two minutes, everything is fine between us and my world feels right. I can lose a lot—my job, Derrick, my apartment—but not Gina.

"Are you still the queen to my bee?" she asks.

"Always. Now, did you come back home to get away from your sister? Or did you come to a decision on what to do about Mack?"

Gina solemnly looks to the window before regarding me. Then a wide grin splits her face. "I'm going to marry him!"

She was holding her hands behind her back, but now she holds her left hand out, and a beautiful princess-cut ring glimmers on her finger.

I cover my mouth with both hands. "Gina, congratulations!" I reach for her hand to get a closer look at the flashy diamond. "This looks too shiny to be an heirloom. What happened with Mack's mom?"

Gina's smile doesn't falter as she tells me the story. "He showed up to my sister's on the third night and asked if we could walk and talk. He apologized for not doing enough to step between his mom and me over the years and said even though he hasn't shown it, I'm the number one priority in his life. He's even willing to go no-contact if his mom can't respect our relationship." She begins tearing up. "Then, while Mack Jr. played in the water, he got on one knee and asked me to marry him."

"I am so happy for you."

"Me too. But he's not off the hook. If he backslides even a little, I'm out. If his actions back up his words and we make good headway in couples counseling, we're eyeing a wedding in early November. And Mimi, I would love it if you not only helped me plan it but were also my maid of honor."

I press a hand to my chest. "I would love to." My best friend glows, and I couldn't be happier for her if I tried.

Gina is already prepared to plan the wedding of her dreams as we continue catching up while she helps me with the rest of the balloons.

The heavy door to the hall opens, and I turn around, expecting to see the building manager or another worker.

"Mimi, is that . . ." Gina trails off beside me.

"Hey, you," Vincent says as he reaches us. With a bouquet of flowers in one hand, he grips my waist with the other and bends down to kiss me.

Who would have thought I'd be the type to enjoy PDA?

"Hey. What are you doing here?" I ask him. I thought his not responding meant he was tied up and I wouldn't be hearing from him until late in the evening.

"I thought you might need help loading up the throne."

I open my mouth to respond, but Gina clears her throat impatiently to remind us of her presence.

Vincent smiles at her. "Let me guess, you must be Amerie's friend Gina? I'm—"

Gina recovers quickly from her shock. "Don't be silly. I already know. You're her Mr. Sex— Er, you're Vincent," she finishes, for once responding to my death glare. "It's nice to finally meet you."

Vincent smirks at me. Gina's words clearly did not go unnoticed. "Yes, I am her Mr. Sexy Vincent."

"I was going to say 'Mr. Sexy Astronaut.'" Gina shrugs, then grins. "But Vincent works too."

"Oh no," I say, shaking my head at them. "See, this? We are not doing this." First I look to Vincent. "You may enjoy letting your family clown on you and all, but not me." I point a finger at Gina. "And you know way better than to try and act up in public." Gina pouts, but I raise my eyebrow in warning. I'd rather not, but she knows I can just as well bring up some embarrassing stories Mack has yet to hear the next time I see him. "Now, I need to have this place cleared in the next fifteen minutes. You said you came for the throne? It's right over there." I point him to where the gold throne I set up so the mom could sit and open her presents remains on the other side of the hall.

Vincent hands me the flowers with one more smirk before going off to put those muscles of his that he likes to talk up so much to good use.

Gina and I both watch him pick up the chair like it's nothing and walk away before she turns to me and squeals. "I did not know you two were gettin' down like that now!"

"See what happens when you shut your bestie out?"

"Argh, I know! But I'm back, and now you know I've got to have all the deets. ASAP, Mimi. I'm serious."

"I'll give them to you," I promise. I'm just as eager to talk to her about Vincent. More than that, I want to tell the world about him. At the very least, maybe I can tell my mom and dad about him, as anxious as the thought makes me.

"How about we finish catching up this weekend?" Gina asks. "I want to go wedding dress shopping, and I'll need my maid of honor there."

"You've got it."

CHAPTER TWENTY-FIVE

My petty side may have been showing a little bit when I chose the drabbest gray I could find for the guest room walls, but now that I see it in action, I'm pleased with the outcome.

After a finishing touch, I put the paint roller down and take a look at my work.

I hear Vincent's footsteps on the stairs, and seconds later he comes strolling in.

"What do you think?" I say, gesturing at the walls.

He nods. "I like it."

I walk to the middle of the room and stop under the fan. Closing my eyes, I point to the left side of the room. "We need some art here. Two eleven-by-fourteen prints would work. White frames, I think. A green plant here." I point to a corner. "An accent chair here. Black or navy will give the room some dimension. Oh, and curtains. Vincent, you really need curtains."

"Anything else?"

I tip my chin and point to the fan. "Change this out for a chandelier."

"I'm sorry, exchange a fan for a chandelier? In South Texas?" His *Woman, have you lost your mind?* look is back.

"I don't know." I lift one shoulder. "I've always had this thing for chandeliers. When I moved into my apartment, one of the first things I put up was a painting of one behind my bed. I still have it in storage, so maybe I'll just get it out."

Vincent grabs my hand and squeezes. "Or maybe we can keep a portable fan in the closet that can be brought out whenever guests are hot."

I grin up at him. "Really?"

"I aim to indulge and please."

"Well, in that case . . ." I slide my hands up his shoulders. "This house could really, really do with a chandelier above the bathtub."

He throws his head back and laughs. Once it dies down, his eyes are still twinkling and his dimples are on full display, and I can't get over how much I love his smiles. Each one. His mischievous smile. The happy one. His satisfied smile. The one he gives his momma. They're all uniquely beautiful and him.

"I'm not sure how safe having a chandelier hanging above water is, but we'll circle back to that," he says. "I'm about to set up the telescope. Want to have a look with me?"

I perk up immediately. Even though it was just the one night when I saw the wonders of the galaxy, I miss looking up at the night sky and being able to see more than a handful of stars. "I'd love to. Give me a minute to put the paint up and I'll meet you out there."

When I step outside a few minutes later, Vincent has finished setting up the telescope and is standing over it.

"What are you checking out?" I ask.

"The moon. We've got perfect conditions. Ready to take a look?"

I walk forward. The telescope is taller than I am, so I

have to stand on my toes to peer through it. I frown. "All I see is black. What am I doing wrong?"

"That's the viewfinder. Back up and look through the eyepiece."

Heat rushes to my face, but one look at Vincent's patient smile and my embarrassment disappears. There's no mocking in his gaze, and I wonder why I ever thought he was so patronizing.

I find the correct part and lean forward. "Will you tell me about it?"

"The moon is the easiest target for us to observe, being so close. Not to mention impressive."

"It's bright," I remark, blinking as I come away from the telescope.

"Like the planets in our solar system, it reflects the sun's light. On a night like this, the moon makes it too bright to observe the other planets. But that's okay. There are so many things to see on its surface."

I put my eye back against the piece and take in the different shades of gray where there are mountains and craters. "It is pretty cool. Would I be able to see you through this telescope if you were there right now?"

"No." He chuckles. "For that, we'd need a much, much larger telescope. One that wouldn't fit in this yard."

"Bummer."

I back up again and look toward the sky. The moon appears so close and yet so far. It's amazing how a huge chunk of rock can stay locked around Earth, but there's nothing there. No trees, no oceans, no civilization.

"And you're really not afraid to travel there?" I ask. What if his mom is right and his going is a big mistake?

"I'm really not," he says confidently, and I can't bring myself to look at him.

Instead, I rub a spot on my chest where I feel heartburn rising up. Or more like a physical manifestation of heartache. I've been happy existing in this little bubble, with my days focused on building up my business and nights spent in Vincent's arms. I don't want it to pop and drop me into a reality where he's leaving soon.

While we haven't talked about it since the first night we made love, his words of wanting forever with me have become a favorite song I play over and over in my mind. I've built myself up and then talked myself down from calling my parents and telling them about Vincent, wanting so much to take that leap and hope for a future with him. But I don't know if my heart can handle having to say goodbye, even if it's temporary.

"You want to know what I love about the moon?"

No. I want him to decide he no longer wants to travel there and will instead stay home indefinitely and become a tax accountant.

"Sure."

"It gives me perspective. The moon was here when Earth was still forming. She is billions of years old and still there. She can be testy sometimes, and why not? She's been hit with blow after blow. But she still rises. Still stands strong. She's truly beautiful, in all her phases."

His gaze is on me, I feel warm from my head to my toes, and like a miracle, all the fear and doubts are pushed to the back of my mind. While watching Gina try on wedding dresses, I couldn't help but imagine myself in one, marrying Vincent. It's so wild. Before, all I wanted to do was throttle him whenever we crossed paths. Now I see—recognize— that it wasn't annoyance that set me on edge around him. At least, not all annoyance. It always caught me off guard the way my body went into hypervigilance mode when I saw him. No man has ever caused that reaction, and I didn't know what to do with myself but push him away. Erecting a border around my heart made the most sense, but as I've gotten to know him more, it's dissolved as easily as the walls of a sandcastle under the force of the tide.

I don't just want these three months with you. I want forever, he said.

And now *I* want forever.

"I want to introduce you to my parents," I say.

"You do?"

I nod. Before forever can begin, Vincent needs to meet the most important people in my life, and I want to share with them one of the best things to happen to me in a long time.

"I do. That is, if you want to meet them."

Vincent cradles my cheek in his hand before bending down to kiss my lips. He nuzzles the crook of my neck and inhales like he's breathing me in. "I'd love to meet your parents."

I exhale a relieved breath, and my happiness swells so much I can taste it as I run my hand over his shoulder. "Good. They'll be in town next week."

"Good." We kiss again until he pulls back and looks up to the moon. "Did you want to see the Copernicus crater?"

I almost laugh, but for the sake of his ego, I manage to hold myself in check. As much as I've been enjoying his teachings, I have my limits. I bunch up his shirt until his abs are bare. "I'm tired of these lessons. It's time for recess, don't you think?"

His nostrils flare as my hands travel lower. "Now that you mention it, I'm pretty sure I heard the dismissal bell."

He picks me up by the waist and strides inside, straight for the bedroom.

I'VE COME UP WITH A SIMPLE PLAN. MY PARENTS WILL BE IN TOWN FOR a week to check on their house and go to Mom's doctor's appointments. I'm meeting with them for lunch first to come clean about everything: That Derrick and I have broken up. That I was fired from Jacob and Johnson after giving them some of the best creative years of my life. They'll be concerned, but I imagine they'll also be proud that I'm making a way for myself in the business. And when I tell them about Vincent, whew boy!

Mom and Dad will get an absolute kick out of the fact their daughter, who always had a hate-hate relationship with science in school, is in love with an astronaut.

There I go again. *Love*.

A giddy smile fights to break loose. It's like each time I think of him, my brain forges little connections between the words *Vincent* and *love*, growing stronger and faster each day, where previously the word *love* has been associated only with Mom, Dad, and Gina.

No doubt, Mom will be dying to meet Vincent, and Dad will have all the questions about Vincent's favorite football team, so we're already prepared to have them come to the house for dinner.

While I sit at a table within viewing distance of the door, waiting for them to arrive, a waitress comes up. "Can I get you anything to drink?"

"I'll just have water for now. I'm waiting for two more people to join me."

She walks away, and my heart pounds with anticipation and trepidation. I haven't been this nervous to tell them something since that time in high school I hit Sheldon Miller's truck while leaving for lunch. At least this confession won't have me scrubbing every surface in the house for two months, down to the window blinds. But what will my parents' reaction be once they realize I've been lying for so long?

I turn my attention to the door, where a family of four walks in. A man, woman, and two bouncing kids holding electronic tablets. The man looks back, then rushes outside to hold the door open as a tall, lean man pushes a woman seated in a wheelchair through.

Once the door is closed and the sun no longer throws everyone into shadow, I stop breathing. That's *my* dad pushing *my* mom in a wheelchair.

Dad spots me right away and makes his way to the table. Running on autopilot, in a near out-of-body trance, I stand up and greet them. I lean in as Dad embraces me, then bend down to hug my mom.

"It's so good to see you, Mimi," Mom says as Dad moves one of the chairs to an empty table to make room for her. "Your hair looks beautiful. You'll have to show me which products you used to get it to curl like that."

I swallow as I look her over. The media would have you believe that every woman blessed with melanin ages like fine wine. However, no one will ever mistake my mom for anything but her age. She's always had the strongest spirit I've seen, but there's something almost frail about the way her collarbones stand out. Her skin, the same almond brown as mine, remains a tad dull no matter how much water she drinks. She does, however, have beautiful hair. When stretched, her tight coils reach the middle of her back, though they have more gray than black these days.

The only time she doesn't tend to her hair is when she's

in a crisis and it's too painful to move. I've always been impatient with my own head, but while I was growing up, it was during those times when I had to help her that I learned how to do hair. Mom would let me give her two-strand twists or gently untangle the mass so it wouldn't loc while she was unable to care for it.

Is today's low-maintenance style—a high ponytail wrapped in a scarf—for pure aesthetics, or did she not have the energy to do anything else?

As soon as everyone is situated at the table, the waitress comes back to take drink orders, and I use the time to re-center myself. I've seen Mom in a wheelchair before. When she gets discharged from the hospital, for instance. Dad always pushes her down the long corridors since he and the nurses don't allow her to walk to the car, which Mom hates.

Once the waitress leaves, I strive to maintain an even tone. "Is this a new development?"

Mom fusses with her hands, looking resigned. "Not exactly. I spoke with my doctor before your dad and I began our RV trip, and she insisted I use the wheelchair to get around."

I suck in a breath. "Wait. You mean to tell me you've had it since you and Daddy left? Why didn't y'all tell me?" And what else have they been keeping from me about her health?

Each time we spoke on the phone, my mom insisted she was fine. Now I realize any pictures I received were usually selfies of my dad or the two of them sitting in a restaurant. No joint activities or pictures of my mom standing up. I've been so caught up hiding my own life that I missed the signs I should have picked up on.

Dad unwraps Mom's utensils and places the cloth napkin

in her lap. Suddenly I'm back at the hospital. Gone are the inviting aromas of cornbread and fried okra filling the air, replaced with cold antiseptic. I'm back on that small, lumpy couch with a low back while Dad fixes a blanket over Mom as she lies curled in pain.

"We were traveling all around the country," Mom says, bringing me back to the present. "What would telling you about the wheelchair have done but make you worry? It's not like we were going to cancel the trip. And, if I'm honest, it's not that bad. I haven't had a crisis since we've been gone, and I'm able to get around without using too much energy."

And there is the crux of it—that she *needs* the wheelchair to conserve energy. It's a sign of how her health is degrading, and I don't know how to deal with it. I didn't when I was a kid, and as an adult, nothing has changed. I'm paralyzed with the familiar fear that I'm going to lose my mom.

She reaches out and takes my hand. "Truly, Mimi, I feel good. Touring the states and seeing the beauty of this country has been such a blessing. I'm feeling like a brand-new woman."

I can't deny that the joy brimming from her face is as real as the warmth of her hand, but I'm not all right with this and I can't find it in me to muster a smile. I feel my mind spiraling, throwing everything in my world off-balance, and I need to get out of here before my parents and everyone in this restaurant can see how not okay I am. I don't care that it proves them right, that I can't handle it. All I know is I have to go.

I squeeze her fingers back and grimace. "You know what? I forgot I have a meeting with a client today. We're going over the final details of the celebration, and I still have a few things to tie up on my end."

As far as excuses go, it's weak and more transparent than an open window. Still, after exchanging glances with each other, my parents nod in understanding.

I stand up. "Call me before y'all head back out on the road, and I'll try to come by the house."

I bend down to hug my mom, holding the air tightly in my lungs so I don't cry. My dad stands up and wraps his arms around me. For just a second, I let myself find comfort in his warmth like I'm once again his little girl and he's assuring me everything will be fine. Like then, I want to have the same faith he does, but I can't. After inhaling the familiar scent of his aftershave, I pull away.

"I'll talk to you later," I say, and walk out the door.

CHAPTER TWENTY-SIX

I didn't exactly lie to my parents this time. I do have an appointment with Mrs. Rogers and Camille to go over the details of the vow renewal ceremony; however, it's not for another two hours. Rather than drive around aimlessly, I pull into the first home-goods store I come across.

How could Mom keep this from me? Her and Dad. They know how much I worry about her and would want to know about any changes.

I know it's a long shot, but I send Vincent a text message, asking him to call me when he gets the chance. I just need something to help drown out the noise in my head.

An associate walks by to ask if I need help with anything. I realize that I've been staring at the same nightstand for who knows how long and walk away with a muttered "No thanks."

My phone buzzes in my purse, and I pull it out, only to see my mom's picture. That same one where she looks so cute holding a ball of yarn. I took that picture when she first took up crocheting two years ago, long before the hospitalization and before we all started keeping secrets from one another.

I let the call roll over into voice mail, then power off my phone. I can't face her now, while the revelation of her diminishing health is still so fresh, though I know everything will have to come out in the open at some point.

When the same sales associate asks if I have questions about the small candleholder that's been in my hand as I've stood here, I realize that once again I look suspicious and should just buy the damn thing and get out of here. It's time to head to Camille's house anyway.

Camille welcomes me with a bright smile as soon as she opens the front door. "It's so good to see you. Welcome to my casa." She ushers me in. "Let's go to the sitting room. Mom told me she's running a little behind, so it's just us for now. Dad likes to joke about Auntie Shelly always being late, but it actually runs in the family. You didn't hear that from me though."

I force out a laugh. As much as I like Camille, being around anyone is the last thing I want at this moment. I suspect if I told her I wasn't in the planning spirit and asked for a rain check, she would eagerly oblige. But, for the sake of my business, I have to see this through. Clients first.

"I'm going to get some refreshments," Camille says. "Make yourself comfortable and I'll be right back."

When she leaves the room, I use the time to get my thoughts in order, falling into the familiar routine of pulling out my organizer filled with hard copies of plans and mock-ups. I turn to the section for the Rogerses' ceremony, then close my eyes and take a deep breath.

I look around the house. The ceilings are so tall it feels like I'm at Carnegie Hall. The walls are a white that gleams from the natural sunlight filtering in through large open windows. There's a curved staircase with a black railing, and I wouldn't be surprised to see Lance strolling down the steps in a red robe while smoking a cigar.

This is the exact kind of house I dreamed about purchasing someday. Though as I'm sitting on her spotless cream couch, that dream feels like it was part of a different lifetime. I can't see myself settling anywhere but Vincent's three-bedroom fixer-upper in a charming neighborhood.

I wish I were there now, wrapped in Vincent's arms.

Camille returns with a plate of croissants and a cold pitcher of water infused with berries. "Since seeing the pictures you've been texting, Mom has been so excited. She keeps bringing all these bridal magazines to work and shoving them in my face between patients. You'd think we were planning for a five-hundred-person affair and not an intimate party on a boat. Speaking of . . ." She wiggles her eyebrows at me.

Ah yes, the yacht. I've just about gotten over the fact that I'm planning a vow renewal ceremony. While it may be similar to a wedding, Mrs. Rogers is nothing close to a bridezilla, and I'm confident the day will go off without a hitch. But why, oh why, they want to hold the celebration on a boat, instead of on dry land or, better yet, here at Camille's house where there's plenty of space, is beyond me. They are the clients, however, so their wish is my command.

"I found our yacht," I announce, forcing a smile.

Camille's eyes light up. "You are a miracle worker! I knew you'd come through for us."

The doorbell chimes through the house, and she stands up. "That's Mom. She's going to flip when she hears the news."

My smile drops when she's out of sight. I hate that my mind isn't all in. Excitement that I'm fulfilling my clients' wishes and thankfulness that my business is moving forward should have me floating on air, but my mom's face keeps popping up in my mind, and all I feel is sorrow. Maybe I should make an excuse to cut this meeting short.

When the door opens, the last thing I expect is to hear Camille say, "Hey, Vince. I didn't expect to see you here."

All the same, I whip around, and the sight of him walking into view is like a balm to my bruised soul. Without hesitation I get up and walk to him, throwing my arms around his neck.

I did well enough keeping my emotions in check, but now everything is threatening to burst out. Vincent must pick up on the quake that ripples through me as I fight back tears and he rubs my back.

"Are you okay?" he says.

"I'll give you two a minute," Camille says before her steps grow faint.

I focus on the steady pounding of his heart against my cheek. Once my emotions are firmly under control, I pull back and clear my throat. "What are you doing here?"

"I've been trying to call you, but it went straight to voice mail. I knew you were meeting with my sister though." He studies me for a moment before running a hand over his face. "There's an issue with the orbiter that's threatening to scrub the whole mission. I have to go to Florida."

I frown. "When do you have to leave?"

"I'm heading to the airport now."

My heart seizes and I take a step back as his words hit me like a physical blow. "You have to leave *now*?"

"Yes. I'm sorry, I won't make it for dinner with your parents. I hope I can make it back in time before they leave."

I forgot all about us having dinner this evening. I didn't even get a chance to tell them about Vincent before bolting out of the restaurant at lunch.

Vincent runs a warm hand up and down my arm. "But something else is bothering you. What's wrong?"

"I met up with my parents earlier, and my mom was ..." I shake my head. I don't want to get into the specifics now. And I don't want Vincent to leave.

"Is your mom in the hospital?"

"No. Thankfully, no. It seems, however, that she's been keeping the severity of her condition from me." Apparently, keeping secrets is a new theme for us all.

"I'm sorry." He doesn't hesitate to close the small distance I tried putting between us and places a kiss on my forehead with a sigh. "I wish I could stay here with you, really, but I have to go."

I close my eyes to fight against the hurt. "You don't have to apologize."

Of course Vincent has to go. As close as we've become these past few weeks—the laughter we've shared, the time we've made for each other; all so, so good—it's all been temporary.

I was fooling myself into thinking we could have forever, when we can't even have tonight. He's leaving, and though it's only for a few days while they manage a crisis, soon he'll be gone for six months. And after that? Who knows. The life of an astronaut is not stationary, even for one grounded on Earth. There are always long hours of training and traveling. So much unpredictability. I've wanted Vincent to be the one person I can rely on to pick me up when I'm feeling low. To hold me if for no other reason than I want to feel his arms around me. To tell me my mom will be okay, just to help keep hope alive. With the career Vincent's chosen, I may as well be counting on the stars not to shine.

I suck in a gulp of air as I back out of his hold. "Don't worry about me, Vincent. Do what you need to do."

I seriously allowed myself to become dependent on

him, all to keep the truth from my parents. Maybe if I had been more forthcoming with them, they would have returned that trust.

"Of course I'm worried about you," Vincent says. "I know how upset you must be about your mom, and I want to be here for you."

"But you have to go. I get it." I wrap my arms around my middle. "We both have our own priorities to focus on."

He stares at me like he's just lost a piece of a puzzle that had been right in his hand. "What is that supposed to mean?"

"It means I need to go be with my parents. It's time for us to quit playing house. We came into this agreement so that you could focus on your job, and I could focus on mine. Well, mission accomplished, don't you think?" Hurt and confusion play across his face, so I avert my gaze to the wall. "We can stop pretending things between us are real." I suck in a deep breath to get out the next words. "Let's stop pretending that we're really engaged."

"What?"

At the sound of Mrs. Rogers's voice, my stomach drops.

There's no telling when she arrived, but she steps from behind Vincent with a bridal magazine clutched in her hand. She glances between us, waiting for an explanation.

Unable to hold her gaze, I look helplessly to Vincent. He's barely reacted to his mom's unexpected appearance, but he finally takes his eyes off me and shakes his head. "Momma, please. Not right now."

"What's going on?" Mrs. Rogers demands. "What did she mean by stop pretending you're really engaged?"

"Not right now, Momma. I'm trying to talk to Amerie."

Mrs. Rogers's laugh borders on hysteria. "Oh, you mean your *fake* fiancée?"

All I hear is blood rushing through my ears. I might throw up right here on the marble floor, as horrible as I feel. God, please don't let me mess up this beautiful floor after being caught in my lie.

Vincent turns to his mom and picks up the hand she isn't using to strangle the magazine. "I know you have questions, and I have not only some explaining but also a lot of apologizing to do. But please, let me talk to Amerie."

Allowing herself to be momentarily placated by Vincent's earnestness, Mrs. Rogers purses her lips before walking away without so much as a glance at me.

Vincent sucks in a deep breath and turns to me, jaw tense like he's steeling himself for a fight. I want to smooth the tension from his face, but I know touching him would undo all the resolve I have.

"I want to make something abundantly clear," he says, voice firm and unyielding. "We are *not* playing house. What I feel for you isn't fake. You know that."

Of course I know Vincent has feelings for me, but that doesn't change how we both want, *need*, different things. He needs to concentrate on his mission, his career. I need to be with my mom. My mom, who's been keeping me in the dark, leaving me with no clues about her health.

I need to remember how close I came to losing everything before I ever met Vincent. Because with his life that's anything but stable, if something were to happen and I lost him . . . I'd never recover. I need to protect my heart.

Before I can say anything else to make him see it's best we part ways now, as friends, he cups my cheek and lowers his voice. "I'm in love with you, and I'm pretty sure the feeling is mutual."

My breath hitches and I look at him with wide eyes.

"I know whatever happened to your mom today must

have scared you, but don't pull away from me. Let me be there for you."

The moment is interrupted by the light tunes of Vincent's ringtone as his phone goes off in his pocket. It's out of place in the heavy stillness surrounding us, but it helps to serve as a wake-up call. Vincent wants to be here for me. But how is that possible when he'll be gone any minute?

He pulls his phone out, staring at the screen for a few seconds before he silences it. It's selfish and stupid, but hope blooms that he'll tell me he's going to cancel the trip and stay with me. Then he lets his head fall and runs a hand along the back of his neck, and I know we're only delaying the inevitable. I can't bear to watch how dejected he looks, so I let my gaze slide to the window. His Benz is parked on the side of the street, and I see his suitcase in the back seat.

"You have to go," I whisper. "Today it's Florida. Tomorrow the moon. What's next after that? Mars? You can't always be here for me."

I know I must sound just like Vincent's mom, because a pained grimace flashes across his face before he shakes his head.

"No. After I get back from my mission, we continue building this life we've started. We enjoy every single second we have together for as long as we can." He leans his forehead against mine. "Tell me you'll be home when I get back. Please, Amerie."

From the beginning, every other time he's asked me to do something, I haven't been able to resist. But now my throat hurts from the pressure of holding back tears. It's just all too much. My mom. Vincent's profession of love. No doubt I've just made everything ten times harder for him with his mom now that she realizes the game we've played. I can also say goodbye to planning their vow renewal. Hell, I can say goodbye to planning anyone's events. I'm not cut out for doing anything but letting people down.

Grabbing the hand he still has resting against my face, I breathe him in one more time. "Thank you so much for giving me a place to stay. For being a great friend. But we both knew this wouldn't last." I slide the ring off my finger and place it in his hand. "Please, concentrate on your mission and just forget about me."

Vincent's tormented gaze pierces right through me as I rush to grab my purse and bolt from the house.

Once I'm out of the neighborhood, I pull into the nearest parking lot and finally let all my tears fall. It's a year's worth of sadness and anger and regret, and when I've cried so much my body is weak, I pull out my phone. Taking in a deep breath I power it up and place it to my ear.

My mom answers on the third ring. "Mimi?"

"Hey, Mom. Is it okay if I come stay with you and Daddy?"

CHAPTER TWENTY-SEVEN

I find myself drifting past my parents' bedroom for the fifth time in thirty minutes. The door is wide open, so I'm able to see my mom knitting something with green yarn while she reclines in bed watching TV. I may be on the verge of developing some sort of compulsion disorder, but the trade-off is breathing easier each time I stride by, so I'll take it.

As I make another pass on my way to the kitchen for no other reason than I'm restless, she looks up at me deadpan. "Well, you might as well come on in here instead of trying to wear down my carpet."

I'm busted, but I make my way to the bed and crawl into the empty spot on my dad's side, snuggling under the heavy comforter. Mom smirks and presses Play to resume the cupcake competition. We both wince in full sympathy when the camera cuts to a man taking a pan out of the oven only to reveal a batch full of sunken centers.

"That poor man," Mom says. "Reminds me of the time you and Gina made all those cupcakes in my kitchen. If I recall, y'all had more than a few batches that were a little concave."

I huff out a laugh. I definitely remember that day. Gina was running for prom queen. Instead of a popularity contest, our high school's tradition was to crown whoever raised the most money for their charity of choice. Gina wanted to raise money for our local humane society and was sure baking would turn a huge profit. It would have gone better if either of us had experience in the kitchen. In the end, we filled the less-than-stellar cupcakes with icing and spent hours restoring the kitchen, and Gina lost to the president of the French club, who had the genius idea to sit outside Costco and ask for donations, netting her charity a few thousand dollars and no mess.

"And you couldn't even help us," I say. "You came out of your room to see what we were up to and walked right back in."

"Not my monkeys, not my circus," she says with a laugh.

I take a deep breath and lean closer to her on the pillows. "You know, I still cringe at the thought of ever making cupcakes again."

"You never did like the idea of giving something a second chance once you decided it wasn't for you. Or someone."

I may have kept the majority of my life for the last year from her, but my mom still knows her child. She's right. After one bad experience, I swore off baking cupcakes forever. Years before that, it was bikes. Dad taught me after I'd begged and begged him to take off the training wheels. I was able to balance easily enough, even dared to take my hands off the handlebars like I'd witnessed the cool kids at school do. For a few seconds, it was amazing. With my hands up high and the wind whipping my face, it felt like I was flying. Then my tire hit a crack in the uneven sidewalk, and I really was airborne, over my bike and onto the ground. I never touched a bike again.

It seems that crashing just when it feels like I'm flying has become the terrible metaphor of my life.

Once the initial panic subsides on the show, the baker speaks to his partner, and they decide to fill the cupcakes with a strawberry compote. Disaster is averted, and they escape elimination.

As the next round begins, Mom mutes the TV. "Are you ready to tell me what's been bothering you? It's been a week, and you're still moping around like the world has fallen apart. I know you loved your job, but this isn't only about Jacob firing you. Or your breakup."

There are so many things weighing me down, I might as well be an anchor bound to the ocean floor. It's been a week since I asked my parents if I could move back into my old room. So far, I've come clean about my breakup with Derrick and not being able to afford my apartment. I even told them about the hospital bill. As expected, they weren't happy to learn I took it upon myself to bail them out, and surprised me with the news that they were expecting the bill and had saved up enough already. They want to pay me back, but I'm insistent they keep the funds and use them on an even bigger vacation. The money I used will serve as a lesson that even though I'm an adult, I shouldn't keep things from them. Especially when it has to do with their finances.

And now, in the face of more questions, I still can't bring myself to talk about the reason my heart is slowly bleeding.

I turn to her and ask my own question. "Why didn't you and Daddy just tell me about the wheelchair?"

She sighs and remains silent for a long time. Long enough for the show's judges to perform taste tests. "I didn't know how to," she finally says. "Your dad and I always tried to teach you the value of honesty, but last year in the hospital, it hit me that we may have failed you in other areas."

"What are you talking about? You and Daddy never failed me."

"Amerie, I'd watch you sit across the room like you were in a trance, only to go to the restroom and come out with bloodshot eyes from crying behind closed doors. I realized that we never taught you it's okay to be vulnerable. You don't have to be strong for me. You don't have to hold in the fear that you'll lose me so tightly that it suffocates you."

A tear escapes from my eye and I quickly wipe it away.

"So, to answer your question, we didn't tell you because I don't want you worrying about me day and night. I want you to live. Travel the world. Fall in love and give me some grandbabies to love on." Mom covers her mouth. "Wait, in this day and age, we're supposed to let our children choose their own path. Oh well, I meant it. Give me some grandbabies."

A watery laugh escapes me. Trust Mom to support whatever path I choose while also making her wishes known.

Back on the TV, the bakers are now furiously assembling a cupcake tower while the timer ticks down. It's a melee of icing as contestants pray that the cupcakes are cool enough, adding finishing touches and decorating the backdrops, all the while knowing just one mistake could cost them everything they've worked so hard for.

"What took you so long to tell us what was going on with everything?" Mom says.

"I didn't want you and Daddy worrying about me." My smile is full of the absurd irony of it all. "I didn't want to be the reason you gave up your dream of traveling, because I knew if I asked for help that's exactly what you'd do." I give her a pointed look.

Sure enough, once my parents knew I was out of a place to stay, they decided to stay home against my protests that I would be fine.

Mom laughs. "What a pair we make. Amerie, I understand you not wanting Daddy and me to worry, but it's what parents do. As for not wanting us to give up our dream, Daddy's already mapping out our trip to the East Coast. We'll be out of your hair in a few weeks, I promise."

I close my eyes and sigh. "Good. I just want you and Daddy to be happy and enjoy every second you have together."

"Mimi, I know you do. And *I* want *you* to feel comfortable coming to us about anything."

I nod. It's like a weight has been lifted from my chest, knowing that my parents are still determined to resume their trip. It's almost like I caused myself so much stress keeping secrets over nothing.

She reaches for the remote, but I stop her before she can turn the volume back up. The team with the almost-ruined cupcakes in the first round won, and now they're celebrating under an explosion of confetti and money.

"How do you and Daddy do it?" I ask.

"Do what?"

"Live and love so freely, knowing your time together may be limited." I hate to acknowledge out loud the reality of my mom's health, but I have to know.

"When it comes down to it, you dad taught me that our love has to be bigger than our fears." She smiles like a woman waking up on her wedding day. "I never thought I'd get married and have a beautiful family, but your dad is stubborn. He wouldn't let me push him away, and here we are thirty years later. And make no mistake, as hard as some of them have been, they've all been good. Tomorrow isn't promised for any of us, Amerie. My health just serves as a daily reminder."

"I've been scared of losing you," I say quietly, and it takes everything in me to admit it. Growing up, I always thought it would hurt Mom to know how much anxiety I had each time she was stuck in bed due to pain or had to go to the hospital for a blood transfusion. My parents always seemed so brave through it all, but now I realize it wasn't bravery but simply a will to continue living no matter what curveballs life threw.

For a year—longer, if I'm honest—I haven't been living. Not fully.

And not until Vincent.

I take a deep breath. "I have something to tell you. I didn't lose my apartment last week. I actually moved out two months ago . . ."

Once I'm done speaking, Mom looks at me for a full minute. "You mean to tell me you and *an astronaut* were engaged?" She holds up a hand as I open my mouth. "Excuse me, *fake* engaged. And you let him get away?"

I certainly don't need to wonder how she feels about the situation. It's obvious she's questioning where my common sense disappeared to.

"I had to let him go. Our deal was always temporary." In the past week, I've repeated those words in my head so many times, hoping my heart would finally agree that I made the right decision. "And our lives are on two different trajectories. I'm still trying to get my life in order, and he's got a career headed for the stars. Literally. I had to let him go." I sigh.

"You already said that," Mom says softly. She opens her frail arms, and like I did so many times when I was younger, I burrow into her side, careful not to put too much weight on her. "And maybe you really believe it. But do you want to know what I believe? I believe you'll get this business you've started back on track, and it will thrive because you're too talented to let it fail. You get that from me, you know? I also believe that once you decide the fear of losing someone you love is too high a cost, you'll find the greatest love of all."

─────────

"OKAY," GINA SAYS. "SO YOU'RE GOING TO GO WITH THE GOLD FRAME for your booth?"

"Yes. And look at this." I swipe through my phone's gallery to show her a screenshot of my slogan. *Unforgettable moments in time for unforgettable memories.* "It took me forever to come up with that."

"Mimi, I love it. Here, have some roses. Roses, roses, roses." She mimics like she's tossing them at me and I smile. She has been doing the most to talk with her hands and show off her engagement ring.

It's so good to see her finally getting what she deserves. I take a sip of my coffee, then let out a shaky exhale.

"Are you sure you don't want me to stay? I can move tables so it doesn't look like we're together."

"No, I have to face them myself. I can do this."

I don't care what anyone else says—I have the best mom in the whole world. She's beautiful inside and out, and with her pep talk, I had the guts to not only book a Bridal Extravaganza booth but also reach out to Mrs. Rogers. If I really want my business to thrive, I need to take chances and face everything that comes my way.

By now, I'm sure Vincent has come clean and admitted the truth of our relationship. Self-preservation tells me to leave the family alone, but an illogical part of me has been screaming over all the other voices in my head that I need to complete this job. Or at least I need to try.

No one ever kicked me out of the group chat, so I sent a message asking to meet in person and talk. Instantly, Camille was the one to reply with a yes and suggested we meet for coffee. It's the smallest of wins so far, and I'm praying luck will carry me through our meeting.

I asked Gina, my favorite and only hype girl, to meet me at Moon Bean to mentally prepare. Without her here, I'd be wondering if there were some undetected gas leak at my parents' house that made me lose my mind. Because is this really the best course of action? *This?* To approach the people I knowingly lied to and ask for my job back? Maybe I should call the gas company and have them come out to the house.

No, I'm not freaking out. I'm here. I'm doing this.

"I'll let you know how everything goes," I tell Gina.

"Okay. Call me later."

After she leaves, I use a napkin from the dispenser in the middle of the table to wipe away any microscopic crumbs. Can't have them think I don't think they're worthy of a clean table. Maybe I should get one of those cardboard carafes of coffee. I realize how rude it looks for me to be sitting here with a cup and nothing to offer them.

Before I can get up, the bell above the door rings and it's too late. Camille and Mrs. Rogers have arrived. Both ladies are in black scrubs with white jackets, and I realize they must have come over their lunch break. I should have at least thought of some scones or something.

Camille at least offers a small smile, but Mrs. Rogers's face gives away nothing.

I wipe my sweaty hands on my jeans and stand up as they approach. "Thank you for meeting me today."

Mrs. Rogers opens her mouth, but Camille clears her throat and speaks first. "We were surprised to hear from you and, I must admit, curious as to what you had to say."

I wait for them to sit down before taking my own seat. "Can I get coffee or tea for either of you?"

"We're fine," Mrs. Rogers clips.

"Right." I clear my throat. I can do this. "First, I want to sincerely apologize for my role in deceiving you. I knew full well walking into your house that I'd be lying about my relationship with V-Vincent." I trip up on his name but manage not to wince. "While my intentions weren't to hurt anyone, I realize that's exactly what happened. If at all possible, I'd like to make amends."

"What did you have in mind?" Camille says.

I should have layered on the deodorant before coming. My skin prickles, and I wrap my hands around my cup to keep from touching my necklace. They aren't softening toward me at all, and it feels like I'm about to pointlessly make a fool of myself.

"Well, uh, yes. This close to the ceremony, it would be almost impossible to find another planner."

"Would it?" Mrs. Rogers says. She raises an eyebrow and I gulp.

"It would be difficult to bring someone in this late in the game. But if you'll let me, I'd like to finish the job I started. I want to make the vow renewal the event of your dreams. No charge. Just a beautiful celebration." Money and other opportunities to expand my business will come later. This will be all about Mr. and Mrs. Rogers. I owe them that much.

Mother and daughter regard each other, exchanging a silent communication, before Camille faces me and pins me with her gaze. "First, I want to know something." She leans closer to the table. "Was everything between you and Vincent really an act?" There is no accusation or hostility in her tone, only curiosity.

The air is sucked from my lungs. I close my eyes. I have to guess they are as upset about me lying to them as they are with the thought that my affection toward Vincent was all fake. Maybe if I tell them the truth, it will ease the ache I've felt in my heart every minute of every day since walking away from him.

"No, everything wasn't an act," I say. "I care about him. I never intended to see him as more than a friend, but he made it infuriatingly hard not to." I force down my queasiness and meet Mrs. Rogers in the eyes. "I know I've already inserted myself in your family more than any stranger has the right to, but you have to know, the reason Vincent lied was because he wanted to make things easier for you. He loves you so much, he just didn't know how else to convince you not to worry about him."

"Amerie, I'm going to assume that when you said you're close to your mother, that wasn't a lie," Mrs. Rogers says.

"No, ma'am," I say quickly. "It wasn't a lie."

"What both you and Vincent fail to realize is that, as a mother, it is my right to consider the welfare of my children."

"Wow. That's almost word for word what my mom said."

"She's a wise woman. You'd do well to listen to her." The lines around her mouth soften, and her shoulders lose some of their edge. Suddenly she looks vulnerable and every bit the woman who already lost one child. "But even I can see I've been pushing my son away, and it's something I need to work on."

Mrs. Rogers and Camille exchange another wordless glance, then Mrs. Rogers nods.

Camille reaches into her bag and pulls out the planner I forgot at her house. "I figured you'd need your notes if you were going to finalize everything."

CHAPTER TWENTY-EIGHT

Two weeks later, I get ready for the Rogerses' ceremony while Beyoncé's *Homecoming* plays on the small TV mounted above my old dresser. The dresser was a staple in each of my rooms as we moved around, and I've found comfort in the nostalgia of being surrounded by my old furniture these past weeks.

I'm sitting at my desk-turned-vanity with light strips adhered to the mirror, turning my head side to side as I inspect my hair and makeup. Gina would be impressed that I managed to nail the halo braid without her help. Or a full-blown meltdown.

Normally, an easy morning like this would indicate I'm in for a smooth event, but today . . . no. No *but*s. This event *will* be smooth. It will be a success. I may be plagued with thoughts of Vincent while I'm around his family, but he stalks my mind and dreams all the time anyway. And now that he's launching today, the only thing I can do is try to move on. After the ceremony, I'll be out of their lives for good. And I'm totally fine.

After grabbing my portfolio bag and stuffing my binder inside, I'm ready to head to the pier. I walk to the living room, where my dad is rummaging through his desk in the corner.

"What are you looking for, Daddy?"

He raises his head with a scowl etched into his handsome face. "Have you seen the battery to my trimmer? I had it charging here last night. Your mom wants me to finish the yard before Tony does."

I smirk. "Momma wants you to finish? Or *you* want to win this weekend's competition?"

Who knew homeownership in the quietest of neighborhoods was so cutthroat over yard work? Mom told me how, now that the weather is consistently warmer, the minute one neighbor on the street revs up their lawnmower, three more are sure to follow. Whoever finishes first celebrates their victory by silently cracking open a beer and lording it over the others from their porch while everyone else labors on. While my parents were traveling, they paid a teenager to take care of the grass, but now Dad's back in the yard work bracket. Mom thinks it's hilarious how he and their neighbor Tony Mendoza seem to head outside earlier each weekend in a bid to beat the other. If my parents stay in town much longer, Dad is liable to start at the crack of dawn so he can win.

"Is that it?" I point to a rectangular orange-and-black box sitting on the bookshelf. I recognize it only because I saw something similar in Vincent's garage.

As I move to the bookshelf to pick it up, my eyes snag on the picture placed behind it. In the picture I'm a kid, probably about nine years old, and my head is sticking out from the opening of a homemade fort. I'm grinning harder than any child has the right to, showcasing a missing incisor, with my hair sticking out of a weeks-old braid.

I hand the battery to my dad as he walks up. "Was this taken at the apartments on Bridgewood Street?" I ask.

"Oh yeah. You remember that?"

"Yes. Those apartments were just a few blocks from the bread factory." I can still see the old stucco exterior. "The slide was broken the whole time we lived there, but at least I got to smell bread every day on my walk to school."

There's another picture on the top shelf. I'm standing on the couch with a toy microphone in front of a burgundy wall. I pick it up and use my finger to get rid of the small layer of dust on the frame. "This was at the condo by Ellis Elementary. No, no. Camelot."

When our neighbors were at work, Mom would let me sing at the top of my lungs as I did chores so I wouldn't complain the whole time.

"You're right," Dad says, stroking his chin. "I thought you would've been too young to remember. Lord knows I'm too old to recall every place I've lived."

I remember them all. I may not know the exact street or the name of each apartment complex, but I can recount dozens of memories of what my parents did to make each space ours so that I never felt like a stranger wherever we were. All these years, I've felt untethered, like I was missing out by not having a childhood home full of love and memories. But now I see I don't need a physical place when the love and comfort my parents have always provided are tangible things I carry with me everywhere I go.

I throw my arms around my dad. "Thank you for a great childhood."

He doesn't ask me to explain. He simply holds me in the strong, reassuring way he always has to let me know I'm not alone.

It makes me think of the way Vincent held me that first night at the New Year's Eve party, and a wave of homesickness I've never experienced before washes over me. It threatens to drown me with its intensity, and I grip my dad tighter. I do not need to fall apart on today of all days, when I'm overseeing Vincent's parents' vow renewal. But here I am.

I'm not sure when it happened, but I came to think of Vincent's home as *my* home. That guest room I decorated was for our future guests. That marvelous bathroom was just waiting for me to talk Vincent into installing a chandelier. And Vincent . . . Vincent, who was always so patient with me and caring and dependable, offered me a place in his home. And I told him not to contact me.

We hear the start of a lawnmower and Dad stiffens.

I smile and release him. "I guess you better finish before Momma gets on you," I tease.

"She thinks I'm some kind of workhorse. Hey, where are you off to looking all nice?"

"I have an event today. Do you like it?" I twirl to show off my navy jumpsuit.

"You look beautiful. Go knock it out, Mimi."

I DON'T KNOW WHOSE SMILE IS BIGGER: MINE OR MRS. ROGERS'S. I'M sure Mr. Rogers could be in the running, but he's barely been able to take his eyes off his wife as she stands there, regal in her vintage cream dress. They're obviously as much in love now as they were thirty-five years ago.

And me? Well, I've truly outdone myself. I can now introduce myself as Amerie Price: event coordinator and yacht expert. Well, not exactly an expert, but I did have to take a tour and go over the safety precautions before the event setup could begin. I was shown each staircase and the exit procedures, and it was heavily stressed that guests are not to jump off the side. It's no cruise ship, but at sixty-eight feet above the water, it may as well be the distance to the moon. If any of the guests are like me, jumping won't be of any concern.

The exterior of the ninety-foot boat is white, and the guests are free to roam between the open upper deck, where the ceremony will be held, and the main deck for the reception.

As the couple walks around talking to their guests, I move to inspect the chairs, making sure the covers are flawless. After, I walk to the edge to straighten some roses on the flower garland that wraps around the railing. I make the mistake of looking down into the water, and immediately my stomach flips. Placing a hand on my stomach, I back away, breathing slowly. I took some medicine, hoping I wouldn't throw up in front of everyone, but if the boat is not even moving yet and I'm already feeling it, I know I'm in for one hell of an evening.

Downstairs in the main cabin, tables are set up, and there's a small area for dancing. More roses and greenery fill the room, outlining the walls and windows, and Mrs. Rogers loved my idea of a bouquet of the same roses in tall gold vases for the centerpieces. String lights along the ceiling finish the look, shining like hundreds of stars. I snap a picture of the room and send it to Gina. Before I can put my phone away, it buzzes with an alert to let me know it's almost time for the ceremony to start.

I take the stairs back to the deck, where I have the DJ change songs, then make sure I have eyes on the photographer, who is already standing near the flower-decked altar. Once the song changes, Brianna is the first to find her seat, followed by Camille and Lance. The rest of the guests follow suit as a hush of anticipation settles over the boat. This song will be over in two minutes, followed by a piano cover of Mr. and Mrs. Rogers's song, "Always."

Speaking of, I need to check on the couple. I look at the time on my watch as I spin around. After taking three steps, I come up short when I spot a familiar smooth walk and topaz gaze headed my way.

"Vincent," I gasp out. Adrenaline floods through me in a mixture of shock and elation. "What are you doing here?" I shake my head, not wanting to sound rude. "I mean, I thought your launch was today."

He briefly scans me from head to toe, and I swear there's a flicker of emotion before he regards me with a neutral gaze that shows none of the heat or teasing he always directed at me before. "The launch was rescheduled, and I knew it would mean a lot to my parents if I could make it."

"They're going to be thrilled you're here."

He offers a polite smile, then looks behind me to where the guests are. "It looks like everyone is already sitting down. Should I sit up front?"

"Oh yeah. Of course." I realize I'm blocking his way and slide over to give him room to move. "We set up two chairs in honor of you and your brother. They're next to Camille."

"Thank you."

He walks away, and I'm left feeling small as I blink after him.

But really, what did I expect? That after he poured his heart out and asked me to stay, we'd exchange exuberant hellos like long-lost friends? No. Vincent is giving me exactly what I asked for, even if I regret it with every fiber of my being.

"Always" begins playing, and I fortify myself with a deep breath. Now is the time to focus on my job.

Mr. and Mrs. Rogers don't need to be herded to their spots. They're already standing hand in hand, ready to walk down the aisle, so I move out of the way toward the railing, careful not to get too close. I paste on my perfectly practiced smile and shoot them a thumbs-up, careful not to show the pain of what I lost.

CHAPTER TWENTY-NINE

By the time Mr. and Mrs. Rogers are exchanging vows, my emotions are firmly under control.

"It's been a beautiful thirty-five years," Mrs. Rogers says. "And I am so, so thankful for my family. My beautiful daughters, Camille and Brianna, who have hearts for helping people. And my son Vincent. In case y'all haven't heard, he's an astronaut." Laughter ripples through the crowd. "He's brilliant, and I'm truly proud of him." She looks up and fans her face to keep her tears from ruining her makeup. The effort is in vain, however, as they stream down her face. Not that it takes anything away from her beauty. "I'm so proud of all of you. And I just know Octavius is smiling down on us."

There's a knot in my throat. I hope Mrs. Rogers's acknowledgment of Vincent's career means their relationship is on the mend. I won't be around to see it, but I wish them all the best.

The guests are dismissed to mingle and eat the mounds of mini lobster rolls, caprese kebabs, and stuffed mushrooms the caterers set out. I ensure cocktails are available, then find my way back to the deck where family pictures are being taken.

It's that beautiful hour when the sun is beginning to set, casting a gold-and-purple glow in the sky that reflects off the sparkling water. I stop before I get too close, watching the photographer direct their poses. They're taking a full-family photo with Mr. and Mrs. Rogers and their kids. I can't take my eyes off Vincent. He looks so good in his fitted tan suit and white shirt, his skin tone providing the perfect canvas for the neutral colors.

They go from full family to Mrs. Rogers and the siblings, then Mr. Rogers and the siblings, then just the siblings.

I can probably find something else to oversee, but I don't want to budge from this spot. Even if I do look like an unwanted outsider intruding on the family's special moment.

Once the photographer has gotten all the photos, she invites the family to join their guests below. I affix a smile as they walk past, but something breaks inside me when Vincent doesn't spare me a glance. I close my eyes once I hear their footsteps on the stairs. God, I just know I'll be crying for months after this day is over.

Why did Mrs. Rogers agree to let me finish this event? Was it actually some sort of diabolical plan to get back at me for the role I played in lying to her? Maybe she somehow knew Vincent would be here and wanted to torture me by forcing me to spend time around the family I'm no longer welcome to be part of and the man I gave up.

"Are you okay? You don't look so well."

I'm broken out of my thoughts by a soft touch on my arm.

The photographer holds a black camera in her hand as she regards me. "Make sure you get something to eat before you pass out. I learned to stipulate in my contract long ago that a meal and break be provided. Yes, we're here to provide a service, but we're only human."

I give her a weak smile. Food isn't the answer to my problems, but I appreciate the concern. "Thanks. It's just a bit of seasickness. Me and water aren't exactly friends."

She gives me another sympathetic pat on the arm before walking away, and I check the time on my phone. Still three hours before the night is over. One more hour until the boat sets off for a small cruise around Clear Lake. Everything is under control, so I could stay up here until it's time to cut the cake. However, the need to see Vincent is like a tether pulling me downstairs. I find a spot in the corner, near a window, to post up and watch him. Here, with my dark clothes against the dark wood, I should blend in.

Contrary to his claim of not liking crowds or parties, Vincent is quite the social butterfly. In the span of ten minutes, he has conversations with six different people—yes, I'm counting. Each time he moves away from one person, someone else pops up, probably full of questions about his upcoming mission. And patient as he is, Vincent answers them all and then some, happy to educate the masses. As much as he moves throughout the room, he doesn't look my way.

My mom encouraged me to move past my fears and claim the life I desire. I've managed to take control of my business's future, preparing for the Bridal Extravaganza and being brave enough to reach out to Mrs. Rogers. So why is it so hard to go after Vincent? Maybe if I stepped out from the shadows and he just looked at me, gave me a small hint with his eyes that everything between us isn't lost, then I would be able to take that first step into the unknown.

"Amerie, there you are," Mrs. Rogers says, approaching arm in arm with a woman clad in a beautiful bright magenta dress and matching hat that would rock in the front pew of any church. "Let me introduce you to my friend Jeanine. I was telling her how you put this all together on such short notice."

"After four boys, my daughter is finally having a girl," Jeanine exclaimed. "It'll be the first granddaughter on both sides of the family, so we're going all out. I'd love to hear your ideas on the celebration."

I immediately reach for one of my newly printed business cards, and my first genuine smile breaks through. "I'd love to chat with you about it. Please, e-mail or text me and we'll set up a meeting."

Jeanine plucks the card from my hands as her eyes transform and take on a starry look. "I'm thinking pink. And glitter. Lots of glitter." She shakes her head as if coming back to reality. "I'll be in touch!"

I'm still smiling as I turn to Mrs. Rogers, but it quickly dims under her scrutiny. Yes, she allowed me to finish the event, but I'm under no illusion that all is forgiven. Or sure that this isn't a calculated, perfectly executed bout of revenge.

"You really did a beautiful job, Amerie," she says after a moment. "I can't sing your praises enough."

"Thank you, Mrs. Rogers. That means a lot coming from you."

"Remember, dear, it's Cheryl."

"Okay." I smile. "Cheryl."

We stand in silence and watch the guests move around. Well, I presume she is looking at the guests, but I'm still zeroed in on Vincent.

Mrs. Rogers lifts her left hand and wiggles her fingers. "I don't think I got a chance to show you my ring yet. I told William I didn't need an upgrade, but he insisted, and who was I to deny him?" Her finger is adorned with glittering diamonds that sparkle even in the low light.

"It's beautiful."

"It's a bit flashy if you ask me. I would have been happy wearing my old ring, but Vincent wouldn't give it back." She lets out an incredulous laugh. "When I asked for it back and he said no, I could have strangled him."

I lower my head to the ground as all the guilt from the last couple of months comes roiling back. "I'm so sorry about everything. I truly am." I know I can apologize a million times and it still won't make up for what I did.

Mrs. Rogers continues like I haven't spoken. "He said it belonged to someone else now."

What? That doesn't make sense.

She places a hand under my chin. I raise my head and see so much warmth radiating from her gaze I want to cry.

"We all make mistakes, and I would be making one of the biggest mistakes of my life if I didn't tell you what a beautiful and kind woman you are to try and fix a mother and son's relationship. And I would be honored to someday call you daughter."

I do cry then, and Mrs. Rogers pulls me into her embrace. I'm not worthy of her forgiveness, but thankful nonetheless. As we break apart, I look around to ensure no one has noticed the event planner falling apart. But all at once, panic sets in as I realize I've lost track of Vincent. He's not seated at a table or talking to anyone.

"If you're searching for my son, I saw him leaving. He'll be heading back to Florida."

All I hear is the word *leaving*. And I know that I have to get to Vincent before he reaches his car. I may never get another chance to tell him I love him and that I made the biggest mistake of my life by walking away. Without another thought, I rush to the small doorway at the back of the room, dodging guests and caterers. My heels clack against the wood once I hit the lower deck, and I see Vincent has already made it to the pier.

"Vincent!" I shout. He's too far away to hear, so I shout his name again as I race to the loading dock. "Vincent, wait!"

I get to where the ramp should be, only to see they've already pulled it in to prepare for the cruise.

"I need to get off right now," I say to the attendant.

I must look a sight because instead of arguing he holds his hands up in surrender. "Okay, just give me a few minutes. We'll get the ramp set up for you." He walks off, presumably to get the ramp. Or maybe he doesn't get paid enough to deal with hysterical guests. Either way, I can't wait. In a few minutes the love of my life will be gone.

Vincent stands at the edge of the pier but has turned around to look at me. If he turns back around, that's it. "Don't go anywhere," I yell to him. "I'm coming to you!"

I reach down to unstrap my heels and kick them out of the way. Before good sense can catch up to me, I rush to the side and pull myself up on the boat's thick ledge, settling into a crouch. My first mistake is looking down from my new vantage point. This part is only supposed to be twenty feet high, but what seemed like small ripples earlier, now move ominously as the sun begins to set and the water darkens. All at once, I feel dizzy, a chill sweeps down my back, and my chest tightens. I grab the railing with one hand while covering my mouth with the other as my stomach heaves.

"Ma'am," the alarmed attendant calls.

My foot slips and my heart leaps into my throat. Breathing hard, I turn my head and glare at him over the railing. "Don't come near me!"

Wide-eyed, he backs up and pulls out his walkie-talkie. They will never let me back on this yacht. Hell, the tale of the event planner jumping from a boat will probably make headlines and I'll lose whatever good standing I've managed to gain.

If this is the end of my event planning career, so be it.

I look back up to Vincent. He's still there. He's alarmed, though he's trying not to show it. His eyes are wide, and he's significantly closer than he was before. Is this enough to get him to wait? If I tell him I'll be right there and wait until the ramp is back out, will he stay where he's at until I can reach him? Judging by the tenseness in his jaw and line of his body, I'd guess yes.

But my mom's words come back to rally me. My love has to be bigger than my fear. For Vincent, I will overcome every mental obstacle. So while I'm scared out of my mind, somehow it's also the bravest I've felt in my whole life.

I take a deep breath, plug my nose, and jump.

The water is cold, shocking every muscle in my body as I'm plunged into never-ending darkness. After the initial shock wears off, I kick my way to the surface, gasping for air when I get my head above the water. Through the burn of water mixed with mascara dripping into my eyes, I see Vincent standing at the edge of the pier and swim to him.

When I reach the pier, strong arms haul me up and out of the water. I sink to my knees, simultaneously catching my breath and thanking the Lord for solid ground. Sweet, flat, solid ground.

"Are you okay?" comes Vincent's anxious voice from above me.

I nod and hold my hand out in a staying motion. I just need one more minute.

As I stand up, Vincent watches me with wide disbelieving eyes that scan from my dripping hair to my bare toes at least three times.

"Are you okay?" he reiterates.

I nod.

"Amerie, what—" he explodes, then stops and looks up to the sky. He's panting as hard as I am. "What were you thinking? There's a reason they don't allow diving close to so many boats. You could have gotten hurt. You could have been killed!"

He turns his back to me, shaking his head.

"I had to talk to you before you left," I say.

Vincent turns back around and regards me warily. "What could you possibly have to say that was worth jumping off a boat for?"

I swallow hard. Now that I'm standing in front of him, I'm at a loss for words. There was no plan when I raced after him, only great need and the knowledge that if he left, I'd never see him again. "My parents have that NASA education channel you told me about. Did you know that as big as the galaxy is, there's actually more trees on Earth than there are stars in the Milky Way?"

He runs a hand over his face and inhales deeply. "You jumped off a boat to talk about trees?" he grits out.

"No." I shake my head, flinging water from my hair, some of it landing on his chin. I can only imagine how I must seem to him. "No. What I really wanted to say is that I'm glad I met you. I could have wished on all the stars, planets, and moons and still never could I have imagined being led to someone like you."

His gaze is steady but unreadable. It might be too late for us, but an asteroid could crash right in front of us, and I wouldn't stop until I told him how much he means to me.

"You're brilliant. You make me laugh. You handle each of my mood swings with the patience of a saint. And you gave me something I never thought I'd have—a home. Not just the structure, but the happiness, contentment, and love." Forget about it being too late. I'm not letting him leave until he's mine again. "I'm sorry I walked away from you. So sorry. If you give me the chance, I'll prove how much you mean to me." His eyes soften, but he still hasn't let his guard down. It's time to bring out the big guns. "And if we're being honest, don't you think you owe me?"

He raises an eyebrow and cocks his head. "How do you figure that?"

Slowly, I close the gap between us. He doesn't back away, so I reach for his hands. The cuffs of his shirt are wet and plastered to his arms from when he pulled me out of the water, but his skin is so warm. I raise his hands to my lips and kiss his knuckles the way he did to mine. It's hard to stop there. I missed touching him and want to gorge myself.

"Well," I whisper, "you did steal my heart. It's only fair you give me a second chance to prove it's worth keeping." I pause, hoping he'll say something. Anything. But the seconds tick by and he stares at me in silence. "I know you're leaving soon," I rush out. "If you need to focus on the mission now, I completely understand. Just know I'll still be here and—"

He crushes his lips to mine.

He cradles my head in his hands, and I'm shaking as I wrap my arms around his neck. This kiss is everything. It's full of promises and forgiveness and love. So much love. It's been part of every kiss we've shared, but now I can fully recognize it.

"Every step," Vincent says as we break apart. "Every step I've taken has brought me to you. From the moment we met, I knew you were the one I'm supposed to spend my life with."

My heart stutters. "You did?"

"Yeah. That's probably why I made such a fool of myself when you spoke to me. You've been my hardest challenge so far." His thumb caresses my bottom lip. "But also the most worth it."

Relief hits me so hard it causes my body to quake. "I thought I'd ruined everything. That you were leaving the party and I'd never see you again."

Vincent flashes that beautiful smile that makes my heart race. "I was coming back."

Teeth chattering, I shake my head. "But the boat is about to leave."

He looks behind me at the boat and his eyebrows jump up. I turn around to see the yacht is already moving away. The attendant and another worker look at me with disapproval while Mrs. Rogers stands behind the rail blowing us kisses.

I turn back to Vincent. "I guess we both missed it."

He takes off his blazer and drapes it around my shoulders. "I guess that means you're coming home with me."

"*Back* home with you."

CHAPTER THIRTY

I step into the foyer and take a deep breath. Home sweet home. So many homes I've left and never come back to. But with this one, my heart never left, even when my body did.

Vincent closes the door behind us, and the lock clicks into place. He turns around, and I reach for his hand, interlocking our fingers. "I'm glad to be home," I say.

I want him to take me to the bedroom and make love to me for hours. But before I can make my request known, he leads me farther into the house. "We need to get you out of those wet clothes and warmed up."

We go to the bathroom, bypassing the bed, where Vincent begins filling the tub with steaming water. He's been quiet since the car ride. Sure, he held my hand the whole way, but it's like he's holding himself back. As if he doesn't fully believe I won't up and leave again, so he needs to brace himself for impact. I need to find a way to assure him I'm right where I want to be.

He's leaning over the tub to check the temperature with his hand when he glances back and catches me watching him. "What?"

"Is that the same shirt I spilled coffee on?"

He looks down and shrugs. "Oh yeah, I guess it is."

"You said I ruined it."

He ducks his head to hide a smile. It's too small, but the room already looks brighter. Then, happy with the water, he straightens and comes to me. "I had to think of something to say to get you to my sister's party."

I shake my head, then drop my arms so Vincent can remove the blazer still wrapped around me. He moves on to my zipper next and peels off the jumpsuit that's sticking to me like a second layer of skin. My bra and panties are next, and I'm left standing bare.

My skin prickles with goose bumps all over, but getting warm can wait. "Come in with me," I say to Vincent. I don't want to be away from him for a moment.

He gets undressed, and soon we're both submerged in the warm water. Vincent leans against the bathtub while I sit between his legs and rest against his chest. I want to soak in this moment forever. He kisses the side of my neck, and it's the sweetest thing to be surrounded by him.

I run my hand along his forearm. "How did the conversation with your mom go that day once I left?"

"It actually didn't go. Once you left, so did I. I contemplated chasing you down until we worked it out, but decided to give you time instead. By the time I spoke to my mom, she'd pretty much figured out why we did the whole fake boyfriend, fake girlfriend thing. Then I told her that I love her, but her guilt trips make it hard to want to be around her. She's been making a real effort to change these past few weeks."

"I'm glad to hear it's working out. So how long do I get to keep you home?"

He pauses for a beat while his body stiffens behind me. "The launch is rescheduled for three weeks from now. I have to go back to Florida in two."

"Your mom made it sound like you were heading back tonight."

"Did she?"

I'm not even mad at her.

The water sloshes from side to side as I change positions so we're face-to-face. With me straddling him, my knees on either side of his hips, I interlock my fingers behind his neck and lean forward. "Okay. Two weeks. Enough time for me to move my things back in. And to introduce you to my parents. I came clean to them too, and Mom especially has been dying to meet my amazing astronaut."

"You'll be here when I return?"

I kiss him, trying to erase the doubt from his eyes. "I'm not going anywhere. You're right, I was scared before. Scared of losing my mom. Scared of losing you."

"And you're not scared anymore?"

"Parts of me will always be afraid of the unknown, but I already know what it feels like to be without you. I hate it. I want to be with you whenever and wherever I can. So even with you being millions of miles away, I'll be right here waiting for you to come back. Every time." I kiss him again.

Vincent smiles against my lips. "The moon isn't millions of miles away. Just 240,000."

There's the smart-ass I love.

He runs his hands along my back. "And this career isn't forever, Mimi. It's just what I do now. *You* are my forever, and I want to build my life with you."

"I can't wait, Vincent. I love you."

I press our lips together again. I want to commit the way they feel to my tactile memory so that when he's on his mission, all I have to do is think of him to feel like he's with me. I pull at his bottom lip with my teeth, and he groans, growing harder under me by the second.

He grips the back of my neck to bring our bodies impossibly closer. Against my chest, his heartbeat races in tandem with mine. Two weeks was too long to be away from him, and we're both desperate to make up for lost time.

I'm on top, but he's the one setting the pace as he licks and drags kisses along my neck. Against my skin, his voice is rough and gravelly as he says, "I need you, Mimi. I need you here with me."

I lift my hips and sink down onto him. We are two stars merging. Becoming bigger and greater. Brighter.

He grips my hips, and we're moving so hard and quick that water splashes over the sides of the tub, dousing the floor. It doesn't take long before we're both coming apart together. And when I regain my breath, I caress the nape of Vincent's neck and lay a kiss on his shoulder.

"I love you," I say. "I'll be right here when you get back."

Finally, his body relaxes.

I lie against Vincent's chest while he runs his hand up and down my back. When the water has long since cooled down, he asks, "Where did you sign your name?"

I'm so sated and comfortable I can barely keep my eyes open. "What?"

"You sign your name in every place you live. Where did you leave it here? I looked everywhere and couldn't find it."

I smirk. "If you really looked everywhere, you would have found it. I'll tell you what, put a chandelier in here"—I point to the ceiling—"and I'll tell you where I did it."

He laughs, and the sound does everything to my stomach. "How about this? While I'm gone, you can do anything you want to this house. This is your home, Mimi. How does that sound?"

"It sounds like you've got a deal."

EPILOGUE

Six months later

My eyes are glued to the room full of long desks, black computers and chairs, and men and women wearing headsets as they monitor their screens.

"Is that man wearing cowboy boots?" Brianna says from her position behind the couch.

I lean forward and squint at the TV. She's right. The man on the right edge is most definitely in white cowboy boots.

"Well, yeehaw," Camille says, and Brianna snickers.

"Would you two stop?" Mrs. Rogers says. "I'm nervous enough as it is."

I admire Camille and Brianna's ability to joke right now, because I'm in Mrs. Rogers's camp. I haven't been able to eat all day, even though Camille has set out a wonderful spread of fruits and Mrs. Rogers arrived with her homemade pizzas. I don't think my stomach will settle until Vincent is home, safe and sound.

They announce on TV that splashdown will be in two minutes and thirteen seconds, and my heart lurches.

Mrs. Rogers looks at me from the love seat she occupies with her husband and clasps her hands against her chest. "I can't stop shaking. I'm so nervous."

"Me too," I say. My voice is shaky, and my hands are sweaty. It won't be long now. "But he'll be okay."

Mrs. Rogers nods and turns back to the TV.

My dad rubs my back. "That's right, Mimi. He'll be okay."

Vincent and Dad took to each other as well as I thought they would, with my dad quickly letting him know he's the perfect future son-in-law for his daughter. And Mom is enamored with his sweet and easygoing nature. And his being an astronaut.

Sandwiched between my parents, I reach out for their hands, holding on for dear life.

Five seconds after the astronauts reach the sky over the Gulf of Mexico, the screen cuts out from Mission Control, and the capsule comes into view. It's quickly slowing as the parachutes deploy, and I think I stop breathing.

After what feels like forever, the capsule splashes into the ocean. Then we're all out of our seats, erupting into applause and cheers. Hugging one another. Breathing again.

Camille rubs her belly, which is barely beginning to show. "Guess what, little one. Uncle Vince made it home safe."

Yes, he's safe. And he's home. Well, almost.

IT'S A BEAUTIFUL DAY WHEN THEY FLY VINCENT AND HIS CREW BACK to Houston. We wait beside a white barricade with the other astronauts' families at the spaceport for the plane to land. The air is filled with anticipation and excited chatter.

The door to the airplane opens, and the first person to disembark is a woman. She begins waving as soon as she's out. I hear a toddler next to us shout "Mama!" But then Vincent steps out and everything fades away.

We were able to chat over video and phone calls, but nothing beats seeing him in the flesh. His hair is a little longer than his usual tapered waves, and he's in serious need of an edge-up. Still, it's the most striking sight I've ever seen. His eyes search the gathered crowd, and when he finds us, finds me, the smile that transforms his face is a thing of beauty.

Once we're given the all-clear to approach, it's a race to cross as much ground as humanly possible. At least it is for the families; the astronauts, not so much. It seems some of them can barely walk as their bodies readjust to Earth's gravity.

If Vincent is feeling any ill effects, he doesn't show it. His arms wrap around me, as strong and steady as ever, and I think of the night before he left. When, as we lay in the dark, we made future plans for the house and vacations we'd spend with both our families. I woke up the next morning, and the ring was back on my finger. I use my left hand now to stroke along his face and kiss those beautiful lips. He's right here, right now. And he's my forever.

ACKNOWLEDGMENTS

I have been falling in love with romance novels since I was a kid, but never dreamed that someday I would be bringing my own characters to life. I know for a fact this would not be the case if not for the following amazing humans.

Thank you to my wonderful agent, Jem. Your support of Amerie and Vincent, and your belief in my words and storytelling abilities allow me to believe in myself. To my dream editor, Esi, thank you for being a joy to work with. I am beyond grateful for your guidance that pushed me to dig deep and helped bring this story to life in a way I could only dream.

To the team at Berkley: Sareer, thank you for your kindness and support. Jessica, Elise, Kristin, Kaila, and everyone working on everything behind the scenes, thank you for all you do that allows me to focus on writing.

Thank you to the wonderful friends who've been there to pull me back when I was on the verge of a meltdown, and who constantly prove writing doesn't have to be lonely. Maggie and Sarah, thank you ladies for being my first "yes" and seeing past that first draft to the heart of the story. To my beta readers, Kiarra and Christine, thank you for your encouragement that had me hype for days. To my RWAG group: Tiff, Quiana, Aaliyah, and Jadesola, thank you for your friendship. Gwynne, thank you for your wisdom and encouragement that is unmatched. To my fellow KP mentees, I couldn't have picked a better group to have gone through those three months with, and will forever be grateful we found one another.

To my biggest supporters, my husband and A Squad. Thank you for giving me my own happily ever after.

And finally, thank you, readers, for giving Amerie and Vincent a chance.

THE KISS COUNTDOWN

ETTA EASTON

READERS GUIDE

QUESTIONS FOR DISCUSSION

1. Amerie's bad day initially colors the lens through which she sees and reacts to Vincent. After spending time with him, she changes her opinion and she realizes he isn't so bad. When has your opinion about someone changed after getting to know them?

2. What does "home" mean to you? Is it a place or a feeling?

3. Even though Amerie was over her ex, she felt she had to prove that she was doing just fine after the breakup. Would you/have you ever tried to show off in front of an ex?

4. Amerie made the executive decision to pay off her parents' hospital bill after remembering how much they struggled financially when she was a child. Would you have made the same decision?

5. What are the similarities and differences in Amerie's and Vincent's respective relationships with their moms?

6. Amerie is so surprised when Vincent sets up the luxury picnic for her. What is the most romantic gesture a partner has made for you, or vice versa? What would you like them to do?

7. Vincent's mom is terrified of him going to the moon. Would you board a spacecraft and ditch Earth for six months if given the chance?

8. Amerie finds it easy to lie to everyone about her life and work concerns except Vincent. Do you ever find it easier to open up to strangers than those closest to you?

9. One of Amerie's most important relationships is with her best friend, Gina. When she goes MIA, Amerie is hurt, even though she realizes Gina isn't upset with her. Could you easily get over your friend ditching you, then be ready to celebrate their good news once they return?

10. By the end of the novel, Amerie is ready to accept that Vincent won't always be around physically. Would you/ have you ever pursued a long-distance relationship?

11. Amerie is committed to getting a chandelier installed in the bathroom. What one item would be in your dream home?

ETTA'S TO-BE-READ LIST

The Art of Scandal by Regina Black

Rules for Second Chances by Maggie North

When I Think of You by Myah Ariel

Sunshine and Spice by Aurora Palit

Love and Other Conspiracies by Mallory Marlowe

Say You'll Be Mine by Naina Kumar

Literally anything by Nalini Singh

ETTA EASTON is a certified hopeless romantic who now writes contemporary romance. Her stories are full of humor, relatable heroines, swoon-worthy heroes, and Black joy. *The Kiss Countdown* is her debut novel. She lives in Central Texas with her husband and two young kids, who get all of their sweetness and attitude from their momma. When not reading or writing, Etta indulges in her s'mores obsession and searches for her next favorite love song.

Ready to find
your next great read?

Let us help.

Visit prh.com/nextread

Penguin
Random
House